Dark Provenance

DARK PROVENANCE

Michael David Anthony

Felony & Mayhem Press • New York

All the characters and events portrayed in this work are fictitious.

DARK PROVENANCE

A Felony & Mayhem mystery

PRINTING HISTORY
First UK edition (HarperCollins): 1994
First U.S. edition (St. Martin's): 1995

Felony & Mayhem edition: 2011

Copyright © 1994 by Michael David Anthony

All rights reserved

ISBN: 978-1-934609-83-5

Manufactured in the United States of America

Printed on 100% recycled paper

Library of Congress Cataloging-in-Publication Data

Anthony, Michael David.
Dark provenance / Michael David Anthony. -- Felony & Mayhem ed.
p. cm.
ISBN 978-1-934609-83-5
1. Clergy--Fiction. 2. Canterbury (England)--Fiction. I. Title.
PR6051.N77D37 2011
823'.914--dc22

2011024336

With love to my sisters,
Mary, Jane, Judith and Helen

ACKNOWLEDGEMENTS

For their painstaking reading of the manuscript and detailed suggestions and advice, I am indebted to my friends and fellow writers, Clare Harkness and Tim Howley. Also I would wish to acknowledge my former editor at HarperCollins, Elizabeth Walter, without whose promptings and patient encouragement this book would not have been written.

The icon above says you're holding a book in the Felony & Mayhem "British" category. These books are set in or around the UK, and feature the highly literate, often witty prose that fans of British mystery demand. If you enjoy this book, you may well like other "British" titles from Felony & Mayhem Press.

For information about British titles or to learn more about Felony & Mayhem Press, please visit us online at:

www.FelonyAndMayhem.com

Or write to us at:

Felony and Mayhem Press
156 Waverly Place
New York, NY 10014

Other "British" titles from

FELONY & MAYHEM

MICHAEL DAVID ANTHONY
The Becket Factor
Midnight Come

ROBERT BARNARD
Corpse in a Gilded Cage
Death and the Chaste Apprentice
Death on the High C's
The Skeleton in the Grass
Out of the Blackout

DUNCAN CAMPBELL
If It Bleeds

PETER DICKINSON
King and Joker
The Old English Peep Show
Skin Deep
Sleep and His Brother

CAROLINE GRAHAM
The Killings at Badger's Drift
Death of a Hollow Man
Death in Disguise
Written in Blood
Murder at Madingley Grange

REGINALD HILL
A Clubbable Woman
An Advancement of Learning
Ruling Passion
An April Shroud
A Killing Kindness
Deadheads
Exit Lines
Child's Play

ELIZABETH IRONSIDE
The Accomplice
The Art of Deception
Death in the Garden
A Very Private Enterprise

BARRY MAITLAND
The Marx Sisters
The Chalon Heads

SHEILA RADLEY
Death in the Morning
The Chief Inspector's Daughter
A Talent for Destruction
Fate Worse than Death

L.C. TYLER
The Herring Seller's Apprentice
Ten Little Herrings
The Herring in the Library

LOUISE WELSH
Naming the Bones

Apart from the historical characters and incidents referred to, the events of this book are completely fictitious, and the city and diocese of Canterbury depicted, along with all their various inhabitants, are but '*the baseless fabric of a dream*'.

Dark Provenance

provenance or (chiefly U.S.) **provenience** *n.* a place of origin, esp. that of a work of art or archaeological specimen. [C 19: from French, from *provenir*, from Latin *próvenìre* to originate, from *venìre* to come]

from COLLINS ENGLISH DICTIONARY,
Second Edition, 1986

Part 1

Die Schwarze Kapelle

Chapter One

Great Dunstan struck the hour.

As the final stroke faded, a tall figure, grey-haired and spare, emerged from the shadowed archway of Bread Yard. Stepping into the sunlit quadrangle, he glanced up at the Bell Harry, the massive central tower of the cathedral, soaring ahead, honey-brown against vivid blue.

Striding on briskly, he followed the path round the central lawn until the twin western towers came into view. As they did so, his feet faltered and he halted, looking up with an expression of distaste. Distorted and swollen by their cladding of scaffolding and plastic sheeting, the shrouded shapes loomed before him, visual reminder that he was back, facing the tedious round of committee meetings, struggles with architects and builders and all the other frustrations of diocesan business. Suddenly, there on the path, the faint tang of a bonfire in his nostrils, he was conscious as never before of the encircling precinct walls, of being trapped within a miniature world.

Green Court was even quieter than usual: the King's School was still on holiday, its buildings shuttered and closed. Croquet hoops drooped and slumped across the parched lawn, while the mallet chest beside the path, one varnished shaft protruding from beneath the lid, added further to the impression of an outpost forsaken and a garrison fled.

Boarding the ferry at Calais that morning, he'd read in *The Times* of the government's decision to send an armoured division to the Gulf; thereafter, as the boat churned through a lake-like calm, and later on the drive up from Dover, he'd been haunted with visions of camps stirring for action, the gathering of equipment and men—it was what his father and grandfather had known, what he'd himself dreamed of, and what, in the end, denied. Now, looking up from the discarded game to the plastic-clad towers above, resentment flooded against the years that had left him behind, abandoned to a moth-like existence among rotten woodwork and crumbling stone.

His thoughts were disturbed by the sound of high-pitched voices. A knot of small boys emerged from the Selling Archway ahead—probationer choristers returned from their short summer break. Almost immediately one broke away and hurried towards him, and a few seconds later he was looking down at the grinning upturned face of Simon Barnes.

'Colonel Harrison, sir, you're back! And how's Mrs Harrison, sir? Did she like Italy?'

'Thank you, Simon. We're both of us very well—and my wife got a lot of painting done.'

Barnes's smile broadened, then with a glance at his approaching companions, he leaned forward confidentially. 'The news is jolly exciting, isn't it, sir? Do you think the Iraqis will fight?'

Harrison stiffened, thinking suddenly of that long-ago winter morning more than forty years before when he was driven from the Charlottenburg Station into a moonscape of rubble and ruin; looking down at Barnes's eager face, he again saw the thin scarecrow children running beside the jeep, hands stretched towards him—he himself hardly more than a schoolboy, sitting there, gripping hard at the gleaming swagger-stick in his hands. Wincing at the memory, he shook his head. 'War is a ghastly thing, Simon—an absolute blasphemy! Whatever happens in the Middle East, let's pray it doesn't actually come to fighting.'

The excitement in the boy's eyes died. 'Yes, sir, of course.' He stepped back. 'Excuse me, the others are waiting.'

Harrison watched the small figure race from him, and continued to gaze as the boys headed away round the lawn. Finally, as they disappeared beneath the Mint Yard Arch, he turned to stride on towards the deanery gate.

A bonfire had been lit in the orchard. Trapped between the walls, the smoke oozed and curled among the trees, gradually drifting in layers across the lawn and vegetable beds. Sunlight beamed through the haze, illuminating and tinting it, so that Harrison, entering the garden, saw the three figures before him as through a faintly lutescent veil.

Dean Ingrams was at work in his shirtsleeves, digging in a plot of cleared earth. Crouched beside him, one of his young daughters was heaping potatoes into a plastic bucket while her twin sister struggled to push a loaded wheelbarrow towards the source of the billowing smoke.

As the gate clicked to, the dean glanced round. Seeing the newcomer, he immediately thrust down his fork and, beaming broadly, hurried to meet him. 'Richard, my dear fellow, welcome back!' Having shaken hands, he stepped back, surveying the other with satisfaction. 'I must say, you look positively blooming. Your holiday has clearly done you the world of good. And Winifred, how is she? Not too weary after the drive, I trust?'

'She's fine,' answered Harrison, 'and already looking forward to beginning another of her art courses next week. I've left her sorting through her mail.'

'Margaret's away visiting her mother at the moment.' Ingrams glanced round as his daughters joined them. 'Jane and Judith have been helping me lift this year's very late potato crop.'

'Worst luck!' Both girls pulled faces.

Their father smiled indulgently. 'Why don't you both go and make us tea while the colonel and I have a quiet chat.'

As the twins disappeared, Ingrams went to where his jacket hung from a plum tree beside the lawn. Extracting pipe and tobacco, he looked at the swathes of undersized potatoes spread out to dry in the sunlight. 'Not a good year for the garden,' he murmured ruefully, stuffing his pipe.

'At least the dry weather should speed work on the towers,' remarked Harrison. 'I notice they've already made a start.'

'Yes, indeed,' grunted Ingrams, applying a match. 'In fact, George Davidson called about it only today. Apparently the stonework is in worse condition than we feared: it means sic months' work at least.'

'Six months!' burst out Harrison indignantly. 'Nonsense! I shall be speaking to Davidson about that!'

Ingrams's face broke into a smile. 'Would you? My dear fellow, how kind.' Taking the other's arm, he directed him towards the orchard. 'Richard, I can't tell you what a relief it is to have you back! What with Davidson's bleak prognosis on top of everything else, I felt I was reaching the end of my tether at last.'

Harrison looked round at his usually equable friend with concern. 'Why, whatever's been happening, Dean?'

'In three words—our new archdeacon!' Halting before the bonfire, Ingrams mournfully shook his head. 'I'm afraid young Michael Cawthorne has not made the most auspicious of starts.'

'Cawthorne here already!' gasped Harrison. 'But surely, he wasn't due until October!'

'Southwark was prevailed on to release him early, it seems.' Ingrams moodily stirred the smouldering greenery with his boot. 'How did the archbishop describe him—a live wire?' The speaker gave a snort. 'Well, he's certainly that! In the short time amongst us, he's given everyone quite a shock!'

'What's he done?' asked Harrison with mounting apprehension.

'Done! Virtually accused us all of prodigality and waste!' The dean again prodded the now-crackling foliage with his foot. 'It seems he has Lambeth's mandate to cleanse the Augean stables and generally set the diocese on a sound financial basis—and that apparently means a further amalgamation of parishes and closure of churches!'

Harrison gazed gloomily down at the blackening potato-fronds at his feet as the other continued. 'Anyway, apparently not content with setting the diocese by the heels, he's begun to sow discord and controversy here in the precincts.' Ingrams looked round. 'In Chapter, he as good as ordered me to denounce the government in my sermon tomorrow.'

'Denounce the government!' repeated Harrison. 'Dear God! In heaven's name, why?'

'Because of this decision to commit troops to the Gulf, of course. Warmongering! Neo-Imperialism! I don't know what else he called it!' The speaker gave a wan smile. 'You should have seen Canon Richards's face—I really thought the poor man was verging on cardiac arrest!' Turning from the bonfire, Ingrams walked on through the orchard, Harrison at his heels. Halting, he drew down a branch containing a few shrivelled pears. 'Heaven knows,' he murmured, tapping the fruit with his pipe-stem, 'we both had our problems with his unfortunate predecessor, but this appointment is very much, I fear, a matter of out of the Anglo-Catholic frying pan into the evangelical fire!'

The outside telephone bell began to ring. 'What now?' murmured the dean, releasing the branch and frowning as he turned round. 'Are we never to be left in peace?'

The ringing stopped, and a moment later, Jane, the slightly shorter of the twins, appeared at the back door. 'Colonel,' she called, 'that was your wife. She says you've a visitor and would you return home at once.'

'Visitor already!' chuckled Ingrams, brightening immediately. 'Dear me, it sounds as if news of your return has already reached our archdeacon's ears.' Laughing, he led Harrison towards the gate. 'Come on, dear chap, don't dawdle! Dr Cawthorne has been keenly anticipating your return, for some reason.'

Bread Yard was as deserted as when Harrison had left it. Apart from a cat drowsily half-raising its head from the cobbles, nothing moved among the huddle of cottages, and as he fumbled for his keys, the only sounds were the murmur of bees among the roses and the plaintive tinkle of a piano from next door.

The clink of cups and the sound of voices met him as he entered the house. Squeezing past the suitcases in the hall, he made towards the sound, but reaching the sitting-room door, he halted in surprise.

Returning from the deanery, Harrison had wondered who had been so inconsiderate to call this soon. Despite the dean's jocular suggestion of the archdeacon, he'd decided it could only be Major Coles, the King's School bursar, who, seeing the familiar orange Volvo enter the close, had hurried round, eager to inflict an account of the latest of his annual tours of the Burgundian vineyards. In place, however, of the bristling moustache and purplish cheeks of the indomitable major, he found himself gazing instead at a tall, thin-faced, dark-haired young woman in her early thirties who sat on the sofa, teacup in hand.

'Ah, there you are!' Winnie smiled up from her wheelchair as he entered. 'This is Miss Miller from the United States, darling. She has some questions to ask.'

'I hope, Colonel,' burst out the visitor, rising to meet him, 'you don't mind me calling like this, but your secretary said you were due back either today or tomorrow—and as I had something to drop off in the precincts, I thought I'd call by. You see,' she went on, hardly pausing for breath, her gaze fixed on his face, 'the Coroner's Court is on Monday morning.'

'Coroner's Court!' repeated Harrison, taken aback.

'It's my father,' continued the girl, feverish unhappiness in her eyes. 'His body was discovered beside the train-track outside Canterbury on Tuesday—it seems he'd been lying there for a month.'

'I'm so sorry,' murmured Harrison, glancing helplessly at his wife. 'One reads of people falling from trains, of course,' he added, 'but nevertheless one hardly...'

'David Miller, Colonel,' interrupted the girl, 'does the name mean anything to you?'

'I'm sorry, no.'

'You're sure?'

Momentarily overcome by the intensity in his interrogator's eyes, Harrison stared back, then breaking away, he went to the window and looked out across the yard. 'David Miller, you say?' He shook his head. 'No, I'm afraid not—the name doesn't ring a bell. In fact,' he said, turning back, 'apart from the occasional tourist, you're the only American I've met in recent years.'

'Rachel is trying to find out what brought her father to Canterbury, Richard,' intervened Winnie. 'So far the only thing the police have discovered is that he attempted to get in touch with your office during the time he was here.'

'The Dilapidations Board office!' exclaimed Harrison in surprise. 'Good Lord! But why?'

'That's what I hoped you'd be able to tell me, Colonel,' said Rachel despondently. 'All anyone seems to know is that he checked in on Friday, August 10th at the Old Swan Hotel for the one night. And next day took the room for an additional two days and got the desk clerk to find your office number—then he left a short message on your answerphone asking to be called back.'

'I don't understand,' said Harrison, frowning, 'the Dilapidations Board is responsible for the maintenance of diocesan property—we don't have direct dealings with the public.' Pausing, he knotted his brow—then suddenly brightened. 'But wait a minute, I think I might have the answer: since I've been honorary treasurer to the Cathedral Friends, we've used my office as their forwarding address. And as the Friends are basically a fundraising body,' he continued, smiling at his visitor, 'and knowing how generous you Americans are, I would have thought it highly likely, Miss Miller, that your father was thinking of either joining the Friends or perhaps planning some little donation.'

Somewhat to his surprise, the girl shook her head emphatically. 'No, Colonel, that's not it—it wouldn't be that.'

'Rachel,' said Winnie gently, breaking the silence that followed, 'why is it so important discovering what your father was doing in Canterbury?'

'I need to speak to someone who can tell me what state he was in.' Biting her lip, the girl sat back down on the sofa and stared across the floor for a moment or two before looking round at her hosts. 'The cops don't think Dad's death was an accident, you see.' There was something verging on anger in her voice, and her hands clenched as she spoke. 'They think he intentionally jumped from the train.'

'Suicide!' Seeing Winnie's warning glance, Harrison softened his tone. 'Forgive me, but why should they think that?'

The girl shrugged. 'Because Dad knew he was sick, I guess. He was operated on for cancer two years back—that's why he was semi-retired from his law practice—and since then he always had regular check-ups, both in the States and then over here when he moved to London ten months back. Anyway, he came from a trip abroad about six weeks ago complaining of internal pains, and a scan showed up extensive secondary growths.' Pausing, the speaker looked across at Winnie. 'It seems Dad demanded to know exactly what his chances were; when he was told, he left the hospital—and that same evening arrived here in Canterbury.'

As she ended, the declining sun sank below the surrounding wall of the courtyard outside, sending a shadow sweeping across the cobbles; for moments, the only sound in the darkened room was the steady beat of the grandfather dock from the hall.

'One thing I don't understand,' ventured Winnie at last, 'is why he moved to England at all, especially so soon after a big operation.'

'I guess he'd always wanted to come, but what with his

law practice and Mom being an invalid, it wasn't really practical until...' Reddening perceptibly, Rachel broke off, her gaze falling on her hostess's wheelchair.

'Until after your mother's death—yes, of course!' Winnie smiled. 'But go on, dear, you haven't really explained: what was the attraction of Europe?'

'Culture, I guess: Dad liked museums, galleries—those sort of things. Back home, he bought a lot of paintings and pottery, and I know he was planning to write something to do with antiques. Anyway,' continued Rachel, 'after he'd sold out his share in the partnership, the firm found they needed a real estate lawyer over here in Europe on a part-time basis, so he took the chance to come.'

Winnie frowned. 'Yes, but none of that explains his dashing up here straight after hearing the diagnosis at the hospital. That does seem very odd.'

'Coming to Canterbury when you're sick—is it so odd?' said Harrison, turning back to the window. 'God knows,' he murmured, gazing up at the cathedral, 'tens of thousands have done just that.'

'Really, darling!' protested his wife with a smile. 'Rachel's father was a twentieth-century American, not one of Chaucer's pilgrims!'

'Pardon me,' intervened their visitor, 'but you can forget any spiritual motive for Dad coming to Canterbury.' She smiled faintly. 'We're Jewish, you see—that's why, Colonel, I don't think he was contacting your office about joining the Cathedral Friends.' She looked away. 'That's why Dad and I weren't really close—we used to fight about religion.'

There was absolute silence in the room for a moment, then Rachel burst out, 'And that's the whole point: apart from not leaving any message for me, Dad wouldn't have killed himself—he was devout, he would have thought it morally wrong.' Dark eyes burning, she looked from one to the other. 'It's got to have been an accident, whatever the goddamned cops say!'

'What's wrong, darling?'

Looking round, Harrison found his wife studying him with concern from the bureau where she'd been answering letters in the fading light. 'Nothing,' he answered. 'Why do you ask?'

'Because, my dear, you've been restless and abstracted all evening, and for the last ten minutes you've been sitting there just staring into space.' Easing the chair round, Winnie pushed herself towards him. 'What are you brooding about? This new archdeacon?'

Harrison shrugged. 'Perhaps—when Ingrams first told me about the dust the fellow's kicking up, it did cross my mind to chuck in the towel.'

'Resign, you mean?' The other burst out laughing. 'Don't be so silly! What would you do with yourself all day?'

Despite himself, Harrison smiled. 'Oh, I don't know—if the worst comes to the worst, I suppose I could always tog myself out in boater and blazer, and go bowling with Major Coles.'

'Seriously though,' said Winnie as her smile faded, 'what's on your mind? Is it that poor girl?' She paused, sudden anxiety in her face. 'I take it it's true what you told her—that you've never heard of her father?'

'Of course it's true!' Disengaging her arm, Harrison rose and went to peer out into the fast-darkening yard. In the distance, the cathedral clock struck the hour; as if in answer, the hall clock launched into its own brisk, staccato chimes. Harrison checked his watch and looked round. 'If you don't mind,' he said, 'I'll slip over to the office to glance at the mail.'

'Now?' His wife stared at him in disbelief. 'But that's absurd! It's almost dark!'

Harrison gave a shamefaced smile. 'I could do with a breath of fresh air and a chance to stretch my legs.'

'All right,' she said, reluctantly, 'go and have your walk, but get back in time for the news: you'll want to hear what's happening about the Gulf.'

'Right!' He went to the door. 'You know, Winnie,' he said, looking back, 'whether it's all this talk of war or what, I have this sense of something hanging above our heads.'

'You're just tired,' said Winnie, smiling. 'Go and get some fresh air, then get straight back for a nice hot milky drink and an early night.'

Dusk had long fallen and lights already shone round Green Court. After the day's heat, the air was still warm, and in the gleam of the overhead lamps, a myriad of tiny moths and similar insects whirled and streamed. Passing the deanery, Harrison thought back to the moment when, opening the gate, he'd spied Ingrams and his daughters in the garden. Now, he thought, his friend would be either at his desk, head bowed over the morrow's sermon, or sitting with Margaret and the twins, the family Siamese sprawled on his lap.

Remembering Cawthorne, he looked across the lawn to where the archdeaconry reared in the gloom, lights burning, not only on the ground floor, but among the windows upstairs. He halted, guessing what they meant: young Michael Cawthorne, as Ingrams had termed him, was clearly also a family man, and that ungainly old house, so long shuttered and dark, was alive again, ringing that very moment perhaps with the squeals and laughter of children.

In the gathering darkness, Harrison continued to gaze towards the archdeaconry, suddenly feeling separate and apart: quarrel and dispute as they might, Ingrams, Cawthorne and the rest of the cathedral clergy were rooted in their families and the Church; he, on the other hand, was an outsider, a refugee from both his own calling and the restless world lapping about the now-locked precinct gates.

The son and grandson of military engineers, the choice of the army had been made for him before he was born; from Wellington, he'd entered into its disciplines as naturally as any novice moving to final vows. Studious and painstaking, he'd excelled in training, then with the fighting ended in Europe, he'd been posted to Germany, taking up his duties with the confidence of one following a path already reconnoitred and mapped. In the end, however, the golden road had led merely to bewildering thicket: with the Cold War deepening, he'd been transferred to Intelligence, and gradually, in a world riven by political divide, he'd been sucked, simultaneously fascinated and disgusted, into a vortex of espionage and counter-espionage, one tiny drop in an ocean of trickery and lies.

In his marriage, also, the expected future had eluded him with polio striking down Winnie. Their separate anguish, the overseas postings and the secrecy of his work had drawn them apart until they were almost lost to each other: she crippled and confined to a wheelchair; he caught like one of those tiny insects blindly circling in the glare of the lamps, mesmerized by the fatally compelling attractions of power and intrigue.

To save his marriage, he'd wrenched himself free, resigning his commission and retreating to these cloisters and the dull decencies of diocesan work. Now, with him already disquieted by the news of possible conflict in the Gulf, had come this other outsider, this wandering Jew, who had also apparently fled to Canterbury—and there, unaccountably, had attempted to get in touch with his own little guarded private world.

The squeak and flutter of a bat jerked him from his reverie. Glancing up, he saw the tiny creature flit over his head and flap away into dark. As it vanished, he walked on towards the great shadow of the cathedral. Moments later he was heading, feet echoing along the tunnel-like passage of Dark Entry, to where the solitary light burned outside the diocesan offices.

As he let himself in, Harrison noticed an envelope in the mail cage. Withdrawing it, he noticed it was addressed to his secretary and had been delivered by hand. Feeling the weight of an object inside, he gave the packet a rattle, and vaguely wondering what it was, carried it with him up the short flight of steps to the door of the outer office.

The striplights flickered on as he entered, bathing the cluttered interior in harsh light. All seemed in order: the ranks of box files and marbled ledgers, faded and time-worn, lining the walls from uneven floor to slightly bulging ceiling. One thing was startlingly different, however: instead of the familiar old upright typewriter on his secretary's desk, there now perched an ivory-coloured word processor.

So unexpected and so garishly at odds was this modern piece of technology with both the furnishings and antiquity of the room that Harrison stared, first in shocked distaste, then with a combination of resentment and unease. Knowing this could only be the archdeacon's doing, he realized the implications: his new superior was clearly not only interested in speed and efficiency, but was a man who acted without thought of the susceptibilities of any who stood in his way.

Back in the house, he'd talked lightly of resignation. Now, gazing down at this technological cuckoo, he wondered if in fact he'd have any choice in the matter: what possible use, he thought, would someone like Cawthorne have for an outmoded antique like himself? What had Ingrams said about the archdeacon keenly awaiting his return? The reason seemed obvious: like the sturdy old Imperial typewriter, he too was to be swept away!

Leaving the package beside the phone, he gloomily walked on to his own office. Going to the desk, he switched on the anglepoise lamp. As expected, his in-tray was full to overflowing. Dropping into his swivel-chair, he began sorting through the pile of already opened envelopes. They were utterly predictable: surveyors' reports; builders' estimates; a letter from the cathedral accountant, another from Lloyds Bank. Each in turn passed through his fingers and was dropped back into the tray—then suddenly his heart gave a jolt. Replacing what remained of the post, he stared down at the unopened envelope in his hand, on which, above his name, was printed in red: MOST PERSONAL AND PRIVATE—FOR THE EYES OF ADDRESSEE ONLY.

Intrigued, he held the envelope under the lamp. The handwriting was unfamiliar; it was postmarked Canterbury, and, according to the date, had been posted a month before. Harrison felt a flutter of excitement. Unadmitted to Winnie, only half admitted to himself, he'd left the house with the faint idea that somehow David Miller might have managed to communicate before taking his final journey. It seemed now that he had—and that, according to the insistent instructions, his message was for himself alone.

Reaching for his paperknife, he sliced open the envelope. Pulling down the lamp, he laid the written-over sheets in the pool of light. Bending, he peered at the erratic scrawl. For a moment he was unable to make out a word, then his eye caught the printed address, *The Rectory, Long Ashendon*. Numbly, he turned to the bottom of the second page where, under a wisp of a signature, appeared the words, *The Reverend Thomas Dove MA (Oxon)*.

Leaning back, Harrison closed his eyes. He, of course, knew Thomas Dove—or Tom Dove as he was always called. Small and lean as the proverbial rake, the recently retired rector of Long Ashendon had made a national name for himself in the anti-nuclear marches of the 'fifties and 'sixties: in black beret and raincoat, his diminutive figure was almost as much part of the annual procession from Aldermaston as the logo of the CND—and though now well into his seventies, until his recent stroke, had still addressed the odd meeting and even trod the symbolic mile among the dwindled remnants of the peace movement.

Unfortunately, Dove's enthusiasm had never been confined to politics: having retreated from an Oxford fellowship to the living of Long Ashendon years before, he'd developed an overweening pride and concern for its massive barn of a church. Indeed, before his retirement, a typed letter from Dove was a regular occurrence—so regular that it had often felt to Harrison as if he and the Dilapidations Board existed for no other purpose than to serve the insatiable appetite of Holy Trinity church and its rector.

His first impulse was to drop the letter back with the others, but curiosity as to why Tom Dove should now be writing to him personally made him turn back to the first sheet.

Dear Colonel Harrison,

From my sickbed—excuse my ghastly handwriting but at present I can't get at my faithful old 'tripewriter'. As you doubtless remember, when I was prevailed on to surrender my living, it was agreed by the late Dr Crocker that, as Long Ashendon was to be added to the responsibilities of Canon Bedford, I should be allowed to retain the use of the rectory for my lifetime. You may imagine my shock, therefore, to receive a missive today from the new archdeacon, informing me that the matter of my future residence was under review!

Harrison frowned: that Cawthorne could consider going back on the firm undertaking of his predecessor was a shock. If this was to be the future, he thought, it boded ill, both for himself and the diocese. Wearily, he bent again to the script.

Of course, I realize I have no legal leg to stand on, but I wonder, Colonel, if you'd be good enough to use your undoubted influence on my behalf. Please remind Dr Cawthorne that I remain here by gentlemen's agreement (if that has any meaning for him!). Also tell him that I need space for my books—and finally, inform him that my wife and I have not the slightest intention of making use of the sheltered accommodation he had the gross impertinence to suggest!

Harrison's reading was interrupted by the phone in the outer office. Rising, he made for the door, but before reaching it, the ringing cut off to be replaced by his secretary's taped voice. Hurrying to her desk, he switched off the answerphone and lifted the console receiver.

'Richard, whatever's happening?' came Winnie's voice. 'You said you were going to be just a few minutes.'

'Sorry, my dear—I was on my way out as you rang.'

'So it's safe if I put on the milk to heat?'

'Fine! I'm on my way.' Replacing the receiver, he switched the answerphone back on. As its tiny red eye gleamed, his gaze fell on the envelope he'd left on the desk, knowing suddenly what it contained. Picking it up, he ripped it open, allowing the object within to slide out into his hand. Withdrawing the enclosed note, he found, as expected, that it was from Rachel Miller thanking his secretary for the loan of the tape-cassette.

Ejecting the existing tape from the answerphone, he replaced it with the one in his hand, and dropping into his secretary's chair, he pressed the playback button. The first voice was Davidson's, requesting the return of his plans for the crypt conversion at St Giles. This was followed by an embarrassed complaint from the Reverend Gleeson about the state of his roof—prompted no doubt by his wife. Then the third message began.

The name's David Miller, speaking at 7 p.m. on Saturday, 11th August. I'm staying at the Old Swan Hotel here in the city until Monday. I'd be obliged if you'd contact the desk cleric saying when you're available and I'll get back to you.

There was a click as the receiver was replaced.

Switching off the machine, Harrison sat motionless. As Rachel had indicated, the message gave not the slightest clue as to what her father had wanted—but it was not the content of the message, but the voice itself that held Harrison gripped. Rewinding, he replayed the tape, and as he listened, beneath the relaxed American drawl, he heard again a faint cadence of something altogether harder and sharper.

Brows contracted, he stared down. Something stirred in his memory. Getting up, he went over to the window and looked out.

Night had now fallen, moonless and black. Beyond the light in the passage below, all lay shrouded in a darkness so profound that it seemed that, instead of acres of stone, he was looking into a barren void. Bowing his head, he pressed his forehead to the glass, straining to remember: any second now, he was certain, he would place that voice—and then, once again, the phone burst into life.

Harrison jerked round at the sound, his mind at once empty of anything but the thought of Winnie's furious face and the stink of burnt milk pervading the cottage.

Chapter Two

Luther's hymn 'A Safe Stronghold our God is Still' echoed through the nave. The sky above the cathedral was as clear as the day before, and the sunlight, streaming through the tiers of lancet windows, cast radiant pools across the pavings beneath. Dappled in shadow and light, the double line of fluted columns soared up through slanting shafts of dustmoted brilliance to the criss-crossed rib vaulting under the roof, where at every intersection the gilt bosses gleamed down like huge golden eyes on the heads of the unusually large congregation eighty feet below.

Having slept badly and woken late, Harrison had been half inclined to stay at home; grumpy and irritable, he'd lingered over breakfast until, goaded by duty and habit, he'd set out for Matins at the final bell, leaving Winnie to enjoy the Sunday papers in peace. So far, however, the beauty of service and setting had been quite wasted on him: for the last thirty minutes he'd clambered from his knees to his seat, from his seat to his feet, and back again to his knees in almost mechanical rotation, repeating the long-ago-learnt responses and prayers automatically, his mind preoccupied again with the voice he'd heard on the answerphone the previous evening. Now, however, as the hymn drew to a close, his attention was caught by the sight of the rotund form of Simcocks, the head verger or vesturer as he was titled at Canterbury, progressing in stately fashion, silver-tipped staff in hand, towards the foot of the carved wooden pulpit a few rows in front, leading a decidedly pensive dean.

'I seek my brethren.'

Amplified by a dozen tannoy speakers, the preacher's words echoed through the nave. Having waited for the inevitable coughing and clearing of throats to fade, Ingrams leaned forward again to the pulpit microphone. 'These words from Genesis, chapter thirty-seven, were taken by the late George Bell as the text at his installation as dean here in 1924 in the presence of his friend and mentor, Archbishop Randall Davidson.' Pausing, the dean surveyed the faces before him. 'Some of you may wonder why, when our young men are setting forth possibly to face the dangers of war, I should speak of one whose ashes have lain in this cathedral for over thirty years. What, I hear you ask, has this long-ago dean of Canterbury and later bishop of Chichester to do with the dilemmas facing us today?'

As if in confirmation of this thought, there was a short outburst of coughing and blowing of noses among the congregation; even Harrison, lulled by the warmth of the slanting sunlight, allowed his eyelids to droop as the unimpassioned tones of the preacher resumed. 'Ironically for such a peace-loving man as George Bell, war was to dominate his life: having lost both his elder brothers in action in the Great War, Bell dedicated his life to the cause of universal brotherhood, tirelessly working through the ecumenical movement for international Christian unity and reconciliation. Though his hopes were tragically dashed by the rise of the Nazis and the outbreak of war in 1939, he nevertheless continued to preach the gospel of love and forgiveness, not only losing all chance of future preferment by doing so, but bringing upon his head the anger and scorn of many, including numbers of fellow clerics and friends.'

At these words, Harrison was suddenly transported back to that morning in his final school year when his housemaster had appeared on the wash-landing, brandishing a copy of the *Daily Telegraph* and trembling with rage. To see a master, famed for his stoic calm, reduced to incoherent fury boded the worst: Churchill's murder or the devastating arrival of Hitler's long-threatened wonder-weapon. It had been, therefore, an anticlimax to learn that 'Podge' Brown's almost apoplectic fit was the result of nothing more than a bishop's speech in the Lords on the subject of the RAF's bombing campaign, one in which the apparently traitorous cleric not only questioned the morality of flattening German cities, but had even expressed pity for those enduring the horrors nightly lavished upon them by Bomber Command.

'...thus with Germany in ruins and his friend, Dietrich Bonhoeffer, dead on the gallows of the Flossenburg concentration camp, George Bell set out once again to seek his brethren in that embittered and devastated land.'

The emphasized repetition of the opening text brought Harrison back to the moment. Feeling guilty at having let his thoughts stray, he looked up at the preacher with an expression of intense concentration and interest.

'Just as he'd pleaded for the Jewish refugees, Bell now pleaded for the German nation, begging on behalf of a starving, defeated people for forgiveness and reconciliation. Just as he'd personally arranged the escape of many Jews and so-called non-Aryan Christians in the 'thirties, Bell went to Germany as soon as the fighting ceased to give what help and encouragement he could.' Laying aside his notes, Ingrams leaned over the lectern.

'Recently, one who worked closely with Bell described to me the occasion when he preached in the famous Marienkirche in Soviet-occupied East Berlin.' The preacher paused. 'I want you to imagine the scene: the damaged church, a packed congregation standing in candlelight, listening with rapt attention while outside Russian soldiers stood on guard amidst the acres of desolation and ruin that was the Berlin of those days.'

At these last words, Harrison gave a start—and then, clenching his fists, exclaimed aloud in a barely suppressed undertone, 'Of course, Müller, damn it! Müller, not Miller!'

Having struggled in vain and virtually given up hope, miraculously the answer had come: the voice on the tape belonged to the man who'd shared his office in the soulless concrete monstrosity in Fehrbelliner Platz. Just as the dean's words had previously conjured up the trembling jowls and furious eyes of the long-dead Podge Brown, so Harrison was now back forty years, sitting in that dingy cluttered little room in what had been Luftwaffe headquarters, seeing again the rather melancholy face and raven-black hair and, below, the bright strip of those so envied ribbons on the battledress blouse of Staff-Sergeant Müller.

'…and thus it behoves us, in war as in peace, also to "seek our brethren", whether Christian, Moslem or Jew,' concluded the preacher, folding his notes. Next moment, dazed and excited, Harrison was stumbling to his feet for the offertory hymn.

'Everything all right, Colonel?'

Matins over, Harrison had slipped into the north-west aisle. Seeing many he knew among the congregation and being unwilling to socialize, he watched from the shelter of one of the columns as they began filing out through the south-western porch, his mind still reeling with the possible implications of his ex-Staff-Sergeant's reappearance after more than forty years. Startled by the voice at his elbow, he swung round to find the cathedral venturer standing behind him, bald scalp gleaming in the light, a look of concern on his round and rubicund face.

'Ah, Simcocks!' burst out Harrison with feigned pleasure. 'Good to see you again. All well, I trust?'

'Well enough, I suppose,' was the grudging reply, 'all things considered.'

'Oh?'

Before Simcocks had a chance to voice whatever resentment was clearly gnawing within his corpulent bulk, his attention was distracted by faint cries and a stirring among those still waiting to leave. With one accord, he and Harrison swung round to view the commotion.

Whereas until then, the still-sizeable crowd had been passing out in an orderly stream, their progress was now impeded by a boisterous flow of young Italian tourists noisily thrusting their way in. With those at the front forced back, and those at the back still moving forward, the demurely-clad recent worshippers at the centre found themselves increasingly pinned and crushed between van and rear.

With the crowd beginning to surge alarmingly, Simcocks hurried towards the mêlée, waving a youthful sidesman to his aid. Harrison watched the gowned figures rush to and fro, soothing the ruffled ranks, until he caught sight of Major Coles.

Standing slightly apart, his back to the now quietening throng, the bursar was talking animatedly to Ruth Hodge, owner of a thriving market garden and nursery business, and Tom Dove's longtime churchwarden—and, since the beginning of the year, also steward to the Cathedral Friends. Through their joint work, Harrison had come to respect her greatly—a respect that now increased as he observed her smiling and nodding with customary politeness at what, he guessed, was a colourful account of the major's recent adventures in France.

Thankful he'd not risked mingling with his fellow worshippers, Harrison remained where he was until Simcocks returned. 'Yes, a good crowd in this morning,' he remarked, stepping out to greet the now perspiring vesturer. 'I'm sure the dean's very pleased.'

'That's as may be,' muttered the other, dabbing his neck with a handkerchief, 'but it don't make my life no easier.'

Puzzled at what could have upset the normally amiable man, Harrison nevertheless deemed it prudent to make no inquiry. In silence he accompanied him towards the chancel steps, and only as they began ascending did he risk the question he'd really been waiting to ask. 'I don't suppose, Simcocks, you recall anybody asking for me while I've been away?'

'No, sir,' was the reply, 'but then I don't rightly see as I could—not with two men short and the crowds we've had through here all summer.'

'Oh, quite,' murmured Harrison. 'I merely wondered—the person I've in mind would have spoken with an American accent.'

Despite the studied casualness of the inquiry, the vesturer paused, giving his companion a curious glance, then looked back towards the column behind which he'd discovered the other at the end of the service. 'What is it, Colonel?' he asked with new-found interest. 'Someone you're trying to avoid?'

'Of course not,' answered Harrison, continuing up the steps to the transept. 'As I say, just a friend. But tell me,' he hurried on, seeing the vesturer's sceptical glance, and anxious to deflect his interest, 'how are you finding life with our new archdeacon?'

It was clearly an unfortunate question; with a sharp intake of breath, Simcocks halted on the marble flooring, breathing deeply, his complexion growing volcanic red.

'Nothing's wrong, I trust?' ventured Harrison. As he waited in vain for an answer, all about him came the murmur of voices and tramp of feet. 'Of course, he added, taking a surreptitious glance at his watch, 'it's always difficult for a new boy. It may take Dr Cawthorne a little time to find his feet.'

Instead of soothing, the diplomatic oil seemed merely to inflame the already smouldering fire, for Simcocks, swinging round, burst out bitterly, 'Expensive folly! That's what he called it, sir, right to my blooming face!'

'This is something the archdeacon said?' said Harrison, quite lost. 'I don't understand—to what was he referring?'

'This, Colonel! This!' The vesturer waved towards the roof. 'The cathedral itself!' Taken aback, Harrison could only stare as Simcocks continued. 'The things that man says, you wouldn't believe! He's all for cutting down even more on the staff here—

rationalization of resources!' The speaker struggled for breath. 'I tell you, sir, if it wasn't for his cloth, I'd like to turnstile him!'

'What?'

'Yes, Colonel—turnstiles!' Simcocks nodded emphatically, sudden savage exultation in his face. 'You wait and see, sir—it will be tickets here soon!'

'Entrance charges to the cathedral, you mean!' Harrison laughed. 'Nonsense, man! The dean would never permit it.'

'The dean! The dean!' repeated the other. 'What can he do? I tell you, Colonel,' continued the vesturer, lowering his voice and glancing furtively along the shadowy north choir aisle, 'the way that man's going on at present will end in blood, just you wait and see!'

'Oh, poor Mr Simcocks!' laughed Winnie, breaking the silence that had fallen over lunch. 'What was the phrase—expensive folly?' She giggled. 'I can just imagine his face!'

Her husband merely grunted and continued gloomily to contemplate his suet pudding and custard.

'I must say, darling,' she continued, looking across the table with a mischievous grin, 'this new archdeacon of yours does seem a trifle short on diplomacy.'

'He's not my archdeacon! I didn't appoint the fellow!' Taking a spoonful of pudding, Harrison scowled through the window, catching sight of the scaffold-clad towers above the yard. 'Mind you,' he said, clearing his mouth, 'Cawthorne has a point—the money the Church puts into the upkeep of these places, and for what? Herds of tourists to be everlastingly tramping about!'

'Yes, dear,' answered his wife placidly, bending to her plate and continuing her meal.

Harrison regarded her bent head with mounting irritation. 'Well, say what you like,' he said after a moment or two, 'but I don't see why the Church has to be the unpaid custodian of our national heritage.' Eliciting no response, he returned to his pudding, but after another mouthful, he lowered his spoon and sat frowning at the already congealing remnants in the bowl.

'I take it,' Winnie's voice broke into his thoughts, 'that this grumpiness is to do with this poor man, David Miller or Müller or whatever you call him?'

'What do you mean?' answered Harrison sharply, looking up. 'I've hardly mentioned him.'

'Exactly.' Winnie smiled, then, becoming grave, reached over to touch his hand. 'Seriously, what's wrong? I know it's horrible the way he died, and you feel bad not being here when he called, but all the same, you haven't met him for over forty years.'

Harrison shrugged. 'It's just I don't understand why he should turn up like that after all this time.'

'Is it so odd? As you were just saying yourself, Canterbury attracts thousands of tourists. It's hardly surprising that one of them is someone you used to know, or that he should try to look you up.'

'Oh, come on, Winnie!' burst out Harrison. 'After being given a virtual death sentence, a person doesn't go cavorting off just to look at a lot of old buildings!' He shook his head. 'Why come to Canterbury, and how, in God's name, did he know I worked here? And what did he want with me after all this time?'

With a troubled look on her face, Winnie regarded her husband for a moment. 'You say he was someone you knew in the army,' she said at last. 'I don't understand: I thought he was an American.'

'Not then, he wasn't!' Harrison pushed away his bowl. 'Then he was nothing—a stateless refugee.' He sat back. 'Just after the war, the British Army was full of Jews and displaced people like Müller who had fled to Britain in the 'thirties and whose families had perished in the Holocaust—it was their only home, I suppose.' Pausing, he shook his head. 'That's why I took so long to put a face to that voice: it wasn't only the accent and the anglicizing of his name, but that even now I find it difficult to associate a retired New York lawyer with the young homeless orphan I knew in Berlin.'

'He worked with you at the British Control Commission?'

Harrison nodded. 'Yes, on that so-called de-Nazification programme.' Leaning back, he gave a snort. 'Christ, what a bloody hopeless job it was—sifting the entire German civil service down to the local postman for those who had been truly Nazi at heart! Talk about trying to separate sheep from goats! To have got it right, we'd have needed a moral Geiger counter!'

'And David Miller?'

'Officially, he was my interpreter. In fact, he virtually ran the section. I was a new boy, completely out of my depth. I depended on him for everything, right down to getting hold of blackmarket coffee!'

'Go on—tell me about him.'

'Well, from what I remember, he was from Vienna originally. His parents packed him off to Britain after the *anschluss* while they tried to sell off the family business.' Harrison paused and looked out at the yard for a moment. 'In the end, they never had the chance to join him: like the rest, Britain had its refugee quota system, and the war started before they got their visas.'

'And what happened to the boy?'

'Placed in some sort of farm community until he was old enough to join the army—and, as a so-called enemy alien, that meant the Pioneers, of course. Finally, he got into the infantry as he wanted and actually won the Military Medal at the crossing of the Rhine. At the end of hostilities he was posted as a military interpreter to Berlin—though, as I say, he was far more than that.'

'You mean he actually helped with the investigations?'

'Oh yes, and he was damned good at it too: patient, painstaking and with a good eye for detail.' Harrison smiled. 'No wonder he became a lawyer—he was made for it!'

'But was that fair,' said Winnie, frowning, 'using a man who couldn't help being bitter? Surely he was bound to be biased.'

'But he wasn't,' protested Harrison, 'that's the funny thing!

He was always absolutely objective—polite, even understanding, with people who were all contaminated, at least to some degree, by that vile creed which had slaughtered his family!' Turning, Harrison sat a moment staring out at the cobbles. 'You know,' he murmured, shaking his head, 'I can hear him now, pleading the case of some poor frightened little schoolteacher who'd over-enthusiastically preached the virtues of racial purity!' Grimacing, he looked back round at his wife. 'Damn it, Winnie, I tried and failed to get him the commission he deserved—now again, all these years later, I wasn't on the spot when he needed my help!'

At that moment, the telephone began ringing down the hall.

'Colonel Harrison?'

'Yes?'

'Michael Cawthorne speaking. I heard you were back. I wonder if you could possibly slip round for a chat?'

'Now?' Harrison was incredulous: difficult and exacting as his predecessor had been, never once had Dr Crocker actually summoned him on a Sunday afternoon!

'I'd be most obliged if you could,' continued the flat voice. 'There are some matters we need to discuss as soon as possible.'

Harrison tightened his grip on the instrument, enforced retirement staring him full in the face. He felt his fury grow: nevertheless, to his surprise, he heard himself say, 'Yes, of course, Archdeacon—only too delighted! I'll be with you as soon as I can.'

So familiar was the walk that Harrison hardly glanced up as he trudged round Green Court. Unlatching the gate, he entered the grounds, exchanging at once the heat of the quadrangle for the shadowed coolness of the ancient covered walkway or pentise that zigzagged between the lawns and shrubberies to the front door.

Despite the variety of foliage and blossom, a faint melancholy settled upon him as he entered the garden. Since Dr Crocker's death, he'd not visited the archdeaconry: now, following the well-remembered pavings between the double line of withered timber supports, the forbidding appearance of the building ahead, with its incongruous tower-like chimneys, flint walls and deep-set windows, was unbearably emblematic of the solitary, austere late archdeacon. A blackbird began singing from among the leaves of the mulberry. Sweet and poignant came the notes: a daytime Philomel calling from the regions of dust. Halting, Harrison thought of Crocker buried beside his sister, and of his own dead staff-sergeant, locked that moment in some stainless-steel mortuary drawer—then, all at once, there burst through his thoughts the melodious deep warmth of cello and violin—and then, almost immediately, joining in and soaring above them, the light, bright trippings of a treble recorder.

So unexpected and at odds was the breezy joy of Purcell with his mood and the melancholy associations of the house, that Harrison peered in astonishment towards where, behind the open french windows, appeared the three players.

Nearest was the cellist, a slim woman in a floral summer dress with short curly blonde hair. Facing her was the very miniature of herself, a girl of about ten, standing solemnly before a music stand, violin to her shoulder. It was, however, the sight of the last of the trio that held him rooted, gazing in mesmerized disbelief across the twenty feet of grass.

In complete contrast to the serene gravity and stillness of mother and daughter, this third was all fire and movement: a short, ginger-headed man in his mid-forties, lithe and wiry, in open-necked shirt, sleeves rolled to the elbow, he played, lips pursed to the mouthpiece, dipping and rolling like some crudely controlled marionette. Aghast, the watcher stared at the Pan-like figure swaying and bobbing above the bent heads of the females:

if he'd visualized Dr Cawthorne as anything, it was certainly not this—this demented pixie; warbling and trilling before him on that wildly oscillating pipe!

Unwilling either to advance or retreat, Harrison remained gazing towards the house. A moment later, however, the young violinist, looking down the strings towards him, nudged her father, nodding towards their visitor. Still playing, swaying and rolling to the beat, the archdeacon—if archdeacon it could possibly be—moved to the window, then, recognizing the newcomer, immediately lowered his instrument and called out brightly, 'Colonel Harrison? I'm sorry, I didn't see you there. Do come over and join us.'

Stiff and self-conscious, the visitor crossed to where Cawthorne waited, freckled, boyish face wreathed in smiles.

'So we meet at last!' Harrison's hand was gripped and pumped. Releasing his hold, Cawthorne smiled round. 'Now, Colonel, Janet and Emily are dying to meet you.'

As woman and girl stepped forward in turn, Harrison received from each the same hesitant smile and shyly extended palm—cool and limp as lettuce. Next moment, still dazed by the welcome, he was being ushered through the open windows into what had been the late Dr Crocker's study.

In the past, the room had been sombre and dark; now, cleared of heavy oak desk and bookcases, it was bright and airy, perfumed with beeswax and lavender, gleaming with new paint and polished floor. Sofas and chairs in matching powder-blue were arranged round a wide pine table, and instead of the yellowing photographs of university rowing teams, there hung large poster-like pictures of sunflowers and poppies, while over the fireplace, in place of the crucifix, an unearthly white gull soared above an azure sea.

Disorientated, Harrison looked about him, then, conscious of the eyes apparently awaiting a response, he managed a smile. 'Yes, very nice—a remarkable transformation!'

A flush of joy immediately lit all three faces. Exchanging a smile with his wife, Cawthorne stepped forward. 'Now, Richard, isn't it? How about a cooling drink? Janet has some of her delicious homemade ginger beer in the fridge.'

Jug and glasses were carried in. After some desultory conversation on the subject of Tuscany, the drought and the state of the garden, Harrison at last found himself alone with his immediate superior, who, perched on the table, was pouring himself a second long glass of the ginger beer. Bracing himself, Harrison cleared his throat. 'You wish to discuss the future, Archdeacon?'

'Do call me Mike.' Cawthorne took a deep draught. Wiping his lips with a freckled hand, he grinned. 'Yes, I wanted to get our strategy planned.'

'Strategy?' repeated Harrison weakly.

Leaning back, Cawthorne pulled over a red box file and, flipping it open, drew out a stapled wad of paper. 'I found this among my predecessor's files,' he said, passing it over.

Harrison recognized it at once: it was his own diocesan rationalization scheme, reluctantly demanded by the previous archdeacon under the pressure of spiralling costs. Baffled, he looked at Cawthorne who sat grinning down at him from the table, swinging his legs like some mischievous Puck on a toad-stool. 'I don't quite follow,' he murmured, and cleared his throat. 'Do you wish to implement some of this?'

'Some?' The other laughed. 'Richard, I wish to adopt your entire plan—it's a masterpiece: comprehensive, radical, daring—everything the diocese needs.'

Harrison was speechless. Now he understood the unaccountable warmth of his welcome: Cawthorne obviously saw him as an ally and friend, a fellow iconoclast, sharing the same ghastly vision of a fully rationalized Church composed of nothing but encounter groups, hand-clapping and purpose-built ecumenical halls! This was bad enough, but what made his blood run cold was that this grinning little man actually intended to implement the entire sixty-four separate recommendations of the board.

So great had been the financial crisis, and so unlikely Dr Crocker's acceptance of the smallest cutback or innovation, Harrison himself had proposed to the board that they should, as it were, loose off a whole volley of proposals in the hope that two or three might find some chink in the implacable armour of Crocker's High-Church conservatism. Thus, by his recommendation, they'd proceeded in the manner of a Dutch auction or eastern bazaar, in the hope—vain, as it turned out—that the more inflated the opening bid, the more positive the final settlement.

Harrison regarded the document with horror: if implemented in full, it meant the decimation of the most ancient and prestigious diocese in the Anglican communion. But what could be done? With the report signed and sealed, he and the board were caught, hoist on their own petard—helplessly allied with a man whose policies and outlook were anathema, not only to hidebound traditionalists like Simcocks and Canon Richards, but even to moderate men like his old friend, the dean.

Miserably, he stared down. His impulse was to resign, but how would that help? With or without him, Cawthorne would push through his plans, using the board's own recommendations as both lever and shield. That was unthinkable. No, like it or not, he must stay where he was, working from within, slowing and watering down each proposal as best he could.

The archdeacon's voice intruded. 'Before we tackle the future, however, we must finish the business of the past—I mean sell off already redundant buildings, especially surplus vicarages and rectories. In fact, I've already notified those concerned that all grace and favour occupations must end.'

'So I understand,' answered Harrison. 'Among the letters awaiting my return was one from the Reverend Dove of Long Ashendon. I'm afraid,' he continued, 'he's rather unhappy as he was prevailed on to surrender his life tenure in the living on the strict understanding he'd have the future use of the rectory.' He paused. 'In the circumstances, Archdeacon, forcing him out would mean a degree of upset in the diocese.'

'Upset! My dear friend,' replied Cawthorne, smiling, 'if we're going to push through your proposals, we must prepare ourselves for a widespread wailing and gnashing of teeth!'

'Quite,' murmured Harrison, reddening. 'Nevertheless, a little diplomacy might...' His voice trailed away as his listener slipped from the table and went to the window. 'Richard,' began Cawthorne, staring out across the lawn, 'you know better than me the state of diocesan affairs: we must act ruthlessly. After all,' he continued, turning to face him, 'the Church is here to serve the entire people—the destitute, the homeless, the masses in their anonymous tenements—not just a retired couple wishing to remain in a house designed for an eighteenth-century gentleman, complete, I believe, with stables and coach house for carriage and pair.'

Harrison made no reply: the logic was irrefutable; there even was, although he hated to admit it, at least a modicum of justice in what had been said.

'So,' continued Cawthorne briskly, returning from the window, 'much as I'm sorry to inconvenience the Reverend Dove and his wife, they must be out by Lady Day next—that gives them well over six months to find a new home. You'll please write informing them.' Pausing, he smiled. 'Yet perhaps, on second thoughts, a little of your diplomacy mightn't go amiss.' The speaker's smile broadened. 'Why don't you drive over to Long Ashendon tomorrow morning and break the news to the old couple as gently as you can?'

For the second time that afternoon, Harrison surprised himself as he heard himself say: 'I'm sorry, Archdeacon, not in the morning—that, I'm afraid, I've already set aside to attend the inquest of an old comrade from army days.'

Chapter Three

Although the huge golden hands of the cathedral clock showed it was not yet quite quarter to ten, Harrison felt that he'd already accomplished a morning's work as he hurried along the path beneath. Having reached his office early, he'd made a good start on his mountainous backlog of correspondence before Miss Simpson's arrival. Cancelling his appointments, he'd signed a number of urgent letters before phoning Tom Dove, interrupting the old man's breakfast to ask if he might see him that afternoon. Deflecting Dove's questions, he'd rung off to contact the diocesan architect's office, requesting George Davidson to call next day. Only then had he felt free to leave and thankfully escape his secretary's rhapsodies on the subject of word processors.

Comparatively early as it was, the day was already growing hot. In brilliant sunshine, he passed through the Kent War Memorial Garden. Ducking through the narrow passage of the Queningate, he negotiated the still dew-damp steps down into Broad Street and was soon hurrying past the ruins of St Augustine's Abbey towards the city law courts and prison.

With its austere grey walls and pew-like benches, there was something of the nonconformist chapel about Court Number Four. Nevertheless, as Harrison, flushed and hot, pushed through the glass-panelled swing doors, there was little sign of the reverent hush and solemnity he'd expected. Instead, he entered an atmosphere verging on that of a cocktail party—a somewhat subdued party, admittedly, and one at which the vast majority of the guests were male, middle-aged and, apart from uniformed policemen, almost exclusively dressed in limp baggy suits. Clerks, lawyers and official witnesses stood chatting and laughing in groups, and as he took a seat at the back, Harrison found it hard to believe that this cheerful gathering had anything remotely to do with death, or that somewhere in the bustling city outside, a dissected corpse lay in a mortuary refrigerator. Indeed, sitting alone at the back, he felt rather like a stranger among a congregation of talkative rustics awaiting harvest thanksgiving—an impression reinforced by the sight of Dr Brooke, the city pathologist, who, flamboyant in tweeds and bulging yellow waistcoat, with long side whiskers and long curly blond hair, towered above his dowdy companions like a prosperous farmer cattle auctioneer.

The swing doors opened. At once there was a slight but perceptible drop in the noise level; laughter faded, and with a hurried final word, officials and witnesses dispersed to their positions before the dais and royal coat of arms. From the direction of their glances, the catalyst of this transformation was clearly one of the figures standing at the entrance. From his position, Harrison's view was blocked, so all he could make out were dim phantom shapes behind the frosted panes. Next moment, however, Arthur Cave-Brown, a local solicitor, entered, talking in whispers to a tall, lantern-jawed, youngish man, whose blue suit and scrubbed boyish face instantly proclaimed him to be American. Behind followed Rachel Miller in a formal dark suit, her pale face and dark eyes more striking than ever with her hair drawn severely back and knotted behind her neck.

Noticing Harrison, Rachel gave a surprised half smile. His heart gave a painful jolt at the sight: just as the previous afternoon, he'd witnessed the close resemblance between the fay-like Mrs Cawthorne and her daughter, in that hesitant smile, he now saw a feminine version of the young man who had shared the Fehrbelliner Platz office. For the first time he understood why he was attending the preliminary inquest. It was not, after all, mere defiance, a token resistance to Cawthorne; nor was it irrational guilt or a sentimental wish to mark a comrade's passing. He'd come for himself, knowing he'd have no peace until he knew why the dying David Miller had mysteriously reappeared in his life, apparently so eager to seek him out.

'Be upstanding!'

The clerk's command burst across his thoughts, bringing him stumbling to his feet.

Having sat and greeted the court, Dr Benham, Kent county coroner and local secretary of the National Beekeepers' Association, paused to leaf through the papers before him. With half-moon glasses slipping forward on his thin nose, his curly grey hair haloing his face, he scanned the documents with a placid smile, as if, instead of refreshing his memory on the grisly details of the discovery and dissection of a putrefying corpse, he was perusing a pleasing monograph on hive maintenance or the efficient bottling of honey.

'As this is only the preliminary hearing,' he began at last, 'today I intend hearing only the autopsy report and the police evidence.' Dr Benham's benign gaze rested momentarily on Rachel. 'And because the deceased's next of kin resides abroad, I'd like to set an early date for the full hearing.' Pausing, he peered over his desk at the sandy-haired clerk below. 'I suggest, Mr Hartley-Taylor, we hold it exactly four weeks from today.'

Half rising, the clerk answered with something between a nod and a bow; having done so, he slid down again to begin laboriously and noisily scratching a note to himself.

'And now,' resumed the coroner, 'I would like to begin with the testimony of Inspector Derby of the Transport Police.'

A uniformed officer strode to the front and began his evidence. 'A suitcase was found left in a first-class compartment of the eleven-fifteen Dover to London train on the night of Monday, the 13th August, belonging to one D. R. Miller of 106d Manresa Road, London, SW3. Although a note was sent, informing the owner, the item remained unclaimed. Then, on Tuesday last, the body of an adult male was discovered…'

'One moment, Inspector,' interrupted Dr Benham. 'Where exactly was the corpse found?'

'Ten miles west of Canterbury, sir,' answered the policeman, 'between the villages of Old Wives Lees and Chartham Hatch. A party of maintenance engineers clearing under growth in a cutting discovered the body lying nine yards from the track, concealed among the brambles round the base of a road bridge close to the Red Bull public house. In the inside pocket was a wallet with money, cash cards and a single ticket from Canterbury to London dated the same day.'

'I presume, Inspector,' said the coroner, 'that the train on which the luggage was found would have travelled along that particular stretch of line, having previously stopped at Canterbury?'

'Yes, sir.'

After a further few questions, Dr Benham dismissed his witness. 'Now, Dr Brooke, if we might hear your autopsy report.'

Until then the pathologist had been sitting slumped, his eyelids closed, a look of weary indifference on his face. Now, however, he rose with alacrity and, smoothing back his leonine hair, came forward to take the customary oath. This done, he began reading from the typescript in his hand, elbow resting nonchalantly on the witness box. 'The cadaver was in a generally poor condition, premature putrefaction having set in due to the unusually hot weather. However, apart from the severe injury to the back of the head and numerous small lesions, the external damage was entirely post-mortem—the result of the attentions of rodents and carrion crows.'

Harrison saw Rachel flinch, and as Brooke proceeded to list an entire ghastly catalogue of ruptured organs and broken bones, he watched her gradually hunch forward, as it through that hot, muggy courtroom, a chilling wind was blowing on her alone.

'Thank you, Dr Brooke,' said Dr Benham as the pathologist

mercifully lapsed into silence. 'I see,' he continued, burrowing among the papers on his desk and extracting a document, 'from your written report, you note cancerous growths in both kidneys, the bowels and pancreas. May I then take it that you fully concur with the prognosis given by the Westminster Hospital?'

'Yes, I'd say that the victim had months to live at most.'

'I further notice,' continued the coroner, 'you give the exact cause of death as "Massive intracranial haemorrhage". How, in your view, was that caused?'

'From the impact of the base of the skull against the bridge support—traces of the brickwork being found in the wound and the hair. The other internal injuries were caused by the initial impact with the ground.' Brooke glanced at his notes. 'Soil and traces of vegetation were embedded deep in the right ear cavity and in the various lesions, as well as ingrained in much of the exposed skin and clothing—all indications of the extreme force with which the body struck the ground.'

'In your opinion, would these injuries be consistent with a fall from a fast-moving train?'

'Yes, indeed.' The pathologist hesitated. 'But, of course, in these matters there is always an element of chance. If the deceased's intention was immediate oblivion, then it was perhaps fortunate that the base of the skull struck the brickwork, otherwise he might have lingered for anything up to an hour.' Brooke smiled round the courtroom. 'Leaping out of trains is, in my experience, not exactly the most intelligent way of despatching oneself into the Great Beyond.'

Harrison glanced at Rachel's bowed head, then looked back to the pathologist. Observing his supercilious smile, he felt an angry disgust.

Dr Benham was also clearly none too pleased with Brooke's remark. 'May I remind you, Dr Brooke,' he said sharply, frowning over his spectacles, for all the world like some indignant sheep, 'that it is not for you or me to determine the reason for the victim's unfortunate fall. As this is a railway fatality, under the terms of the Coroners Act of 1887, a jury alone can decide whether the deceased fell by accident or design.' Having delivered himself of this, he dismissed the clearly amused Brooke, and as the latter returned to his seat, Harrison saw him actually wink at a couple of his cronies.

Dr Benham looked about the court. 'As that concludes all I need to hear today, I propose, if the police have no objections, to now sign the burial certificate.'

With the morning's sessions drawing to a close and the various courts disgorging their occupants, the entrance hall was thronged. Disappointed by the paucity of information at the preliminary hearing, and feeling he'd wasted his time, Harrison pushed towards the entrance. Doing so, he spotted Rachel and her two companions in a corner, she looking paler and more feverish than ever after the strain of, the hearing. Harrison wondered if he should go over and speak, but imagining what she was feeling, and not knowing what to say, he continued pushing towards the exit.

Before he reached it, however, Rachel turned towards him. As she did so, Harrison saw again the unmistakable genetic imprint of the man whose gutted remains temporarily lay in the care of Dr Brooke. Hardly conscious of making any decision, he immediately turned and made towards the small group.

'Excuse me, Miss Miller—I wanted again to express my sincere condolences.'

'Thank you, Colonel Harrison. It was good of you to come.' Rachel's mind was clearly still occupied with what she'd heard in the courtroom for her smile was automatic and her eyes didn't quite meet his. 'I think you know Mr Cave-Brown who will be representing me at the final inquest. This,' she said, turning to the lanky American, 'is Joe Eisenberg from Dad's old firm who's taken over his European work.'

Having shaken hands with both her companions, Harrison turned back to Rachel. 'Part of my reason for attending today is that, since you called on Saturday, I've remembered who your father was: he and I served in the army together just after the war. Presumably that's why he attempted to look me up.'

'Of course!' said Rachel. 'From your military rank, I should have guessed that was the connection: I knew Dad had been in the British Army before he was taken on by ours, though I don't recall him ever mentioning your name.'

Despite the slight jolt he felt at her final words, Harrison smiled. 'My dear, why should he have? It was all a long time ago, our time together in Berlin just after the end of the war.'

'You were with Dad in Berlin!' There was a sudden sharp interest in Rachel's face.

'Oh, yes,' Harrison nodded. 'We worked together for the British Control Commission. Well,' he said briskly, 'I won't keep you, but I'd like just to say how much I admired and respected your father, and to express my condolences. If there's anything I can help you with, please get in touch.' With a nod at the two men, he turned and made for the door, and within moments was back in the sunshine, retracing his steps along Longport. He hadn't taken a dozen paces, however, before he heard Rachel's voice behind, calling his name.

'Sorry to delay you, Colonel,' she said, catching him up. 'I want to ask a few questions.'

'Of course—only too delighted.'

Rachel glanced about her. 'Do you know any quiet place around here? Somewhere we could talk in peace?'

Mounting the steps to the Queningate, the two figures entered the war memorial garden. The lawns and flowerbeds around the tall central cross were as deserted as when Harrison had hurried between them earlier. Apart from the incessant chirp of birds and the drone of the traffic passing along Broad Street, nothing disturbed the peace of this sequestered corner of the precincts.

'Right,' said Harrison, stepping from the shadow of the bastion set in the high wall behind them, 'I think we can talk here safely.'

On the walk back, Rachel had said not a word. Now, however, looking around the symmetrically laid out garden, with its severely-cut grass, trim bushes and rosebeds, her expression softened, and she murmured, 'It's perfect.' She gave her companion a weary smile. 'You've certainly found yourself a perfect retreat, Colonel.'

Harrison gave a short laugh. 'Things aren't always quite as they seem.'

'I guess not.'

'Come on,' he said, leading her to the nearest of the benches under the wall. 'Let's get out of this damned heat.'

For a minute both sat in silence. Finally, Rachel turned. 'Colonel, did you know Dad well—personally, I mean?'

The other shook his head. 'Not really—though, as I said earlier, I liked and respected him: he was a capable and conscientious man.'

Harrison saw the pain flash through Rachel's eyes as he spoke; jerking her head away, she stared across, the lawn, her throat convulsing. Distressed and feeling absurdly clumsy and out of his depth, Harrison looked across the lawn—suddenly he was thinking of Tom and Joyce Dove, and of the afternoon trip to Long Ashendon, determining that moment to have Winnie with him when he broke the bad news.

'Tell me straight, Colonel,' Rachel's voice broke into his thoughts, 'do you think my father was someone to commit suicide—to kill himself on an impulse, without bothering to leave me or anyone else a note?' Her dark eyes were fixed on his. 'Do you really think he could be that mean—your conscientious man?'

Though he'd expected the question—in fact, he'd been dreading it—so direct and abrupt did it come, and so intense was the questioner's face and eyes as she spoke, that, colouring, Harrison dropped his gaze to the path.

'Well?' pressed the other. 'Was my father a man to kill himself without even bothering to say goodbye?'

'It's difficult to say,' murmured Harrison, profoundly wishing suddenly that he'd never agreed to this private meeting.

'Is it?' There was angry accusation in the other's voice. 'I thought that was something you military people prided yourselves on, being able to judge how an individual is likely to act!'

Raising his head, Harrison gazed up to where, above the inner wall, the cathedral towers reared against the sky. With the chirp of birds, the hum of bees, the drowsy purr of a distant mower in his ears, he thought back to the vast blackened ruins of Berlin and its bedraggled inhabitants as he began assessing the likelihood of the suicide of the man who'd shared his office. Certainly the person he'd known as Müller had not lacked courage, the Military Medal was ample testimony to that. But is courage, he thought—moral or physical—an enduring trait? Don't the years wear down the bravest and the best? And anyway, he wondered, what is the courageous action when facing what David Miller had faced? Is it to surrender passively and accept the inevitable indignities of physical infirmity and pain—or to leap clear, to escape the grip of disease?

As if reading his thoughts, Rachel spoke. 'Remember, Dad was a religious man, Colonel—and even if you discount that, could he have ever been cruel enough to leave me feeling so rejected and so loaded down with guilt?'

Harrison cleared his throat. 'There is,' he said slowly, 'always the possibility of an accident. I remember reading something about faulty door catches on a number of trains.'

A look of disappointment crossed the other's face. 'I wasn't thinking of an accident, Colonel.'

For a moment, Harrison didn't take in the implication of her words, then he burst out, 'Good God! You're surely not suggesting that your father was killed deliberately?' Incredulous, he stared at her. 'Some sort of thuggish attack, you mean? Hooligans on the rampage?' He shook his head emphatically. 'No, no—it's quite impossible! If there had been anything remotely like that, it would surely have shown up in the pathologist's report.'

Opening her bag, Rachel withdrew a white envelope, creased and stained. 'This was found in Dad's back pocket,' she said, handing it over. 'The police aren't interested in it at all.'

Harrison squinted down. It was addressed to her father and posted from New York; above the sender's printed address were the gold-embossed words: 'Schumann-Hope, Lawson, Eisenberg & Miller—Attorneys at Law.'

'Look at the other side.'

Doing so, Harrison saw that the back was jotted over with odd words and numbers, some circled, some underlined in pencil or biro, and in one corner, a heavily boxed-in date. He knew at once what it was: a crude *aide-mémoire*, the evidence of a problem puzzled through on a journey or in an airport lounge—indeed, just the sort of thing that he himself habitually scribbled at board meetings whilst enduring some rambling diatribe on the merits or otherwise of plastic piping or the synthetic tile.

Taking out his reading glasses, he scanned the envelope. The words FULL ORCHESTRA—22 were written in capitals and underlined. Below were six names in a vertical list, each with either a number or circled word beside it. 'Goering 10,' he read aloud, then proceeded slowly down the list. 'Canaris 1, Menzies 1, Treeck 7,' he read, sounding exactly as if he was announcing unbelievable football results. Breaking off, he turned to Rachel. 'What's all this about?'

'You tell me, Colonel. When you said you'd worked with my father in Berlin, and knowing he'd tried to get in touch with you, those numbers and words seemed suddenly important. Especially,' she continued, dipping into her bag again and withdrawing a coloured postcard, 'having got this from Dad six weeks ago—it's from Dresden and it says he was there going through some recently opened state archives.'

'Yes, damn it! Of course! How stupid! The *Schwarze Kapelle*!'

Harrison had wandered out on to the lawn, bent over and frowning down at the scribbled figures and numbers. Now, however, as he spoke, he straightened and smiled round at Rachel who'd followed him, confident realization shining in his face. 'This,' he said, waving the envelope, 'explains everything.'

'It does?' Surprise, disbelief and disappointment rang in equal proportions in the other's voice.

'Yes, I believe so—didn't you mention something on Saturday about your father planning a book?'

'Yes, on art antiques.'

'No,' said Harrison, shaking his head, 'it wasn't about antiques he was going to write—at least, not the sort of antiques you've in mind.' He smiled briefly. 'It was history he was going to write on. That's why he was in Dresden, researching the recently opened East German archives—and also why he wanted to speak to me.'

'History?' repeated Rachel, bemused. 'What sort of history?'

'In a way, his and my own—the reason why we two found ourselves in post-war Berlin.' Harrison glanced again at the envelope. 'It is clear from this that the book he was planning was on the *Schwarze Kapelle*.'

Bewildered, Rachel shook her head. 'I'm lost: what is this *Schwarze Kapelle* thing?'

'It simply means Black Orchestra,' answered Harrison, returning to the bench. 'It was the Gestapo's name for the group of high-placed bureaucrats and military officers opposed to Hitler. You've heard of the July Plot, I imagine?' he said as Rachel sat down beside him. 'Count von Stauffenberg's attempt to blow the Führer to kingdom come?'

'Vaguely—but what makes you think Dad was interested in that?'

Harrison smiled. 'Because we all were—everyone involved in the de-Nazification programme. The history of the *Schwarze Kapelle* and the numbers of people involved in it was a gauge to the extent of the German people's opposition to the Nazis—and that brought into question the extent of their culpability. That, as you can imagine, straight after the war, was a red-hot potato, politically speaking. From what's scribbled here,' he continued, holding out the envelope, 'it seems your father managed to dig up some astonishing new facts regarding the true extent of that opposition—information presumably suppressed by the old GDR because it stemmed from an upper-class right wing.'

'You've worked all that out just from that scrap of paper!' said the other with an incredulous look. 'In God's name, how?'

'First from the title here, ORCHESTRA,' said Harrison, 'then there's this boxed-in date: July 16th, 1944—just four days before Stauffenberg exploded his bomb. Now look at these names—Canaris, for instance, is Admiral Canaris, head of the Abwehr—Military Intelligence—that was rather like our own MI6. It's now generally accepted that he was a prime mover behind the *Schwarze Kapelle*. In fact, the Nazis hanged him as a traitor just before the end of the war.'

'Yes, but for God's sake,' burst out Rachel, 'you're forgetting the first name—Hermann Goering was Hitler's deputy, wasn't he? You're not seriously saying he was secretly plotting against his own regime!'

Harrison's face clouded. 'I agree,' he murmured. 'The notion of the Reichsmarschall being behind the July Plot does seem rather difficult to accept.'

'Difficult! Impossible, I'd say!'

Frowning, Harrison gazed across the lawn, then shook his head. 'No, it's not impossible—Goering was a very different bird from the other Nazi leaders: like von Stauffenberg and Canaris himself, he was from the aristocratic class. He certainly had doubts about the war from the start. Who after all,' he continued, 'has ever fathomed the fellow—his extraordinary personality, that mix of courage and cowardice, intelligence and childish vaingloriousness?'

The doubt in Rachel's face had not disappeared, and she again pointed at the envelope. 'All right, what about this third name then—Menzies? It doesn't even sound German.'

'Nor is it, my dear. It's pure Scots,' said Harrison, laughing, 'just like my own! General Sir Stewart Menzies was head of MI6 from just before the outbreak of war until into the 'sixties. He's the famous M in Fleming's James Bond books.'

Rachel's eyes opened wide. 'I don't get it—are you saying that the head of British Intelligence was part of German resistance?'

Harrison shrugged. 'Who knows—he certainly would have known about the *Schwarze Kapelle*, I imagine, and, after all, von Stauffenberg's bomb was British.' Smiling, he leaned back on the bench. 'Dear old Sir Stewart certainly had his finger in many a pie.' For a moment, he sat in silence, remembering his own long-ago stay at the General's Cotswold home—the delicious pleasure he'd experienced, watching his host poker-faced at the church lectern while reading aloud of Moses's own difficulties in the selection of reliable spies.

Rachel's voice intruded. 'But what about these last three names: R. Treeck, F. J. Mendelssohn and J. Lipmann—and what are these words ringed beside the last two, *Fiddler*, *Fifer* and *Drummer*?'

'They're cover names, obviously,' answered Harrison, 'though why this chap, Mendelssohn, has two I can't imagine.' Pausing, he frowned. 'And, as for the names themselves, I'm afraid they don't ring any bells for the present.'

Rachel looked away. 'You may be right, but it doesn't explain why Dad fell from that train or why he ever came to Canterbury in the first place.'

'As I say,' began Harrison, 'in coming here, he might well have thought I had some useful...'

'Come on, Colonel!' Rachel swung round, eyes blazing.

'Surely he would have contacted you before he came—and anyway, he was here three nights! What was he doing all that time? What was so urgent that it brought him rushing here on a Friday night? And why, however horrible it was to learn that the cancer was back, should he kill himself without a word to me?' She turned back to stare across the lawn. 'With those names on the list, and when I heard you had worked with him in Berlin, I thought perhaps...' Her voice tailed away.

'What?' said Harrison gently. 'That he was on the track of some escaped Nazi leader, and so was killed?' He shook his head. 'My dear, it's all too long ago: we're in the last decade of the twentieth century—and this is Canterbury, not somewhere in South America!' He gave a short laugh. 'Anyway, any old Nazi leaders still on the loose would have job enough now to set a mousetrap, let alone thrust a struggling man out through a train door!'

'I guess so.'

There came the boom of the cathedral dock. 'I'm afraid I must go,' said Harrison, getting up. 'My wife will be waiting lunch.'

Rising, Rachel held out her hand. 'Anyway, Colonel, thanks for sparing so much time.'

'Look,' said Harrison, wondering if he'd been too hard on her, 'let me keep this envelope for now: I'll find out whose are those names I don't recognize. If nothing else, it will prove that your father was indeed researching the *Schwarze Kapelle*.'

'All right, but I don't know what the point is.' Rachel grimaced. 'I'm still left with the burden of Dad killing himself, and having to remember that bastard's stupid joke back there in court.'

Harrison nodded sympathetically—the image of the pathologist's wink rising in his mind. 'Tell you what,' he said, 'now the burial certificate has been signed, your father's body is yours to dispose of: you could always arrange for a private autopsy. Who knows,' he added, 'it's always possible Dr Brooke missed some tiny clue.'

Chapter Four

'Damn it, woman! What else could I have done?' Harrison glared at the back of the lorry ahead. 'And anyway, where's the harm in getting a second opinion?'

'I told you, it just puts off her having to come to terms with her father's suicide, and so delays the healing process.' Winnie paused. 'And anyway,' she went on, 'what will Dr Brooke think if he finds out it was you who planted the doubt in Rachel's mind regarding his competence?'

'Confound Brooke!' exploded Harrison, slamming down a gear. 'The fellow's nothing but a self-satisfied brute!'

The clock had struck two before the Volvo passed under Mint Yard Arch. Nearly half an hour then went by before it was clear of the crowded streets and trundling south-west along the banks of the Stour. Even on the so-called 'open road', the going was slow as the heavily laden trucks began their snorting haul up on to the rolling North Downs.

'Can't we just take our time?' pleaded Winnie as the Volvo, like an impatient elephant calf, edged out from behind the lumbering herd. 'We're not due in Long Ashendon until four.'

'I want to make a small detour,' replied the other. The car hesitated, then fell back before the oncoming traffic.

Winnie inwardly sighed, but said nothing more: from long experience, she knew the inevitable delays any drive through the diocese involved, due to Harrison's insistence on using the opportunity to inspect any recent church repairs in the area—and, almost as inevitably, then fulminating against the builders for half an hour afterwards.

In less than a mile, they thankfully turned off the main road, and bisecting the ancient Pilgrims Way, headed through quiet country lanes, occasionally glimpsing Canterbury as a dark smudge in the distance below. Insects splattered across the windscreen in yellows and reds; in the fields, cattle sprawled, languorously flicking their tails against a torment of flies. After the overlong summer, there was a parched, weary stillness to the landscape—broken only once by a maddened dog exploding from a dusty farmyard to rush barking after the car—and as pasture gradually gave place to orchard, the effects of the drought grew even more evident: limp leaves hung prematurely yellowing, while the ripening fruit was as wizened and undeveloped as that in the deanery garden.

Lulled by the warmth, Winnie allowed her eyes to droop. Almost as she did so, she felt the car brake. Sitting up, she found they were puffing on to the verge of a lane. 'Where are we?' she asked, looking round for the expected spire or steeple.

'Nowhere particular,' answered Harrison, opening his door. 'There's just something I want to glance at.' As he spoke, there came a raucous two-toned blare of a klaxon; a moment later, the ground seemed to tremble as, with a roar and clatter, a train thundered past, invisible below the line of the hedge.

'I take it,' said Winnie coldly, 'that this is something to do with the inquest?'

Her husband nodded. 'That's the Red Bull,' he said, pointing towards a distant roof. 'Apparently it was below the bridge ahead on the right that poor Miller was found. I just want to take a quick look at the place, that's all.'

'Go on then,' said Winnie wearily, 'if you really must.'

Although the bridge was lower and narrower than Harrison had expected, below was just as he had imagined:

steep banks dropping down to the twin sets of rails, with the recently cut nettles already blackening on the slopes and wide smears of ash marking where the cleared vegetation had been burnt.

Leaning out over the parapet, he looked directly down. Below, on the shorn ground around the brickwork supports, were signs of recent trampling. However, apart from that, and a length of striped tape tangled among the close-cut nettle stems, there was no other indication that a human body had lain there for nearly three weeks. A sense of futility rolled over him. What was the point of this visit? What had he hoped to find? However it had happened—spasm of despair or unlikely accident—nothing here could explain how Miller had come to plunge from the train.

He straightened to leave. As he did so, there came the sound of a car door.

Gazing forlornly down into the shorn, blackened cutting, Harrison had not been conscious of any vehicle passing. Thus, at the sudden metallic slam, he looked round in surprise. Above the hedge bordering the lane there now protruded, not only the roof of the Volvo, but also the gleaming red top of a second car. It was parked close to the turning on to the bridge—and, as he turned, above it appeared a waving grey-sleeved arm and a formal, black broad-brimmed ecclesiastical hat.

'Good afternoon, Mrs Harrison. All well, I trust?'

The greeting rang through the quiet air. With a muttered curse, Harrison hurried back into the lane, emerging behind the short, rotund and instantly recognizable figure of Canon Bedford, the local rural dean.

'Ah, Colonel Harrison! There you are!' exclaimed the cleric, turning at the sound of his footsteps. 'I guessed you must be somewhere at hand.' He stretched out his hand. 'I stopped when I noticed your car. Not a breakdown, I trust?'

'Oh, no,' replied the other, 'I stopped merely to…to …'

'Oh, quite,' interrupted the other. 'My dear fellow, you need not explain.' Bedford's grey-green eyes twinkled. 'Even our esteemed Dilapidations secretary is subject, I fear, to the inconvenient demands of poor Brother Ass!'

Either from embarrassment or deference to the speaker's old-fashioned broad-banded clerical collar and the tiny black rose on his hatband, reddening, Harrison shook his head. 'No, Canon, you misunderstand. As I was in the vicinity, I stopped to pay a short tributary visit to where an old colleague was recently killed.'

'Indeed?' The rural dean looked grave. 'A colleague, you say? Not a member of the board?'

'No, someone I served with in the army years ago.'

'Ah, in the army—yes, of course,' said the canon, managing to sound as if military service, past or present, was sufficient explanation for sudden violent or untoward death. 'Poor soul! A road accident, I presume?'

'No, he apparently managed to fall from a train.'

'Really! A train?' Canon Bedford's interest sharpened perceptibly. 'Ah, yes!' he exclaimed, striking his brow. 'Now I remember! A parishioner mentioned that a body had been found beside the railway in the locality. And the poor man had been an old friend of yours, Colonel?'

'Well, an associate, certainly,' answered Harrison, glancing towards the indistinct form of Winnie behind the windscreen.

'The accident happened below in the cutting, did it?' continued the cleric, attempting to peer through the hedge. Next moment, he was striding towards the end of the bridge. With an appeasing wave back at the car, Harrison hurried behind. 'No, not that side, Canon,' he called as Bedford headed across, scanning westwards. 'The fall was over here.'

'Ah—on the up-line?' The rural dean hurried back.

Harrison pointed down. 'The body was found here directly below.'

'Yes, indeed,' said Bedford, holding on to his hat as he craned over. 'But when exactly was this tragic fall?'

'Nearly a month ago now—back at the beginning of August.'

'Really—early August, you say!' exclaimed Bedford, still gazing down with interest. Straightening, he turned, perplexity in his face. 'But, Colonel, I had been given to understand that the body was badly smashed.'

'It was,' answered the other. 'I was at the preliminary inquest this morning. Apparently, the force of the impact broke every bone.'

'Every bone!' Frowning, Bedford turned and gazed away along the rails stretching straight to the horizon, then looked back round. 'Colonel, you're sure about this—the entire bone structure smashed?'

'Quite sure.'

'Really! Well, I must say, I find that absolutely fascinating.' The cleric again peered over the bridge. 'Fascinating,' he repeated, staring down at the rails.

Shocked by the apparent ghoulish interest, Harrison frowned. 'If you'll excuse me, Canon,' he said stiffly, 'I must get back to my wife.'

'My dear fellow, of course,' said his companion, turning at once from the bridge. 'This unfortunate comrade, Colonel,' he resumed, accompanying the other back into the lane, 'may I ask his name?'

'David Miller.'

'Miller?' repeated Bedford, halting. 'Not one of the Faversham Millers, surely?'

Harrison shook his head. 'No, David was an American; he had no family connection with this locality at all.'

'Indeed! Again you amaze me, Colonel—a Miller, you say, with no relations in this locality!' Bedford shook his head. 'Extraordinary! At this end of the diocese, Millers are positively thick on the ground—ah, but now I must pay my respects to your wife.' Bedford hurried forward towards the Volvo, doffing his hat.

'It was very kind of you to stop, Canon,' said Winnie, shaking hands through the window.

'Not at all. I've been having a fascinating talk with your

husband. In a matter of minutes, he's managed to surprise and interest me more than I can say. But tell me, Mrs Harrison,' continued the cleric, beaming down, 'may I ask to what do we owe the pleasure of your presence in this far-flung corner?'

Winnie smiled. 'We're on our way to one of your own parishes, Canon—Long Ashendon.'

'Long Ashendon!' repeated the rural dean with a sudden look of concern. 'I hope, Colonel,' he said turning, 'this is nothing to do with this unpleasant rumour that the Doves are going to be asked to vacate the rectory. As you doubtless know, they were guaranteed life tenancy by poor Dr Crocker.'

Harrison inwardly winced and, colouring slightly, shook his head. 'Nothing was put in writing, I'm afraid.'

'Nevertheless,' protested the other, 'Dr Cawthorne must be informed that Crocker gave his word on the matter.'

'I assure you, he has been told,' murmured Harrison unhappily and glanced at his watch. 'Canon, you'll have to excuse us—I'm afraid we're already late as it is.' A moment later he was pulling away, the rural dean staring after the car, hat raised in salutation, a look of grave and bewildered perplexity on his normally genial face.

'Confound it!' burst out Harrison savagely, as the figure in the rear-view mirror was mercifully blanketed as the car swung right across the bridge. 'What was the blasted fellow doing in this out of the way place!'

'If you mean Canon Bedford,' answered Winnie drily, 'I don't see how you can blame him for travelling round his own rural deanery. Anyway,' she added, 'I don't know why you're so upset. Sooner or later, he had to know the truth.' She paused. 'Or is it that you simply don't like being seen in your new role as archdeacon's bailiff?'

Gripping the wheel hard, Harrison stared rigidly ahead.

'I really don't know why I agreed to come,' resumed his

wife after a few seconds. 'I don't know if I want to be a party to this errand you've agreed to run.'

'Damn it, woman!' exploded Harrison. 'I've told you—there's nothing else I could do! If I'd refused Cawthorne outright, it would have meant resignation. What's the use of that?'

'At least you could have kept everyone's respect. What's Matthew going to think when he hears of this visit?'

Receiving no answer, Winnie leaned back and listlessly stared ahead as they sped on through the sultry afternoon. Just as previously pasture had given place to orchard, apple and plum tree now gave way to hop garden. Harvest had begun, but in place of the bygone hoards of cockney and gipsy pickers, huge machines, garishly painted in red and yellow, crawled like gigantic praying mantises along the green avenues, their mechanical hands roughly tearing and gouging at the high-growing bines; and whereas in the past the air had been filled with the soporific tang of drying pods, now it stank of exhaust fumes. Winnie's spirits sank further: the whole scene—the huddles of redundant oast houses, the hideous devouring machines—seemed all too painfully symbolic of the spirit that was forcing the sick elderly man and his wife from their home.

'Thank God! Holy Trinity at last!'

Her husband's voice broke into Winnie's thoughts, and looking round, she saw a solitary tower raised like a finger above the fields.

In one of the great medieval cities like York, Norwich or Canterbury, Long Ashendon parish church might have been passed with hardly a glance; set where it was, however, among low-lying hop fields and scrubby orchards, its only rivals a few distant dumpy spires and steeples, its graceful high-pinnacled tower soared in eye-catching splendour, a thoroughbred tossing its head over a straggle of nags. Curiously, the church stood well outside the village, a good quarter mile from the nearest building—almost as if, after its original patron had first raised it up (doubtless, long-nosed Norman himself), it had snootily looked down its own long tower and, seeing in what dreary and nondescript setting it was cast, had stalked off in high dudgeon to stand, back turned on a community it deigned not to see or acknowledge.

'Oh, it *is* a lovely church!' murmured. Winnie appreciatively as they headed towards it. 'Dr Cawthorne can't really be thinking of closing such buildings!'

Harrison gave a noncommittal grunt. For years he'd regarded Holy Trinity as an extravagant drain on tightly stretched resources. Peering up through the windscreen and seeing on the tower the marks of its most recent repairs, he felt a sneaking sympathy for the archdeacon: after all, he thought, what was the point of such massive barn-like churches in villages where now the average congregation would hardly fill a mini-bus?

Beside the lychgate, a weathered noticeboard faced the open fields. As the car swept by, its occupants glimpsed a crudely painted representation of the church—its tower wrapped in a bloodstained handkerchief, and above it, the faded words: Help our Patient—Holy Trinity Tower Appeal.

A few yards beyond the noticeboard a number of children's bicycles were heaped against the churchyard wall. Instinctively, Harrison slowed and, glancing left, caught sight of their owners running about the overgrown graves and clambering over the pile of scaffolding pipes and planking heaped against the outside of the nave. Frowning, he hesitated. Normally he would have stopped and ordered them out, but conscious of already being late, he reluctantly contented himself with a double blare of his horn.

A few modern bungalows and a row of drab council houses

slipped by before the village proper was entered. Despite its name, Long Ashendon consisted in the main of a scatter of buildings round a broad grassy expanse, over which at present a phalanx of ducks were racing to and fro in short bursts, trailing their wings and quacking loudly.

'Whatever's happening?' exclaimed Winnie, peering ahead at the knot of villagers gathered round the wide pond at the further corner of the green, apparently absorbed in watching a couple of shirtless, mud-splattered youths wading through the muddy water in thigh-length waders.

Squinting into the sunlight, Harrison saw two of the spectators turn at the sound of the car and immediately begin heading towards it, one waving a walking stick.

'Stop, Richard! There's Tom and Joyce now!'

Winnie's words were unnecessary; even at that distance there wasn't the slightest chance of mistaking the couple: the short, slight figure of the ex-rector in panama hat, clerical collar and yellowing cotton jacket; beside him, steadying him as he limped towards the car, his wife—who, incongruously at odds with her wide-brimmed straw hat and floral summer dress, was carrying in her free hand a stumpy, mud-caked object roughly the shape and size of an Oscar trophy.

'Oh dear!' murmured Winnie as the engine was turned off. 'Tom's stroke has certainly told!'

Harrison saw at once what she meant: in the few months since he'd last seen him, a subtle yet terrible change had overtaken Dove. Though recognizably the same impish rebel who for so long had plagued him, the man limping towards them seemed, like the ripening fruit, to have withered and shrivelled in the summer drought. As long as Harrison had known him, his face had always had a decidedly wizened, puckish look; now, however, the deeply etched lines, the chalky-grey pallor and prominent cheekbones created an impression of fragility never there before.

'Damn Cawthorne!' he muttered: until now he'd regarded the serving of notice on Tom and Joyce Dove as a painful embarrassment—now he saw it as gratuitous cruelty, a vile cowardly body blow to a literally tottering septuagenarian. Grimly he clambered from the car and, with heavy heart, began crossing the grass to meet them.

'Ah, there you are at last, Harrison!' called Dove cheerily as he approached. 'Joyce and I were beginning to think that more important business than a couple of old fogies had waylaid you!'

'Nonsense, Thomas!' laughed his wife. 'Richard, don't take any notice of his ridiculous teasing.'

'Well, as it happens,' replied Harrison, somewhat stiffly, 'I did run into Canon Bedford on the way, and he took the opportunity to raise one or two small matters.'

'Indeed!' Dove's eyes sparkled. 'First, a mysterious phone call over breakfast, now deanery conferences in country lay-bys!' He grinned. 'I must say, Harrison, diocesan management is becoming positively Byzantine!'

Disconcerted, the other reddened: clearly, for all his physical frailty, Dove's mind and personality remained frighteningly intact. 'I assure you,' he began, but broke off as a sudden scream from the direction of the pond rent the air. Looking round, he was in time to witness one of the wading youths hurl a second sodden, decayed segment of what once had been a feather mattress towards a group of teenage girls.

'Ah, there you have it, Harrison!' said Dove, grinning broadly. 'Our simple rustic existence—rather different from the polished life of a cathedral close, I imagine!'

'I'm going to talk to Winnie,' interrupted Joyce, laughing. 'Thomas, you come in your own time—and allow Richard to help you.'

'As you see,' continued Dove, nodding towards the pond as his wife walked on, 'unusually, our Parish Council has heeded my advice and is taking advantage of this drought to clear the water. Joyce and I thought we'd survey progress while awaiting your arrival.'

Even from a distance of twenty yards or so, the wisdom

of the ex-rector's advice was evident: the usually broad pond was half dry, caked mud showing the extent of its usual limits. Heaped among the young ash saplings on its banks was an array of salvaged articles, prominent among which were an ancient mangle and a surprisingly shiny supermarket trolley.

'Fascinating, isn't it!' exclaimed Dove. 'How do these things ever get there, one wonders?' He grinned at his visitor. 'What do you think: a wish to hide secrets or some primitive form of libation? A throwback to water nymph worship, perhaps?'

Knowing he was being teased, Harrison smiled, then looked back at the car where Joyce was showing the object she was carrying for Winnie's inspection. 'I see,' he said, 'that you found something of interest in the pond.'

'Of interest?' Dove shook his head, his face suddenly serious. 'No, my dear fellow, merely a depressing symbol of personal failure—that piece of hideous kitsch Joyce is presently showing Winifred is the triumph of ridiculous jealousy and spite over my obviously wasted forty years in this parish.' Turning, he glanced to where a middle-aged woman was heading towards them, shooing and flapping at the ducks as she came. 'Come on!' he said, urgently, hobbling on. 'Let's beat a strategic retreat. That's Mrs Boyle. If she sees what secret the pond has revealed, there's every chance of blood flowing in the village before nightfall!'

Whereas the parish church stood boldly on a slight rise outside the village, Long Ashendon rectory did the very opposite, lurking behind a thick curtain of laurels that simultaneously robbed it of light and screened it completely from passers-by. For Harrison, standing at the drawing-room window, tea-cup in hand, the dark, impenetrable foliage had a peculiarly depressing effect, reinforcing as it did, his sense of being hemmed into a quite intolerable situation.

Behind him, the women were laughing at the absurd story

Dove was recounting about the broken china ornament he'd brought back to the house. Harrison, however, hardly took in a word, so entirely was he occupied with the question of exactly how and when to bring up the news of the archdeacon's decision. Sipping his tea, he glumly stared out at the aged Morris Traveller parked on the overgrown gravel outside, its rear windows decorated with a variety of stickers, including those of Greenpeace, CND and Save the Whale.

'Oh, no, surely not!' he heard Winnie suddenly exclaim. 'Richard, did you hear that?'

'Sorry,' he said, looking round. 'Hear what, my dear?'

'Tom was saying there was a quarrel at the church fête here back in June. Two of the village women both wanted to buy the figurine, and the one who eventually got it later threw it into the pond.'

'Good Lord! For heaven's sake, why?'

Dove laughed. 'I told you, Harrison—good old-fashioned malice, nothing else! Our own dear cleaner, Mrs Taylor, was determined to have it at all costs, simply to make sure that Mrs Boyle didn't. Once she had the thing, she only wanted to get rid of it—and what better place than the village pond!'

'Oh, come on now, Thomas!' interrupted his wife. 'That's pure supposition. You have no proof.'

'My dear, however else could Miss Hodge's little donation have found its way to the water?' Grinning, Dove shook his head. 'No, that's clearly how it happened. And as for proof, my forty years incumbency here is all the evidence I need.'

'Well,' laughed Winnie, 'I still don't believe it!'

'Of course you don't!' The old man's eyes twinkled. 'Dear lady, how on earth could you be expected to? After the refinements of cathedral living, weaned as it were on the dean's best sherry, what could you possibly know of the primitive passions of we simple rustics!' Clearly enjoying himself, Dove rubbed his hands. 'If you don't believe me, ask Joyce: there are feuds in this parish that would embarrass the Borgias—superstitions that the less enlightened of the pharaohs might have baulked at!'

Chuckling, he pointed at the table next to Harrison. 'No, mark my words, that's how Miss Hodge's little donation got into the pond—like faithful good Sir Bedivere returning Excalibur to the lake, Margery Taylor crept out one night and hurled the awful thing out into the pond with all the strength of a long and carefully nurtured spite.'

Frowning, Harrison looked down at the bizarre piece, of porcelain. Still encrusted with mud, it lay now half wrapped in a back number of the *New Scientist*. It was certainly hideous enough—a grinning, bearded monkey dressed in an eighteenth-century wig, frock coat, satin waistcoat and breeches. Now, with its two arms snapped off, it had the appearance of a grotesque parody of the Venus de Milo. No wonder, he thought, Ruth Hodge had donated the thing to the fête—and as for throwing it away, the murky depths of a duck pond seemed an eminently suitable place for such a ghastly piece of junk.

'What are you going to do with it?' asked Winnie.

'Get rid of it before Miss Hodge comes round,' answered Joyce. 'Apparently, it belonged to her mother, and it would upset her to see it broken.' She smiled over at Harrison. 'Now, Richard, can't I tempt you to a slice of this fruit cake? So far you haven't eaten a thing.'

'Thank you, no.' Laying down his cup and saucer, Harrison braced himself. 'Yesterday afternoon,' he began, 'I had the opportunity of discussing the financial affairs of the diocese with our new archdeacon. In the course of conversation, he happened to mention…'

'One moment, Harrison,' interrupted Dove, raising a hand. 'As this sounds like a diocesan matter, I think it better discussed in private.' He struggled up from the sofa, helped by his wife, then came over and picked up the statuette in its wrapping paper. 'I'll take this vile thing away before anyone else sees it.' He smiled back as he made for the door. 'Come along then, my dear chap—we don't wish to burden the ladies with the grislier details of ecclesiastical administration.'

Avoiding the women's eyes, Harrison followed the

ex-rector out into the hail, feeling uncomfortably like one of the Emperor Caligula's fatal emissaries.

'Welcome to my little *sanctum sanctorum*—excuse me a moment while I clear you a perch.'

Placing the monkey figurine among the untidy heaps and books and box files on his desk, Dove began removing a pile of typewritten papers from a chair. Behind him, Harrison glanced about. Though he'd visited the rectory before, this was the first time he'd actually entered the study. A single-doored French window in the further corner provided the light, while the sombre, gloomy feel of the room was heightened by the faded décor and the crammed bookshelves that completely covered two walls.

Facing him was Dove's cluttered desk, where among a welter of papers stood the very twin of that faithful old Imperial typewriter so recently and peremptorily snatched from his office. An assortment of cupboards and filing cabinets, together with a venerable gestetner duplicator, occupied most of the remaining space. Dominating the room was a fireplace surmounted by a high ornamental mirror, the mantelpiece covered with a miscellany of objects, including a brass microscope, tub of pencils and scissors, postage scales and some pale, indescribable thing in a bottling jar. Both sides of the mirror were similarly utilized, with postcards, letters, bills and receipts slotted between the tarnished glass and the once-gilded moulding. Books, magazines, papers and files were piled on every available surface, including most of the floor, so that, as the Reverend Dove now proceeded round his desk, he moved with exaggerated care.

Oddly, for a person so fastidious and fussily tidy as Harrison, he felt quite at home in this dusty, untidy nest: here was a world he recognized—the visible embodiment of reclusive Anglican scholarship stretching back to the Reformation; in such rooms as these, between the dual calls of parish and glebe, the country parson had found time to throw off a devotional sonnet, translate Homer or pen a learned monograph on anything from magnetism to the life cycle of the common newt.

Thinking back to Cawthorne's airy, spacious room of the afternoon before, he looked around the cluttered space with affectionate respect. This feeling was rapidly overtaken, however, by a wave of horror as he realized that the death warrant he was to deliver was destined to fall, not just on the scrawny neck of the man now shakily lowering himself into his swivel-chair, but on all that this room represented—a tradition of scholarship and literary achievement as glorious and irreplaceable as the English parish churches themselves, a heritage encompassing men as varied and gifted as the great White of Selborne, Hooker of Bishopsbourne, Sterne of Coxwold, Hubert of Bemerton, Smith of Combe-Florey and doomed poor young Kilvert of Clyro.

'Harrison, are you all right?' Dove was looking up from the desk with concern. 'For heaven's sake, do park yourself, my dear fellow. For a moment then I really thought you were next in line for a stroke.'

'Thank you,' murmured the other weakly, taking the chair in front of the desk. 'I must admit I find this heat oppressive.'

'Now, before we descend to business, forgive me if I roll myself a much-needed cigarette.' Dipping into a drawer, Dove drew out a flat battered tin. 'Highly illicit, of course,' he added with a mischievous smile. 'Nevertheless,' he said, glancing significantly towards the door, 'I'm certain I can trust the discretion of as seasoned an old campaigner as yourself.'

As he began fiddling with paper and tobacco, Harrison couldn't help noticing how severely Dove's hands trembled. Was it merely age or the result of the stroke, he wondered, or could he—horror of horrors—be simply terrified of what he was to hear?

Unable to bear the sight of those clumsy, quivering fingers, Harrison raised his gaze to the large framed black and white photograph immediately above Dove's head. It was of a seated, white-haired cleric in full canonicals, with black tabs at his throat and episcopal cross on his chest. Whoever he was, he was certainly a striking figure with those compelling large eyes beneath the unusually prominent brow. From the size of the portrait and its position, he wondered if it could be the ex-rector's own father; after all, having a bishop as a parent might explain Dove's lifelong rebellion against established authority.

Turning his head, Harrison looked up at the bookshelves, catching sight of a faded white cap with black peak protruding over the topmost shelf. There was a decidedly rakish, nautical look to the thing, and Harrison immediately took it to be part of pre-war yachting attire. He gazed up at it curiously. All else in the room fitted: the dusty fossils used as paperweights, the microscope, the collections of scissors and pencils, even what he took to be the preserved remains of a frog in formaldehyde—all these, he felt, were the proper impedimenta of a scholarly parson. But a pre-war yachting cap! How could that be explained? In his mind, a vision rose of the bishop's rebellious young son attending a long-ago Cowes Week, striding the snowy decks of an ocean racer in white cotton ducks.

Blinking away the image, he returned his gaze to the shrunken old man in front of him, now licking and rolling his cigarette like a wizened little dormouse over a walnut. It seemed incredible, the thought of Dove as a playboy, playing baccarat and rubbing shoulders with the likes of the Aga Khan, Lord Brabazon, Mrs Simpson and the Prince of Wales.

'Now, let's get straight to the nitty-gritty.' Wiping a strand of tobacco from his lower lip, Dove faced him across the desk. 'How long is Dr Cawthorne giving us?'

Harrison was dumbfounded. For twenty-four hours he'd been worrying exactly how to break the news; now here was Dove already clearly knowing the archdeacon's decision! Had Cawthorne after all had the decency to phone the old man and inform him himself?

Dove laughed. 'My dear chap, don't look so surprised. Ever since receiving Cawthorne's original missive, Joyce and I have known there was the strong possibility we might have to leave—then, with your mysterious phone call this morning and the look on your face as you got out from your car, we were both absolutely certain why you and Winifred had taken the trouble to come and see us personally.' Pausing, Dove placed his sagging approximation to a cigarette to his lips. 'I'm afraid, Harrison,' he said, applying a match, 'you're entirely transparent.' Coughing and gasping, he tapped at his chest, then smiled. 'Luckily, you never had to be either a secret policeman or a country parson; both callings, I fear, demanding an ability for deception quite impossible in a straightforward military man like yourself.'

Harrison looked away as the cleric broke off, coughing and gasping again alarmingly. 'I'd like you and Joyce to know,' he said as Dove recovered himself, 'that I pressed your case with the archdeacon as strongly as I could.'

'My dear chap, I don't doubt it.' Dove inhaled again, then coughing violently, stubbed out his cigarette. 'But you haven't told me how long before the bailiff's boys arrive?'

'Dr Cawthorne is giving you until Lady Day.'

'Really!' Dove smiled. 'Lady Day! What a charmingly old-fashioned notion—pure Thomas Hardy! Despite all evidence, it seems there's a touch of poetry in our new gauleiter's soul!'

'Quite,' murmured Harrison uncertainly, fearful of displaying the slightest disloyalty to his immediate superior.

Swivelling round, Dove looked out through the French window. 'Not that it won't be a great wrench to leave,' he continued, 'but I can't complain—I've had a good innings here.'

Though he'd guessed what was coming, now the notice to quit had been actually spelt out, Dove was clearly having to struggle to control his feelings: head bowed, he gazed out towards the laurels, his knuckles white on the arms of his chair. Embarrassed, Harrison dropped his gaze. As he did so, his eye caught the author's name on the spine of one of the books lying hotch-potch on the desk before him—Frederick Mendelssohn. He stared at it intrigued: F. J. Mendelssohn, he remembered was one of the names on the back of the scrawled-over envelope he'd borrowed from Rachel.

Dove still sat hunched, gazing out. Quietly, Harrison reached over and, taking the volume, flicked it open and peered at the title page. As he did so, his heart gave a leap at the words *Das Bruderhaus* printed in large Gothic script. His German was rusty, but the translation was simple: The House of Brothers or the Brother House. But what was that, and did this mysterious-sounding establishment have anything to do with the equally mysterious *Schwarze Kapelle*?

'My dear Harrison, you amaze me! I didn't know you read high German!' Looking up, he found Dove had turned and was grinning at him impishly. 'What did I call you just now: a straightforward military man? Yet I hardly turn my back before I find you seizing a book and boning up on recent German Lutheran history!'

'I'm so sorry,' muttered the other, hurriedly replacing the volume. 'I just happened to notice the author's name coincides with one on this rather curious list,' he said, drawing Miller's envelope from an inside pocket, 'which a late army friend recently drew up while researching the famous July Plot against Hitler in 1944.'

'May I see?' Taking the envelope, Dove swivelled round to catch the light, then immediately burst out laughing. 'What's this—Goering?' Grinning, he glanced round at his visitor. 'The late Reichsmarschall might have been a cultured man and a great collector of art, but surely the chap was an absolute moral coward and hardly liked to oppose Hitler on anything! Anyway,' he continued, 'isn't it generally accepted that by 1944 he'd largely slipped into a self-induced world of alcohol and drugs?'

'That could have been a cover,' said Harrison defensively.

With a sceptical laugh, Dove turned back to Miller's list. Uncomfortably, Harrison watched him studying it. 'If you look at the bottom,' he murmured, 'you'll see Mendelssohn's name and the obvious codeword *Drummer* circled beside them.'

Dove didn't answer for a few seconds. 'This late friend of yours,' he said finally, 'I take it he was a brother officer?'

Harrison shook his head. 'No, Miller—or Müller as he was known then—was a Jewish refugee serving as a military interpreter in Berlin.'

'Jewish?' Frowning, Dove again studied the list of names.

'It appears he became an American citizen later,' continued the other, 'and practised as a real estate lawyer in New York.'

'A property lawyer, you mean?'

'Yes, that's the reason he'd been over here in Europe this last half year: until his tragic accident a month ago, he'd been combining some researches of his own in Eastern Germany with some part-time legal work.'

Dove turned to gaze at the mud-coated monkey figurine on the desk. 'A tragic accident, you say?' he said, finally looking up. 'May I ask exactly how he died?'

'It seems he fell from a train when returning from a short visit to Canterbury during August. Sadly, the police appear to believe it was suicide, although no note has yet been found.'

'I see.'

Harrison cleared his throat. 'You don't think, Rector, that the Frederick Mendelssohn who wrote this book here on the desk could possibly be the person referred to on Miller's list?'

Dove glanced again at the envelope in his hand, then passed it back. 'As to that,' he said, 'all I can safely assert is that, whatever the truth about Goering and the others, the person you refer to took no part in the July Plot.' A faint smile flickered over his lined face. 'You see, I happen to know that throughout the war years, Frederick Johann Mendelssohn was acting as a temporary assistant curate in Hove.'

'A curate!' exclaimed Harrison incredulously. 'In Hove—the place next to Brighton?' He paused, then added flatly, 'Well, in that case, I can see it would have been rather difficult for him to have had much of a hand in planting bombs in East Prussia.'

'Quite.' Dove suddenly seemed very tired and drawn. 'Now,

if you don't mind, Harrison, I'll ask you to let yourself out. It's not your fault, but I'm afraid your tidings this afternoon have rather knocked me back. I'd like just to sit here for a while and sort things out in my mind.'

'Of course.' At the door, Harrison turned and looked back. Dove had again swivelled round in his chair and was staring out into the garden, his back towards him. He cleared his throat. 'May I just say before I go, how much I personally regret the archdeacon's decision.'

Without turning or speaking, Dove half raised a hand and waved it limply. Turning away, Harrison let himself out and headed back through the hall towards the distant murmur of the women's voices.

Chapter Five

With a sigh, Harrison rolled over and stared up at the ceiling. He felt hot and sticky under the blankets, and every portion of his body seemed to itch in turn. Not since he'd crossed the Channel, he thought miserably, had he passed a decent night's sleep; and here he was once again, at nearly two o'clock in the morning, dog-tired, yet as awake as if strung on the rack.

Outside not a breath of air stirred. Through the orange curtains came the livid glow of the yard light; only the sigh of Winnie's breathing broke the silence. With a mix of irritation and resentment, he lay listening to its soft, even cadence, until, unable to bear it longer, he impatiently turned on his side and, edging as far as possible from the heat of her body, determinedly shut his eyes.

It was useless; the closing of his eyelids was the signal for the curtain to rise and the show recommence: in a few seconds he was once more locked in the theatre of his skull, facing the excruciating image of Tom and Joyce Dove making towards him—both knowing why he'd come, yet both so graciously welcoming: the old man gaily waving his walking stick and Joyce smiling bravely as she supported him—even bothering to carry away that repulsive china figurine to spare Miss Hodge's feelings. Another scene rose: the final memory of Dove's shrivelled figure, hunched in his chair, back towards him, staring out of the window, unable to acknowledge his departure with more than a pathetic half-wave.

'Goddamn it!' Feeling like St Lawrence on his grid iron, he thrashed round to stare again at the ceiling. He lay a moment more, then finally making up his mind, slid from the bed and began feeling round for his slippers.

Blinking against the glare of the striplight, he entered the kitchen. Yawning and bleary-eyed he filled and switched on the kettle, then went to stand at the window as it gradually murmured into life.

A full moon gleamed over the cathedral; in its light, a band of high clouds, flat-based and high-topped, reached towards him like an outstretched arm. Clearly, the weather was on the change; the long hot summer building up for a spectacular end. Behind him, the kettle boiled. Dropping a tea-bag in a mug, he made himself a drink, then switching off the lights, returned to the window. Standing there in the dark, mug between his hands, sky spread before him, he thought of the churning propellers and the growing armada of ships steadily heading for the Gulf. War and its preparations seemed far from the silent, enclosed world about him, yet all the same, there was an ominous look to the looming towers with the advancing high-piled clouds behind them, ghostly yellowish-white in the moonlight.

Instead of soothing, the tea served merely to wake him further; and with every sip, the idea of returning to the clammy darkness of the bedroom to lie again at the mercy of his own thoughts grew increasingly repugnant. What he needed was something to occupy his mind. Should he try a book, he wondered, or the day's crossword? Then he remembered again the incongruous list of scribbled numbers and names in his jacket pocket.

It had been an amazing coincidence, the writer of that book on some doubtless esoteric aspect of German Lutheranism having the same name and initials as the penultimate name on Miller's list; equally extraordinary was that Tom Dove had actually known him. Despite the old man's assurance to the contrary, and the dictates of plain common sense, could this obscure temporary wartime curate have, in fact, been a man in deep cover—a member of an inner elite beyond the ken of Himmler's Gestapo, helping to guide Stauffenberg's shattered hands from a small English seaside resort? The idea seemed ludicrous, yet why, after all, should a German Lutheran pastor have been in Britain at all during the war years unless he'd been an opponent to Nazi rule? And what was the nature of that organization about which he'd written, the mysterious Brother House?

Suddenly Harrison found himself regretting he hadn't pressed Dove a little on Mendelssohn's history. He even wondered if he should ring in the morning and try to squeeze the ex-rector for what he knew. He quickly dismissed the idea: the last person he wanted to speak to at present was Tom Dove. There had to be a less embarrassing way of finding out if his original supposition had been correct, and that the six names on the back of Miller's envelope were indeed, all connected to the *Schwarze Kapelle.*

Still gazing up at the cathedral and the clouding sky, he took a final sip of his tea. Beside Goering, Canaris, Menzies and Mendelssohn himself, there were still those other two—the unknown Treeck and Lipmann. Perhaps they could be the means of proving to Rachel Miller that her father had been engaged in nothing more dangerous than turning a further spotlight on the true extent of German resistance to Hitler—and that indeed in the old GDR archives lay proof that the Führer's trusted heir, the Reichsmarschall himself, had waited like a bloated Brutus in the shadows, drawn dagger concealed behind his massive bulk.

It was an exciting thought. Turning to wash out his cup, Harrison hurried back to the bedroom. Slipping in quietly, he stopped and listened. To his relief, Winnie's breathing was as regular as before. Feeling his way to the wardrobe, he groped in the blackness, brushing his hand through the hanging jackets until he felt the weight of his wallet. Drawing it out, he began creeping back to the door, but in doing so, he stumbled over the shoes he'd left placed at the end of the bed, and half falling, he grabbed at the footboard.

'Richard?' Winnie's voice came out of the darkness. 'What's happening?'

'Nothing.' He paused. 'I just wanted to look up some names.'

'Names?' Winnie repeated the word sleepily. Not answering, Harrison waited, willing her quiet breathing to resume. When it eventually did, he tiptoed on to the door. Once in the hall, he went straight to the staircase and began creeping upwards, his sense of guilt increasing at every cautious step.

In all his years at the cottage, Harrison had never once climbed the stairs without feelings of profound unease. The narrow steps were an insurmountable barrier to Winnie; as such, they were a visible reminder of her crippled condition and physical dependence—of everything that should have been, and never was. With the dining-room converted to a bedroom and the kitchen used for eating, the pair preferred to regard the house as a bungalow, and though the rooms above were rudimentarily furnished, neither saw them as part of their home. For this reason alone, every mounting of the stairs represented a departure for him: a separation—perhaps even a betrayal. This latter feeling had been reinforced in recent years by his secret conversion of one of the unused bedrooms to a private study—a sanctuary to which he'd occasionally away, there to relax in the knowledge that he was temporarily unattainable to all—wife, friends, clergy, diocese and the world in general—free for a moment from the demands of duty and love.

It was to this rather dowdy little retreat that Harrison now stole, Miller's envelope in hand. Closing the door, he crossed to the iron-bound wooden trunk which once had been his toy box. Dropping on to his knees, he unlocked and opened the lid. Where—in another existence—there had been a colourful chaos of comic annuals, board games and Dinky cars, there lay instead all that physically remained of his years in Military Intelligence: diaries, letters, photographs and files—and with them, secreted like pornography, his collection of books on various spy rings, traitors, espionage operations and deceptions, most of them soiled, dog-eared volumes obtained from second-hand bookshops and library sales, all surreptitiously smuggled past Winnie into the house.

Bending miser-like over the box, he dipped in, knowing just what he wanted. Soon he'd piled about him all the books he had dealing directly with the July Plot, together with general works on Second World War intelligence. Still on his knees, he went through them, discarding those without indexes. The remainder he carried to the rickety card table beneath the central light and piled them on the moth-eaten green baize next to Miller's mysterious list of names.

Beginning first with the books dealing explicitly with the July Plot and the *Schwarze Kapelle*, Harrison flipped through the indexes, searching for sight of Mendelssohn, Lipmann and Treeck. With each new volume, his disappointment grew: among the familiar names, Canaris, Stauffenberg, Beck, Oster and Rommel, there was not one reference to the three he was looking for. After half an hour or so, and with only general reference books remaining, he paused and looked again at the scribbled-over envelope. Had he been wrong, he wondered—was the orchestra referred to really the *Schwarze Kapelle*? Could it be a separate organization, another secret group altogether? But if so, what sort of group could it have been—and what could have been its purpose, encompassing as it did, not only the heads of both MI6 and the *Abwehr*, but the flamboyant, vainglorious Goering and an obscure assistant curate of Hove?

A sense of weary hopelessness welled up. Yawning heavily, Harrison had to force himself to reach for the first of the remaining books. Certain that his efforts were wasted, and feeling sleepier by the moment, he began running his finger down the columns of names. As he expected, there was no Mendelssohn, no Lipmann. He flicked over a page and glanced down—and there, staring up at him between the names Marshal Tito and General Henning von Tresckow, was the entry: Treeck, Capt. Robert.

Numbly, he stared down: with that homely English 'Robert' and that comparatively humble rank—not even a field officer—it didn't look much like the name of a high-placed German plotter. All the same, he thought, recovering from the shock of actually finding the name, mere captain or not, Treeck had at least been a soldier; above all, he was actually included in a book on the role of wartime deceptive strategy.

Flicking to the pages indicated, Harrison began to read. As soon as he did so, he was transported back to the nineteen-thirties—not, indeed, to what he remembered of that era: icy bedrooms, *William* books, clockwork Hornbys ands Cape Triangulars—but to that dazzling firmament of high society: débutantes, the London season, country house parties—that fairy tale existence to which, incongruously, the young Tom Dove had apparently belonged with the rest of his yachting friends.

Weariness and the strains of the past day were now forgotten as the words conjured in the reader's mind a procession of lorries trundling west down the A4 in the spring of 1935, bearing the servants, chattels and horses of a certain ex-Hanoverian cavalryman and international sportsman: Captain Treeck, weary, it seemed, of London high life, wanted nothing now so much as to ride to hounds in the blue and buff of the Duke of Beaufort's famous Badminton Hunt. In his mind's eye, Harrison followed the vehicles as they turned off at Chippenham to thread their way through country lanes and Cotswold villages to turn eventually into the gravelled drive of Luckington Manor—where, from the adjoining garden, Stewart Menzies, then deputy head of MI6, watched his new neighbour's collection of French wines, Dutch paintings, Dresden porcelain and silver-mounted sporting guns being unloaded and carried indoors.

Harrison rubbed his hands with relish: how far all this was from his experience of espionage: the dreary ploughing through everything from CIA-supplied files to the contents of dustbins, endless waits in freezing vehicles, the stink of formalin and corpses. The world he was reading of was something to savour: late supper parties, the cry of peacocks across the lawns, bugle-horns ringing through autumn woods, and Menzies's ironic cry of *Deutschland über alles* as, according to the book, stirrup to stirrup, he and Captain Treeck thundered over the hedges and walls of the Wiltshire hundreds.

So he had been right, after all! The names on Miller's list had indeed been part of the *Schwarze Kapelle*—Treeck sent ostensibly to sound out the mood of English ruling class, but really to liaise with Menzies and British Intelligence; Canaris, the man who had sent him; Pastor Mendelssohn and the so-called Brother House, the mysterious unknown Lipmann and, most incredible of all, the future Reichsmarschall, Hermann Goering—a man so much like Treeck himself, war hero, upper-class sportsman and art connoisseur—the six of them at the centre of a web, all of them plotting the overthrow of the dangerous little upstart already strutting the marble of the German chancellery!

Too excited to sit, Harrison got up and went to the window. The moon had disappeared; all was black overhead, with clouds covering the sky, and the cathedral appeared as hardly more than dark shadow on dark. The story was sensational—but why, he wondered, had not a hint of Goering's involvement emerged before, and why had the man not mentioned a word of this in his spirited defence at Nuremberg?

Frowning, Harrison stared up through the, glass, but no explanation came. Returning to the table, he thumbed through the indexes of the remaining books in search of the elusive Lipmann. There was nothing—whoever he'd been, his name, like Mendelssohn's, was apparently still unknown to the historians of the Third Reich—as unknown indeed as the part Hitler's deputy had played in the final ill-fated attempt on his life.

Harrison leant back wearily. At least he'd established to his own satisfaction the truth of his original supposition. Tomorrow he'd ring Rachel and tell her the news. Thinking of the morning, he glanced at his watch. It was already nearly three. With so much office paperwork remaining, the diocesan architect's and the cathedral auditor's visits in the morning, and the Friends' council meeting in the evening, the coming day promised to be at least as long and gruelling as the one just past. Getting up, he turned off the light. As he did so, there was a vivid blue flash, then, from the far distance, a low gathering rumble like the growl of some huge beast aroused and stirring from sleep.

'Whatever was going on last night?'

'Going on?' repeated Harrison disingenuously, glancing up from his breakfast. 'Sorry, did I wake you? What with the heat and everything else, I found it difficult to drop off.'

'Maybe,' said Winnie, scrutinizing him narrowly, 'but what was all that about needing to look up names?'

Bending his head, Harrison stared glassily down at his bacon and egg; the last thing he wanted at that moment was to try justifying his lonely vigil.

'Well?'

Clearing his mouth, he looked up. 'It was nothing, my dear—just this Friends' council meeting tonight. I wanted to check the way things are likely to go if it comes to a vote.'

'Vote? About what?'

'Oh, just this stuff of Simcocks's about turnstiles. Knowing him, of course, it's almost certain to be a lot of nonsense. All the same,' continued Harrison, 'it pays to be careful: as archdeacon, Cawthorne has an automatic place on the council, and, who knows, if the figures the accountant brings me this morning are bad, there's just the chance he might try pushing such a proposal through.'

'Introduce cathedral entrance charges? Surely not! That would be outrageous!' Winnie fairly bristled as she spoke: though no churchwoman, her spirit rebelled at the notion of having to buy oneself into any place of worship. 'Anyway,' she continued, frowning, 'such a decision could only be made by the dean and Chapter—and knowing Matthew, he would never permit it!'

Harrison shrugged. 'Who knows—the way costs are

spiralling at the moment, he may not have much choice. The Friends' contribution to the cathedral exchequer is large: if they recommend entrance charges, as dean, he'd be under great pressure to implement them.' He drank down his tea, and smiled reassuringly. 'But don't worry, my dear—I'll do my best to prevent it.' Wiping his mouth, he rose to his feet.

'You haven't forgotten I'll need a lift to my art class this evening, I hope.'

'Art class?' Harrison paused. 'Yes, of course. I'll drop you off before the council convenes.'

'Incidentally,' called Winnie as he reached the door, 'yesterday I managed to talk Joyce into attending the class. I thought it would help take her mind off things.'

'Good idea—just what she needs. Now, you'll have to excuse me if I dash. I want to make another early start.'

Relieved to be free of the house, Harrison strode out of Bread Yard. Despite that single, ominous roll of thunder hours earlier, the morning was as dry as the one before; but whereas the sun had then gleamed from an azure sky, now it was masked by a low-lying, continuous layer of cloud.

Already there was an unpleasant clammy warmth to the air—and as he headed past the deanery, he had to step over a bloated brown slug that had crawled on to the path.

Gone completely was the excitement he'd felt at the discovery of Treeck's name. Now, whether owing to the unpleasant humidity or to his lack of sleep, he felt a general oppression of spirits as he mounted the office steps. The sight of the word processor and the amount of correspondence awaiting his attention added to the feeling, and somewhat dispiritedly he slumped down behind his desk. Curiously, however, from the moment his seat touched the familiar leather, his mood began to change. There was a feeling of reassurance in being back in his comfortable high-backed chair, and he felt once more in control. Pulling out his fountain pen, he reached for the top envelope in the high-piled in-tray with a confidence he'd not felt in days.

Safe from the perplexities, strains and confusions of the world outside—from the nebulous groping after the full extent of long-past conspiracy, from those clumsy attempts to calm the almost frantic girl in the garden, and, worst of all, from the painful necessity of serving notice on Tom Dove—he was soon happily immersed in the nitty-gritty of diocesan business. Surveys, quotations and estimates passed beneath his eyes, and not until nine o'clock, when interrupted by the arrival of his secretary with the post, did he raise his head from his work.

After a short exchange on the weather, the girl returned to the outer office, having reminded him of the visit of the diocesan architect at ten, and that of the cathedral auditor an hour later. Free to resume his study of the details of the damage done by a botched and ill-judged crypt conversion, he bent again to his labours, and was soon so absorbed that it seemed only a matter of minutes before the intercom buzzed to announce George Davidson's arrival.

'Ah, my dear chap! Come in.' Beaming, he rose to shake the architect's hesitant hand. 'Dead on time as usual! Well done!'

Reseating himself, Harrison regarded his visitor with satisfaction. Though no older than Cawthorne, Davidson had been in diocesan employ as long as himself, having been recruited by Dr Crocker—or so it was whispered—partly because he was a clergyman's son himself and partly because of a letter published in the *Church Times*, in which the normally mild Davidson had let rip a blistering blast against every modern trend in church architecture. Whatever the truth of these rumours, he'd proved a competent employee, seemingly content to play his part as technical custodian of the great works of his predecessors in the dual role of diocesan architect and surveyor to the cathedral fabric. That none of his repairs and designs had ever given rise to the slightest controversy or upset, caused Harrison to value him highly, and if he'd never exactly warmed to Davidson's personality, he'd at least learnt to appreciate the conservative qualities of this polite, reserved and diffident man.

'Well,' he said, 'how is the family? Wife and babes blooming, I trust?'

'Thank you, Colonel, we're all of us very well.' The speaker's sallow face flushed as he spoke. 'At the moment we have my wife's sister staying—she's kindly helping Pauline out.'

'Good,' murmured the other, nodding approval. 'I'm sure you will both benefit from a little domestic assistance at present.'

Having embarked on matrimony comparatively late, marrying the daughter of one of the King's School housemasters, Davidson had rapidly sired four children, all sons. The eldest of these was just turned five, while the latest additions, identical twins, were less than three months old—as was amply indicated by the dark patches under his eyes, his generally dishevelled appearance and the discoloration on both lapels of his decidedly crumpled, cheap, ill-fitting suit.

'Now,' continued Harrison, briskly, 'I wish to discuss the matter of the tower restoration work. I share the dean's concern over the proposed length of the task. Six months, I believe, is your estimation?'

'I've discussed the work with the cathedral mason,' replied Davidson, uneasily, 'also with the clerk of works. I agree with them that it's not a job to be rushed.'

'Rushed!' repeated the other, smiling. 'My dear fellow, nobody is asking for rush, merely for a steady, reasonable rate of work. Good God!' he resumed, 'six months for some trowelwork on the parapet balustrades! It's ludicrous!' Leaning back, he regarded his visitor quizzically: safe and dependable as the architect might be, he was a man, he felt, only too easily bamboozled and led by the nose by an unscrupulous workforce or idle clerk of works. 'Tell me,' Harrison resumed with what he hoped was a friendly smile, 'how long do you think it originally took to build the Bell Harry Tower?'

Disconcerted by the question, Davidson shook his head. 'I'm sorry, Colonel, I've no idea—fifty years perhaps?'

'Fourteen!' announced Harrison triumphantly. 'That's all Master Mason Wastell took to design and complete the entire thing!' Pleased that he'd taken the trouble to arm himself with this fact, he continued, 'Dammit, Davidson, fourteen years for the entire caboose, and you seriously suggest six months for a touch of patching-up!'

For a moment, protest seemed to hang on the architect's lips, but then, capitulating entirely, he mumbled, 'I'll have another word with Mr Keates.'

'Good,' said Harrison, appeased. 'Shall we say an absolute deadline of eight weeks from today for the western towers, and we'll have a further estimation on the Bell Harry work when the scaffolding's up? Talking of such,' he continued, looking up from making a note in his diary, 'there's another small matter I must mention: when visiting Lang Ashendon yesterday, I noticed that the builders had left scaffolding piled in the churchyard. Not only is it unsightly, but village children were clambering all over it and generally treating the place as a playground. I'd be grateful if you'd arrange for it to be cleared at once.'

'Of course.' Davidson rose from his seat, then hesitated. 'Forgive me asking, Colonel, but your visit—was it connected with these rumours about the sale of the rectory?'

Harrison stiffened. 'Have you some personal interest in the matter?' he asked coldly, remembering that the architect had bought a number of dilapidated properties around Westgate for redevelopment, and wondering if this interest had a similarly commercial basis.

Davidson blushed. 'It's just that Tom and Joyce Dove are old family friends.'

'Really?' That the dull, self-effacing man before him could have any personal connection with a scholarly eccentric like Tom Dove was a surprise. 'Family friends, you say?'

'Oh yes,' said Davidson. 'Joyce is my aunt on my mother's side and Tom is my godfather—he and my father were close ever since their time together as curates.'

'Indeed! I had no idea.' Remembering that thick file next door on Holy Trinity church, it crossed Harrison's mind that all that work lavished on that prodigal building at Davidson's recommendation might have stemmed in part from a natural desire to please his father's friend. But looking across at the architect's pale, meek face, and remembering his scrupulous reports, he dismissed his suspicions as unworthy: dull and pedestrian as Davidson was, professional misconduct was the last thing to be laid at his feet.

'Why I'm asking,' continued the other, 'is because the worry about losing the rectory is hampering Tom's recovery—at least, that's what Joyce told my wife.' The speaker forced a smile. 'Still, Colonel, I'm sure you've been able to reassure them.'

It was now Harrison's turn to drop his gaze; he sat for a moment frowning down at his desk. 'As you know,' he began, reluctantly looking up to meet Davidson's anxious eyes, 'diocesan finances have been in a critical state for some time; as a result, it has been decided to extend the policy of selling off redundant property.' Steeling himself, he went on: 'In accordance with that decision, I have been forced to ask your godfather to vacate the house.'

For the first time in their ten-year association, Harrison saw anger flash in the other's dark eyes. However, as fast as it had come, it was gone. 'Thank you for telling me, Colonel,' said Davidson, quietly. 'Now I think I understand the phone call I had from Tom last night, asking me to visit. From his voice, I knew something was very wrong.' The speaker paused. 'As I'm due to be in that area this afternoon, I'll take the opportunity to call on my way home. If nothing else, I might be able to fix some alternative accommodation.'

'Good,' murmured Harrison with relief. 'That's just what he needs—a decent alternative.'

'What he needs, I would have thought,' replied the other, a pink flush rising in his cheeks, 'is to be allowed to live out his old age in peace—not to be driven from his home, especially having been guaranteed the use of the rectory for life!'

Harrison was utterly taken aback: it was as if some long-dead volcanic crater had burst without warning. Temporarily speechless, he felt the blood rushing to his own face. 'It's unfortunate, I agree,' he struggled out, 'but there it is—with the state of diocesan finances as they are, I'm afraid it's a matter of needs must when the devil drives.'

'Quite!' Davidson's face was now chalk-white. 'Well, if you'll excuse me, I shall go and tell the clerk of works you insist on his pushing through the restoration work in two months.' He breathed heavily. 'I shall then arrange to have the scaffolding cleared from Long Ashendon churchyard by the end of the week.' Turning, he went to the door, then looked back, eyes burning. 'As you say, Colonel, it's needs must when the devil rules!'

There was a tap at the door; Harrison turned from the window to see his secretary looking in anxiously. 'Everything all right, Colonel?'

'Thank you, Mary—everything's fine.'

The girl hesitated, but as Harrison turned back to the window, she quietly closed the door, leaving him staring fixedly out through the pattern of diamond panes. He remained looking out until, suddenly slamming a fist into his palm, he exclaimed aloud, 'What a goddamned bloody fool!'

Cursing himself for that unfortunate phrase which had so inflamed and infuriated his, until then, invariably polite and respectful subordinate, he stood clenching his fists and trembling with impotent rage against both Cawthorne and Davidson. From the passage below came the sound of high-pitched voices: the choristers were heading past to their daily practice, among them Simon Barnes, giggling over something with the boy at his side.

At the sight of the little procession, Harrison's fury abated, and he looked down with unwonted affection at this tangible expression of the community in which he'd so long lived and served; and as the ragged crocodile passed on down the passageway, the bobbing heads disappearing into the shadows, he gazed after it as to a world lost. The news of his apparently willing association with the archdeacon and his part in the forced eviction of Tom Dove must, he thought, already be spreading; soon he'd be facing the scorn, not just of Davidson, but of people he respected—including the dean.

At the thought of Ingrams, his face contorted: over the years, their friendship had evolved so gradually that he'd rather taken it for granted; now the thought of losing it, of seeing the affection and pleasure fade from the other's eyes, bit like acid. Returning to his desk, he sat, miserably envisaging the future: Cawthorne raging through the diocese with all the zeal of a Saul, closing churches, amalgamating parishes, doubly armed and unstoppable with the archbishop's mandate and the board's own recommendations—while he, as jackal to the lion, followed in his train, avoiding and avoided by all. Misery overcoming him, he stared down, wishing he'd listened to Winnie and resigned.

The boom of the distant clock brought him back to the moment. He unfolded the letter he'd been opening, when Davidson had arrived, noticing that it had come via the internal mail.

Dear Richard,

A note just to say how much Janet and I (and Emily!) enjoyed meeting you yesterday. I'm confident that we'll make a fine team. To my pleasure, I've just learnt you are also honorary treasurer to the Council of Cathedral Friends, and therefore look forward to seeing you at the meeting tomorrow night. I have a proposal to make regarding the future funding of the cathedral upkeep which I'm sure you'll wish to support.

Mike

PS. Trust the Long Ashendon visit didn't prove too embarrassing.

Crumpling the note in his fist, Harrison sat staring down at his desk. The encounter with Davidson had driven all thoughts of Simcocks's gloomy prophecies from his mind; now, however, he was absolutely sure they had been correct, and that his immediate superior indeed intended to push for admission charges. And what was to be his own position with Cawthorne expecting his support? This was no matter of an obscure country rectory and a quiet chat in an old man's study: this was an almost public matter, a formal meeting presided over by the dean and Miss Hodge, and attended by so many he knew, including—God help him—the already scornful Davidson! There was no escape: tonight he'd be in the open, forced either to blow his cover by supporting the status quo, or to compromise himself irrevocably before them all.

His thoughts were distracted by the sound of voices. He glanced at his watch: clearly the auditor had arrived. A thought struck him: one hope remained, that the general financial position was better than expected—and, what with the money raised by the Friends' fête the month before, he might be able to give such an optimistic forecast that Cawthorne would have no reason to raise such a controversial matter as admission charges.

Rising, he went straight into the outer office to find the elderly accountant uncharacteristically sharing a joke with his secretary. Hurrying forward, Harrison greeted him warmly, noting that the usually dour Calvinist Scot looked well and sunburnt after a fortnight's recent stay in the north. Having exchanged a few words on their respective holidays, he smiled, glancing down at the ledgers under the other's arm. 'Well, Mr Jamerson,' he said with forced brightness, 'I only hope the news you've brought equals the weather you obviously enjoyed in Dunoon.'

The other's smile faded immediately, and he shook his head. 'Nay, Colonel, I've no good news for you.' He tapped the leather-bound volumes with his free hand. 'What I have here would gladden only the heart of the devil!'

Chapter Six

Though the cathedral dock's golden hands continued to move at their usual rate, one chasing after and lapping the other in the monotonous flat-race of time, and though Great Dunstan marked every circuit and quarter with customary regularity, for Harrison, the usually fleet hours plodded past on leaden hoofs. Weighed down by his worries about the Friends' council meeting, time dragged by with little accomplished. After Jamerson's doleful tidings, he struggled to prepare his financial report, but breaking off at the thought of the evening, he'd turned to stare dolefully up at the darkening sky.

Over the parched, yellowing lawns of the precincts and the hot, dusty city streets, the loud gradually thickened. By mid-afternoon, the men working high on the western towers were glancing up with apprehension. Below them, the clock struck four; a few minutes later there came a distant rumble, echoing the sound Harrison had heard in the early hours. Still the men laboured, driven on by the clerk of works, whose face since Davidson's midday visit had matched the sky. Less than five minutes, however, after the first, came a second sharper roll—then, virtually simultaneously with a dazzling flash, a third, this time almost directly overhead. Sixty seconds later the scaffolding was deserted, and water was tumbling vertically in a seemingly solid sheet. As if anxious to compensate for its long absence, the rain continued to pelt; and though its first fury soon slackened, it was still drizzling hard, and lightning and thunder occasionally flashing and rumbling when, three hours later, Harrison returned in the Volvo—its headlights blazing—from dropping off Winnie at the Canterbury College of Art.

Having garaged the car, Harrison hurried into the house. Tense and unhappy though he was at the thought of what lay in store at the meeting, he was nevertheless anxious to contact Rachel before it began to tell her of his success in tracing one of the unknown names on the envelope, and that now, knowing Treeck had been one of Admiral Canaris's agents and had been sent by him to liaise with Stewart Menzies, he was more than ever convinced that her father's researches in Dresden had been into nothing more dangerous than the rather ancient history of the *Schwarze Kapelle*.

Rachel was clearly pleased that he'd phoned. Gone was the frantic note of the day before, that explosive mix of anger and guilt. She was obviously both impressed and grateful that within twenty-four hours of giving him the list, he'd already tracked down one of the names and also had a slight lead on another. On her part, however, Rachel hadn't much to tell him—and the little she had, was somewhat perplexing. The lawyer, Joe Eisenberg, had been round to Chelsea that morning to collect the remaining legal documents that had been in her father's possession. While there, he'd helped her sift through all the papers in the flat, but though they'd searched thoroughly, they'd failed to discover evidence of any historical research, German or otherwise. In fact, the only detailed notes were on numbers of art objects in various galleries and museums, indicating that Miller had, just as he'd said, been planning a book on eighteenth-century European fine arts and ceramics.

'You found nothing at all on the July Plot?' said Harrison, frowning. 'You're sure? No books—biographies perhaps of Goering or Hitler?'

'No, Colonel, the only thing like that were some jottings on the life of someone called Kändler.'

'Kändler?' repeated Harrison, noting the name on the telephone pad. 'You've no idea of his rank, I suppose?'

To his surprise, there was a girlish laugh in his ear. 'He wasn't a soldier. As far as I can make out, he was some sort of artist—a kind of potter, I think.'

'A potter?' Although he knew that opposition to the Nazis had far from been limited to the upper classes—indeed quite the contrary—it was disconcerting, nevertheless, to discover that the secret core of the conspiracies against Hitler embraced such a wide segment of society; not merely a clique of military officers, diplomats and senior civil servants as he'd always supposed, but a staggeringly wide group, embracing Hermann Goering on the one hand, and on the other, an unknown refugee pastor in England; and now, it seemed, also this equally obscure German potter—or whatever this chap Kändler had been.

Rachel interrupted his thoughts. 'Colonel, I just want to say how much I appreciate all this trouble you're taking.'

'Not at all,' he answered, absently circling Kändler's name. 'Despite the circumstances, it was a pleasure to meet you. In fact,' he added, doodling a question mark, 'my wife was wondering if you'd like to stay with us during the final hearing.'

As if in response to this downright lie, there came a rolling grumble of thunder that drowned most of Rachel's answer. 'Sorry,' said Harrison, 'I didn't quite catch that—what report did you say?'

There was surprise in the girl's voice. 'The one you suggested I get, Colonel the one from the private autopsy. Dad's firm has arranged for it to be carried out down here in London. I should have the result by Friday.'

Harrison's heart fell. In the midst of everything else, he'd completely forgotten his unconsidered suggestion of a second autopsy, made for no better reason than to spite Dr Brooke. Remembering Winnie's warning about the pathologist's likely reaction if he ever discovered who had sown the seed of doubt in Rachel's mind, regarding his professional competence he gloomily replaced the receiver: the way things were going at present, he felt, it would not be just the cathedral precincts he'd soon be forced to leave, but Canterbury—or perhaps even the county itself!

Oppressed by this thought as well as by his continuing dread of Cawthorne bringing up the thorny question of entrance charges, he prepared to leave for the meeting in the Christ Church gatehouse. A few minutes later, briefcase in hand, he was striding across Green Court, the dank, dark evening perfectly matching his mood.

'Richard! Richard!'

He had just reached the Selling Archway when he heard his name called. Turning, he saw the dean hurrying to overtake him.

'So glad to have caught you,' panted Ingrams, reaching the shelter of the archway. 'Canon Bedford rang a few minutes ago, and I wanted to find out at once if there was any truth in the unhappy tidings he gave me.'

Harrison stiffened and turned away, unable to meet the newcomer's eyes. 'I take it, Dean,' he said heavily, 'that you are referring to the matter of Long Ashendon rectory?'

The dean blinked up at his friend in surprise. 'Long Ashendon rectory?' He shook his head. 'No, my dear fellow, I meant this sad news concerning your late comrade in arms.'

So much had Harrison steeled himself to admit his own part in the disreputable treatment of the Doves, that he could only reply weakly, 'Ah, Miller's death, you mean? Yes, that was an unfortunate matter.'

'Unfortunate, certainly,' answered Ingrams gravely, concern visibly growing on his face. Taking the other's arm solicitously, he began guiding him on down Dark Entry. 'Clearly, it's been a terrible shock. Bedford is quite worried—it seems he found you yesterday wandering the scene of the accident very far from your usual good self.' He sighed and shook his head. 'I only wish you'd felt able to share your grief with me.'

'I'm sorry,' murmured Harrison, embarrassed. 'I would have spoken, but the circumstances of the death made it rather difficult to mention.'

The dean halted, looking at the speaker with renewed perplexity. 'I don't follow. According to Bedford, your friend fell from a train.' He smiled wanly. 'Surely there's nothing particularly shameful about choosing, to travel with British Rail!'

'I was referring,' answered Harrison, 'to the manner of his fall. Miller was a desperately sick man, it seems, and there's reason to believe that his death might have been intentional.'

'Poor fellow! No wonder, dear chap, you've been so upset.'

Together the two men walked on. Nothing further was said until they'd reached Great Cloister. There Ingrams again halted, and, pulling out his pipe, looked out through one of the latticed arches into the garth where, among the few horizontal gravestones, Dr Crocker's memorial sapling rose, a frail ghost in the drizzle. 'Perhaps I shouldn't say this,' he said, stuffing tobacco into the bowl, 'but in my view, the true evil of suicide lies in the torturing guilt it bequeaths to the living.'

'Quite,' murmured Harrison, thinking of Rachel.

Lighting up, the dean meditatively sucked his pipe for a moment or two. 'But that guilt is unavoidable, I fear,' he resumed, 'for each suicide seems to underline both the limitations of human love and our sheer inability to change the sad reality of this fallen world.' He paused, drawing again on his pipe, then suddenly chuckled. 'And talking of such,' he said, smiling up at his companion, 'rumour has it that Michael Cawthorne is coming armed this evening with some proposal on entrance charges.'

'Yes,' murmured Harrison heavily, gazing fixedly out into the rain, 'I had heard something of the sort.'

'Still,' said the dean, laughing, '*nil desperandum*: with Miss Hodge to aid us, and your masterly grip on the tiller, I'm confident we'll somehow steer safely between whatever Scylla and Charybdis good Brother Cawthorne plants in our way.'

Forced to proceed in Indian file along the narrow path round the northern wall of the nave, Harrison followed the bobbing shape of the dean's umbrella, intermittently inhaling wisps of the smoke that wafted behind. Despite this benediction, Harrison walked in grim silence, if anything more oppressed than ever by Ingrams's complete faith in him. Rounding the West Front, he saw Christ Church gatehouse looming ahead, its windows gleaming through the darkness, and shadowy figures already moving behind the narrow panes. His heart quailed at the sight, and resolve momentarily faltering, he unconsciously slackened his pace.

Ahead, a small group were already clustered in the dimly lit passageway, waiting their turn to duck through the narrow doorway leading up to the committee room above. Through the gloom, it was impossible to make out who they were, but from the repeated brays of laughter, one was certainly Major Coles.

'Thank goodness for that!' murmured the dean as the bursar and his companions ducked out of sight. 'I don't know, about you, Richard, but I need a few moments more of peace before we're finally embroiled.'

Entering the gatehouse, the pair slipped past the foot of the staircase. Going to the hinged-back postern, they halted, looking out into the deserted Buttermarket. The drizzle had eased, and through a fine rain, welcoming lights shone across the square from the bar and snug of the Adam and Eve.

From Mercery Lane, a figure emerged, hurrying towards the tavern door. As it opened, there was a tantalizing glimpse of laughing faces and the gleam of bottles and glasses, a scene which Harrison couldn't help contrasting with the one awaiting him overhead. The dean, however, appeared to have no such thoughts: contentedly sucking his pipe, he appeared for all the world like a short, corpulent innkeeper himself—the epitome in all but dress of the genial landlord, standing, as it were, at the doors of a gigantic hostelry, viewing with benevolent forbearance the sight of a tiny upstart rival.

'Richard, what do you know of your distant forebears?'

Surprised by the question, Harrison laughed. 'Nothing really,' he answered, 'though I remember my father boasting about one of us Harrisons—a Major-General, I believe—who got himself drawn and quartered at Charing Cross.'

'Really!' exclaimed Ingrams, chuckling over his pipe. 'Drawn and quartered, you say, and at Charing Cross!' His chuckles grew louder. 'You amaze me—it's difficult to conceive any relative of yours allowing himself to arrive at such an unpleasantly terminal position!'

Though Harrison laughed politely at his friend's mild joke, he remained preoccupied with wondering what he should do if Cawthorne forced the issue of admission charges to a vote.

'I don't know about you,' continued Ingrams, lighting another match, 'but I find all this interest; especially among our Atlantic cousins, for tracing ancestors quite inexplicable.' He gave a wry laugh. 'All I've ever needed, to know of my pedigree is neatly summed up by that unfortunate pair over there.'

Harrison peered into the gloom, fully expecting to see a couple of ragged outcasts. Seeing nobody, however, he looked inquiringly round at the dean; who, with his pipe stem, then pointed towards the illuminated inn sign, depicting the traditionally naked couple gazing up at a gaily painted serpent coiled among the apple branches above their heads. 'That, I fear,' resumed Ingrams, 'is sufficient family tree for me.' He gave a slight sigh. 'With all this talk of war, that pair of moral weaklings seem appropriate originators of all we humankind.'

Harrison coughed and cleared his throat, wondering why the topic was so preoccupying his friend.

'Yes, indeed,' mused the other, 'roots, bloodlines, genealogy—what does it matter? In the end, our dark provenance is the same—we're all the stock of Adam, the benighted heirs of Cain!' Having delivered himself of these gloomy ruminations, the dean turned again to his companion. 'I suppose there's no chance, Richard, your poor friend was a Mormon?'

'What! Miller, you mean?' exclaimed the other incredulously, staggered by the question. 'Good Lord, no! Why do you ask?'

Ingrams shrugged. 'Only because of their famous zeal in adding names and dates to the rolls of the Latterday Saints. It's the only explanation I have managed to come up with for why a desperately sick man in body and mind should spend his final days perusing church registers.'

Harrison was so stunned that for a moment he could only stare at the other in incredulous disbelief. 'Are you talking of David Miller, Dean? Checking registers, you say? Good God, wherever did you learn this?'

'From Canon Bedford, of course.'

'But how does he know?'

Ingrams laughed. 'My dear chap, there are no better intelligence gatherers in England than your average rural dean! Bedford was apparently so taken with your assertion that Miller had no relatives in the area, that he mentioned the matter to a few of the clergy in his deanery. One of them, I forget which, informed him that an American called Miller had consulted his church registers back in August.'

Harrison struggled to gather his thoughts; before he could speak, however, the dean suddenly exclaimed, 'Ah! This looks like our good lady steward now!'

A moment later, out of the darkness emerged the small, rather dumpy figure of Ruth Hodge. 'Dean, how very kind of you to wait for me,' she said, stepping through the portal. 'And Colonel Harrison too! How very gracious of you both!'

From behind came the first boom of eight. 'Ah, just in time,' said the new arrival. 'I was so frightened I was going to be late.' She began heading for the stairs. As she did so, there came a dazzling lightning flash and a crack of thunder.

'What a night!' she exclaimed, smiling round. 'Let's just hope, gentlemen, they're the only sparks going to fly tonight!'

With his foreboding as to coming events overlaid by the dean's extraordinary revelation, Harrison climbed the winding stairs, his mind whirling in equally narrow circles around the question of why a suicidal man—a sick wandering Jew—should have chosen to spend his final days consulting the registers of some obscure Kentish church. He thus arrived in the glare of lights above like an actor dragged blinking on to the stage, bewildered to find himself torn from one drama and peremptorily thrust into another.

As in a dream, he followed round the square of tables to sit down on Miss Hodge's left, while Ingrams, as council chairman, took the seat on her right. 'Well, ladies and gentlemen,' began the latter, beaming round, 'I first must thank you all for attending on such an unpleasant night.' As if to underline his appreciation, another vivid flash and a crash of thunder accompanied his words. 'Next, I'd like to welcome our latest member, the Right Reverend Michael Cawthorne.' Ingrams smiled. 'Or Mike, as he wishes to be known.'

Somehow Harrison forced himself to look towards the member in question. Cawthorne was sitting almost directly opposite, between Coles and Prebendary Richards. Wearing no jacket or tie, without insignia of rank or calling, he sat as on Sunday with the sleeves of his open-necked shirt rolled to the elbows, looking if anything even more out of place in this austere shadowy chamber than he had in the freshly-painted archdeaconry.

At that moment, Davidson entered, clearly soaked to the skin. His pasty-white face seemed paler than usual, and, as he met Harrison's eyes, the latter saw the same intense mix of anger and contempt as he'd seen that morning; clearly the visit to his godfather had merely inflamed the architect's fury against one whom he obviously now regarded as nothing but the unscrupulous lackey of an uncaring Church.

'Though I know our steward wishes to make a few remarks about this year's cathedral fête,' resumed Ingrams as Davidson took his seat, 'I wish first to express my personal appreciation not only of our members' valiant efforts in manning the stalls on the eleventh of August, but also in acting as cathedral guides and postcard sellers throughout the height of the tourist season.'

Harrison hardly heard a word: the open scorn and fury in Davidson's face had shaken him, and he sat gloomily staring down at the table. However, as Ingrams gave way to Ruth Hodge, and the room filled with murmurs of appreciation at her detailed account of the fête, he was forced to raise his head to nod and smile with the rest, being careful, however, to direct his gaze well above the respective heads of both his superior and subordinate.

Outside the rain was again splashing down; rumbles of thunder rolling and volleying incessantly overhead—and as he gazed up, a flash of lightning momentarily lit the opposite wall. As it did so, he had a glimpse of a solitary framed photograph hanging high upon the rough-hewn stone. He'd vaguely noticed it before, but so high did it hang, and so faded and dusty was it, that he'd never given it any attention. Now, however, as the talk of hoopla, tombola and fortune-telling continued, he remaining staring up, his gaze riveted on the place where it hung.

There came another flash. This time he saw it clearly: he'd been right: the black and white photograph portrait was of the very same man who looked down from above Tom Dove's desk!

There was no mistaking that broad face, the protruding brow, those compelling deep-set eyes. Indeed, the only difference between the photograph in Long Ashendon rectory and the one before him was that this latter had obviously been taken a good twenty years before the first, and that instead of sitting, garbed in the dress of a bishop, its subject stood in a strangely familiar garden, dressed in the charmingly archaic gaiters and clerical morning coat of a formally dressed cathedral dean.

Harrison had little time, however, to consider the curious coincidence of seeing the same man's portrait in such different places and on consecutive days, for Ingrams's voice intruded. 'I now call on our treasurer to render the general accounts and give us an idea of our likely financial position in the coming year.'

Just as his speculations as to what Miller had wanted with parish records had protected him from the full horror of entering the meeting, so now the photograph on the wall, and the remembrance it gave him of Dove's final sad wave, blunted his susceptibilities; hardly sensing the deepening gloom of those about him, he read out the figures, expressionlessly outlining the potentially calamitous gulf between likely income and present expenditure like some mechanical Micawber.

Silence fell, and, with the rain and thunder now finally ceased, Harrison resumed his seat. For a second or two the spell continued until, with obvious effort, the dean spoke. 'It would seem,' he began, 'despite our best endeavours, we have once again rather fallen short in worldly matters. Chapter and I will have to look where we can to make further cuts in cathedral expenditure.'

'Perhaps, Dean,' murmured Prebendary Richards, 'we might request Madam Steward to consider an increase in the Friends' individual contributions.'

Before either Ruth Hodge or the dean could answer, however, Cawthorne's voice rang through the room. 'That's all very well, but as Colonel Harrison has made clear, we are looking at a shortfall of over fifty thousand pounds a year! That's not going to be put right with a few more pence in contribution envelopes!'

Though Cawthorne smiled as he spoke, so sudden was his outburst, and so different was his tone and expression from that normally employed, that his words had a truly electrifying effect: there were audible gasps and a general stiffening; in particular, Prebendary Richards's face appeared to become marble, while on the right, grimacing, Major Coles began to pluck at his moustache.

In the ensuing silence, the dean cleared his throat. 'Perhaps, Archdeacon, you have some particular proposal to make?'

Harrison looked round in dismay: if Ingrams hated the idea of admission charges as much as he imagined, this invitation to Cawthorne was the equivalent of Daniel, not just entering the lion's den, but insisting on wrenching the wretched beast's jaws open and plunging in his head!

Cawthorne, rubbing his hands with apparent relish, began at once. 'As our chairman has made clear, the cathedral is subject to a vast influx of visitors. In view of the financial crisis, I suggest it's high time we make a virtue out of necessity by requiring them to pay towards its maintenance. I, therefore, propose we implement admission charges forthwith, bringing Canterbury in line with the majority of English cathedrals.'

There was a pause as he finished, then from Coles there came a gruff, 'Good idea!' Immediately, from all sides, other voices joined in with similar sounds of approval. As they did, Prebendary Richards's face changed from pale marble to vivid red. 'Ladies and gentlemen,' he burst out, 'aren't we forgetting that Canterbury is mother church to the entire Anglican Communion? Are the children to pay to enter the family home?'

The Chapter secretary's indignation momentarily stilled the archdeacon's supporters, but then with customary smile, Cawthorne calmly rejoined, 'I don't see why, if a mother's in need, her affluent children should not be required to make her adequate provision.' Richards bristled like a turkey cock, but before he could speak, the other went on. 'Perhaps we should remember how Jesus praised the good steward who had a hundredfold profit. In light of that, I believe we have a divine mandate to charge whatever the market will take!'

Richards's mouth opened to speak, but clearly overcome, he merely breathed, 'Really, Archdeacon!' and lapsed into silence.

With one gun knocked out, another now came into play, for suddenly, to Harrison's surprise, he heard Davidson's voice.

'I'd like to remind the council of the wishes of our founder. When, as dean, George Bell established the Cathedral Friends and set aside this room for our use, it was with the intention that the mother church of the Anglican Communion should remain free for any of its members to enter.'

Davidson was pointing directly at the photograph of the man who occupied such a prominent position in his godfather's study. Of course, thought Harrison mid the growing uproar, no wonder that a virtual pacifist like Dove would display the portrait of the man whose ecumenical work and questioning of the Air Ministry's conduct of the war had denied him the primacy.

Above the upraised voices came the dean's voice. 'I think, ladies and gentlemen, at this juncture we could do no better than hear the advice of our treasurer.' He beamed round. 'I'm sure, from long experience, we all agree that Colonel Harrison's good sense and practical expertise can be depended on.'

'Hear! Hear!' rejoined Richards at once, then Cawthorne's eager tones. 'I agree—let's hear from Colonel Harrison.'

Suddenly all was silent as both sides of the conflict waited for the council treasurer to speak, while the dean, with a confident smile, leaned back, arms folded, the very picture of an assured ship's captain relaxing after handing over the command of his beleaguered vessel to a trusted pilot.

If the man stumbling unhappily to his feet represented a ship's pilot, it was one who temporarily had not the slightest idea where to steer, and whose mind was so overcome with the awareness of rocks and shoals, that for a moment all he could do was stare ahead in numb dismay. Before him, the three rows of faces looked up. Among them, he saw the bristling moustache and enthusiastic eyes of Major Coles, and next to him, the confidently smiling archdeacon.

Turning away, he met the cold suspicious look of Davidson,

who alone in the room, sat regarding him with a mixture of dislike and disgust.

Harrison coughed and looked up at the bishop's portrait, as if in those kindly eyes might lie the answer to this agonizing moment that had been racing towards him all day. And then, almost miraculously, gazing at the face of George Bell, he remembered the moment in the archdeaconry drawing-room when he'd conceived the idea of working against Cawthorne's plans while apparently agreeing with his every word. If he could use one civil service technique, why not another? The answer was obvious: he must employ the most time-hallowed and successful of Whitehall's delaying ploys. Next moment he heard himself saying in clear measured tones, 'As this is a complicated and controversial business, I propose we set up a committee to look into the matter thoroughly and report back to the council in due course.'

As he spoke, he saw Cawthorne's face: the confident look changing first to incredulity, then to doubt. On all the other faces around, however, there was no such ambiguity of response. 'Hear! Hear!' rang Coles's voice above the rest. 'Setting up a committee! Masterly! The very thing we need.'

All tension had vanished; the majority of the overwrought opponents of moments before were now smiling and talking amongst themselves as if at a vicarage tea-party. Then came Ingrams's voice. 'As ever, we must all thank Colonel Harrison for his good sense and ability to see straight to the heart of the matter.' He smiled round. 'And if we may further prevail on his good nature, I suggest, Madam Steward, that he should chair the committee and choose among the interested parties for its membership.'

Ruth Hodge smiled round. 'Well, Colonel, would you mind?'

'Not at all.'

There was a brief murmur of appreciation, then the Friends' steward continued: 'Now that's settled satisfactorily, I suggest we move directly on to the important matter of this year's Christmas card design.'

'Darling, the news is just about to begin.'

'I'm on my way.' Adding a plate of biscuits to the mugs on the tray, Harrison carried them through to the sitting-room with the sound of Big Ben echoing through the cottage. Having handed Winnie her bedtime drink, he thankfully slumped before the television.

With the dreaded meeting finally over, and the air cool and fresh after all the rain, he relaxed, sipping his drink and greatly enjoying the sight of a decidedly shifty-looking Iraqi ambassador being hard pressed on the subject of hostages. Film of an enormous American aircraft carrier added further to his sense of well-being, and, in complete contrast to what appeared on the screen, he felt more at peace than at any time since his return from abroad. Cornered as he'd been, he had nevertheless achieved, if not victory, at least the next best thing: a masterly strategic retreat. Thus, with warplanes and tanks hurtling across the screen, he nibbled his biscuits and sipped his cocoa with something like the relief that poor doomed General Moore must have felt, watching the last of his ragged battalions crossing the Mero to the Corunna defences.

Drowsily he lay back in his chair, enjoying the final memories of the evening: Ruth Hodge's words of gratitude when the meeting had broken up an hour earlier than expected and she was leaving to collect Joyce Dove from the evening class; Coles's hearty handshake; the grateful nod from Prebendary Richards and, last of all, Ingrams's kindly words as they parted at the deanery gate—but above all these, what he really relished was the doubt and general uncertainty he'd glimpsed on the archdeacon's face.

His wife, however, seemed to share nothing of his mood; she sat in silence through the news, a frowning, weary despondency on her face. 'Is anything the matter, dear?' he asked. 'What's on your mind?'

'Oh, I don't know,' answered Winnie with a shrug, 'I'm thinking about Joyce, I suppose. She was very low all evening—that's why Ruth was nearly late for your meeting: when she called to give Joyce a lift, she had a lot of trouble persuading her to come at all because she's so worried about Tom.'

'He's still taking the idea of the move badly?' said Harrison, his smile fading.

Winnie nodded. 'Much worse, apparently, than Joyce would ever have guessed. It seems she'd hardly got a word out of him since we left yesterday.'

Despite this interruption to his sense of well-being, so relieved was he with how the meeting had gone, that Harrison switched off the bedside lamp half an hour later with a profound sense of satisfaction. Despite its unavoidable strains, it had been a day of positive achievement: he'd cleared the backlog of work; Keates and his men were now pressing on fast with the tower repairs; above all, he'd successfully wriggled out of any public commitment to Cawthorne's policies—and thus he remained, as it were, free to dine with the angels of tradition and sup with the devils of change.

Lying there in the dark, his mind strayed back to the moment under the gatehouse when the dean had told him of Canon Bedford's information about Miller's perusal of parish registers. Since then, he'd had hardly a chance to consider its implications. It seemed as unlikely now as when Ingrams had so innocently first mentioned it. Nevertheless, he thought, in the morning he would ring and check with the rural dean.

Closing his eyes, Harrison turned over on the pillow, certain he would sleep well and finally get in the eight hours he so badly needed. However, hovering on the frontier of sleep, one last tiny thought occurred—if Miller really had been hunting through church registers, there existed the possibility—extraordinary though it seemed—that his thwarted attempt to contact him through his office might have had less to do with their time in Berlin together, and more with the present-day affairs of the Canterbury diocese. Hardly, however, had that thought touched him before he drifted into unconsciousness, leaving the Dunstan bell to sound the quarters, halls and hours beneath a now rapidly clearing sky.

Suddenly the light was back on, and Winnie was shaking him. 'Wake up, Richard! The phone!'

Drugged and drowsy with sleep, he looked up from the pillow, hearing the insistently repeated sound. Dragging an arm from under the blankets, he blinked at his watch. 'Damn it!' he murmured incredulously. 'It's almost one! Who the devil can be ringing now?' With a groan, he stumbled out on to the floor.

'Yes? What is it?'

From the bed, his wife heard his abrupt tone as he answered the phone, then a moment later, his astonished exclamations. 'What! No! Surely not!'

Half raising herself on the pillow, Winnie found herself straining to listen. Finally, she heard him say, his voice strangely altered, 'Tell her I shall be there as fast as I can.'

The phone rang off, and a moment later Harrison reappeared in the doorway, face ashen-grey, eyes glazed and staring.

'Richard, whatever's happened?'

Instead of answering at once, he slumped on the bed and began, hands trembling, to unbutton his pyjama jacket. 'That was Miss Hodge ringing from Long Ashendon rectory,' he said hollowly. 'Joyce wants me to go over there straightaway.'

'At this time of night! For heaven's sake, why? And what's Miss Hodge doing at the rectory now?' There was dread in Winnie's voice. 'Come on, Richard, tell me—whatever's happened? Why does Joyce want you there in the middle of the night?'

Harrison took a deep breath, then with effort, his face anguished, he looked round. 'It's Tom,' he said slowly. 'Apparently Joyce found him dead when she got home.'

Chapter Seven

As the Volvo crawled between the high laurels, tyres crunching the gravel, the rectory seemed silent and dark, but as the beam of the headlights swept the drive, they picked out two cars, Ruth Hodge's gleaming white Peugeot, and beside it, the diocesan architect's shabby Toyota Estate.

Davidson here! The very thought was unbearable. Grimacing, Harrison drew up behind the Toyota's tailgate with its prominent notice: Keep your distance—children on board, and silenced the engine. As he did so, two figures emerged from the house. Numbly, he clambered out to meet them.

'Thank goodness you've come, Colonel!' exclaimed Ruth Hodge, hurrying to him. 'Joyce wouldn't allow a thing to be touched or the doctor called until you arrived. As I was just saying to George here, I don't know what would have happened if you'd refused to come.'

At her words, the architect's lanky figure materialized from the dark beside her.

'Ah, Davidson! There you are. I noticed your car—how long have you been here?'

'Just a few minutes. Joyce asked Miss Hodge to phone us both.' The shock of that call had still clearly not worn off, for there was a deadness to the architect's tone that gave his voice an almost mechanical quality. Better that, thought Harrison, than the raging and bellowing he'd more than half expected.

'Where's your aunt at the moment?' he asked, looking round at the house.

'Waiting in the drawing-room.'

'It's been a terrible shock for her,' intervened Ruth Hodge. 'I waited for the art class to finish after our meeting, then I drove her home. When we got here, there was no sign of Torn. We looked for him everywhere, even in the garden, until we found the note.'

'Note?' repeated Harrison, aghast. His senses reeled. 'Merciful God! Surely you're not saying…'

'I'm afraid so,' answered Davidson heavily as Harrison's words trailed away. 'It seems,' he continued in an expressionless monotone, 'that my godfather has taken his own life. My aunt and Miss Hodge discovered his body in the garage—apparently he'd asphyxiated himself with exhaust fumes.'

Numbly, Harrison gazed past the speaker's head to where, invisible in the darkness, rose the old coach house used for garaging the elderly couple's car. He couldn't move: in the blackness of the sequestered drive, the thick, Musty scent of the wet laurels in his nostrils, he stood facing nightmare: he was a ruined man, of that he was quite certain—directly implicated in a policy that had driven a sick old man, an ordained priest, a nationally known figure, to desperately end his own life! With Dove having committed suicide and having left a note (God knows how caustic!) there was no escape. Ahead lay the Coroner's Court, hectoring tabloid reporters and inescapable scandal, not just to the diocese, but to the entire Church. And there, in the near future, was himself, bereft of self-respect, honour, position and friends—and yet, even then, standing in the drive with his mind conjuring nightmares, he heard himself calmly ask, 'Are you quite certain, Miss Hodge, that he's dead?'

'Oh yes, Colonel,' came the reply. 'I checked carefully. I had some training with St John's Ambulance—he must have been dead at least an hour before we found him.'

'And you haven't yet called the doctor, you say?'

The other shook her head. 'Joyce insisted that Tom's instructions be carried out to the letter, and that nothing should be done before you and George arrived.'

For a moment, Harrison could hardly take in what he'd heard. 'You mean,' he said hollowly, 'my name actually appears in the final note?'

'Oh, yes, Colonel, very much so. Now, I think,' continued Miss Hodge briskly, turning back for the house, 'that Joyce has been on her own for too long. Let's go in.'

Harrison nodded dumbly and followed across the gravel. Stunned by the additional horror of his name actually appearing on Dove's suicide note—a message that would be publicly read out in court—he walked in silence, and, for the second time in less than forty-eight hours, grimly entered what had been so long the home and workplace of the inimitable Reverend Thomas Dove.

Outside the drawing-room door, Ruth Hodge stopped and turned to Davidson. 'George, I think you and I had better wait in the kitchen. Joyce wishes a private word with the colonel.'

Davidson nodded. In the hall light, he looked dazed with horror, and there was a hopeless deadness to his eyes. As Harrison watched him walk on with Ruth Hodge, for the first time he realized something of the closeness of the bond between that diffident, repressed conformist and his late father's ebullient and famously radical friend.

Finally, as the other two vanished, he turned to the door and, steeling himself, gently knocked and entered.

Apart from a single standard lamp, the room was unlit, and, as Harrison entered, he didn't immediately see the occupant. For some reason, he'd expected to find Joyce either sitting or lying on the settee, but in fact, it was empty. He stood a moment staring about him before a slight movement from the window-bay made him turn.

In the half-light, Joyce stood, her back to him, staring out into the dark. For a second or two, he remained looking at her, wondering why she hadn't turned at his entrance, then, noticing the tension in her body, he had a sick feeling that the next moment she'd swing round with blazing eyes to hurl at him the absolutely justifiable accusations of moral cowardice and cruelty—if not downright complicity, in murder. Instead, however, as she slowly turned, her red-rimmed eyes had in them nothing but the desolation of grief.

The sight of her pain affected him greatly. Unable to face her, rooted in shame and embarrassment, he lowered his gaze, mumbling, 'Joyce, my dear, I'm so truly sorry.'

Next moment she had crossed to him, and, to his surprise, taking both his hands and squeezing them, said, 'It was so good of you to come, Richard.' Her voice seemed to break. 'So very like you!' Releasing her grip, she turned away, and, withdrawing a handkerchief from her sleeve, shook her head. 'Everyone is being so awfully kind.'

Harrison felt as helpless before this older woman's grief as he'd been before the younger's in the memorial garden. Just as then, he had no idea what to say, and could only blurt out, 'Winnie asks me to give you her love.'

'Dear Winifred!' Joyce looked round, smiling through her tears. 'Poor dear, being disturbed like this, and after giving us all such a very nice class tonight.'

Until this moment, Harrison had been concerned with the inevitable scandal in the diocese, and the damage to the reputation of the Church and himself. Now, however, faced with the courage and selflessness of this woman who, in the extremity of grief, could show such concern and gratitude to others, he saw the true enormity and significance of what had happened: that night, her life had been shattered, a lifetime's partnership broken; on top of that, she was faced with the agonizing knowledge that her husband had deliberately taken his own life. Rachel Miller had found the thought of her father's suicide almost unendurable: if that had been true for an estranged daughter, how much more so for this woman who had been, not only Dove's wife and companion, but his lifelong protectress and friend. Suddenly it was not the screaming headlines of the tabloids, flaying and bludgeoning himself and the archdeacon, that horrified Harrison, but Joyce's inevitably continuing pain.

'I'd no idea,' he murmured miserably, 'that he would have taken the news so badly, else I'd never have agreed…'

'No, Richard! No, you really mustn't blame yourself!' Joyce gazed earnestly up at his face. 'You were doing your duty, that's all. Tom said that very thing just after you left. I know,' she continued, attempting to smile, 'he could be an awful tease at times, but underneath, believe me, he always liked and admired you enormously.' She looked down. 'It must have been very difficult for you to come over and break the news personally.'

Again, so different was this response from what he'd expected, that Harrison stood speechless, wretchedly aware that on top of everything else, instead of endeavouring to comfort her as he should, it was she who was trying to cheer him.

'Look,' she continued, going over to the mantelpiece and picking up a sheet of paper, 'this is the note he left; see how well he speaks of you, and how much he valued your judgement.'

Wordlessly, Harrison took it, but, unable to read in the dimness, he went over and held it directly under the standard lamp. As usual with Tom Dove's communications, it was typed—but that quirky, bubbling, sometimes questionable, humour that had been the hallmark of his letters, political speeches and articles had quite disappeared, and what Harrison now read were not the words of the indomitable, provocative battler he'd known, but those of an ultimately defeated man.

My darling,

Forgive me for the pain I now cause. You know the depression I have suffered at feeling so uselessly frail and dependent since my stroke. After yesterday's news, I find I cannot face the inevitable upheaval.

Beyond that, I'm conscious you're wearing yourself out, having to nurse me. On your own, you'll be far better able to deal with the coming move. I therefore leave you, my dear, deeply grateful for our many happy years. In regard to matters practical, I wish you to ring George immediately and ask him to come over, but because he is so sensitive and will take this badly, I want you to call Richard Harrison also. From long experience, I know we can trust that he'll do all that has to be done with complete discretion and integrity. Tell him he will find my body, in the garage.

Finally, my dear darling, once more, forgive me for this sudden departure.

My love and gratitude,
Your everloving,

Below appeared the single written word *Tom*, scrawled in the usual green ink.

Harrison felt a range of emotions: pity for Joyce; relief that Dove hadn't blamed him; surprise at the old man's gracious comments about him, especially after all their battles over the expenditure on Holy Trinity; above all, her felt shock at the strange casualness of this brief farewell note—but then, as he told himself, Dove had always been a mystery to him and everyone else.

Refolding the note, he turned back to Joyce. 'You know, of course, I'll do whatever I can.'

'Will you?' Suddenly there was something like hope in her face. 'Then you'll save him!' she cried, moving towards him. 'Oh, Richard, say you will!'

'Save him?' repeated Harrison, taken aback at this passionate outburst, and wondering if the horror of finding such a note had temporarily unhinged the woman. 'Save him from what?'

'From the consequences of what he's done,' she cried, clutching his wrists and pleading with frantic urgency. 'Save him from his last, mad, momentary aberration. Please, Richard, I know you have the strength. Do what you have to, and allow his spirit to rest in peace.'

Whether from exhaustion or nervous strain, for one ghastly

moment Harrison remembered again those grisly ancient superstitious practices surrounding suicide, and actually thought that this intelligent woman clutching at him was begging him to go out to the garage, armed with hammer and stake. However, with hardly less horror, he began to understand what it was she was really suggesting, as she continued, 'Save his reputation, Richard! Let him have died peacefully in his sleep, as the doctor promised me, not—please not—by his own hand!'

Going to the window-bay, Harrison looked out into the darkness, standing in almost exactly the same position as when he'd endeavoured to summon up the courage to break the news of the archdeacon's decision—and, just as then, the course of his thoughts was continually buffeted by a series of conflicting and contrary winds.

You may trust his discretion and integrity. Is that what Tom Dove had implied in his final note, that he could be depended upon to cover up the cause of death, and so protect both the Church and the old man's reputation from scandal and the damage of venomous tongues? But to break the law! To cover up suicide! Could Dove have really expected that of him? And Joyce, did she have any idea of what she was asking—that he, a law-abiding and trusted church official, should surreptitiously and illegally cart around a corpse like some sort of latterday grave snatcher! That he and—presumably—Davidson should together hump her husband's body through the rectory grounds at night like a second Burke and Hare! It didn't bear thinking of! And what if it ever came out? It wouldn't be a matter of a painful scene with the dean, or an unpleasant half-hour with the archbishop: it would be a police matter, and could well end with a narrow cell in Canterbury gaol with nothing but a bunk and a bucket!

'Please, Richard—help us!'

Harrison groaned inwardly: Joyce's plaintive appeal was an

echo of Rachel's; if he'd felt an obligation to assist the one merely because he'd been abroad when her father had called, how much more so was he duty bound to help this woman—the widow of a sick old man who, whatever she said, he'd helped badger to death! Damn it, he owed her an unpayable debt—and anyway, even if it was illegal to cover up suicide, was it so wrong to protect the reputation of the dead and lessen the mental anguish of their nearest and dearest? What was it that Winnie had told him about the dying Dickens being carted from his mistress's home to die respectably on his own front carpet? True or not, the principle was surely correct: for the sake of society and for the sake of the Church, Dove's reputation must be protected. It was clear: obligation and duty gave him no choice—the indignities of the prison cell must be risked.

Slowly he turned and nodded. 'All right—I'll do what I can.' He paused. 'That is, of course, if I'm able to persuade your nephew and Miss Hodge to aid and abet me.'

'Bless you, Richard.' Going over to him, Joyce bent and kissed his cheek. 'I knew you'd not let us down.'

Surprisingly, Miss Hodge came up absolute trumps. Local magistrate, churchwarden, steward of the Cathedral Friends—the very epitome of old-fashioned provincial respectability, she nevertheless accepted the proposal of illegally moving the body with complete equanimity. Davidson, on the other hand, took the idea hard. Already shaken by the night's events, he seemed to go all to pieces at the very thought, and as Harrison argued, he walked to and fro in the rectory kitchen, shaking his head and muttering variously about the sanctity of the body and a citizen's duty.

In the end, it took the combined arguments of Ruth Hodge and Harrison to persuade him that scandal and gossip, on top of everything else, would likely kill his aunt. Finally, visibly trembling from the idea of the crime he was committing, he reluctantly followed Harrison out to the drive, pathetically whispering that he'd never seen a dead body in his life.

Unspeaking, the two men crunched across the gravel, their way lit by Dove's venerable wood-box torch. Halting before the barely opened sliding doors of the garage, they listened a moment. Around them the village lay in absolute silence, and as they proceeded to heave back the doors, the ensuing rumble seemed loud enough to wake the parish.

Harrison flashed the torch briefly on the grille of the old Morris Traveller, then dropping the beam to the floor, noticed rags and pieces of sacking against the base of the doors. Clearly, they'd been used to help block in the lethal carbon monoxide. Even now the stink of exhaust fumes was discernible above the smell of oil and the various musty exhalations emanating from the numerous tins and cans littering the shelves, benches and floor at the back of the garage.

Automatically, Davidson reached for the light switch as they entered. Before he could touch it, however, Harrison snapped, 'For God's sake, man, leave it! The last thing we need at present is a blasted carnival display!'

'Sorry, Colonel!'

The fear was evident in the other's tremulous reply, and as Harrison began edging between the car and the wall, it occurred to him that one good thing at least had emerged from the whole grisly business: the customary respect and subordination of the diocesan architect had clearly returned. It was a gratifying thought, and gave him the strength to shine his torch down through the glass at the figure slumped over the wheel.

Dove's mouth hung open, though mercifully his eyes were closed. In front of him, the ignition and oil lamps glowed red and blue on either side of the large central speedometer. Harrison noticed that the manual choke beneath was partly drawn open: clearly the engine had run on until either the plugs had oiled up or the fumes in the garage had choked it. Through the sliding rear off-side window; a section of what was obviously garden hose protruded into the interior of the car.

Moving round the half-timbered vehicle's rear, Harrison knelt and shone his torch on where the rubber tubing was tightly secured over the nozzle of a shiny new exhaust pipe with a rusty-looking jubilee clip. He gave the hose a useless tug, then straightening, briefly directed the light round the shelves and over the untidy collection of cans. He then began tapping round his pockets.

'Davidson, have you any loose change?'

'Change?' answered the other uncertainly. 'How much do you need, Colonel?'

'For God's sake, man—just a tuppenny piece if you have it,' muttered Harrison, irritably. 'In lieu of a screwdriver, I need a large thin coin to remove this blasted clip.'

Davidson pressed the coin in his hand. Kneeling, panting from exertion, Harrison attempted to turn the screw of the clip. It was impossible: grunting, he struggled, conscious that both knees of his suit were resting in a patch of oil.

Suddenly the architect's voice intruded. 'Try this.' From somewhere, Davidson had found a screwdriver—and, heaven be praised, one of just the right size. In another moment, Harrison had loosened the clip and jerked it clear of the pipe.

'Right,' he murmured, yanking the hose from the car and passing it and the clip over to Davidson, 'get rid of these—go and throw them on the back seat of my car.'

As Davidson vanished, Harrison stumbled to his feet and again shone the torch round the back of the garage. Its beam revealed a tarpaulin-swathed motor-mower, a collection of aged garden implements, a carpenter's bench on which lay a large roll of green binding twine. Directing the torch upwards, he made out a pair of old wooden stepladders, hung on heavy cobwebbed hooks. Focusing the light on it as the other returned, he said, 'Right, lift that thing down and lay it beside the car.'

Davidson seemed to freeze: the wretched man appeared

to be nearing the end of his tether, and showed every sign of nervous collapse. Harrison, his own nerves taut, felt his blood pressure rise, but before he could express what he felt, he was suddenly remembering that long-ago day in Berlin when he had faced his first dead body—the bound victim in a ruined bakery in Uhlandstrasse, head beaten to pulp. If it hadn't been for Staff-Sergeant Müller's steadying hand and his whispered, 'Just take deep breaths, sir,' he certainly, would have fainted. So, instead of the sharp command he'd intended, he said gently, 'Buck up, my dear fellow. I know it's a horrible business, but now we've started, we must see it through.'

Both words and tone had a great effect on Davidson; with almost dog-like devotion, he helped as Harrison opened the driver's door and, wrapping his aims around the stiffened corpse, dragged it out and laid it down on the horizontal step-ladder. Removing the tarpaulin from the motor-mower, the two men wrapped the body, and finally, taking a length of the garden binding twine, secured their load.

'Right,' breathed Harrison, 'let's get on with it.'

Carefully, without a light showing and not a word said, the improvised stretcher was hurried to the front door where, like a priest at the church porch, Ruth Hodge stood waiting to receive it. Again, like the officiating minister preceding the cortège, she walked ahead as Dove's body was carried across the hall and up the staircase.

Showing the way, she led them into the bedroom, and then with Harrison's assistance, and with Davidson watching with face almost as ashen as the cadaver's, she undressed the body and then struggled the now almost rigid arms and legs into pyjamas. Having done so, they drew the blankets over him. Having finally smoothed down the old man's hair, and spread out a red dressing-gown from his chin like a cloak, turning off the lights, they slipped away, leaving the late rector of Long Ashendon alone in his glory.

Chapter Eight

Just as Harrison had feared at the time, the headlong drive through the pools and puddles of the flooded back roads to Long Ashendon had damaged the Volvo's exhaust system, for now, on his return, its engine noise rapidly increased; and by the time the familiar trinity of towers appeared through the greying light, the respectable family saloon sounded like a teenager's hot-rod. Praying he wouldn't be stopped by the police, and, feeling horribly exposed, he drove through the empty streets, leaving an echoing roar in his wake. Finally, having entered the still-sleeping precincts with all the din of an armoured column, he thankfully switched off the racket and clambered out, ears ringing and almost drunk with fatigue.

Having secreted the hose and jubilee clip beneath his workbench, he locked the garage and stood in the dawn light for a minute or two, stiff and unsteady, vainly trying to clear his head. Doing so, he shivered, partly from exhaustion, partly from cold: less than twenty-four hours after almost tropical heat, the air had a wintry nip, as if the very seasons, along with everything else, were plunging purgatorially from one ghastly excess to another.

'But was I wrong, Winnie?' he cried out thirty minutes later, propped up in bed with a hot drink. 'Should I have gone along with the business—that's the question, damn it!'

'Knowing you, my poor darling,' answered his wife, 'you

hadn't a choice, not after Tom's note and Joyce's pleadings. Anyway,' she continued, taking his mug, 'now's not the time to get all worked up again. You must rest.'

Harrison lay back on the pillow, momentarily closing his eyes before again bursting out, 'God Almighty! Who'd have thought the old fellow would actually do himself in!'

'Shush now!' murmured Winnie, stroking his shoulder. 'Come on! What's done is done—for your own sake and everyone else's, try to sleep: if you don't, you're just going to make yourself ill.'

'Sleep?' he cried. 'How can I sleep with the image of Dove's face in that car!'

Surprisingly, however, within a few minutes of this final outburst, Harrison drifted into unconsciousness and was soon sleeping as soundly as if the night had been innocently spent discussing diocesan affairs with the dean or playing gin rummy with Major and Mrs Coles. When he awoke, the bed beside him was empty and the sun bright in his eyes. For a moment he lay hardly able to believe that the night's events had been anything but a bad dream, apart from the telltale dull heavy weight in his head. Reclosing his eyes, he lay reliving the nocturnal memories, then, in a sudden spasm of apprehension, sat up and looked at the clock.

It was quarter-past nine! Kicking off the blankets, he began feverishly dressing, wondering how he could have slept through the alarm, and angry that Winnie hadn't bothered to wake him. He had just pulled on his trousers to find both knees stained and still damp with oil when his wife wheeled herself into the room.

'Up already? I hoped you'd sleep for another hour at least. Don't worry,' she added, seeing his expression, 'I've phoned Mary Simpson and told her you won't be in until eleven at the earliest. I said you'd got yourself overtired at the council meeting last night.'

'Good God! What the hell did she say?' murmured Harrison hopelessly, surveying his ruined trousers as he spoke.

'Well,' said his wife, smiling, 'to tell you the truth, I think she's relieved. Apparently she's been worried about you this week. In Miss Simpson's words, "Foreign parts don't agree with the colonel." Next year I'm instructed to allow you your customary fortnight in Weymouth.'

Refusing anything but a strong cup of coffee, Harrison insisted on leaving the house within twenty minutes of rising, and was thus at his desk before Dunstan had chance to strike the first chime of ten. All this hurry, however, in the end proved completely useless: once seated, he found it impossible to muster the will to start work. Indeed, the very sight of the morning's post was repugnant, the waiting estimates, quotations, proposals and complaints seeming somehow meaningless after the happenings of the night.

In an effort to divert his thoughts, Harrison reached in a drawer for the latest EEC building directive. For a moment or two he actually managed to focus his mind on it, but in less than two minutes he'd thrown it aside and sat staring up at the tiny-paned window above him, the very picture of his doomed ancestor awaiting the distant clink of the gaoler's keys.

It was already almost half-past ten. Joyce Dove, he thought, must have called the family doctor at least an hour before; by now the death certificate would be signed and the funeral director called—either that, or a couple of police cars were already in the rectory drive and Dr Brooke bent over Dove's body, hunting down clues with bloodhoundly relish.

His blood chilled at the thought. With the sound of his secretary moving about the outer office, Harrison sat with an identical dread he'd experienced at prep school, trooping into prayers to meet the headmaster's gaze the morning after the bootman's unfortunate fall down the cellar steps. Then it had been a simple matter of the removal of a light bulb; now it was the illegal moving of a corpse and the covering-up of an unnatural death. Then it had meant only the traditional six quick burning strokes; now it meant flashing blue lights in the close, heavy boots on the stairs, and the indignity of being hustled outside and publicly driven away.

Gloomy and tense, he continued to sit as the dock hands crept round the dial, wishing, yet not daring, to ring Joyce. Eleven o'clock struck and still nothing. He began reading through a rambling appeal for the renewal of belfry beams; apparently the Reverend Eric Croxted had checked his parish records, and, having discovered that his church had rung for Blenheim, Trafalgar and Alamein, felt in the light of the latest developments in the Middle East, that the Board might thus take a sympathetic view of his request. Harrison had just jotted a polite note of regret when there came the sound of hurrying feet on the stairs. Pen in hand, he sat rigid until the inevitable knock. 'Sorry to disturb you, Colonel.' His secretary was looking in. 'Dr Cawthorne insists on seeing you at once.'

'The archdeacon?' gasped Harrison. 'Yes, of course, Mary.' He began stumbling to his feet. 'Please show him in.'

The instruction was quite unnecessary, for hardly had the words left his mouth before Cawthorne was shouldering past the girl to face him, and without taking the proffered hand, burst out, 'For heaven's sake, Richard, whatever have you done?'

'I?' said Harrison as his secretary hurriedly closed the door. 'I don't understand, Archdeacon. What has happened?'

'Happened! I've just had a call from Canon Bedford: Tom Dove was found dead in bed by his wife this morning, and according to his doctor, his death was almost certainly brought about by the shock of whatever you told him on Monday!'

Despite the unpleasantly accusative tone, Harrison felt a wave of enormous relief. Unlike the time when he'd placed the still-intact bulb on the stone floor eight feet beneath the hanging flex in an ill-judged attempt to make it appear it had fallen by itself, the simple ploy of carrying the body to bed had apparently worked. Dove's doctor regarded the death as natural, therefore no police cars would enter the close after all: the old man's reputation had been preserved, along with that of the Church in general, and also his own and those of Ruth Hodge and poor timid Davidson.

'I don't quite follow you, Dr Cawthorne,' he heard himself say. 'What I told the Reverend Dove on Monday was exactly what I'd been instructed by you to say: that he had no legal right to the rectory and that he had to vacate before Lady Day.'

The cleric gaped, eyes wide with anguished horror. 'Good Lord! If you put it like that, no wonder the poor fellow had another stroke!'

Frowning, but saying nothing, Harrison regarded his visitor with an icy look, before which the lithe fluting man of summer visibly wilted. Apparently sapped of all strength, the visitor sank into a chair, wiping his face. 'I know what I decided,' he murmured, 'but I trusted you to break it diplomatically.'

'I think, Archdeacon,' answered Harrison, 'that even the present Secretary-General of the United Nations would be hard put to soften the facts of eviction.'

A look of protest rose in Cawthorne's face, but then, colouring, he dropped his gaze. 'You're right, of course, Colonel,' he mumbled wretchedly. 'God help me! I insisted on pressing the matter against your advice.'

This abrupt capitulation took Harrison by surprise; for a moment, he stared down at the slumped figure with vindictive pleasure, simultaneously experiencing a strong measure of satisfaction at Cawthorne dropping that impertinent use of his Christian name. Nevertheless, despite himself, he suddenly found himself saying, 'My dear Archdeacon, you mustn't blame yourself unduly. You had a duty by the diocese—and nobody who knew Tom could have ever believed that so courageous and indomitable a fighter as he would have taken the news so badly.'

After escorting his visitor down to the outer door, and having had his hand wrung with touching warmth, Harrison watched him walk away up Dark Entry. He remained until the slight figure disappeared, then thoughtfully remounted the office stairs.

Gratifying as Cawthorne's unexpected collapse had been, Harrison was under no illusion: what he'd won was a battle, not a war. The fellow had proved a moral pigmy, and once the shock of Dove's death had worn off, someone who could rush round like an hysterical schoolgirl to offload the consequences of his own decisions on a subordinate, would rise again, as cocksure, smug and self-satisfied as ever—if anything, made doubly dangerous by his resentment of the humiliating little episode just past. Stung and wishing to reassert himself, he would doubtless attempt to push on with his crude economies with even greater zeal than before. Indeed, he'd said as much, sitting there before Harrison's desk, writhing his hands and babbling on about cruel necessities—and, in almost the same breath, repeatedly bemoaning the inherent conversatism of the majority of his fellow clergy and extolling the common sense and vision of the Dilapidations Board. Certain Cawthorne was but temporarily scotched, and the time would come when he'd spring up again, fangs regrown, to seek to reimpose his authority over himself and the diocese, Harrison thoughtfully returned to his office and closed his door on his wondering secretary.

It was not, however, the revelations into his superior's character that had astonished Harrison most: what had really surprised him was what he himself had said of Tom Dove's. Trying to cheer up Cawthorne, he'd given voice to thoughts suppressed even from himself. He'd called the old man brave and indomitable, and had said Dove was the last person to collapse before the commonplace necessity of finding a new home—and if that was true of any supposed strain on his heart, how much more so was it when it came to suicide and the matter of a mortal sin!

Going to his window, he stared out, aware for the first time just how extraordinary Dove's self-slaughter had been. He found it impossible to accept he'd killed himself just for the sake of a house. Even with the tangible facts like the note and that hose protruding into the car, like Rachel Miller regarding her father's suicide, Harrison felt suddenly certain there was much more to the matter than he yet knew.

Restless, he walked to his desk, then back to the window. Had there been something else on Dove's mind, something more than the loss of the rectory, that had driven him to take his life? If so, what could it possibly have been in the quiet world of Long Ashendon?

Going to his desk, Harrison picked up the phone. A moment or two later his wife's voice was on the line.

'No, everything's fine, Winnie. Don't worry.' Glancing at the door, he dropped his voice. 'According to the doctor, Tom died of a stroke. I heard it from the archdeacon just now. But there's something I want to ask: last night, when you talked to Joyce, apart from the worries about moving, did she happen to mention if there was anything else on Tom's mind?'

'No, nothing.'

'You're sure—just feeling depressed at having to leave the village?' Frowning, Harrison stared up at the window. 'Look, Winnie,' he continued, 'there's something I want you to do: phone Joyce straight away and say we'd both like to come over and see her tomorrow—don't take no for an answer. Tell her we insist on giving her all the support we can.'

Replacing the receiver, he sat thinking for a moment. Tom and Joyce had been a devoted couple, as close as any he'd known. Was it possible, however, that Dove had held something back from her? Had there been something too sensitive, perhaps too terrible, for him to have even confided to his wife?

All at once he felt an overwhelming impulse to ring Winnie back and ask her to forward their visit to that afternoon—but then, remembering his broken exhaust, he instead put on his reading glasses and again reached for his in-tray.

Despite feeling more than usually cribbed and caged in his office, Harrison nevertheless managed to clear his desk before lunch. He was walking home against a blustery wind when he met Ingrams emerging from the deanery.

He'd already learnt of Dove's death from Cawthorne; having left Harrison, the archdeacon had apparently gone directly to see him and, still extremely upset, had broken the news. 'Extraordinary!' mused Ingrams, turning his back on the wind and gazing up at the torn plastic sheeting flapping and billowing about the tops of the western towers. 'What a change! I could hardly believe it. Our erstwhile firebrand was as meek as a mouse! Whatever else,' he added, shaking his head, 'I don't think the diocese has much More to fear from young Michael Cawthorne!'

'We shall see,' answered Harrison guardedly. 'But I agree, this business has clearly shaken the chap to his roots.'

'Yes, indeed.' The dean continued surveying the rather shanty town appearance of his cathedral. 'Poor old Tom!' he sighed. 'It's certainly him we've to thank for our deliverance.' Glancing at the other, he gave a rueful smile. 'Talk about shaking to the roots! With his death, it seems Tom's finally managed to bring the house of his enemies crashing down about their heads!'

As the dean walked away, Harrison continued towards Bread Yard, wondering if there could be any element of truth in his friend's little joke. Could Dove, a shrivelled miniature of the blind Samson, have sacrificed his life to save the Canterbury diocese and his beloved Holy Trinity from philistine schemers? Sick and ailing, had the doughty old campaigner, hearing the rumours of church closures, thrown his body, as it were, over Cawthorne's sizzling grenade before it had chance to explode?

Dismissing such unlikely thoughts, he arrived home to find Winnie had arranged for them to call at Long Ashendon the following afternoon; apparently Joyce had been comparatively bright on the phone and pleased to be rung. With the coming journey in mind, he went and looked up the address of one of the city's exhaust centres.

He'd hardly got back to his office after lunch when Davidson called to discuss developments. The latter was able to confirm that the doctor had safely signed the death certificate, and that his aunt, amazingly resilient, had already arranged with Canon Bedford for the funeral to take place on Saturday afternoon.

Apart from looking even paler and more dishevelled than usual, the diocesan architect seemed much his usual self. Despite his loud protestations on first hearing the plan of covering up all evidence of suicide, now that the deed had been successfully carried out, he seemed, not only pleased, but touchingly grateful to Harrison for having overruled his quite natural reservations about moving the body, thus allowing his godfather to be buried without scandal.

Having obtained permission to take time off to spend with his aunt and to help with the preparations for Saturday, Davidson left. Pleased how well his subordinate was standing up to the emotional strain, Harrison took the unprecedented step of seeing him down to the outer door, and watched him leave with an almost paternal affection.

He was then free to make his own escape; fifteen minutes later he was back in Bread Yard, reversing the Volvo from the garage. His getaway was not completely smooth, however: having driven across to Mint Yard, he found his way blocked by a crowd of boys and their parents. From the youngsters' expressions and the sight of trunks being carried past, there was no doubt as to what was happening: the ancient King's School was swinging wide its doors at the start of yet another academic year.

From bitter experience, Harrison well knew the pent-up emotions of those stiffly shaking hands with fathers and being kissed by tearful mothers. As he swung out into Palace Street, he felt an enormous relief that he himself would never again have to follow his grandfather's venerable military trunk up to a bleak dormitory—and yet, simultaneously and perversely, he experienced a tingle of nostalgia for those long-lost horrors.

So the school's back, he thought. There was a certain mournful satisfaction in the idea: the boys' return set the seal on the unnaturally hot summer past. With the archdeacon's teeth at least temporarily drawn and the tower work progressing satisfactorily, once the funeral was over and Rachel Miller's doubts on her father's death were ended by a second autopsy, things would return to normal. Now rather regretting his decision to revisit Long Ashendon next day, he drove on with the pleasing feeling that, despite all, the cathedral and diocese would soon be settling down for the usual steady pull towards Christmas.

Part 2

Die Affenkapelle

Chapter Nine

Though the wind had dropped, the following day was as grey and chilly as the one past, and as the familiar orange Volvo sped past Holy Trinity, its isolated tower, with rooks wheeling and crying about it, had a sombre look of well-bred melancholy, as if the eight-hundred-year-old church was itself in mourning at the passing of the latest and last of its fully-inducted incumbents.

As half expected, Davidson's Toyota was parked in the rectory drive, almost in the same position as on the fatal night. As Harrison drew up behind, it occurred to him that the architect was displaying the same earnest care and concern for Joyce as he'd always shown in his diocesan work. Nevertheless, as he unloaded Winnie's chair, he couldn't help hoping that the devoted father of four hadn't had the idea of cheering and diverting his aunt by packing his car with his offspring and filling her home with their high-pitched shrieks, wails and screams.

He need not have worried: approaching the open front door, the house was mercifully quiet. Clearly, Long Ashendon rectory was neither the temporary playground of the Davidson children, nor had it yet been given over to the rattle of tea-cups, subdued conversations, ham sandwiches and other appendages of the typical English wake.

In answer to the bell, Davidson appeared, wearing a long striped apron and peeling off a pair of yellow plastic gloves.

His dark hair was sprinkled with dust, as were his shoulders and sleeves, and the remains of a cobweb clung about one of his frayed cuffs; what with the signs of nervous and physical exhaustion in his face, and his more than usually downcast air, he appeared the very epitome of the faithful retainer, sorrowfully and conscientiously fulfilling his final duties.

'How is your aunt today, George?' asked Winnie as he and Harrison manoeuvred her chair into the hall.

'Not so bright, I'm afraid. The shock is starting to tell.'

The diagnosis was clearly correct: they found Joyce slumped at one corner of the sofa, suddenly looking all her years. Whereas in the past, for all the controversies and upsets that had swirled about her husband's ministry like ravens above the hosts of the Norsemen, and for all Dove's sudden unfathomable depressions, she'd always managed to combine the stately dignity of a mature, intelligent woman with the gaiety and lightheartedness of a girl. Now, however, it was clearly as much as she could do to raise her reddened eyes and greet her visitors with a melancholy smile.

'Oh, my dear,' murmured Winnie. Wheeling forward, she took the grieving woman's hands in hers, and they sat, heads bowed, neither speaking. Harrison, helplessly redundant, fixed his eyes on the pattern of intertwined plants decorating the sofa. Beside him, the aproned Davidson stood, dusty head similarly bowed, until Joyce smiled up at them both through her tears.

'I'm so sorry.' She dabbed at her face. 'And you're all being so kind.' For a moment she struggled with herself, then turned back to Winnie. 'George is being an absolute saint: he insists on cleaning the house ready for Saturday even though Mrs Taylor has promised to do a few extra hours tomorrow.'

'Ah, of course—your rather extraordinary cleaner!' said Harrison, recognizing the name of the woman who'd hurled the monkey statuette into the village pond.

'Extraordinarily bad, I'd say!' intervened Davidson sharply, tapping a demonstrative puff of dust from a sleeve.

'I know,' murmured his aunt appeasingly, 'but Tom would never hear of getting rid of poor Margery.' She gave a sad laugh.

'He always said that keeping on an unpleasant and incompetent cleaner was part of his pastoral duty—though, for the life of me, I really don't know why: apart from when her son was married, I don't think dear old Margery has been to church for years!'

Davidson went out to make tea. This done, the four sat talking of everything except the matter uppermost in their minds, moving in turn from the matter of Canon Bedford's difficulties with the cantankerous old parish sexton, the changed weather and, finally, the plight of the Baghdad hostages. Tea over, Davidson returned to his self-imposed tasks, and Harrison, sensing his hostess needed to talk to Winnie alone, said, 'I wonder, Joyce, while I'm here, if there's anything of a practical nature I could do to help?'

'Oh, Richard, that's very kind, but I don't think there's anything. As you see, George is being his usual wonderfully dutiful self.' She paused. 'Unless, of, course, you wouldn't mind…' Breaking off, the speaker glanced away, the hint of a blush in her cheeks.

'Please, if there's anything,' insisted Harrison. 'Anything at all.'

'Well, there is just one little thing,' she said, looking back round. 'I'd ask George, but I don't want to embarrass the poor dear.' She gave a wan smile. 'My nephew, I'm afraid, is just a tiny bit of a prude.'

At the words, Harrison felt himself colouring: for one ghastly, skin-prickling second he actually imagined next moment he would hear the rector's widow asking him to dispose of a collection of girlie magazines or something similar. 'You see,' continued the other, mercifully unaware of his thoughts, 'there are some things locked in Tom's desk which relate to his life before our marriage—things that are not mine to disturb.'

Despite the more than ten years' difference in their ages, Harrison had always imagined that, like Winnie and himself, the Doves had lived their entire adult lives as married partners. It was a slight shock, therefore, to think of Tom as having had a previous single existence, but now, remembering the incongruous yachting cap in the study, he had yet another alarming vision of the dead man's wild bachelor days. He coughed discreetly. 'These things, Joyce, they're in his desk, you say?'

'Yes, you'll need these keys.' From her handbag, the widow produced a heavy key-ring.

'And these things,' began Harrison, 'what exactly would they be…' Catching Winnie's look, he broke off. 'Yes, of course,' he said, rising quickly, 'I'll go and see to the matter at once.'

Out in the hall, he heard a clatter from the rear of the house. Guessing it came from the kitchen, he followed the passage past the study to discover Davidson kneeling, head and shoulders deep in a cupboard beneath the sink.

'I wonder,' he said, entering, 'if there are any large plastic bags in here?'

Davidson's head emerged, his normally parchment-pale face quite pink, presumably partly from his exertions and partly from being found engaged in domestic chores. 'Plastic bag, Colonel?' Even more dusty and dishevelled than previously, the lanky architect stood amidst the welter of dusty bottles, dustpans and cans of cleaning fluids, obviously bewildered and discomforted by his superior's unexpected appearance.

'Yes, a large bag of some sort. Joyce has asked me to clear your godfather's desk.' Seeing something like surprised hurt on the other's face, he added quickly, 'Apparently there are diocesan papers that should be returned to Canterbury. I'll need something to carry them in.'

'My wife sent over some dustbin-liners with me.' Davidson stepped through the litter round his feet and began rummaging in a cardboard box. As he did so, Harrison glanced about. Clearly, Davidson had been right, the elderly couple and their cleaner had let things rather go of late: the top of the stove was blackened with the residue of years, while dust and grime coated the majority of the cooking utensils.

Davidson saw his look. 'Yes, it is in rather a state. That's why I wanted to give it a good spring-clean.'

'Well,' said the other, taking the bag, 'I'll leave you in peace to your task.'

'Colonel,' called Davidson as he went through the door, 'are you sure you wouldn't like me to help?'

Looking back, Harrison shook his head with a smile. 'Thank you, no. I'll be perfectly all right. You keep up the good work in here.' Grateful that it wasn't him down on his knees with scrubbing brush and carbolic soap, he strode away, keys jingling.

Harrison had wondered what his reaction would be on intruding into the private study of such a strong and independent character as Dove. It was a relief, therefore, to find that, in fact, he experienced no unease at all. Despite the dreary day outside, the room had a welcoming feel, and as he stood before the old man's desk, even though he'd seen the pasty-grey, drooping face of the corpse, and had actually dragged the body from the car, he had the quite illogical feeling that nothing irredeemable had occurred, and that his eccentric old adversary had, as the suicide note suggested, merely slipped away for a while.

Mystified as to why he experienced no aversion to either the sight of the long-carriage typewriter on which the note had been written or the poignantly empty four-legged swivel-chair, he glanced round to suddenly meet the only other set of eyes in the room. Immediately he understood the unaccountable sensation of welcome he felt: from its place directly over the late rector's chair, the photograph of Bishop Bell smiled at him with benign and confident trust.

Having removed the typewriter, he sat under the bishop's portrait and began sifting through the desk. The middle drawer was full to overflowing with all the clutter expected of such a squirrel-like hoarder as Dove: along with birth certificates, insurance papers, passports and the like, was a collection of letters, outdated receipts and bills—the whole mass of papers overlaying a motley collection of sealing-wax stubs, candles, rulers and buttons lying in a layer of tobacco and dust.

Checking each document in turn, Harrison worked steadily,

deciding what should go straight into the wastepaper basket and what merited a place on one of the various piles growing on the desk. Having cleared the top drawers, he began working down through the three on the right, until unfolding yet another outdated receipt, he noticed the logo of the same exhaust centre to which he'd gone the previous day. Curious to know what the trio of grimy young bandits who ran it had dared charge the notoriously caustic Dove, he glanced at the totalled sum.

What began as a glance became an incredulous stare: when he'd vigorously protested the amount demanded for a new silencer and piping, he'd been insolently informed that if he didn't want to pay high costs for spare parts, he shouldn't have bought a foreign vehicle—yet here in his hand was the oily and thumbmarked evidence that Dove had paid six times more than he, and all on as typical and popular a British car as the venerable Morris sitting that moment out in the garage!

In indignant disbelief, he gazed at the receipt, trying to decipher the exact words scrawled on the grubby piece of paper. Giving up on the illegible scribble, he decided that the young rapscallions must have foisted a new clutch and set of shock-absorbers on the old man in addition to a complete new exhaust system. Relieved that he himself had escaped so comparatively lightly, he threw the receipt away.

Having completed the clearing of the right-hand drawers, he turned to the left. Only when reaching the second of these had he need of the keys—and then, as it slid open, he realized at once that this was what he'd been sent to find.

Unlike all the rest, the drawer was neatly arranged and only half full: looking down at the bundles of envelopes within it, each tied with red ribbon like so many miniature legal briefs, he knew he was gazing into the secret heart of what the old cleric had called his *sanctum sanctorum*.

All the while, Harrison had been wondering what embarrassing or painful evidence he'd been sent to remove; he'd even wondered if it would prove an additional reason for that agony of mind that had driven the old man to take his own life. Joyce had said that, whatever the secret, it belonged to the period before she and he were married—and he could not help wondering if some dreadful fetish, weakness or perversion, inherited from bachelorhood, had re-emerged, returning, a forgotten Hyde, to haunt and overwhelm a finally weakening Jekyll. Now, however, looking down at the faded ribbons round the thin bundles, he knew that here was nothing of scandal or shame: what lay before him was a treasured shrine, a sanctified burial chamber of long-past events and emotions.

Having cleared additional space on the desk, he began laying out the envelopes. As he did so he had a shock: they had all been posted in Germany, the majority, as he saw from the postmarks, sent to Dove at a Berlin address between July 1937 and January 1939—and the rest directed twice weekly to Wadham College, Oxford, until finally ceasing in September 1939.

Harrison sat for a moment gazing down at the envelopes, each bearing its own portrait of a greasy-haired Adolf Hitler sternly gazing into some remote terrible distance of his own. Having neither the slightest intention nor wish to read their contents, he gathered them together and dropped them into the plastic sack, ready for incineration. Finally, he reached for the single large brown envelope lying at the bottom of the drawer, bearing on its unmarked surface the ghostly rectangular shapes of the letters which had rested undisturbed upon it so long. As he picked it up, he felt its weight and knew at once what he'd found. Photographs, unlike letters, he felt belonged to a public domain, and slipping his hand in, he drew out the small collection within.

Intrigued, he gazed down at the large top photograph. It was obviously a wartime desert scene, in which three Churchill tanks were drawn up under the shelter of palm trees, the nearest bearing the word *Corston* boldly printed on its turret, and the other two similarly adorned with the words *Rodbourne* and *Foxley*. Resting against the foreground tank was the young troop commander, above whose smiling, sand-dusty face, the cap badge of the Wiltshire Yeomanry peeped from beneath a pair of goggles. Who he was, or why his photograph should be in Dove's drawer, Harrison had not the slightest idea.

Laying it aside, he turned his attention to the next picture. This, in total contrast, was a carefully staged studio portrait, showing two young men standing each side, of a pedestal bust of Goethe. One was the youthful Tom Dove, typically grinning and provocatively resting an elbow on the poet's head. His companion was a stranger, and the only real oddity about the whole thing was that, although they were formally dressed in high-buttoned three-piece suits, both, for some extraordinary reason, were wearing rakish black and white peaked caps identical to the one protruding from the top shelf of the study bookcase.

Glancing at the back, Harrison read the photographer's Berlin address stamp, then, with the faint sound of Davidson's clatter from the kitchen, he looked at the third. It was far smaller than either of the first, obviously taken with a cheap box camera. On its brown, faded surface appeared a group of young men and women framed against a mountain range. They all had packs on their backs and carried sticks, but it was the couple on the far left of the group that gripped his attention.

One of the two was Dove, wearing lederhosen and plumed hat. As before, his puckish face was grinning at the camera, but this time he stood, arm round the waist of a blonde, curly-haired girl. For seconds, Harrison sat pondering the touchingly innocent-looking young couple before turning to the final photograph.

This was as large as the first two, but mounted in a cartridge paper folder. As Harrison opened it, he gave a slight gasp. It wasn't so much the head and shoulders shot of the same girl that made him draw breath, though close up and properly in focus, she was strikingly attractive, with a delicate face haloed round with curly, blonde hair. It was the man, obviously her father from his age and his features, who sat at her side, arm round her shoulders, that staggered him—and even then, it wasn't his face that riveted him, but his clothes, for he wore the full dress uniform of a major-general of the German Wehrmacht, with the white-enamelled cross of the *Pour le Mérite* or *Blue Max* at his throat, and on his breast, the stark Iron Cross.

Earlier, Harrison had been shocked by the size of Dove's garage bill, but to discover in a quiet Kentish rectory study someone wearing so familiar, yet so alien a uniform—one, indeed, diametrically opposed to that homely crumpled khaki shirt and shorts of the unknown tank commander, was a shock of quite different proportions. It was almost as if the diocesan architect had rushed in to announce the discovery of a loaded Luger automatic in one of the kitchen cupboards. Stunned, he held the photograph up to the light and made out the signature, *Gerhard von Leiper* and, below it, the single word *Anna*.

Getting up and taking a chair, Harrison drew down the faded peaked cap from the bookshelf. Turning it over, he read without surprise the name of the Berlin outfitter. At last he understood: all his absurd fantasies about Dove's youth were gone: there had been no Cowes Week, no oysters and champagne, no dancing on tables in the Café Royal—the cap was simply the graduate cap of a pre-war German student. Obviously Dove had studied abroad—and equally clear was that, beside a Bavarian lake or one evening in a candlelit cafe on the Unter den Linden, an idealistic young Englishman had lost his heart in a darkening, dangerous land.

Having dropped the photographs into the plastic sack along with the letters, he turned to the bottom left-hand drawer. It too was locked, and again he had to experiment with a variety of keys before it finally opened. Within was the usual muddle of objects: a pre-war stapler, a tin of carpet nails, a few dried-up bottles of Tippex fluid. Stuffed on top of these, however, was a large object, wrapped in a copy of the *New Scientist*.

Pulling it out, Harrison found the crude parcel contained the armless, mud-encrusted figurine that Joyce had carried away from the village pond. Now, with the oddly poignant memory of that lovely young girl in the photograph etched in his mind, the grinning monkey, in its incongruous velveteen coat and satin breeches, seemed more grotesque than ever. Why, he wondered, had Dove bothered to lock it away? Even for such an eccentric hoarder, the action seemed as bizarre as the hideous thing itself. But as he sat looking down at the curiously lopsided angle of the creature's head and its exposed fangs, an answer came. Of course, he thought, Dove decided not to throw it into the dustbin in case Margery Taylor should see it and know that her spiteful perversity in throwing it away had been brought to light by the drying out and subsequent clearing of the pond.

Thrusting the figurine down on top of the now bulging wastepaper basket, he began clearing the final drawer. Before he had chance to finish, however, there came a loud ring, and a moment later Ruth Hodge's voice calling, 'Hello! Anyone home?'

Remembering the trouble Dove and his wife had taken to protect the churchwarden from knowing the fate that had overtaken her contribution to the village fête, Harrison snatched it and its wrappings out of the basket. Davidson's footsteps passed the study door; he heard Joyce and Winnie greet the new arrival; next moment the latter was calling for him from the hall. Hurriedly rewrapping and stuffing the figurine into his plastic bag, he hurried to the door.

'Ah, there you are, Colonel! I was just hearing that you and George were both hard at work.' Ruth Hodge beamed as he approached. 'I trust though,' she added, glancing down at the bag with a smile, 'you're not purloining any of our parish records!'

'No, not at all,' he answered, laughing. 'These are all diocesan matters. Now, if you'll excuse me,' he continued, catching Joyce's eye, 'I think I'll go out and lock them in the car for later disposal.'

Closing the tailgate, he looked up at the house, wondering what money it would make for the diocesan funds. Not much, he thought glumly, surveying the dilapidated guttering and the crack that ran down the façade from roof to ground like the torn veil of the temple, and thinking of the present poor state of the property market. He began recrossing the gravel, but then diverted towards the garage. Sliding back the door, he gazed in at the elderly Morris, on which, like the parish church, such disproportionately large sums of money had been recently lavished.

Looking in, he remembered in detail the ghastly half hour he and Davidson had spent there: the torchlight falling on Dove's slumped figure, the bloodless pallor of the cleric's face, the struggle to loosen the jubilee clip, then the ghastly dragging of the head-lolling corpse from the driver's seat. He remembered the photographs: the young tank officer beneath the palms; the two young civilians in those absurd suits and caps; the couple standing together, the mountains behind; the handsome Wehrmacht general officer proudly embracing his daughter.

It was almost too terrible to think of the unbridgeable gulf stretching between that faraway time and the present—the young theological student could never have dreamt, hiking with Anna von Leiper and his fellow *wandervogels* among the Bavarian mountains, what nightmare would soon fall across that lovely land—or that one night, half a century later, despairing and alone, he'd sit in a converted coach house, drowsily breathing in carbon monoxide.

Lost in thought, Harrison didn't hear the crunch of wheels on the gravel. Startled, he looked round at the sound of his name to find Canon Bedford smiling up at him through the open window of his car. 'Ah, what a pleasant surprise, Colonel. I never expected to find you once again so far from home.'

'My wife wished to give poor Joyce all the support she could,' said Harrison, blushing at the thought of what the rural dean must be thinking of him—one who had aided and abetted in the serving of the fatal notice to quit.

'Yes, indeed,' said the other, his face showing not the slightest sign of any such thought. 'How very kind!' He looked towards the house. 'She knew it was on the cards, of course, but nevertheless, Tom's death must have been a terrible shock. Anyway,' continued Bedford, brightening, 'from the cars, I see everyone is clearly rallying round. Look, Colonel, with so many here, I won't intrude. Would you inform Joyce that the sexton and I have chosen a suitable place for the grave. Tell her, it's close to the chancel. I hope that will be some comfort.'

'Of course, Canon. I'm sure it will be.'

Turning, Bedford looked into the garage. 'Ah, the poor chap's car! How he used to wrestle with his conscience about whether or not to keep the old jalopy!'

'He was considering replacing it?'

'Replace his faithful old steed! Perish the thought!' Bedford laughed. 'No, what I meant was that the dear fellow used to wonder if he should go on polluting the atmosphere by driving at all. He was, of course, very green in his final years.'

'Yes, so I'd gathered,' replied Harrison, thinking of the stickers on the back window.

'Trouble is, there's no bus service to speak of in these villages nowadays,' continued Bedford, turning back to his own car. 'But you'll excuse me: if I hurry I'll just be in time to give a blessing at the end of our Mothers' Union meeting.' He started the engine, then looked round. 'But forgive me! In my rush, I'm forgetting your own sad loss. Your friend's extraordinary death has been much on my mind—though I've not yet managed to make sense of the matter.'

'I don't understand, said Harrison, frowning. 'Was it really so very unusual? I believe there have been quite a number of fatal falls from trains.'

'Oh, yes indeed,' answered the cleric, smiling. 'In recent years, our national rail service has, I fear, allowed many of its customers to literally fall by the wayside.'

'Then why do you find David Miller's death so strange?'

'Only because of the fearful injuries you described, Colonel,' said the Canon, engaging a gear. 'Injuries which, in the circumstances, I can't help but regard as simply incredible.'

For a moment, Harrison stood rooted to the gravel as the red and white car reversed round the curve of the drive. Then suddenly he was running after it. Reaching the driver's window, he looked down at the rural dean's startled face. 'Excuse me, Canon, but what did you mean when you said Miller's injuries were incredible? Surely on that straight stretch of track, the train would have been travelling at full speed, and his injuries were merely consistent with that.'

Canon Bedford smiled. 'My dear fellow, quite obviously you don't follow the tortuous saga of British Rail with the same interest as myself. You've heard of its struggles against fog, ice, snow and leaves? Well, this summer they've had to contend with nothing less than the fiery chariot itself!'

Baffled, Harrison stared blankly down at the smiling, good-natured face. 'Fiery chariot?' he repeated, bewildered. 'Are you saying that they're reverting to coal?'

'If only, Colonel!' laughed Bedford. 'If only! Unfortunately not—I was merely referring to Apollo's chariot.' Once again, the other's incomprehension made him laugh. 'The sun, my dear chap! Dean Donne's unruly sunne! Prosaically put, we're talking of heat expansion: that stretch of line beside which your friend was found was badly afflicted by buckling during August.' Smiling ruefully, the speaker shook his head. 'British Rail wages an unequal struggle, I fear, against the whims and perversities of that wicked old lady that dear old Tom insisted on terming Good Mother Gaia!'

As he talked, Bedford continued to ease the car back by fits and starts, so that Harrison had to move and pause with the vehicle. Now, however, as the full implications of Bedford's words hit him, his look of horrified amazement forced the driver to a temporary halt. 'Buckling of the line! Canon, surely you're not saying there was a speed restriction?'

'Yes, Colonel—twenty miles an hour. Your friend could have almost jumped out and run beside the train.'

'You're absolutely sure?'

'Quite sure—I've checked with one of my railway parishioners.'

Dazed, Harrison stood stock-still as the car moved away, then squeezed himself between the laurel bushes and the creeping vehicle. 'Excuse me, Canon—one more question: what was it that you told Dean Ingrams about Miller checking parish registers?'

By this time the car had reached the top of the drive, and as Bedford halted to answer, its bumper and boot protruded into the road. 'Ah yes, that was a strange coincidence! I happened to mention to Peter Gleeson your curious notion that your friend was not related to our local families, and he told me that an American of that name had indeed checked the Kington St Laurence parish registers in early August—but now, Colonel, you'll really have to excuse me. You would not wish me to disappoint the ladies, I'm sure.'

Harrison watched the car go. As it disappeared, instead of returning to the house, he remained in the gateway, looking across the green. The only movement on the dreary stretch of grass was of a small procession, composed of a woman pushing a child in a buggy, followed by two tiny figures who ran in similar eccentric circles to those previously practised by the ducks.

Towards this distant group, he gazed, lost in thought while the woman continued to push her load and the two children to run ever further from her. Suddenly pausing, she looked back. Though a slight woman, she obviously had powerful lungs for her yells echoed now across the green. 'Tom! James! Come back 'ere, you little buggers, or I'll murder the pair of you!'

The shouted words broke Harrison's spell. As the boys ran towards their furious dam, he swung round on, his heels and strode purposefully back along the rectory drive.

Chapter Ten

Evensong over, in the falling dusk, the last of the day's visitors tramped out through the Christ Church gateway, leaving the precincts to darkness and peace. High in the niches and crevices of the cathedral, rooks and starlings settled themselves on their draughty perches, while the massive Bell Harry and its lesser companions gradually faded and merged into night. One after another, round Green Court, lights flicked on, the windows of the deanery, archdeaconry, the King's School prep rooms greeting each through the fading light, and soon the wide quadrangle was like an estuary or harbour road lit by the lamps of an anchored fleet.

Over Bread Yard the same outward tranquillity had also fallen. A piano tinkled in one cottage, a cat gipped across the cobbles, and behind a sitting-room window a figure sat beside a shaded table-lamp, deeply absorbed in a book.

No more firing was heard at Brussels—the pursuit rolled miles away. Darkness came down on the field and city: and Amelia was praying for George, who was lying on his face, dead, with a bullet through his heart.

With a satisfied sigh, Winnie leaned back in her chair, momentarily close to tears at the image of the kneeling girl and the irony of those hopeless prayers. For a few seconds, she continued to sit, then closing the book, wheeled herself out into the hall and looked into the kitchen.

Except that his eyes were open, and that he intermittently turned to flick back and forwards through a large volume beside him, the solitary occupant could quite well have been praying himself—for he sat head bowed over an open book, his lips moving soundlessly, his animated face giving every appearance of his journeying that moment through the very torments of hell.

With a frown of distaste, Winnie regarded the scene, then wheeling forward, broke in sharply, 'For heaven's sake, Richard! What are you meant to be doing? You'll give yourself a cerebral haemorrhage, the way you're going on!'

Harrison looked up briefly, but instead of answering, his gaze returned to his book and, grimacing, he muttered, 'Goddamn their tortuous syntax and these confounded verbs!'

'I take it,' said his wife coldly, 'you're attempting to read that book you borrowed?'

There was no answer: irritated, Winnie sat in the doorway, watching him alternately mouthing and frowning as his eyes moved between the book he was reading and the battered old German–English dictionary that had followed them through their married life, gathering dust and uselessly occupying space. On the drive back from Long Ashendon that afternoon, he'd been more abstracted and preoccupied than usual, and she hadn't managed to obtain any coherent explanation of why he'd been suddenly so keen to borrow a dowdy little volume in German from the rectory study—and then, when she'd innocently asked what it was about, he'd snapped that he hadn't got the faintest idea. As a result, hardly another word had been said, and as soon as they were home, she'd thankfully escaped to enjoy her rereading of Thackeray's *Vanity Fair*.

Now, however, curiosity overcoming her annoyance, Winnie manoeuvred her chair until she was sitting beside him and able to look past his shoulder at the open books and papers spread on the table.

'Aren't these David Miller's jottings on the Black Orchestra?' she asked, reaching out for the scribbled-over envelope. Picking it up, she glanced at the apparently meaningless list of names with their strange circled numbers and codewords, then looked at the volume that her husband was poring over. 'Is that what the book's about, the German resistance to the Nazis?'

Instead of ignoring her or making her the subject of a furious outburst as she half expected, Harrison leaned back with a sigh. 'I think so—trouble is, after all these years, my German is just so damn rusty.'

'Then, for goodness' sake, why try to read it? You can always borrow something in English on the subject.'

'It's that name there—F. J. Mendelssohn.' Harrison pointed at Miller's envelope. 'It's the same as the writer of this book—he's the chap who, according to Dove, was once a temporary assistant curate in Hove.'

'Hove—the place next to Brighton?' Winnie burst out laughing. 'Really, darling! Curates in south coast seaside towns and this mysterious *Schwarze Kapelle* or whatever it's called! What is all this nonsense about?'

Harrison, however, didn't smile in response. 'It's complicated, but far from nonsense,' he answered stiffly. 'From what little I've gleaned, Mendelssohn's book recounts how a number of German Lutheran pastors and students, frightened at the way things were going in the 'thirties and the silence of their Church regarding Nazi policies, established a sort of seminary in Finkenwalde in Pomerania known as the Brother House which became the nucleus of the so-called *Kennende Kirche*—Confessing Church.'

'Confessing Church?'

'The name for the group of pastors who refused to be incorporated into the Nazi State Church—those, like the ex-U-boat commander, Martin Niemöller, who refused to toe the Nazi line and publicly denounced the anti-Jewish decrees until they were either arrested or dismissed.'

'You've learnt all this just from this book?' said Winnie.

Harrison shook his head. 'I knew something of the business from the time Miller and I were in Berlin. You see, it wasn't just postmen and schoolmasters who were forced to be in the Nazi Party—practising Protestant clerics were also regarded as state officials, and so also had to become party members merely to keep their posts. Our de-Nazification programme, therefore, included the cleansing and reconstruction of the German Church. But what I didn't know until now,' he continued, thumbing through Mendelssohn's book to expose a photograph of a group of earnest young men in a garden, 'was about this Finkenwalde community and the part it played in anti-Nazi opposition, or that this chap here,' he said, pointing down at the picture, 'was the instigator and inspiration behind this clerical resistance.'

Winnie looked down at the figure indicated: he was a bespectacled, slightly tubby and prematurely balding man of about thirty who, dressed in a sports jacket and open-necked shirt, stood at the centre front of the group. 'Who is he?' she asked.

'Dietrich Bonhoeffer—the famous theologian whom the Nazis hanged along with Admiral Canaris for their assumed association with the *Schwarze Kapelle*.'

'And this Frederick Mendelssohn who wrote the book? I take it he was also a member of the Brother House?'

'Apparently—though he must have got out of Germany early for some reason if he spent the war years in Hove.'

'Well,' said Winnie, 'the reason why he fled Germany seems only too obvious—his name is the same as the composer's.'

'So?'

'My dear, Mendelssohn is a Jewish name.'

'Jewish!' Harrison shook his head in disbelief. 'But I don't understand, how could he have been? Damn it, I told you—the Brother House was a seminary for Lutheran pastors.'

'Come on, Richard—there are such people as Christian Jews,' protested Winnie. 'In fact, I believe at least one of the present Anglican bishops is of Jewish descent, and didn't you tell me that Bishop Bell helped rescue numbers of so-called non-Aryan Christians from Nazi Germany. Perhaps Mendelssohn was one of those. After all, Hove must be in the Chichester diocese.'

'Good Lord, you're right,' murmured Harrison flatly, staring again at the scribbled-over envelope.

'Anyway,' resumed Winnie brightly, 'I don't see why you're so worried. Surely that Mendelssohn was actively anti-Nazi is further proof that what you originally told Rachel was correct: that her father was planning a book on the German resistance to Hitler.'

Harrison again picked up the scribbled-over envelope. 'Yes, I know,' he answered, 'but a refugee cleric in England linked closely with Goering, Menzies and Canaris—is it possible? And there is still this name Lipmann here at the bottom—a person with double codewords, *Fiddler* and *Fifer*.' Frowning, the speaker shook his head. 'I don't know why, Winnie, but the longer I look at this list, the more uneasy I get.'

Getting up, he went over to the window and stared out. Reflected in the pane, Winnie saw the wrought-up intensity of his face. 'Richard,' she said, wheeling forward, 'what is really on your mind? Why were you so snappy in the car, and why suddenly all this worry about Miller's list? I thought all that was more or less settled in your mind.' She paused. 'Something happened at the rectory today, didn't it? Was it something Canon Bedford said when you met him outside on the drive?'

'I told you,' murmured Harrison, still gazing out, 'he just dropped by to inform Joyce about the site of the grave.'

'Yes, but it was after speaking to him that you came back and asked Joyce if you might borrow Mendelssohn's book.' Winnie reached up to touch his sleeve. 'Come on, darling, tell me—what did Canon Bedford say to you?'

Harrison sighed. 'It was nothing, damn it! Just a small detail which everyone appears to have missed.' Breaking from his wife's touch, he went to the sink and stood a moment staring down at the taps. 'According to Bedford,' he said at last, 'there was a twenty-miles-an-hour limit on the section of track when

Miller fell. At that speed, it seems impossible for his body to have been so badly smashed.'

Apart from the tick of the hall clock, there was silence as the initial shocked amazement in Winnie's face crumpled into distress. 'For goodness' sake, Richard,' she cried out, 'a small detail! Why didn't you tell me this straightaway?'

'I don't know—didn't want to upset you, I suppose.' Harrison looked round at his wife. 'God knows, we've both had enough on our minds of late, what with poor old Dove's death and everything else.'

'If what Canon Bedford says is true,' said Winnie after a pause, 'you must get in touch with the police.'

'I want to check with the railway people first; I also want to hear the result of the second autopsy,' answered her husband, rubbing his forehead wearily.

'So you're just going to wait—is that it?'

Harrison took a deep breath. 'There's something else I haven't told you: according to Bedford, Miller consulted the Kington St Laurence parish registers before he died. I therefore rang Peter Gleeson when we got in to say I'd be coming over tomorrow to have a look at that blasted roof he's always complaining about. When I'm there, I'll try and have a quick shufti at what interested Miller.'

Winnie sat hunched forward, staring down at the floor. Harrison went over and stood behind her. 'Look,' he said gently, 'I knew you'd find it upsetting, me poking into things again—that's why I didn't want to say anything.' Obtaining no response, he continued. 'Winnie, whether we like it or not, the past seems to have somehow re-emerged—and if there really is something fishy behind Miller's death, I want to find it out.' He paused. 'It's a moral duty, damn it! After all, he was my staff-sergeant, and the poor fellow came here seeking my help.'

Winnie remained hunched forward, neither moving nor saying a word a moment or two longer before looking up. 'You're not in the army any more, Richard,' she said, 'and though I'm still stuck in this awful chair, I refuse to go back to that life and playing again the part of poor, silly, passive Amelia on her knees in Brussels.'

'Brussels?' repeated Harrison, utterly lost. 'Amelia who?'

Suddenly smiling, Winnie reached up for his hand. 'I only mean, darling,' she said, squeezing it, 'that, whether you like it or not, I'm coming with you tomorrow to help look through these parish registers.'

'It was flowing through there.' The outstretched finger swung remorselessly left. 'And there! And again there! Pouring through like a waterfall!'

'I'm sure, my dear, Colonel and Mrs Harrison don't want to have every small leak pointed out.' Tousling his grey hair, the Reverend Gleeson smiled apologetically at his visitors.

'Every small leak!' Geraldine Gleeson gave her husband a withering look. 'That roof up there might as well be a colander for all the good it is!' Pink in the face, she continued. 'I can't imagine, Colonel Harrison, what the diocese was thinking of, employing a builder like Harker!'

'My dear,' intruded her spouse with a pained smile, 'do remember that Fred Harker is one of my parishioners.'

'He can be churchwarden and chairman of the parish council for all I care!' was the angry retort. 'Just let him come over and see the damage Tuesday's downpour did to my lounge!'

Harrison's long-held view that face-to face meetings with the clergy, and especially their wives, were best avoided was confirmed by this interchange. Frowning, he gazed up at the cheap unseasoned timber used for the skylights, and was still wondering how best to defend the Dilapidations Board when Winnie intervened. 'Oh, water does make such an awful mess, doesn't it! Darling, do you remember that lovely Turkish carpet of Mummy's that we had ruined in Aldershot when the tank burst?'

Unable to remember any such thing, Harrison looked round in surprise, but seeing something in Winnie's face warning him to agree, he managed to get out, 'Quite—very distressing indeed!'

Amazingly, these few words had as soothing effect on the vicar's wife as his suggestion of a committee had had on the council off Cathedral Friends: her anger disappeared instantly, and a few moments later she was wheeling Winnie through to the hall, actually laughing at her own account of the family rushing about with buckets during the height of the storm. Gleeson and Harrison followed to the sitting-room where the two women, aided by the vicar's teenage daughters, lamented together over the still-damp carpet and curtains before discussing the intricacies of fabric repair.

Having promised that George Davidson would survey the roof and give him a personal report, Harrison stood silently by, sipping coffee and staring glassily at the pair of RAF squadron crests hanging on either side of the mock-Georgian fireplace—one depicting a mailed fist brandishing forked lightning, the other, a hooded cobra poised to strike above the somewhat unnecessary motto: *caveant omnes*.

'Mr Gleeson,' he ventured at last, 'I wonder, while I'm here if my wife and I might have a glance through your parish records. I'm curious to know what my old friend David Miller found out about his relatives when he visited you in August.'

If Gleeson was surprised by the request, innate politeness prevented him from expressing it. He immediately offered to take his visitors straight over to the church to inspect the registers. In a matter of minutes, therefore, Harrison was trundling Winnie across what had been until recently the old vicarage orchard and hen-run, but was now already a trim, well-kept garden, having as centrepiece or *épergne*, an ancient stone font, planted with straggly, rain-beaten geraniums.

Once clear of the house, Gleeson grew talkative. 'I'm afraid the recent rain damage has rather upset Geraldine. You see,' he continued, 'we rather thought we'd left that sort of thing behind us when we finally made our hop.'

'Hop?' Winnie smiled up from her chair.

'Over the garden wall, dear lady.' Gleeson laughed, pointing up at the roof looming above the high wall on their right. 'Our escape from the tyranny of a draughty Victorian vicarage. At your husband's instigation, the diocese sold the place to a local dentist. Such a happy change for us,' continued the vicar, 'despite our continuing little problem with the leaks, but not so good for him, I fear: the poor man's had his fingers well and truly burnt with the spiralling cost of mortgages and the drop in property values.'

As Gleeson talked, they passed through the garden gate, and ahead rose the stumpy spire of the parish church. Despite its rather grand-sounding name, Kington St Laurence consisted of little more than a couple of farms, a few cottages, an unprepossessing public house called the Dun Cow and a general store. In contrast to Long Ashendon, the homely little church stood central to this small community, and as Harrison wheeled Winnie through the graveyard, he smelt the acrid stink of a farmyard. Manoeuvring the chair into the porch, he couldn't help contrasting that vast desolation of ruin in which Miller and he had first met with the sleepy hamlet about them. How strange it seemed that he should be searching into the mystery surrounding the death of the man who'd long ago shared the cramped office in Fehrbelliner Platz here in this obscure little church.

Wrapped in such thoughts, he wheeled Winnie down the nave and halted to allow Gleeson to open the glass-panelled doors into the vestry.

'There you are! Now do please come in.'

Harrison gave an audible gasp and stared past the beckoning cleric, amazed disbelief in his face, as if, rearing up from the pile of discarded hymn books on the floor, swelling its hood and baring its fangs, was the archetype of that very serpent, incongruously decorating the Gleesons' living-room.

'Colonel, are you all right?'

Too flabbergasted to reply, Harrison continued to gaze

past Gleeson's face at the large, board-mounted map of Berlin resting against the vestry wall, the four original military zones differentiated by variously coloured ribbons, and a thick purple strip showing the track of the infamous wall.

'Ah yes, the remains of our celebratory exhibition!' exclaimed the vicar, glancing round. 'We constructed it as a thanksgiving for that wonderful night last year when the East Berliners poured into the west.' Sliding a second board out from behind the first, he smiled bashfully. 'This is my eldest daughter's contribution—as you see, Helen's inherited all her mother's practical skill.'

Mounted on this second board was a hand-drawn map of Germany, the old east–west border prominently indicated with a tinsel strip, and the soon to be completely reunited nation illustrated with postcards of the Brandenburg Gate, Cologne Cathedral and various Rhine castles—the whole dominated by a centrally placed magazine photograph of a youth, face striped in green and white, silhouetted against a sky bright with fireworks on top of the Berlin Wall, swinging a huge pickaxe like a demented harlequin.

'Germany,' continued the vicar, 'has always had a special place in my heart. It's where Geraldine and I met when I was a very green young chaplain indeed and she already a highly regarded ATCO with Strike Command.'

'ATCO?'

'Air. Traffic Control Officer, Mrs Harrison.' Standing in his cluttered vestry, among piles of mouldering hymn books and hanging cassocks, the Reverend Gleeson shook his head, a dreamy look in his eyes. 'Yes, indeed! Dear old RAF Mannheim! Wonderful days!'

Harrison coughed. 'I wonder, Vicar,' he said, 'if we might make a start: I need to be back in Canterbury as soon as possible.'

'Of course, Colonel—I'm so sorry. If you'd like to wheel Mrs Harrison in, I'll get out the registers.'

Having now recovered from the shock of coming face to face in such an unlikely place with a map of the city so much in his mind, Harrison manoeuvred Winnie into the vestry while Gleeson knelt and groped among the skirts of the hanging cassocks for the church safe. 'Well, here we are!' said the latter, extracting four hefty volumes. 'At home,' he continued, carrying the pile to a table, 'I have facsimiles of registers as far back as the fifteenth century, but strangely enough these current ones were all your late friend was interested in.'

At these words, a terrible thought struck Harrison. 'You mean you don't know what he was looking for? Surely Miller told you why he needed the registers.'

Gleeson shook his head. 'No, he merely asked if he could inspect the parish records for the last fifty years, which everyone has a right to do on the payment of a small charge.' The cleric smiled. 'Not, I hasten to add, that I shall be demanding any charge of you, Colonel.'

Despite the graciousness of the vicar's words, Harrison made no reply; instead, he gazed in dismay at the four huge, musty volumes, thinking that even if he knew what he was looking for, it would take hours to find it.

'I don't suppose, Mr Gleeson,' interposed Winnie, 'you have any idea of the particular volume Mr Miller was interested in?'

'I'm afraid not. As I was up to the elbows in the parish magazine at the time, I merely laid out the registers and asked him to lock up in here when he finished.'

'And how long did that take?'

'Yes, well, that was another rather odd thing, Mrs Harrison—Mr Miller was back with the keys in less than half an hour.'

'And do you think he'd found what he wanted?'

'I'm sure he did,' was the emphatic answer. 'Indeed, from his mood and his generous donation to parish funds, I'd say whatever he'd discovered had pleased him mightily.'

'And you have no idea what that might have been?'

Gleeson shook his head. 'I'm sorry, no. In fact, when I hinted an interest, I had the distinct impression it was not something he was keen to disclose.' The vicar smiled brightly.

'Anyway, I'm afraid I have a number of ailing parishioners to attend. I'll therefore leave you to your researches in peace.'

'This reminds me of something.'

'What have you found?' Harrison looked up eagerly.

Winnie shook her head. 'Nothing, I'm afraid—I only meant that sitting here in a church vestry, looking for some clue in a marriage register reminds me of some Victorian novel or other.' She paused, wrinkling her brow as she tried to remember the title. 'I know it involved a false entry squeezed into a blank space at the bottom of a page.'

With a noncommittal grunt, Harrison gloomily returned to perusing the handwritten columns recording, in a variety of inks and hands, the names of those buried in St Laurence's churchyard since 1937. So far he'd discovered no squeezed-in entry, no missing page, no foreign name or unidentified body—indeed, nothing of interest whatever.

From the moment Gleeson had indicated that he had no idea what Miller had been looking for, or even which of the four registers he'd consulted, Harrison had felt defeated. Now, with the evidence of yet another annual winter cull of the frail and the elderly passing beneath his forefinger, a sense of futility overcame him. With an exasperated sigh, he sat back and gazed at his wife, who, unconscious of his scrutiny, continued to read through the marriage register, irritatingly absorbed. Turning away, he looked down at the propped-up map of Berlin, thinking again of the blackened ruins and funereally silent streets. Faint from the distance came the repetitive buzz of a chainsaw.

'You've given up then!'

Winnie's voice brought him back to the present. 'It's useless,' he answered defensively, turning to face her. 'What's the point of going on without an idea of what we're looking for?'

The futile search and the chill of the vestry had obviously taken its toll on Winnie, for her irritation now spilled over.

'Well, can't you at least try and think what Miller might have been looking for? Have you no theory at all?'

'Nothing beyond the obvious,' answered the other. 'If he was researching the resistance to Hitler, I suppose it's just possible he was on the track of some war criminal, or perhaps just someone connected with the *Schwarze Kapelle*.'

'What—and then traced him to Kington St Laurence?' Scorn rang in his wife's voice. 'Really, Richard—doesn't a Kentish hamlet seem a rather unlikely alternative to the anonymity of a South American city? The last place to hide, I'd have thought, is among a lot of suspicious bumpkins! And another thing,' she continued remorselessly, 'why choose to comb through the burial register, for heaven's sake? If the person in question was already dead, surely there wouldn't have been any reason for Miller's urgent request to get in touch?'

'I would have thought,' answered her husband, bristling, 'that a stranger being buried here is slightly less ludicrous than the notion of Dr Mengele or Martin Bormann selecting St Laurence's for their late-life nuptials!'

Despite herself, Winnie laughed. Then she drew the two as yet unopened registers towards her. 'Confirmations' and 'baptisms' she read aloud, glancing at their long-faded spines. 'I must say-neither of these would seem of obvious interest to a Jewish lawyer tracking down some octogenarian Nazi grotesque!'

'Quite,' answered Harrison, smiling. He got to his feet. 'Come on,' he said, 'this is useless. All we can do now is just wait and see if the second autopsy comes up with anything out of the ordinary.'

Having helped Winnie into the car, Harrison slipped back to deposit the keys at the vicarage. Geraldine Gleeson answered the door, arms and hands white with flour, and before he'd turned from the house, he'd thrice repeated his earlier assurance that the matter of her roof would receive immediate attention.

He returned through the garden in reflective mood. The sight of the ancient font, incongruously standing out on the lawn, made him think of the unfathomable twists of destiny: the Viennese boy becoming a British soldier, then an American lawyer—finally ending his life, smashed at the bottom of an obscure Kentish railway cutting; himself, all ambition gone, reduced to returning to Canterbury, to deal with the matter of the Gleesons' roof; the vivacious, lively young Winnie becoming virtually overnight the crippled prisoner of a wheelchair. Finally, he thought of the woman to whom he'd just handed the keys: could the WAAF officer of twenty years before ever have imagined, he thought, that instead of practising fighter intercepts over Europe, she'd be one day baking her cakes, bottling her jams and, generally mending and making do in the best traditions of the impoverished country parson's wife.

Lost in such thoughts, he rejoined Winnie in the car. Starting the engine, he prepared to drive off. Before he had chance to do so, however, there was a tap on the glass beside him, and looking round, he found Canon Belford smiling in and raising his hat.

'Ah, Colonel and Mrs Harrison!' The rural dean beamed as Harrison wound down his window. 'After Mrs Gleeson's unhappy phone call on the night of the storm,' he said, 'I felt obliged to drop by.'

'Ah yes, the leaking roof,' replied Harrison, relieved that there was no further need to explain their presence. 'I've managed to reassure her that the diocese will speedily remedy matters.'

'Excellent! Then I won't need to disturb the good lady—but speaking of the diocese, I presume you'll both be at Tom Dove's funeral tomorrow.'

'Yes, indeed.'

'And have either of you had time to read the wonderful obituary in today's *Telegraph*? If not, you really must. Most illuminating! Tom was always a public figure, of course, but I never guessed that he'd played such a pivotal role in great events.'

'Great events?' Harrison frowned disapprovingly, thinking of the chanting columns marching under BAN THE BOMB banners, and those scandalous newsreel pictures of the younger Dove lying stretched out beside the aged Sir Bertrand and Lady Russell on the Trafalgar Square roadway before the old philosopher and the rest were carted like sacks of firewood into the waiting Black Marias.

'Yes, indeed,' continued Bedford, nodding emphatically. 'You see, among other things, he actually accompanied his great mentor on his famous wartime mission.'

Completely at a loss, Harrison shook his head. 'I'm sorry, Canon, I'm lost—what wartime mission?'

Bedford laughed. 'Come, Colonel—you must have heard of Bishop Bell's secret journey to Sweden in 1942. After the Norwegian pastors and bishops had so openly and bravely defied Nazi rule, Bell was sent to make contact with representatives of the German Church opposed to Hitler—and it was then, while he was in Stockholm, that he had the famous clandestine meeting with Dietrich Bonhoeffer.'

For a second or two, Harrison couldn't speak, but then he burst out incredulously, 'Surely, Canon, you're not saying that Tom Dove was connected with the *Schwarze Kapelle*?'

For a moment Canon Bedford looked confused, then his face cleared. '*Schwarze Kapelle*—Black Orchestra, of course! How stupid of me! Yes, I believe the phrase occurs in the obituary.'

At these words, the lane before them, the trees, the huddle of barns, the spire of St Laurence's, the very parish itself seemed to dissolve and melt, and Harrison was seeing nothing but the old man swivelling round in his chair and holding up Miller's list to the light. As from a remote distance, he heard Winnie's voice, 'You said Tom Dove played a pivotal role, Canon?'

'Yes, Mrs Harrison—almost literally so. You see, for all his ecumenical work, Bishop Bell didn't speak a word of German. As a result, Tom Dove was forced to act as interpreter, and therefore was not only physically central to negotiations, but, of necessity, privy to all the deepest and most delicate of secrets.'

Chapter Eleven

Over the silent precincts echoed the dying fall of the bell. From the kitchen came the sound of running water and the brisk scrub of a brush. Apparently unaware of either sound, the figure remained bent over the books and papers spread before him.

Apart from the reader's marble calm, and that he sat at the sitting-room bureau, the scene was almost identical to that of the evening before: dusk falling over Bread Yard, Harrison absorbed, head bowed in his hands, German dictionary open beside him. This time, however, in place of Mendelssohn's history of the Brother House, stacked about him there were now piles of books brought down from the toy-box overhead, together with the heap of neatly bound bundles of envelopes removed from the dead rector's study.

Refolding and replacing the letter just read, Harrison extracted another. Holding it to his nose, he sniffed the faded, yellowing paper: across more than half a century came the now familiar odour of the long-entrapped perfume. Once again, he drew it in, then looked down at the photograph of the girl smiling up from her father's side. For a few seconds he continued to gaze at Anna von Leiper's thin, boyish face under its halo of blonde hair, then suddenly grimacing, he roughly thrust the letter back into the envelope unread.

From beyond the open door there came again the sound of scrubbing and running water. He listened a moment, then reaching over, took from the back of the sofa the copy of the *Daily Telegraph* he'd bought directly after parting from Canon Bedford that morning.

The obituary was long and detailed, and between it and the letters, he now felt he had a good idea of the tragic events that had shattered Dove's early life, destroying all hope of an academic career, and finally stranding him—the moody, maverick, quirky, sometimes sardonic and always ever-so-slightly ridiculous rebel of Long Ashendon. Staring down at the article, he winced, remembering the scene in Dove's study: the old man joking and laughing, then turning away to hold up David Miller's list to the window—then the last sight of him, bowed in the chair, giving that final, pathetic dismissive wave of the hand.

'Darling, whatever's the matter?'

Again, just as on the previous evening, Harrison looked round to find his wife regarding him from the doorway. 'Nothing,' he said, 'just thinking how blind I was not to see the obvious—that it was something about Miller's list that upset Dove, not the message from Cawthorne.' A spasm of anguish crossed his face. 'For God's sake, didn't the fellow actually tell me himself that he'd already prepared himself for the loss of the rectory!'

'My dear, you really can't blame yourself,' said Winnie, manoeuvring into the room, 'you had no reason on earth to think Tom had ever had the remotest connection with the *Schwarze Kapelle*.'

'No? Not with that student cap looking down at me! Not with Mendelssohn's book in front of my nose!'

Winnie wheeled to his side. 'Have you finished reading Anna's letters?' she asked gently.

'Most of them—as many as I could bear.'

'And?'

He shrugged. 'They merely confirm what's hinted at in the obituary. Dove met Anna von Leiper in the summer of 1937 after being sent to continue his theological studies in Berlin; obviously both were much in love, and Anna was at least as anti-

Nazi as himself, though obviously she didn't share the majority of his left-wing views.'

'In that case,' said Winnie, frowning, 'why, for goodness' sake, didn't she return to England with him? According to the obituary, they were engaged. Surely they could have married.'

'Anna was of good Junker stock,' answered Harrison. 'From these,' he said, picking up a pile of the envelopes, 'it's clear that, like her father, she felt it her duty to serve the Fatherland, not abandon it to its fate.'

'So Tom had to return home alone!' Leaning forwards, Winnie reached for the obituary and, glancing through it, shook her head. 'With the war beginning, he must have felt so terribly helpless and alone back in Oxford. No wonder he leapt at Bell's invitation to serve as a curate in Chichester.'

'Quite,' murmured Harrison, 'and being German-speaking, he was the ideal person to help the Bishop in his work on behalf of the German anti-Nazi and Jewish refugees, and later to accompany him to Sweden.'

'Ah yes! The secret meeting with Bonhoeffer!' Winnie glanced at the books. 'Did you manage to find out any more about that?'

'It seems that Bonhoeffer was serving in the *Abwehr* at the time. Presumably it was Canaris who was the inspiration behind the meeting.'

'Bonhoeffer was in military intelligence!' Winnie stared incredulously. 'What, an internationally-respected theologian?'

'I'm afraid, my dear,' answered Harrison with a smile, 'a clerical collar has never been impediment to the secret services—quite the contrary. Anyway, Bonhoeffer was the ideal go-between: he'd met Bell in England before the war, and the two men trusted each other implicitly.'

'But whatever was the purpose of the whole thing? What did the German resistance hope to obtain from this meeting?'

'Peace terms—before attempting a *coup d'état* against Hitler, the senior members of the *Schwarze Kapelle* wanted Britain to drop the demand for Germany's unconditional surrender. It's one thing to ask serving military officers to act against a dictator, quite another to expect them to deliver their country, lock, stock and barrel into the hands of its foes—Bonhoeffer had therefore to ask Bell to persuade Britain to change its war aims and agree to negotiate a peace with Germany once Hitler was out of the way.' Pausing, Harrison leaned back in his chair. 'Trouble was, Churchill was bound by his agreements with Roosevelt and Stalin; by 1942 he couldn't have taken unilateral action even if he'd wanted to. Anyway,' he went on, 'though Canaris forwarded through Bonhoeffer a list of the leaders of the *Schwarze Kapelle* as a sign of good faith, there was still the strong possibility that it was all just a devilish trick to split the Allied coalition.'

'So the war continued?'

'Yes.' Getting up, Harrison walked over to the window. 'The killing went on,' he said, staring out into the darkness, 'and Miller's family, along with other millions, were herded like animals into the concentration camps and destroyed.'

'And the *Schwarze Kapelle*?'

He shrugged. 'They staggered on, with the Allied demand for unconditional surrender tying one arm behind their backs. Nevertheless, as things got more desperate for Germany, they tried to kill Hitler on various occasions, but for one reason or another always failed. Finally, with Bonhoeffer arrested and the Gestapo closing in, von Stauffenberg took the gamble of placing a bomb in the Rastenburg conference room—and when that also failed to kill Hitler, that was the end for them all.'

'Including Anna and her father?' added Winnie quietly.

Harrison nodded, then turned to face her. 'Tell me in all honesty, do you really think just being reminded of that would have driven Dove to take his life? The obituary says that he suffered a nervous collapse in 1945: I can understand that—the woman he'd loved tortured to death in a Gestapo cellar! But I still don't see why Miller's list of names should have affected him so badly.' He paused and picked up the envelope. 'Could I really have killed the old fellow, Winnie, just by handing him this scrap of paper?'

'By reminding him of Anna, you mean? No, of course not. With Joyce's help, Tom had made a new life for himself. Anyway,' continued Winnie, 'whatever pains Tom still carried from that time, he'd already lived with them for nearly fifty years.'

'Then, for the love of heaven, what was it that drove him to kill himself?' Slapping his fist in his palm, Harrison turned once more to the darkness. 'And why,' he murmured, pressing his forehead to the glass, 'hide the real reason for it from his wife and everyone else?'

Winnie sat silent a moment more, then said, 'Come on, you'll just make yourself ill continuously racking your mind with these things. Come out to the kitchen: I've got a pleasant surprise for you.'

'Good grief, woman! What in hell's name is that monstrosity doing here?'

If the earlier scene of Harrison bent in the lamplight, absorbed in his reading, had echoed the one of the night before, the one now, with him in the doorway staring aghast at the kitchen table, was an almost exact replica of that outside St Laurence's vestry—though, instead of Helen Gleeson's enthusiastically beribboned map of Berlin, facing him was merely the broken little figurine that Tom and Joyce Dove had brought back from the Long Ashendon pond.

Incongruous as the medieval font on the Chiron St Laurence vicarage lawn, the armless, dandified monkey stood before him, looking over its shoulder and baring its teeth in what appeared to be an open-mouthed snarl. Smeared and mud-encrusted, the thing had been hideous enough; now, cleaned and gleaming in pristine colours, with yellow satin breeches and coat, snow-white wig, ruffles and cuffs, it seemed if anything more bizarre and repulsive than before.

'Don't you like it?' said Winnie, wheeling up to the table and rotating the statuette so that its polished surface caught the light. 'I found it in the plastic sack you had the letters in, and as I wanted something to do when you were reading, I thought I'd give it a scrub.' Picking it up, she studied it. 'Oh, it really has come up beautifully! Look,' she said, holding it out. 'See the amazing detail of these tiny pearl buttons—they're absolutely perfect!'

'Absolutely bloody horrible!' grunted her husband, gazing at the object with unmitigated disgust.

'Why don't you like it?' Teasingly, Winnie smiled up at his face. 'Because it's an ape trying to be a man?'

'No, damn it! Because it's a man who is an ape!'

Winnie frowned. 'Whatever do you mean?'

'For Christ's sake, look at it!' Snatching it from her, Harrison held it up. 'Does that look anything like those pathetic little beach photographer's monkeys you see in grubby velveteen jackets and trousers? No! And why not? It isn't because of these fine clothes, but the way they're worn.' Thumping the figurine down on the table, he pointed. 'Look—the creature stands elegantly upright; its clothes hang well. That's not a monkey—that's a monster! A blasphemy! A man with the clawed feet and bared fangs of the beast!'

Dazed by this passionate outburst, Winnie stared at the statuette. 'I see what you mean,' she said, 'but really, Richard, I don't understand why you're quite so upset.'

'Good God! What have we just been talking about? Dove's fiancée done to death in a cellar; Bonhoeffer strung naked on a gallows; Canaris the same—and Miller's family and all those others, men, women and children, herded to their death—and now Miller himself, apparently smashed to death over absolutely nothing!' Harrison jabbed at the figurine. 'Whoever created this was saying just one thing: that for all our fine clothes and manners, our culture's a sham—that, at heart, we're all soulless beasts, nothing but a damned pack of monkeys and apes!'

Distressed, his wife shook her head. 'That's all in your head, Richard—just your interpretation.' She again picked up the statuette and turned it in her hands. 'Look at all this intricate delicacy—can't you just appreciate it as a piece of art, never mind what you think it says?'

'No, I bloody well can't!'

'Well, I still think it's sweet,' she said, replacing the figurine on the table, 'and, anyway, I think it's smiling, not snarling.' Easing back her chair, she surveyed it appreciatively. 'That head's tilted at a curious angle though,' she murmured. 'It's bent over just as if the poor creature has some awful crick in its neck. Do you think it's meant to be listening to something?'

'To me,' scowled Harrison, 'it looks nothing so much as if it's stretching out its neck for the butcher's knife.'

'It's a funny thing,' continued Winnie, appearing not to have heard, 'but the angle of that head reminds me of something—I just can't think what it is.' Leaning forwards, she rubbed her finger over the broken end of one stump. 'If only the poor thing still had its arms, then I'm sure we'd see what it's meant to be doing.'

'Good God! Yes, of course! How stupid of me!'

Winnie looked round to find her husband staring down, not at the figurine as she expected, but at the torn sheets of the *New Scientist* in which it had been wrapped.

'What now?'

'This.' Sliding across a crumpled sheet, Harrison pointed down at an article circled in red, entitled: The Catalytic Converter—Friend of the Earth or Wolf in Green Clothing?

'Well, what about it?' said Winnie, puzzled.

Unexpectedly, Harrison laughed. 'It's the answer at least to one little puzzle. Going through Dove's papers, I couldn't understand why he'd paid so much for an exhaust system: obviously he'd bought himself a catalytic converter—one specially made, I imagine, for that old Morris of his. I should have realized. Bedford said something about the old fellow tormenting himself about polluting the atmosphere.'

'Catalytic converters—aren't they the things that cut down on exhaust fumes?'

'That's right.' Harrison again laughed. 'Typical Dove! The fellow worried over his small contribution to the greenhouse effect while quite happily smoking those ghastly cigarettes of his!' His laughter was cut off by the ringing of the phone. 'What now?' he muttered, making for the door.

As he disappeared, Winnie pushed the figurine aside; in its place, she drew over the crumpled sheet, and, with the monkey statuette grinning fixedly at her, began reading the encircled article, a frown increasingly darkening her brow.

'Winnie!' Harrison's excited voice rang down the hall. 'Bedford was right! That was Rachel! She's had the second autopsy report!'

Having finished the article, Winnie was still sitting at the table when her husband reappeared in the doorway. Almost reluctantly she turned and looked up at his triumphant face.

'It wasn't a fall from a train that killed Miller,' he cried, entering the kitchen. 'According to the London boys, the fragments of masonry embedded in the skull don't match the cladding of the bridge; also, the clothing stains are not consistent with the vegetation in the cutting. Added to that,' he continued, 'there are indications that the body was moved after death.'

'I see,' said Winnie flatly.

'My God,' burst out Harrison, rubbing his hands in relish as he strode about the room, 'what wouldn't I give to see Brooke's face when he hears! This will wipe away that smug grin! With all his complacent preconceptions, the fellow's obviously kitten-blind, and as much good as…as…' He struggled for a phrase, then laughing loudly, pointed at the statuette on the table. '…as that confounded armless monkey of yours!'

'How's Rachel taking the news?' asked Winnie without a trace of a smile.

'Oh, very relieved—now she can return home without all that guilt.' Going to the sink, Harrison began filling the kettle. 'And talking of relief,' he added, turning off the tap, 'I'll be damn glad to pass Miller's note over to the police and leave the whole matter to them. You know what,' he said, returning to the table, 'after all this absurd hunting through church registers and trying to make sense of that list, I wouldn't be surprised if the whole thing doesn't turn out to be a simple matter of greed: some local lout hears an American accent and strikes out for the sake of a few dollars.'

'I thought,' said Winnie quietly, 'that Miller's wallet was still in his pocket and that his luggage was found on a train.' Harrison's smile faded, but before he could speak, she went on, 'Clearly someone went to a lot of trouble, first to hide the body, then to make it look like suicide if it was found—that seems hardly the behaviour of a casual thief. Anyway,' she continued, 'how on earth did this local lout of yours manage to break every bone in his body?'

'God knows!' said Harrison impatiently. 'Thank God, it's not my business any more: it's a police matter now.'

Saying nothing, Winnie looked away.

With only the murmuring stir of the kettle breaking the silence, Harrison regarded the back of his wife's head with a frown. 'I don't understand,' he said, 'you complained enough about me getting involved in the first place; now you seem unhappy just because I want to leave things to the proper authorities and live our lives in peace!'

'Peace?' Winnie spun round, gazing up in what looked like pitying wonder. 'Richard, don't you see? It's too late! You're implicated—you helped to disguise an unnatural death!'

Dazed as much by the passion of the outburst as by what had been said, for a moment he could only stare back, then his face paled. 'You mean, Dove's death? What in hell's name has that got to do with Miller's? Christ Almighty, woman!' he went on, his voice rising over the rapidly increasing sound of the kettle, 'there's no possible connection between them!'

'No connection! For goodness' sake, darling, wake up!' Seizing his wrist, Winnie stared into his face. 'What about Miller's list of names? Half an hour ago you were berating yourself for not seeing it was that which upset Tom—there's a connection for a start! Then isn't your *Schwarze Kapelle* another? Miller appears to have been researching the subject for a book, and Tom had direct personal contact with it through Bishop Bell and also through the woman he loved.'

'Coincidence, damn it! Pure chance!'

'What? Just like Mendelssohn's book on Dove's desk, I suppose!' Pale herself now, Winnie paused, then burst out again. 'Talk about Dr Brooke being—what did you say—kitten-blind! What about you!' Harrison's face reddened, but she continued, tears suddenly in her eyes. 'Oh, Richard, why do you refuse to see the obvious? Is it because you're frightened of the consequences?'

Behind them, the kettle automatically switched itself off. In the ensuing silence, Harrison got to his feet and, returning to the sink, stared down as if mesmerized. Winnie pushed across to him. 'Please, my dear, for me: go and ring Joyce, Ruth and George Davidson. Tell them you've decided to make a clean breast of the covering up of Tom's death—I'm sure the police will understand the pressure all of you were under.'

Harrison shook his head. 'Winnie, you don't know what you ask: the lot of us would be charged with a felony. Think what that would mean! Ruth Hodge would be all right with her market garden business and I've got my army pension—but what about Davidson? Between us, Ruth and I virtually forced the poor devil to join us. Now, if this gets out, he'll be chucked from his job with virtually no chance of another—and him with those four wretched little children to feed!' He paused, then continued: 'And what about Joyce, for heaven's sake? I thought you regarded her as a friend? Hasn't she had enough to bear without all the scandal that would follow if I did what you ask?'

'My dear, for your sake and theirs, you've just got to insist.

If the police make a connection between Miller's death and Tom's, it will be ten times worse.'

'Damn it!' cried Harrison, 'There is no connection—except in your head, Winnie!' Breathing heavily, he turned away and stood, fists knotted. Finally managing to calm himself with an effort, he again looked round. 'No, I can't do it—not with the death certificate signed, the funeral tomorrow and half the diocese coming as well as the press: I can't suddenly chicken out because of a vague theory.' He paused. 'When I agreed to do as Joyce asked, I made a moral commitment, and what with others involved, I'm obliged to see it through.'

'Look,' pleaded Winnie, wheeling forward, 'at least go over and speak to Matthew. Explain it to him and get his advice. You needn't worry about confidentiality. He's a priest: if you call it confession, he's bound to keep it secret.'

'No! I'm not going to burden Ingrams with this. The poor chap's enough on his plate as it is.' Harrison strode to the door. 'Now I'm going to take all those damn books back upstairs and then burn those letters and photographs as I promised Joyce.'

'Please, Richard, listen! There's one other thing.'

'No, Winnie, damn it! That's enough now! I've made up my mind. Tomorrow I drop Miller's list off with the police on our way to the funeral. After that,' he called, striding out to the sitting-room, 'I never want to hear another word of this whole sorry business!'

Harrison's hands were still shaking with pent-up emotion when, having collected together the bundles of letters, he eased the photograph of Anna von Leiper and her father back into the envelope. As he did so, he heard the wheelchair entering the room.

'Richard, I want to ask something.'

'No, damn it! No!' Not looking round, he waved the envelope arm as if attempting to ward off a wasp. 'For Christ's sake, woman, leave it now!'

Instead of withdrawing, however, the wheels crossed the carpet to his side. 'I only want to know one thing—just one.' His wife's voice was strangely quiet. 'What colour was Tom's face when you found him in the car?'

Harrison froze, the photograph envelope still in his hand. So unexpected, so extraordinary and bizarre was the question, yet so earnestly asked, that he felt a premonition of horror—a dread that shivered through him to solidify in the pit of his stomach. 'Why do you want to know?' he asked defensively, turning to meet Winnie's gaze. With the wheelchair blocking his path, her eyes staring up into his, he felt trapped and hemmed in the corner of the sitting-room like an animal brought to bay.

'Just tell me, Richard—what colour was Tom's face?'

'Grey,' he murmured, remembering the sight of that head slumped and lolling against the wheel, the streak of dribble from one corner of the open mouth—and later, the bloodless pallor of the wizened features against the pure white of the pillow. 'Grey, dammit!' he repeated, his anger recovering. 'Ashen-grey! What the hell bloody colour would you expect!'

Winnie didn't flinch: her eyes remained fixed on his. 'Red,' she said slowly. 'Cherry-red—the colour of carbon monoxide poisoning—that's what I would expect.'

Momentarily, the colour heightened in Harrison's cheeks, then the marks of his fury faded and disappeared. Aghast, he stared down at her in bewildered horror. 'Is it true?' he struggled out at last. 'Cherry-red, you say? Heavenly God! How do you know?'

She shrugged. 'It's common knowledge—I thought everyone knew.'

Feeling his knees growing weak, Harrison reached for the arm of the chair, his wrist trembling as he gripped it.

'Just before Rachel rang,' continued Winnie, 'you said you thought Tom had fitted a catalytic converter on his car. Well, just listen to this.' Picking from her lap the sheet of the *New Scientist*, she began reading aloud.

'The increasing use of the catalytic converter will have another small but significant effect on our national life: just as the conversion of the domestic stove to natural gas ended one traditional means of British suicide, so the catalytic converter, cutting down nearly ninety per cent of monoxide emissions, will block off yet another convenient shortcut to the great free-parking in the sky!'

In dazed disbelief, Harrison shook his head. 'It's not possible!' he breathed.

'Exactly—it's not possible for Tom to have gassed himself to death in that particular car.'

'But then...' His voice died away.

'Yes, my dear.' Pushing forward, Winnie took his hands and, squeezing them, gazed earnestly up into his face. 'Now you see why I wanted you to go to the police and what I tried to avoid having to tell you: I just didn't want you to know that, for the kindest and most understandable of motives, you, my poor darling, have managed to help cover up murder.'

Chapter Twelve

With the bell ceasing to toll, a hush settled over Long Ashendon graveyard; apart from the muffled crunch of feet on gravel, not a sound disturbed the dank autumn afternoon. Indeed, as the procession filed from the church, it seemed that even the birds, whose joyous outpourings had accompanied the solemn ritual within, had been finally silenced by the sight of the plain deal coffin being trundled on its stainless steel bier towards the waiting grave.

Wheeling his wife at the rear of the column, Harrison noticed that not only had the pile of scaffolding pipes and planking been removed as he'd asked, but someone—presumably the sexton—had cut the tall, straggling grass which until recently had half hidden the majority of the tombstones. In spite of the horror knotted within him, he couldn't help feeling a measure of satisfaction as he glanced at the bevy of press photographers stalking among the stones: with the churchyard tidy, the choir leading in cassock and surplice, and the majority of the local clergy in attendance, the Church, whatever her past tussles with the deceased, was demonstrating that, if nothing else, she at least knew how to bury her own.

'Forasmuch as it hath pleased Almighty God of his great mercy to take unto him the soul of our brother here departed...'

Canon Bedford's voice rose above the crowd about the grave. From his place on the path below the chancel windows, it was impossible for Harrison to make out much among the cluster of heads. As the interment continued, he stared over Winnie's head towards them, hardly able to concentrate on a word being said.

Since the devastating revelation of the evening before, a paralysis had overwhelmed him. Despite all his wife's pleadings and the tormenting voices in his head, through a sleepless night and a long morning, he'd let the funeral creep towards him, unable to make the single phone call that would have prevented it taking place. Caught between conflicting loyalties, he'd allowed the minutes and hours to draw him relentlessly to the present moment—to this helpless watching the evidence of murder being slowly lowered on creaking ropes from the sight of the massed ranks of clergy and laity.

'*Enter not into judgement with thy servant, O Lord.*'

Over the grass came the mumbled response, '*For in thy sight shall no man living be justified.*'

Lowering his head, Harrison stared down at the gravel. What excuse, in God's name, could he give when eventually it came to light that he'd not only organized the illegal removal of a corpse, but stood idly by, virtually a knowing accomplice to murder? What justification had he for protecting with his silence the killer or killers who, with the guile of the serpent, had stolen into this quiet world to do to death two sick men? All at once his mind was made up: whatever the consequences, he had no choice but to inform the police that day.

With shock, he found that, with the final *amen*, the interment was over. Impatient to inform Joyce of his decision, he looked round to see her emerge from among the mass of mourners, escorted by Canon Bedford and closely followed by George and Pauline Davidson. As he watched them go, he felt Winnie's hand on his sleeve. 'Richard,' she whispered urgently, 'we must go over and speak to the archdeacon and his wife.'

Though he'd seen them in church, he'd not given either a thought. Now, however, glancing towards them, he saw at once why Winnie had spoken: with the officialing minister and family mourners gone, a metamorphosis was overtaking the-until then—subdued mourners, transforming them to animated guests and spectators; from the ensuing chatter and activity, however, Michael and Janet Cawthorne stood self-consciously apart. Whether by accident or design, every back seemed turned against them, every head turned away, so the couple remained as if behind an invisible barrier, tense and unhappy-looking spectres at an increasingly social feast. The reason was only too easy to guess: obviously the diocese was alive with the whisper that Dove had died a martyr to Cawthorne's monetary principles, and the latter's appearance at the funeral was casting a Caligulaian shadow which even the most generous hearted of his fellow clergy were only too anxious to avoid.

'Come on,' urged Winnie. 'Wheel me over.'

Manoeuvring the chair on to the grass, Harrison pushed towards the solitary pair.

Despite their obvious relief, there was a wary watchfulness in both the archdeacon's face and his wife's as they greeted Harrison and Winnie—and the former couldn't help contrasting their present reserve with the guileless spontaneity of the welcome they'd given him on the archdeaconry lawn. Clearly Dove's death had bitten deep, and the spectre of a sick, dying old man denied his home haunted them both. Nevertheless, Harrison sensed beneath Cawthorne's restrained smile more than a hint of that resentment towards himself he'd expected, and it was clear that his attendance at Dove's funeral was, in part at least, both an act of defiance to diocesan opinion and an assertion of his previously stated intention of sticking to his original policies.

Allowing Winnie to bear the brunt of the conversation, Harrison stood back. Doing so, he became aware of the critical glances he was attracting. He cared nothing: against the murders of Miller and Dove and looming personal disgrace, any small damage to his reputation now was like a flea-bite to a baited bear.

'My dear Richard, there you are! Margaret and I were wondering where you and Winifred had got to.'

Turning, he found the dean and his wife approaching. Genial as ever, Ingrams shook hands with all four. Within moments, Winnie's wheelchair was surrounded as the lesser clergy edged into the aura of their apparently reconciled superiors—the whole scene creating the happy impression that, having buried its dead, the diocese of Canterbury was, literally and metaphorically, once more closing ranks.

'Yes, indeed—a very successful funeral!' Dean Ingrams beamed complacently round the crowded room. With the aroma of coffee suffusing the air and the sound of voices filling the entire ground floor, Long Ashendon rectory was, for the last time, playing host in its quasi-ecclesiastical role. As if its very plaster and stone radiated the residual spirit of generations of quiet, industrious lives, the house had seemingly accomplished the work begun in the churchyard: peace and reconciliation now apparently existed where previously had been bitterness and strife. The archdeacon and his wife stood talking with Margaret Ingrams; Winnie and Joyce were grouped with Canon Bedford and an extremely spruce Major Coles—while Davidson and his wife, tailed by their two eldest children and aided by Ruth Hodge, moved among the guests with steaming jugs, and laden plates. Greetings and handshakes were exchanged, conversations ranged back and forth, and as the volume rose and the refreshments circulated, the old rectory droned increasingly with all the harmonious accord of one of the good Dr Benham's hives.

To whatever beneficent effect the building might be shedding on the gathering, Harrison remained impervious; for him, the funeral had been bad enough, but the almost festive spirit of the reception was well nigh unbearable. Conscious of the reality behind the smiles and chatter—two sick men done to death—he stared down at the untouched cup in his hand. In his pocket was that incongruous list of names, numbers and codewords which he'd borne like a death warrant or plague bacillus from the one to the other; and with absolute certainty that, in some way, history had stretched forth skeletal hands to pluck both down, he stood locked in nightmarish thought.

'You know, Richard, there's a certain irony to this situation.' Ingrams leaned over, smiling. 'Who would imagine that anything connected with Tom Dove could breed such harmony!'

Harrison forced a smile.

'Poor old Tom—how he loved this house!' The dean paused to sip his coffee. 'Now that Joyce has accepted Davidson's offer of one of those properties he's renovated in Westgate, I imagine you'll soon be putting the place up for auction?'

'I suppose so.'

'One always knew that Joyce was strong, of course,' resumed Ingrams, 'but I must say, she's displaying remarkable courage.' Pausing, the dean looked appreciatively across at his hostess who stood, nodding and smiling at whatever Janet Cawthorne was saying. 'Still, it's good of Davidson to be giving her such support—and dear Miss Hodge too, of course.'

Automatically, Harrison followed his friend's benevolent gaze towards his unlikely co-conspirators as they ministered among the guests. To every appearance, both were their normal selves: Davidson gravely refilling cups; Ruth Hodge offering round a plate of ham sandwiches with her customary social ease. As he looked from the lofty form of the one to the dumpy appearance of the other, it seemed impossible to believe that only four days earlier they'd aided him in smuggling Dove's body into the house, and that upstairs in the shaded lamplight, they'd struggled, tugged and levered the stiffened limbs of the old man's corpse.

'You're not eating anything, Richard! You really must try one of these sausage-rolls—they're absolutely delicious!'

'Excuse me, Dean, but I really must get some air.'

'My dear fellow, are you all right?' Hardly aware of Ingrams's startled voice, Harrison pushed towards the door, glimpsing Winnie's look of concern as he went. In the hall, Gleeson and

Bedford were locked in solemn conclave, but as the pair turned towards him, he brushed past towards the front door.

It was blessedly cool in the drive. He stood a moment breathing in deeply; then, to escape the muffled voices within, he began walking away from the house. Apart from the crunch of gravel and the crying of rooks in the distance, the silence was absolute as he threaded between the parked cars. What he needed was peace—somewhere to still his racing thoughts, a refuge from prying eyes and wondering stares. Seeing there was still no lock on the garage, he went over, and, dragging back the heavy sliding door a shade, squeezed himself into the dim oil-scented interior.

As soon as he was in, he knew he'd found the sanctuary he desired. Slipping round the shadowy shape of the Morris, he went to the rear of the vehicle. There, resting his hands on its metallic surface, he stared down at the faded Save the Whale sticker. The reception had been a tormenting dream, a delusion of normality—there his knowledge of intrigue and double murder had seemed but the sick fantasy of a diseased mind. Here, however, was the material proof of his sanity: the stained concrete was where he'd knelt, struggling to release the jubilee clip from the gleaming stub of the new exhaust system.

Careful of his best suit trousers, he crouched down and gripped the smooth end: it had been such a struggle to twist and tug off the plastic tubing; how much harder, therefore, must it have been to force it on? Whether or not there was a catalytic converter under the car didn't matter: he was absolutely sure no frail old man, however desperate for death, could ever have stretched the plastic tubing over the diameter of that pipe.

Absorbed in his thoughts, he didn't hear the approaching footsteps until the last moment. He was, therefore, still crouching behind the car when the garage abruptly darkened further as a figure filled the narrow opening and a voice called, 'Colonel Harrison? Are you in there?'

At the sound of the footsteps, Harrison's first thought was that Ingrams or Bedford had come to seek him out. It was, therefore, with surprise that he heard Ruth Hodge's voice. Rising quickly, he made for the door, wondering how to explain his skulking like some disgruntled adolescent in the garage.

Oddly enough, the newcomer didn't seem at all disconcerted as he emerged, beating a cobweb from his sleeve. Smiling apologetically, she merely said, 'I'm sorry to disturb you, Colonel, but when I saw you slip out, I thought I'd take the opportunity of a quiet word.'

'Of course, Miss Hodge—delighted!' Puzzled as to what she could want, he dragged the door shut, then accompanied her as she began walking away from the house.

In silence, they followed the curve of the drive until all but the roof of the rectory was curtained by the laurels, and before them stretched the green, broken only by a row of cottages in the distance and the few ash saplings beside the pond.

'I'm afraid today is proving a strain for us all,' said Ruth Hodge, halting in the gateway. 'How Joyce is coping so well, I can't begin to guess! And George too, bless him!'

'Yes, indeed.'

'I hope, Colonel,' resumed his companion, looking earnestly round, 'you realize how appreciative Joyce is of your courageous action on Tuesday night. Without your moral leadership and practical abilities, nothing could have been done: the honour being shown to her husband's memory is entirely due to you.'

Harrison looked away: at the funeral and afterwards, Ruth had obviously read in his face something of what he'd been going through. 'I wonder, Miss Hodge,' he said, 'if you'd mind strolling a little way on. There are one or two matters causing me slight concern.'

‘Of course.’ Ruth Hodge smiled. ‘May I suggest we conduct a short tour of inspection of our pond: I believe it’s recently undergone an almost miraculous transformation.’

Since the interment, the clouds had thickened and darkened, and now stretched round the entire horizon. In miniature to the sky overhead, the cleared water, denuded of its traditional sheen of algae and weed, lay a blank sheet of iron-grey. On its muddy perimeter, the ducks huddled beneath the now almost leafless saplings, their tails determinedly turned on this barren nakedness. One dismal quack alone greeted the approaching intruders as they turned from the road and crossed the few yards of spongy turf separating the pond from the highway.

Oblivious of the discomfiture of the ducks, Harrison halted beside the water and stood gazing down to where, at his feet, the waterlogged ash leaves hung in motionless shoals, appearing through the translucent liquid like clusters of tiny eyes. ‘Tell me, Miss Hodge,’ he said at last, ‘as his longtime churchwarden and close friend, were you surprised that Tom should have taken his own life?’

‘I was shocked,’ she answered. ‘I don’t know if I was surprised.’ Pausing, she looked away across the pond. ‘I realize that’s a terrible thing to say about an ordained priest, but somehow one always sensed that Tom trod on thin ice.’

‘Mentally, you mean?’

Ruth nodded. ‘He was always a moody man. Joyce, I know, had a difficult time with him on occasions. That’s not, of course, to say that he was a bad parish priest. On the contrary, whatever the demons within, and whatever his political commitments, he was always conscientious and hard-working—and speaking personally, he was unfailingly kind both to myself and my mother.’ Pausing slightly, the speaker smiled. ‘And my mother, Colonel, wasn’t exactly the easiest of people herself.’

Harrison stared again into the water, wondering why he couldn't speak of what was now his certainty that Dove had been murdered.

'My dear Colonel,' intruded his companion after a moment or two, 'you really mustn't torture yourself. Everyone in the diocese realizes that you had no option but to carry out Dr Cawthorne's bidding.'

'You are very kind,' he answered, shaking his head, 'but that's not exactly what's weighing on my mind.'

'No?'

'I have an idea that the cause of Tom's death lies deep in the past, and involves events which, I believe, led to his original breakdown at the end of the war. In the strictest confidence, Miss Hodge, did he ever talk to you about that period of his life? Did he, for example, ever allude to a certain Anna von Leiper or of his connections with what he may have termed either the Black Orchestra or the *Schwarze Kapelle*?'

'Never!' The other shook her head vigorously. 'Of course,' she continued, 'I know from Joyce there had been another woman in his early life, someone he met in Germany before the war, but he never once mentioned a word about her to me. As for his involvement in German politics, all I know is what I gleaned from the obituaries.'

Harrison felt a pang of disappointment: clearly, for all his strange humour and garrulous nature, Dove had hoarded the most delicate and sensitive areas of his life from even his closest friends. 'So you have no reason,' he said, frowning down again into the frozen sea of eyes, 'to think he carried any secret burden from the past—no guilt, remorse or whatever?'

The question was little more than a token, the murmured expression of his fading hope of ever smashing through the apparently impenetrable barrier keeping him from the truth of that mysteriously scrawled-over envelope. However, his words had an immediate effect on his companion: half turning, she gazed away towards the distant tower of Holy Trinity. 'Until recently,' she said, 'I'd have said definitely not. Now, however,

I'm not sure—there may be an element of truth in what you suggest.'

'Indeed! You think there was something on his mind?'

At the sudden eager interest in Harrison's voice, Ruth shook her head. 'No, it's nothing dramatic, Colonel: just that I noticed about a year ago a rather distressing change in him. As you know, except in his dark moods, he was normally a genial, open man. Gradually, however, I noticed he'd become somehow guarded and reserved with me. Superficially, he was as friendly as ever, but on some deeper level, I felt a veil had descended.'

'And this change, Miss Hodge? You have no idea what brought it about?'

'None at all, but you see, I'd been so preoccupied with looking after my mother during her final illness that I hadn't seen much of Tom for months. It wasn't until after Mother's death last November that I noticed anything at all. I thought it might have been something to do with me—something I'd inadvertently said or done.' The speaker paused. 'Anyway, I decided to broach the matter one day when we were alone together in the study.'

'Really! And what did he say?'

'Nothing—just sat there looking down at his desk.' Clearly distressed by the memory, Ruth looked across the green. 'I pressed him, of course, but he still didn't reply—then, finally, he asked me a rather odd question.' Turning, the speaker looked directly up into her companion's face. 'Colonel, he asked me why Judas Iscariot betrayed Christ.'

'Good Lord! Whatever did you, say?'

'Oh, I don't know, something about it clearly not being for the thirty pieces of silver, as those were later thrown back at the chief priests—but that Judas must have been hoping for a different outcome, a rising against the Romans or whatever, and that the poor misguided man must have been attempting to serve some higher good, as it seemed to him. I hope, Colonel, that doesn't sound too blasphemous.'

'No, of course not! But please go on—what was Tom's response?'

'He just nodded and swivelled round to look up at that photograph of Bishop Bell above his chair. Then he said something I've never forgotten. "My dear Ruth," he said, looking up at the picture, "the time may come when you'll need to remember that the Judas kiss had love in it, and that the greatest betrayals are carried out with breaking hearts, and that the cruellest rack the traitor knows is the one he or she winds for themselves."'

'Extraordinary!' Taking a step or two along the water's edge, Harrison stood visualizing the scene: Dove staring up at Bell's face, speaking of betrayal, weighed down by something he couldn't speak of even to his trusted churchwarden and friend. All this, ten months before—the very time when the television screens were filled with pictures of the East Berliners surging through the Brandenburg Gate, and when, over in Kington St Laurence, the Gleeson family were busy joyfully snipping round the photograph of that painted bacchante smashing through that graffiti-strewn wall! Clenching his fists, he took another step, scattering the cowering ducks. As they rushed out on to the green, cackling loudly, he felt an overwhelming exhilaration: an answer had come—obviously poor murdered Miller had indeed uncovered some secret in Dresden in which Dove had been involved. No wonder that the ex-rector had become so unusually reserved with his respected churchwarden when he must have known that, with every crash of the hammers, a little more light was reaching into those places where the compromising information had been hidden so long.

'Colonel?'

'Forgive me.' Swinging round, he strode back to his wondering companion. 'Miss Hodge: may I ask, apart from the composer, does the name Mendelssohn mean anything to you?'

The other wrinkled her brow. 'I don't think so, no.'

'And Lipmann? I don't suppose you've ever heard that name?'

A look of incredulity rose in the other's face. 'Good heavens, Colonel! How extraordinary! To tell you the truth, I never really expected to hear it again.'

'You know it!' burst out Harrison, taken aback. 'Presumably you heard it from Tom,' he continued excitedly. 'In what connection, may I ask?'

'No, no, Colonel, it wasn't from Tom I heard it,' answered Ruth, shaking her head. 'It was from someone who came to the nursery inquiring about rose bushes one Sunday afternoon a month or so back.'

So unexpected, yet apparently so banal and ordinary was the answer, that momentarily blank disappointment overcame Harrison. Next moment, however, realizing the implication, he said, 'A month or so back, you say? Good God, Miss Hodge! This person wasn't an American called Miller, by any chance?'

'Yes, Colonel, that's right—David Miller.' Ruth laughed. 'Such a charming man, though it wasn't really about rose bushes he'd come. That was all just an excuse: what he really wanted to know was the history of Holy Trinity—though for the life of me I can't see how an English parish church could be of any interest to a Jewish lawyer from New York.'

'Miller told you he was Jewish?'

'Oh, yes, that was one of the first things he said—in fact, he was very chatty altogether: he told me about his wife's death and his rather difficult relationship with his daughter. Then we talked a long time about my involvement with Holy Trinity and the Church in general.'

Harrison glanced back towards the rectory gateway where a car was turning on to the road. 'All this talk of Holy Trinity,' he said, turning back to the other, 'would I be correct in guessing that it led eventually to a discussion about Tom?'

'Oh, yes, naturally we talked a lot about him. I said how kind he'd always been to Mother and me. In fact, as he was leaving, I had the strong impression that Mr Miller would have visited Tom if he hadn't been still so weak after his stroke.'

'Really! And this name, Lipmann? In what connection did that come up?'

'It was the very last thing he asked—had I ever heard the name mentioned? When I said no, I remember he smiled and said, "Well, Miss Hodge, I think I can safely guarantee you'll hear it again." ' Ruth laughed. 'Funny thing, Colonel, I'd almost forgotten about it, then suddenly, out of the blue, you come along and make that odd little prophecy come true!'

Apart from the mournful lowing of cattle in the surrounding fields and the sounds of a departing tractor, nothing disturbed the quiet as Harrison wheeled Winnie through the churchyard. As if in recompense for the general dreariness of the day, the lowering sun had burst through the clouds; now it blazed low among the stripped bare hop gardens, haloing the western sky in various ambers and reds, and as the two figures rounded the chancel, the church tower loomed over them, a gigantic black pillar frozen against an inferno of flame.

'Really, Richard, I don't understand!' Twisting herself round, Winnie looked up at her husband. 'What's the point of this? We're just both going to end up getting very cold.'

Seeing his abstracted look, and receiving no reply, she slumped back in her seat with a sigh. Regretting that she'd allowed the spectacular sunset to seduce her from the car, she wrapped her rug more tightly around her and sat in silence as they finally halted before the now filled-in and flower-heaped grave, its Michaelmas daisies, carnations and lilies showing up in the shadow of the tower like the foam of a night-breaking wave.

Harrison's apparently perverse refusal to answer his wife's question had a simple explanation: even to himself, he couldn't explain why, on this chilly evening, he'd stopped to take a final farewell of the man who had occupied such a disproportionately large portion of his thoughts in life, and who now, in death, was doing the same. For some reason, he felt a strong disinclination to leave the village until he'd properly come to terms with Ruth Hodge's extraordinary revelations beside the village pond.

That Dove had been burdened by the knowledge of some ancient betrayal was evident; that Miller, after his Dresden researches, had made his way to Long Ashendon to inquire after Bishop Bell's wartime interpreter—and doing so, had made significant mention of the final name on the orchestra list, suggested that, whatever the actual betrayal had been, it was linked to the overthrow of those who had contacted Churchill's government through Bonhoeffer and Bell. On the other hand—and this was the primary reason for this vigil—although the origin of Miller's and Dove's fates had clearly been spun long before and far away, Harrison nevertheless sensed that in this obscure Kentish village lay the end of a thread stretching directly back to Bell and the *Schwarze Kapelle*. Somewhere here, he felt, dangled a strand of that labyrinthine web his ex-staff-sergeant had obviously discovered—and which, in jerking, had awoken some still-living spider, sending the hideous thing slipping down the dusty netting to seize and crunch him to the bone, leaving him finally a rotting husk, secreted beneath the undergrowth of a railway cutting.

A shiver of apprehension went through him as it occurred to him that, by retracing Miller's footsteps—inspecting the Kington St Laurence registers and asking questions in Long Ashendon—he himself might have inadvertently twitched the same invisible string as his ex-staff-sergeant had done, and that even at this very moment, the same hideous, bloated creature that had killed both him and Dove might be gliding towards himself.

'Listen!' Winnie's hand was suddenly on his arm. 'I think there's someone creeping around!'

Straining his ears, he heard the soft crunch of gravel—the sound of someone moving stealthily along the side of the church. For the first time in years, he felt an almost physical grip of fear, and, partly from instinct, partly from training, he immediately slipped a hand in his pocket and, drawing out his car-keys, clenched his fist about them, leaving a half-inch of their ends protruding between his fingers as gouges.

'Wait here,' he hissed, and pulling free of Winnie's grasp, he dodged between the gravestones to the shelter of the chancel. Reaching it, he listened, and hearing the crunch on the gravel more distinctly, he moved along the wall until he reached the corner. Heart beating hard, he then waited for the stalker to draw level, and only when he could actually hear the other's breath did he launch himself round the corner with a yell, his pronged fist raised to strike.

The short figure fell back before him with a terrified cry, hands raised before his face.

'Who are you, damn you?' Seizing the intruder's arm, Harrison dragged the cowering man from the shadows.

His bellowed words, his iron grip and still-raised fist reduced his already trembling prisoner to shaking ague. 'It's just Hoskins, sir,' came the tremulous reply, and as he lowered his hands, Harrison found himself gazing with astonishment into the wizened and virtually toothless face of Tom Dove's long-time verger and sexton.

'Good God, man!' he exclaimed, releasing his hold. 'What the devil are you playing at, creeping round the place like some blasted Peeping Tom?'

'I was just stoking the church boiler for the morning,' answered the other, recovering himself. 'I thought you were them ruddy kids again after the rector's flowers.' He pointed towards the dim shape of Dove's grave. 'What I didn't expect,' he added, resentfully rubbing his arm, 'was a gentleman pouncing out like a blooming tiger!'

Thankfully, Winnie appeared at this moment, wheeling out of the dusk, and was soon smoothing the ruffled septuagenarian with praise of his recent work in the churchyard.

'No, ma'am, that wasn't nothing—a bit of mowing was the last service I could give Rector.'

Having recovered from the shock of discovering who had been creeping up on him, Harrison was looking for a chance to fish for whatever information the old verger had; he now cast a tentative hook. 'I don't suppose, Mr Hoskins,' he said with apparent casualness, 'that you happened to meet an American visitor to the village a while back?'

'The Yank? Oh aye! I met him wandering around in here.'

'In the churchyard?'

'Aye, and long chat we had—like most of them. Yanks, he was very interested about the church and the village as it used to be.'

Harrison took a deep breath. 'And the Reverend Dove—what sort of questions did he ask about him?'

'Rector, you mean?' The elderly verger looked surprised. 'He didn't mention him—as I say, he was more interested in times past and all the old un's resting out here.' The speaker waved towards the irregularly placed tombstones about them, some with their surfaces still garishly illuminated by the sinking sun, the majority now steeped in profoundest shadow.

With every word spoken, Harrison felt himself further out of his depth: why, when talking to Dove's longtime verger, had Miller not even mentioned him? And why, here in Long Ashendon, as in Kington St Laurence, this odd interest in the mundane details of a backwater rural community? What, in God's name, he thought, raising his head to stare up at the tower above him, could be the connection between the lives of a handful of humble rustics and whatever subterfuge Miller had unearthed in the old GDR?

His thoughts were interrupted by Winnie. 'Speaking of the locals, Mr Hoskins, isn't this the grave of Miss Hodge's parents?' She was peering at the inscription on the polished marble headstone almost directly beside her wheelchair.

'That's it—and I'll say this of Miss Hodge, ma'am, she do keep it nicely.' The speaker briefly contemplated the neatly kept rectangle of white gravel between the kerbstone surround. 'Not, of course,' he continued, 'that either of them lying there were proper locals—they were Canterbury folk rightly. Old man

Hodge was a gardener at the cathedral before he came over this way to start up his nursery and market garden business.'

'Well, his wife certainly lived to a good age,' remarked Winnie, peering closely at the inscription. 'What was she—ninety-one?'

'Aye, but perhaps too good an age and all,' came the rather mysterious retort. 'She was a right strict churchwoman to the end and a tartar with it, if you take my meaning.' The verger chuckled. 'Mind you, I remember what they used to say of her-"rightly was she named Sarah-Elizabeth".'

Harrison shook his head. 'I don't follow—Sarah-Elizabeth?'

'You know, sir—the Magnificat: *For he that is mighty hath magnified me*.' Laughing at his own incomprehensible humour, the verger pointed at the headstone; his few teeth gleaming fang-like in his shrunken gums. 'Look at them dates, sir, and tell me if that wasn't a little miracle in itself.' He grinned; and then to Harrison's horror, the fellow actually winked.

Winnie's voice intervened. 'What are these on the kerb-stone?' Stretching down, she began fingering the row of small objects balanced on the marble surround of the grave.

'It's them blasted kids, ma'am: the little buggers are always coming up here throwing stones at the ornamental pots! When I was mowing, I kept picking up the bits in the blades, and had to keep stopping to lay them aside.' As he spoke, Winnie picked up one of the larger pieces and, holding it up towards the horizon, turned it over before suddenly exclaiming. 'Richard! See what I've found! Go on, have a look.'

Taking the small object, Harrison held it up, silhouetting it against the glow of the sunset. 'It looks like…' he began, then burst out, 'Good God, but it is! It's a bit of that damned monkey statuette!'

He held it higher, the distinctive yellow satin-clothed arm tinted now to the colour of blood—and there, clenched in its paw, protruding a quarter inch, was the jagged end of what might well have been a broad-bladed dagger or sword.

Chapter Thirteen

'*He went down also and slew a lion in the midst of a pit in time of snow.*' Having delivered his text, the visiting preacher paused to look round at the disappointing number who had braved the wet streets before launching briskly into a sermon on Christian resolution.

Despite the glorious promise of the previous evening's sunset, a steady drizzle had been falling over Canterbury since dawn, and for all the enthusiasm of the Bishop of Ballarat for the courage and manly fortitude of Benaiah, son of Jehoiada, there was a melancholy gloom to the nave. In the week since the dean had preached in response to the government's decision to commit troops to the Gulf, there had grown in the national psyche a dread of coming slaughter—thus, for all the eloquence and fervour of the preacher, from their expressions, the bedraggled-looking congregation might have been hearing the doleful lamentations and forebodings of an antipodean Jeremiah.

Among the Bishop's listeners, no face was more clouded than that of the secretary of the Dilapidations Board. Indeed, the more the preacher enthused at the skill and daring of his hero in creeping up on, and leaping in at, the trapped beast, the more Harrison found himself sympathizing with the lion—vividly imagining the half-starved creature's terror, facing Benaiah's already crimsoned spear. After all, he thought, in covering up Dove's death, hadn't he dug his own pit, and wasn't his own position much the same as the poor animal's, smelling the twice-shed Moabite blood on the wind, sensing the presence, of the killer, yet unable to guess the shape and intention of his enemy, or even the likely direction from where he would spring.

Though he'd kept it from Winnie, his sense of personal danger had not diminished since experiencing it first in the churchyard. On the contrary, the more he considered it, the more ruthless and resourceful appeared the killer, and he now cursed his loss of control at the funeral tea. If, incredible though it seemed, the murderer had been among the guests, his unusual behaviour could well have alerted him—and what with his visit to Kington St Laurence and his questioning of Ruth Hodge, his own apparent suicide could only too easily be next—with nobody in the diocese greatly surprised, believing as they must that he'd been somewhat unhinged by Dove's death.

His every instinct was to go to the police at once, but still he was held back by the thought of the consequences for the grieving widow, for the universally respected Ruth Hodge and the earnest, well-meaning Davidson. In fairness to them, to Dove's memory, to the diocese—even to himself—he must have some definite proof before he took any irrevocable step.

Apart from the fact that Benaiah's slaying of the lion was the only biblical scene set in snow—clearly, a matter of interest to one from the blazing Australian heat—the sermon taught Harrison nothing new. Still perplexed at what to do next, he rose from his knees as Matins ended and headed for home.

Wrapped in thought, he strode along the roofed-over passageways round the north of the cathedral, the blown rain dampening his face. Pausing under the Selling Archway to unfold his umbrella, he heard an only too familiar voice from behind, and turned to find the stocky form of Major Coles hurrying along Dark Entry towards him.

'Glad to have caught you, Colonel.' Reaching him, the bursar paused to take breath. 'I wanted a word at the funeral tea yesterday, but before I had chance, you were off like the proverbial rabbit.'

'Yes,' replied the other gruffly. 'I've had one or two minor administrative matters on my mind of late.'

'Yes, of course.' Coles's cheeks appeared to deepen in colour, and he coughed. 'Fact is, that's really what I wanted to speak about—I was wondering if you'd finally decided on the exact composition.'

'Composition?' Harrison felt his irritation growing fast. 'Composition of what, now?'

'Your committee, Colonel,' said Coles, surprised. 'The one on cathedral funding you volunteered to set up.'

'Ah, yes! That's been much on my mind.' Amidst the alarms and excursions following the Friends' council meeting, Harrison had, in fact, completely forgotten his inspired delaying ploy; now, seeing the absurd—almost dog-like—anticipation in Coles's eyes, his heart fell: like so many earthly triumphs, that of Tuesday night had returned to plague him in the shape of this eager, garrulous busybody. 'Actually, Major,' he said, somehow managing to smile, 'I'd been meaning to ask: would you consider joining yourself? I could certainly do with your financial expertise.'

'Delighted, Colonel! Only too pleased to do what I can—though I'm rather tied up in the treasurership of Toc H—and there's the Bowls Club committee, of course. Still, I'm sure I can fit in the time somehow—anything to take a bit of weight off your shoulders.' With the major fairly babbling with relief at having got his finger safely ensconced in yet another ecclesiastical pie, the two men set out across the quadrangle beneath Harrison's umbrella. 'To tell you the truth,' went on Coles, looking round at the taller man, 'I was a shade concerned at your precipitant departure yesterday—you looked a trifle liverish to me. Still, not to worry—if nothing else, it gave me the opportunity for a jolly good chinwag with the dean.'

'Indeed,' murmured Harrison, feeling momentary guilt at having abandoned his old friend to the tender mercies of Coles. 'I must say, Major, I was somewhat surprised to see you at Long Ashendon at all. I never realized you were a personal friend of the Reverend Dove.'

'Personal friend? Certainly not!' Scandalized, Coles halted. 'I assure you, I was merely there to represent the school.'

'Oh, I see,' murmured Harrison, 'but what possible connection had Dove with the school?'

'He was an old boy—had a scholarship to the place back in the 'twenties. Apparently, that's how he first knew George Bell: Tom and his brother used regularly to go round for tea and crumpets at the deanery in the holidays. I suppose Bell and his wife felt sorry for the little blighters with their parents away Bible-punching in Bechuanaland.'

'Really?' That Dove had been at the King's School was as much a surprise to Harrison as that there had been a brother—somehow Dove had carried an indefinable sense of isolation with him, and it was somehow difficult to conceive the old man as ever having had siblings, at all.

'Although he couldn't attend himself,' continued Coles, 'the headmaster's view was that the sins of the brother shouldn't be laid at the other's door. After all, whatever one thinks of Dove's ideas, he had made a sort of name for himself. Anyway, the head asked for a volunteer to go in his place.'

'Sins of the brother?' Halting, Harrison looked at the other. 'I don't understand—what sins are we talking about?'

Coles glanced round as if to make sure they wouldn't be overheard. 'Didn't you know,' he said with lowered voice, 'Christopher Dove was one of those damned Foreign Office types from the same filthy nest as Philby, Burgess and the rest?'

'Cambridge, you mean?' said Harrison, quite lost.

'Moscow, Colonel!' Coles bent closer, gleaming intensity in his eyes. 'The fellow went and topped himself while in clink—seems he was in under suspicion of attempting to pass over details of our diplomatic codes to one of Stalin's crew.'

Dumbfounded, Harrison stared at the bursar's exuberant face, then, struggling to suppress his own rising excitement, said calmly, 'Major, may I ask the source of your information?'

Coles laughed. 'Your friend the dean, of course! I told you, I had a long chat with him after the funeral.' The speaker glanced towards the deanery. 'The fellow's a positive mine of information on both Dove and Bell—presumably that's why the *Telegraph* got him to write their obituary.'

'Richard, do calm down and stop pacing around—you'll wear out the carpet! Yes, of course I knew about his brother. Joyce told me years ago—I didn't think it had any relevance.'

'No relevance! A red in the family! A traitor! Good God, woman, don't you see! It's the missing link that explains everything: Dove's original breakdown, all his talk of treason to Ruth, and why Miller rushed here posthaste from the Dresden archives, wanting to speak to me!'

Winnie shook her head. 'I'm afraid I don't see at all—spell out what you mean.'

With an exasperated sigh, Harrison went to the bureau and poured himself a second large pre-lunch sherry. 'We know that the *Schwarze Kapelle* had already been penetrated long before the July Plot of 1944, and that it was the knowledge of the Gestapo's net closing in that finally prompted von Stauffenberg to plant his bomb. Given that this penetration took place after Bonhoeffer's meeting with Bell, and that the British Foreign Office was infiltrated by Moscow agents, it's therefore reasonable to suppose that the names given Bell were betrayed to the Nazis through London.'

'Reasonable to suppose! Really, Richard! It's preposterous! What would have been the point? We and the Soviet Union were both at war with Germany!'

'Ah, yes,' replied Harrison, gulping his sherry, 'but by the summer of 1942 the war had started to move in the Allies' favour, and the German army was on the retreat in Russia.'

'I'm sorry,' said Winnie, 'I still don't see. Why should the Russians betray the German resistance? After all, if Hitler had been overthrown, the war might have ended straightaway.'

'Exactly! And that's the last thing Stalin wanted! You know the fellow's paranoia: he'd have envisaged a separate peace between a new German government and the Western powers, perhaps even we and the Germans joining up and turning on him together. Apart from that, peace would have prevented any hope of expanding the Soviet Empire. To get a stranglehold on Europe, Stalin needed the war to continue until his armies had fought their way right on into the heart of Germany.'

'But surely,' burst out Winnie, 'you're not saying Stalin prevented Hitler's downfall! Not when it would have saved millions of Russian lives!'

'I'm afraid, my dear, old Joe didn't care a tuppenny damn for any of that, just so long as he and his godless regime survived and prospered!'

Winnie gazed down at the carpet for a moment or two. 'So you think Bell's list was communicated to Moscow, and from there, passed to Berlin—and that Christopher Dove was responsible?'

Harrison nodded. 'It's a guess, but it's what I now believe: what else could Miller have dug up in the Dresden archives that would have brought him rushing to Long Ashendon? What other reason had Dove to be bowed down by the knowledge of treason? Either knowingly or unknowingly, he must have communicated Bell's list of names to Christopher, and then later, when his brother was exposed as a Communist agent, he must have realized that inadvertently he'd betrayed them all—not only Canaris, Bonhoeffer and the rest, but also his own bishop and the woman he loved! No wonder the poor devil had a breakdown! It's amazing that the man was able to continue at all!'

'And these names scrawled on the back of the envelope?'

said Winnie. 'You think they're the ones Bonhoeffer originally passed to Bell—the ones that Tom later showed to his brother?'

'Exactly—and that's what so upset the old boy when I showed him the list. According to Ruth, he'd been strangely oppressed and withdrawn ever since the Berlin Wall came down. He must have realized the story would inevitably get out.'

'I see,' said Winnie. 'So you're seriously suggesting that Admiral Canaris, through Bonhoeffer, saw fit to send Menzies's name to the British—the name of its own head of Intelligence?'

So calmly and quietly did she speak that Harrison didn't react for a moment; and then, before he had chance to get out a word, she continued, 'And even if we accept that quite ludicrous idea, who do you think killed Miller and Dove? Why, after all these years, murder to protect an already discredited and overthrown Communist regime?'

Reddening, Harrison began to speak, but stopped, the anger in his face melting into a look of consternation. 'I must admit,' he murmured unhappily, 'put like that, the motive for the murders is rather difficult to see.'

'Rather, yes!'

Avoiding his wife's sceptical smile, Harrison turned to look out through the window at the drizzle. 'It's just possible,' he said slowly, 'that someone's trying to protect Britain's reputation. After all, if it gets round Germany that their own internal resistance to Hitlerism was betrayed through London, it would dangerously strengthen the neo-Nazi right.'

Behind him came a laugh. 'So that's it now! Some good-hearted person's running around Kent, merrily killing off old men to protect western democracy!'

So dismal was Harrison's face as he turned, that Winnie's smile faded; wheeling forward, she took his hand. 'Richard, please do as I ask—get Joyce, Ruth and George together this afternoon and tell them about that exhaust system: they'll see you've no alternative but to go to the police.' Pausing, she squeezed his hand. 'Please, my dear, do it! In the end, it's all going to come out anyway.'

Harrison shook his head. 'No! No!' Breaking away, he went to the mantelpiece. 'I'm going over to the deanery after lunch. According to Coles, Ingrams wrote the *Telegraph* obituary, and knows the full story of Dove's early days. There's just the chance I might get some sort of new lead from him.'

'Come on,' said Winnie after a moment's silence. 'Let's forget it for now—it's time for lunch, and there's something I want you to see: when you were at Matins, I carried out a small repair job on our little friend from the pond.'

'Oh, not that damned monkey again! I wish you'd throw the blasted thing away as I asked!' Receiving no reply, Harrison resentfully followed his wife's chair out into the kitchen.

'There! What do you think?' she said, pointing to where the figurine stood on the table, its missing right arm now glued in place. 'Can you now make out what it's meant to be doing?' she continued, wheeling herself to it. 'To me, it looks like some sort of duellist.'

Harrison saw at once what she meant: with its newly attached arm held out waist high, the fractured end of the blade protruding fractionally above the gripped paw, its head angled back, the fangs exposed in what looked like a terrified snarl, the monkey seemed nothing so much as a grotesque caricature of a swordsman flinching back with fatally lowered guard.

Going over, he picked it up and, turning it over, inspected the base: there, as if to confirm Winnie's impression, appeared a pair of straight-bladed crossed swords and the monogram AR.

'I still don't understand,' said his wife, carefully taking it from him, 'what the arm was doing in the churchyard.'

'I've told you,' said Harrison. 'Dove obviously got it wrong: Margery Taylor, or whatever her name is, wasn't the one who chucked it in the pond. She must have thrown it away somewhere else, and one of the village brats got their hand on the thing—and after hurling it around in the churchyard and breaking it, dumped it where he thought it would never be found.'

'I suppose so,' answered Winnie, replacing the statuette on the table. 'Poor old thing.'

For a moment longer, Harrison gazed at the strangely averted head and the dangerously dropped guard, then suddenly laughed. 'Well, Winnie, I'll tell you something for nothing—if you're right, and that creature is meant to be fighting a duel, I wouldn't rate its chances of survival any higher than mine of learning anything useful this afternoon from the dean!'

'Wouldn't it be better if I returned later?'

'Certainly not! I wouldn't be forgiven if I let you escape.' Margaret Ingrams smiled at the visitor. 'Don't worry, Richard: I'm sure Matthew will regard your arrival as providential.'

The door closed, leaving Harrison alone in the familiar book-cluttered room. Outside the windows was dreary desolation: drizzle falling over the leaf-strewn lawn; an abandoned wheelbarrow beside the stripped potato beds; skeletal arms emerging among the balding orchard trees. As if by some mysterious process of osmosis, the autumnal gloom appeared to have penetrated even the deanery study, giving the normally cosy room a dank, chilly feel.

There came the sound of a door, followed by footsteps. Next moment the dean entered, smiling broadly and brandishing a carved boomerang. 'Ah, Richard! What a pleasant surprise! I wouldn't have expected you to stir from your burrow on such a miserable Sunday afternoon.'

'I apologize for intruding on your lunch,' answered the other. 'I had no idea you were entertaining the bishop.'

'Apologize! My dear fellow, your visit's an absolute mercy! Fascinating as New South Wales doubtless is, one rapidly wearies of the administrative problems of an outback diocese.' With a mischievous smile, Ingrams went to the mantelpiece and balanced the boomerang, apex upwards, between his pipe rack and a framed photograph of his daughters. 'Anyway,' he continued, stepping back to admire the effect, 'I meant to contact you today. I was rather concerned by your sudden departure yesterday from the funeral tea.'

'Yes, I'm sorry about that.' Harrison coughed and looked down. 'I found the situation rather overpowering.'

The dean regarded his visitor with concern. 'Of course, I know what a terrible shock poor Dove's death was for both you and the archdeacon, but as I told Michael at the time, there's nothing to blame yourselves for. As I know from speaking with him shortly before his death, he quite accepted that Crocker had no right to grant him the rectory in perpetuity. Really, Richard, I promise you, he'd quite resigned himself to leaving. In fact,' continued Ingrams, bending to switch on an electric fire, 'I had the distinct impression that he actually saw the move as a blessed relief for some reason, and was actually looking forward to passing his final days back here with us in Canterbury like his great mentor before him.'

'I never realized, Dean, that you were so intimate with Dove.'

Ingrams laughed. 'Hardly intimate, my dear fellow—for such a garrulous man, Tom was amazingly guarded. Nevertheless,' he continued, seating himself at his desk, 'over the last couple of years, I got to know him quite well through his generous help with a private project of my own.' For the first time in their long acquaintanceship, Harrison saw a slight blush in his friend's face. 'It's my dream to bring out a modest volume on the history of my more illustrious predecessors—an updated version of Meadows Cowper's *Lives of the Deans of Canterbury*. Tom's guidance was invaluable to my chapter on George Bell.'

Turning to the windows, Harrison gazed across the lawn to where the roof of the prep rooms peeped above the garden wall. 'I gather from Major Coles that there was an elder brother.'

'Yes, indeed,' sighed Ingrams, tapping his pockets in turn. 'The unfortunate Christopher! Yet another tragic casualty of war! For obvious reasons, I skated round the matter in the obituary.'

'Casualty of war!' repeated Harrison, frowning. 'According to Coles, the chap took his own life after being caught attempting to smuggle diplomatic codes to the Soviet Union.'

The dean paused in the midst of extricating his pipe and laughed. 'I'm afraid the good bursar's imagination grows more lurid by the day! It will soon be the equal of our vesturer's—as I know to my cost, having had rather a close of it yesterday after your escape.' He shook his head ruefully as he filled his pipe. 'No, Christopher's death was nothing to do with politics—at least not directly. The coroner put his depression down to his experiences at El Alamein.'

'The battle?' Harrison stared in disbelief. 'But that was in 1942—six months after Bell's meeting with Bonhoeffer! Surely he was working for the Foreign Office at the time.'

Lighting his pipe, Ingrams shook his head. 'No, Christopher didn't enter the Diplomatic Corps until the end of the war.'

Turning back to the window, Harrison stared across the garden, remembering the photograph of the sand-grimed young lieutenant leaning against the track of his tank. Still staring out through the trickling panes, he said slowly, 'I take it then that there's no question of his being a Soviet agent?'

'None at all,' answered the dean, puffing his pipe. 'Though, of course, like most silly gossip, there's a faint element of truth behind Coles's story. The facts are simply that Christopher came out of the war mentally scarred, and after being picked up one night wandering drunk in south London, tragically hanged himself in a police cell. The gutter press tried to make a sensation from the fact he was carrying sensitive papers at the time, but there was never suggestion of treason.' Pausing, Ingrams gazed smouldering bowl of his pipe. 'I'm afraid, like so m the brain tends to shape reality to his own precon and buried fears.'

Harrison was silent for a moment, then dipping his breast pocket withdrew Miller's list. 'I wonder if glance through these names, Dean. Could they be those Dietrich Bonhoeffer handed to Bishop Bell?'

Clearly bemused, Ingrams took the envelope and peer at it—then stared up at his friend incredulously. 'Bell's lis What, with Goering's name on it? Certainly not!' He burst out laughing. 'My dear fellow, what an absolutely extraordinary idea!'

'You're sure?'

With a slight smile, Ingrams rose from his chair, and going to a bookcase, extracted a worn, red-jacketed volume. 'Bell's official biography by Ronald Jasper,' he said, flicking through the pages. Finally, he looked up with a triumphant smile. 'Here you are! The names George Bell brought back from Sweden—there's no secret about them: Colonel-Generals Beck and Hammerstein, former chiefs of the General Staff, Herr Goerdeler, former lord mayor of Leipzig, William Leuschner, former president of the United Trades Unions and Jacob Kaiser, a Catholic trades union leader.' Smiling, the dean closed the book.

'And Mendelssohn and Lipmann?' asked Harrison heavily. 'No mention of them? Not even of Canaris?'

The other shook his head. 'I don't think I've heard either of those first names. As for the late Admiral Canals, from what little I know of that gentleman, I'd have thought him far too wily an old bird to have ever allowed his name to have appeared on such a compromising list.' Ingrams's face was suddenly grave. 'Richard, what is all this about? Something is obviously troubling you. Why this sudden interest in Bell and Bonhoeffer, and what is this curious list?' Pausing, he looked up at the other beseechingly. 'Dear friend, won't you allow me to share this with you?'

Just for a moment Harrison hesitated, then shook his head. 'I'm afraid, dean, I have nothing to share—everything I've thought real has finally proved a mirage, an insubstantial illusion, dissolving the moment I reach to touch it.' Taking back Miller's envelope, he stared down for a moment at the scrawled numbers and names, then folding it, returned it to his pocket. 'Like you say,' he continued, turning to look out across the grass and rain-sodden earth, 'I've been shaping reality to my own stupid preconceptions—so busy conjuring up demons from shadows, that I've utterly missed the actual serpent coiled somewhere about concrete reality.'

'Oh, not another!' Winnie looked up from her book. 'Really, Richard—it's only going to keep you awake half the night!'

Not answering, Harrison finished pouring himself a liberal measure of whisky. Upending the water jug, he shook the remaining drops into the glass before slumping down into his chair to sit, tumbler cupped in both hands, alternately sipping and scowling. His wife regarded him critically over her reading glasses for a moment. 'Well?' she said. 'What do you intend doing then? Are you going to go to bed or stay up uselessly brooding all night?'

'You go off—I'll follow as soon as I finish this drink.'

With a smile, and showing not the slightest inclination to leave, Winnie returned to the final pages of *Vanity Fair* and to the pleasure of witnessing the purblind Amelia's final recognition of the dear, good Major Dobbin's qualities of heart. Irritated, Harrison took another deep draught of the whisky.

Rationally, he knew she was right: weary to the point of collapse and already muzzy with alcohol, what possible use was there in sitting up, tormenting himself longer with searching for an answer that had eluded him in the clear light of day? Yet with his theory of the *Schwarze Kapelle* betrayal in ruins, and himself facing public notoriety and disgrace, how, in God's name, could he meekly stumble away defeated to bed? Brow furrowed, head aching, he drew from his pocket Miller's soiled and crumpled envelope and blearily blinked down once more at the incongruous list of numbers and names.

Complete Orchestra—22. Miserably, he reread the underlined title. Ever since Rachel had first handed it to him that single word: Orchestra had been the basis of all his thought: upon it, he'd constructed an entire hypothesis, rushing from one support column to the next, trying to make the unwieldy structure stand, with every perpendicular slipping and sliding as if upon sand—until, seizing upon the central pillar by simply consulting Bishop Bell's biography, Matthew Ingrams had brought the whole shaky edifice finally crashing to the ground.

Once again, in weary distaste, he read through the familiar names: Goering, Canaris, Menzies, Treeck, then at the two unknowns, Mendelssohn and Lipmann—the mysterious *Drummer* and *Fifer* of the group. Who were they? And if it hadn't been the Black Orchestra, then to what other clandestine organization had they and the rest of that curiously disparate group belonged? And what could any of them have to do with two small backwater Kentish villages? Above all, how could mere names have led to the separate murders of a semiretired Jewish lawyer and an elderly English country parson? For a moment longer he remained frowning down—then suddenly, in angry frustration, he crumpled the grubby envelope to a ball and thrust it into his pocket and rose to his feet.

'Ah, off then?' Winnie smiled up from her book.

'No, I'm going to get some water.' Pausing in the doorway, he held up his glass. 'If I'm going to think this thing through, I need to dilute this confounded firewater.'

His wife frowned, but before she'd mustered a suitable reply, he'd wandered off to the kitchen.

Wincing against the glare of the striplights, Harrison went to the sink, and topping up his glass, turned to leave. As he did so, he looked down to where on the table stood the cleaned and partly repaired monkey statuette.

Whether from the effect of the alcohol, or merely as a temporary diversion from his endlessly circling thoughts, the grotesque ornament suddenly had a compelling fascination. Swaying slightly, Harrison gazed blearily at the hideous grinning parody of whatever human activity it was meant to represent, then pulling out a chair, lowered himself down and, sipping his drink, squinted at it over the rim of his glass.

There was something about the slightly bent-forward stance and the strangely broken-necked took to the head that he recognized. Reaching out, he rotated the figurine slowly until the creature's eyes were virtually facing his own; so that, with its bared fangs, its lopsided head, its slightly forward stance and the outward bent right arm with its fraction of protruding blade, it seemed the very picture of some mad, deformed assassin.

Taking another drink, he blinked his eyes into focus and turned the statuette just a touch more—and suddenly he was back, standing in the shadow of the pentise roof a week before, looking across the archdeaconry lawn towards the open windows—the sound of Purcell drowning the birdsong, seeing Janet Cawthorne's blonde head bent over the cello, and beside her, the lithe, swaying movement of the recorder player—and between them both, the intense concentrated gaze of the girl with the violin, bow flowing in her hand, chin snuggled tight to the rest, bending slightly forwards over the music sheets, head askew, eyes looking down the length of the strings towards him exactly as the monkey's did now.

'Of course! Of course!' he burst out aloud in delighted discovery. 'A confounded violinist, dammit!'

'Richard, are you all right?' Winnie's concerned voice rang across the hall. 'What's going on in there?'

'Nothing, my dear. I'm fine.' Leaning forward, he peered at the monkey's face and laughed: the exposed fangs represented neither threat nor mockery: they were merely the self-evoked entrancement of imaginary music 'Hold on,' he called again. 'I'm bringing something in to show you.'

With Dove and Miller temporarily forgotten, Harrison picked up the figurine and began getting to his feet—but then all at once, he paused, then sank back upon his chair, holding the broken statuette above his eyes in both hands like a chalice, gazing up as if at the very Grail itself.

'Well, where's this thing you said you were going to…' Voice tailing away, Winnie paused in the doorway in puzzled surprise: whisky laid aside, her husband sat hunched at the kitchen table, clutching and gazing upon the monkey figurine with rapt concentration. 'For goodness' sake, Richard,' she said, 'whatever are you doing?'

Excitement flushing his face, Harrison turned and, raising the statuette, flourished it before her. 'I've cracked it, Winnie! Come and look at this ghastly abomination of yours: I'm certain it's meant to be playing a violin!'

Intrigued, Winnie wheeled forwards and peered at the brandished object—then a smile lit her face. 'Darling, you're absolutely right! You clever old thing! That's just what it's doing—that broken-off bit in the paw is the handle of the bow.'

'Exactly!' Placing the figurine on the table, Harrison contemplated it for a moment, then burst out, 'God Almighty, it's so obvious! Talk about blindness! All this time the answer's been literally staring me in the face!'

Surprised, his wife looked round. 'Richard, sometimes I don't understand you at all! Why get so worked up? What's so important? I thought you didn't even like the poor old thing.'

'Poor old thing!' exploded Harrison. 'Good God! Don't

you see? This grinning little gargoyle here is the cause of everything—it's the damned catalyst behind both poor Miller's death and Dove's!'

Taken aback, Winnie stared at him, incredulity and irritation contending in her face. 'The figurine behind everything? For goodness' sake, Richard, whatever do you mean?' She paused. 'Are you sure this isn't the whisky speaking?'

The scepticism in her look and tone were as goads; knotting his fists, veins swelling in his forehead, Harrison cried out in an ecstasy of exasperation, 'Violinist, Winnie! Violinist! Think! What's a violinist but another name for a fiddler! God Almighty, the thing's as obvious as that crick in the damned thing's neck!'

'What is?' snapped Winnie. 'I really don't understand what you're talking about. Just calm down now and, without shouting, explain clearly what you mean.'

Harrison started to answer, but instead, delving into his pocket, he extracted the screwed-up envelope. Flattening it, he pointed at the word next to Lipmann's name. 'See there, *Fiddler*—I'd assumed that was a codeword, not some actual damned catgut scraper! Don't you see, the list is of a real orchestra, one composed of porcelain models like this one here.'

Frowning, Winnie looked from the paper to the figurine.

'You really think this broken little thing is the fiddler referred to here?' she said doubtfully. 'Darling, whatever reason have you to think so?'

'Reason—our fat friend here, of course!' Harrison stabbed at the envelope. 'Hermann blasted Goering! Hitler's confounded deputy! Think of that grinning show-off in those absurd pantomime uniforms—what's the one thing everyone knows about him?'

Winnie shrugged. 'I don't know—that he commanded the Luftwaffe, I suppose.'

'Yes, yes, but apart from that? Wasn't he meant to be a great connoisseur of the arts? Didn't he ransack the Louvre and the other galleries of occupied Europe to ornament his country houses?' He pointed again at the scribbled, list of numbers and names. 'See—twelve pieces out of the full twenty-two! Typical! The late Reichsmarschall somehow got his sticky little paws on over half the orchestra!'

'And these others? Treeck here has five against his name.'

'Quite—and what was Captain Treeck but another Goering on a lesser scale: not only an upper-class international—playboy and sportsman, but a well-known collector of art. If I remember rightly, among the treasures he brought with him when he moved into Luckington Manor was a fine collection of Dresden china.' Harrison paused, then suddenly drove his fist into his open palm. 'Dresden porcelain! Good God, that's it!' Springing to his feet, he strode to the window, there swinging back round, wild exuberance in his face. 'Dresden was where Miller had been doing researches! And, dash it all, according to Rachel, wasn't her father some sort of art expert, and wasn't his primary reason for coming to Europe in the first place to research a book on porcelain china or something of the sort?' He again slammed his fist into his palm. 'Winnie, I know it—we're on the right track at last!'

'Menzies—one,' read Winnie, bending over the envelope. She looked up. 'So you think Sir Stewart was also an art collector? I must say that that wasn't the impression I gained of him the weekend he had us to stay.'

Uncertainty flickered across Harrison's face: again, he saw the tall, tweed clad figure of his host peering at the lectern through half-moon spectacles; the bleak unadorned dining-room, the Pearly sporting guns, the hunters in the stables, the young Labrador bounding at his master's heels. Winnie was right—Menzies had seemed the archetype of the English country squire—hardly, one would have imagined, an enthusiastic collector of European porcelain. Then the answer came. 'No, it's simple,' he cried, 'Treeck was Menzies's neighbour—they hunted together and were the link between the German and

British intelligence. What is more natural but that Treeck should have given him a gift? The same with Canaris! As Treeck's superior, he was presumably given one piece of the orchestra too.'

Returning to the table, Harrison gazed again at the figurine. 'No,' he said, 'I'm absolutely certain that this is the *Fiddler*—and that before it was broken, it was doubtless highly valuable.' He smiled round. 'Mark my words, Winnie, behind the killing of Miller and Dove is not vengeance or any perverted sense of justice, but simple, common-or-garden greed!'

Winnie shook her head. 'No, but I still don't quite understand. If this statuette was so valuable, why did Ruth have it sold at the fête? And how could David Miller have known about it when it was lying in the pond? And then again, if you think Tom was killed by someone trying to steal it, what was the point? As we both know, it was already broken and therefore virtually valueless when he and Joyce brought it back to the house.'

Doubts clouded back into Harrison's face as she spoke; and as she finished, grimacing, he shook his head. 'You're right—I still don't understand it all; there's something about the whole thing I've missed.' He paused, then reaching over, again picked up the figurine. 'And yet I'm sure this thing lies behind everything.' For a moment he continued to gaze upon it, then burst out passionately, 'Confound it, Winnie! If this gaudy little monstrosity could only talk to us!'

'My dear,' answered Winnie with a smile, 'if you're right and that really is some famous piece of art, it can speak—at least, to an extent.'

'Speak? How do you mean?'

'Art historians will know about it, it will be catalogued—and presumably its provenance, its background history, will have been fully researched.'

'Provenance?' Harrison murmured, remembering the dean's use of the word: what had been his phrase, looking out through the rain at the Adam and Eve—our dark provenance?

'You know, Winnie,' he said, looking round, 'I think you've solved it—or, at least, another part of it. That must have been what Miller was doing when he went out of his way to see Ruth Hodge: he was investigating the provenance of our little monkey fiddler here.'

His wife was silent a moment. 'So what are you going to do?'

Harrison laughed. 'The obvious, my dear! I'm going to do exactly what Miller did—start tracing back where this thing has been and when. Tomorrow I'll go over to Long Ashendon and see this Taylor woman. From her, I'll find out just how the statuette got into the pond. After that I'll see Ruth and ask where she originally got hold of the thing, then just trace back along the same thread as Miller. Sooner or later, I'm bound to...' Breaking off, he glanced quickly round at the window.

'Exactly,' said Winnie, dread in her voice, 'you're bound to come face to face with whoever killed Miller and Tom Dove!' She gripped his arm. 'Richard, for my sake, if not for your own, ring the police and admit what you've done. If you don't, somebody else is going to die—I know, I can feel it!'

Chapter Fourteen

The Malt Houses—a low-roofed, long terrace of cottages—crouched in the extreme north-western corner of Long Ashendon green. Originally built by a nineteenth-century Glaswegian brewer, and long maintained as a charitable trust, this damp, airless warren of dwellings had retained something of the spirit of the pestilential slum from which its original inhabitants had been plucked. Disproportionately peopled by the very young and the old, the feckless and the helpless, it obstinately clung to tradition, its yellow-washed walls and deep-set windows scowling over a criss-cross of washing lines and trodden mud.

As the Volvo pulled up beside the ditch fronting the drab terrace, three small grubby children ran out across the nearest of the crudely-hewn slabs that acted as bridges to each separate front garden; halting, they gazed in at the occupants with a mixture of suspicion and interest. Winnie smiled and waved, but obtaining no response, she looked round at her husband anxiously. 'Darling, are you sure it wouldn't be better if I came as well?'

'I'll be perfectly all right,' he replied. 'It's merely a matter of confirming a few facts.' Leaning over, he reached into the back seat for a large yellow shopping-bag.

Though the local petrol pump attendant had directed them to the Malt Houses, he'd been unable to supply a particular number. Harrison, therefore, approached the silent onlookers.

'I wonder,' he said, smiling down, 'if one of you would be kind enough to direct me to Mrs Taylor's residence.' Receiving blank stares, he tried again. 'Mrs Taylor's house? Could one of you point it out?'

The triple set of eyes surveyed him dubiously, then the smallest, a boy, grinned. 'Come on, mister—I'll show you.'

With his diminutive guide rushing ahead, Harrison crossed one of the uneven slabs and began gingerly making his way up a greasy path towards the front door. To his dismay, the tot, running ahead, thrust inside without ceremony, bawling out, 'Nanny Taylor! There's some old geezer here wants to see you.'

A moment later a large-boned, grey-haired woman appeared on the doorstep, the child at her side. Folding her arms, she surveyed her visitor coldly.

'Mrs Margery Taylor?' inquired Harrison, raising his hat.

'What about it?'

Disconcerted, the newcomer reddened. 'Excuse me disturbing you—I trust I haven't chosen an inopportune moment.' With his free hand, he struggled to extract a visiting card. 'I represent the Canterbury diocese,' he said, holding it out. 'I wonder if I might have a word.'

With arms still determinedly folded, Mrs Taylor squinted at the card, glanced at the bag in the caller's hand, then shook her head emphatically. 'No, I don't want nothing,' she said, backing indoors. 'I've all the dusters and cleaning materials I need.'

'No, no,' cried Harrison. 'Madam, you misunderstand: I'm not fundraising, merely inquiring about a small item purchased at this year's village church fête.' Delving into his plastic bag, he extracted and flourished the monkey statuette. 'I believe you obtained this from the white elephant stall.'

The sudden production of the porcelain figurine had, for a moment, a similar effect as the severed head of Medusa on the court of Polydectes: woman and child froze, staring at it with mystified and open-mouthed incredulity, until Mrs Taylor unexpectedly burst out laughing. 'Good God! He's like enough, but he ain't the one I got!'

'Not yours?' Harrison blinked. 'But I was reliably informed that you bought it at the fête, then threw it away.'

'Threw it away?' Astonishment switched to anger. 'Do I look bloody mad? Think I'm made of money? 'Course I didn't chuck mine away! For Christ's sake, it cost me all of ten quid!'

'Not yours!' cried Harrison. 'Are you absolutely sure?'

''Course I'm sure! Anyway, he can't be mine—not unless them little china legs have walked themselves out of my scullery cupboard!'

The group at the doorway was increasingly attracting attention. Glancing round, Harrison noticed a number of spectators, adult and juvenile, staring towards him with expressions varying from curiosity to downright hostility. 'I wonder, Mrs Taylor,' he said with a pained smile, 'if we might continue our talk indoors—there remain, I fear, one or two tiny aspects of this matter I as yet imperfectly understand.'

An east wind was blowing across the barren expanse of the green. As the minutes passed and the temperature in the car dropped, Winnie's annoyance grew. Try as she might, she couldn't concentrate on her magazine, and laying it aside, she sat back, looking towards the door through which her husband had vanished.

According to the dashboard clock, nearly half an hour had passed since he'd disappeared. Wrinkling her brows, she concentrated her gaze on the obstinately closed door in an effort to will him out—and to her surprise, the moment she did so, the peeling grey surface yielded, opening to reveal the back and shoulders of her husband's familiar brown overcoat as he backed out, still talking to the invisible figure within.

Winnie craned forward: in addition to the original bag, he now carried a second—a blue plastic laundry-bag. Intrigued, she watched him attempt to raise his hat with a loaded hand before turning to make his way back along the garden path, but as he glanced towards the car, she immediately took up her magazine.

'Are you all right? I'm sorry to have been so long.'

With apparent surprise, Winnie looked up from her reading as Harrison opened the door behind her. Twisting round, she watched him arrange the two bags on the rear seat, then, catching his eye, said smiling, 'Taking in washing, dear?'

Harrison grinned and, closing the rear door, clambered in beside her. 'I'll tell you all about it in a minute,' he said, starting the engine. 'Let's just get clear of this place first.'

The Volvo didn't travel far. Bumping out on to the road, it followed round the edge of the green, pulling up facing the pond. Leaving the motor running, the driver leaned over and lifted the laundry-bag to the front. Resting it on the floor between his knees, he carefully drew out a solid object swathed in what appeared to be a grubby strip of bed-linen—something which, from its size, its loose grimy-grey wrappings and upright shape, bore a passing resemblance to an amateurishly mummified cat.

'Well?' said Winnie, mystified. 'What is it?'

With a slight smile, but saying nothing, Harrison spun the loose end of the binding about the wrapped object. As he did so, there appeared first the head, then the gleaming shoulders and body, and finally the legs of a monkey statuette similar to the one in the other bag.

'Oh, Richard! It's beautiful! Let me look!' Reaching out, Winnie took the figurine and held it up. In dress, it was an exact replica of the first, with yellow breeches and jacket, loose waistcoat reaching to the knees and, hanging about the bearded face, the same incongruous long horsehair wig—but unlike the other, this was complete, with its pair of satin-sleeved arms bent back, holding to the creature's lips a stubby horizontal tube.

'What's it meant to be?' she said, twisting the figurine before her face in rapturous admiration. 'A flautist, you think?'

'No, the tube's too short for a flute,' said Harrison. 'I'd bet that thing in his mouth is meant to be an eighteenth-century military fife. Remember—*Fifer*—the second supposed code-word against Lipmann's name.'

A look of confusion rose in Winnie's face. 'But I don't understand: how did Mrs Taylor come to have this second one? I thought she bought only one.'

'So she did—and that's it. Obviously, when the Doves came across a broken monkey statuette beside the pond, heavily encrusted with mud, they naturally assumed it was the same one that had been sold at the fête.'

'You mean this other was never sold at the village fête!' said Winnie, turning round to the rear seat. 'Then how did it get in the pond and where did it come from?'

Harrison shrugged. 'God knows! Mrs Taylor had certainly never seen or heard of it before.'

'Yet this one clearly belongs with the other,' mused Winnie, again studying the figurine in her hands.

'I agree,' said Harrison, taking it from her and displaying the base. 'See—the monogram AR above crossed swords: exactly the same markings as the other. Without doubt, these two we've got are part of the full twenty-two of the set.' He began rewrapping the figurine. 'It seems Mrs Taylor bought *Fifer* here as a peace offering for her daughter-in-law after a row between them—anyway,' he continued, leaning over to replace the bag on the back seat, 'the girl apparently turned her nose up at the gift and so Ma Taylor was only too pleased to sell it me for twice what she originally paid.'

Both sat silent for a moment, staring out over the pond. The wind was ruffling the water, corrugating the surface with concentric ripples, through which a pair of ducks swam together, rising and dipping like miniature ships riding a miniature gale. 'So what do you intend doing next?' asked Winnie, at last. 'Now you've found *Fiddler* wasn't the figurine Ruth gave to the village fête, what's the point of going on to see her?'

'Because *Fiddler* and *Fifer* are as much a pair as those

two out there.' Harrison pointed at the ducks. 'On Miller's list they're both linked to Lipmann's name, and as you say yourself, they clearly belong together. My guess is, that if Ruth owned the one, she must also have owned the other.'

Winnie stared at the two bobbing shapes. 'It's a funny thing about Ruth,' she said thoughtfully alter a second or two, 'but don't you think there's something of the proverbial ugly duckling about her?'

'How do you mean?'

'I don't know—I find her curious, that's all. On the one hand, she's the archetypal village spinster—devout churchgoer, faithfully devoting herself to her mother for the greater part of her life; on the other hand, she's an unusually intelligent and capable woman who runs her own business, is a local JP and a member of Lord knows how many boards and committees: all this after being brought up in this backwater place by elderly parents who, according to Joyce, were a decidedly limited pair.'

'Come on,' said Harrison, engaging a gear. 'We've got enough on our hands at the moment without worrying about the mysteries of genetics. What's important now is for this unlikely swan of yours to tell us what she knows about our two little friends back there on the seat.'

'Nonsense! You're not inconveniencing me in the slightest.' The speaker gestured towards the window. 'See—my busy little bees are getting on perfectly well on their own.'

'Well, if you're sure,' answered Harrison doubtfully, gazing out at a huge lorry being loaded by a squad of women and girls. 'As I say,' he continued, raising his voice as a young Amazon in green overalls swept past on a miniature tractor, hauling a massive pile of cardboard flower-boxes, 'we could always return at a quieter time.'

'Mondays are our quiet time, Colonel,' laughed the other. 'I'm afraid life here lacks the tranquillity of your precincts.'

Perhaps because he associated Ruth Hodge with the Friends' quaint committee room above the Christ Church gateway, Harrison had always imagined her business as little more than a genteel hobby in which the lady steward of the Cathedral Friends desultorily wandered ornate Victorian glasshouses, with basket and secateurs. It had been, therefore, a shock to confront a signboard proclaiming Long Ashendon Garden Centre and Nurseries plc, then enter something like a military depot—a neat, ordered, extensive concern with a barrack ground of a car park. Disconcerted, he'd then driven as directed, along a concrete roadway, past ranks of modern glasshouses, to be finally rewarded by the sight of the Friends' steward, clad in day-glow orange dungarees and peaked cap, energetically directing the operations of a fork-lift truck whilst talking on a mobile phone.

'Well, if you'd both like to make yourselves comfortable, I'll bring in our coffee.'

Left to themselves, husband and wife glanced about curiously. The room was incongruous—as unlikely indeed as the unprepossessing breeze block bungalow set amongst the dazzling acres of glass. Apart from the obviously high quality curtains and an exquisite Persian carpet, the furnishings were strictly utilitarian. Plain-edged antimacassars were draped upon a dowdy sofa and chairs, and with neither bookcase nor cabinet, the box-like severity was increased by the nakedness of the walls, bare apart from the picture over the mantelpiece, depicting the drooping crucified Christ—a Victorian reproduction that Harrison recalled with a shudder from childhood, associating it with eau de Cologne and the High-Church piety of an elderly maiden aunt in Tunbridge Wells.

On a corner table, a number of mounted photographs were displayed. Largest was a yellowing highly stylized wedding portrait—a handsome, curly-haired, pleasant-faced man, standing ramrod stiff beside his equally rigid, but altogether more formidable looking bride. Intrigued, Harrison went over and picked it up. From the dress and hairstyle of both, the couple clearly belonged to the nineteen-twenties, and though neither bore the faintest resemblance to the present steward of the Cathedral Friends, he guessed they were her parents. Indeed, from the set of the jaw and the direct, unsmiling gaze of the woman, it seemed clear from whom Ruth had inherited her undoubted strength of character.

'Oh, isn't that sweet!' Having wheeled over, Winnie reached past him for one of the smaller photographs. 'Look, Richard,' she said, holding it up, 'that's Ruth as a child.'

He peered down: bunting-draped trestle tables stood laid out with food on a daisy-covered lawn, around which were seated small children, each brandishing a tiny Union Jack and a spoon—among whom sat a dark-haired little waif of a girl whose shyly smiling face was the miniature of that of the present proprietress of Long Ashendon nurseries.

'What's that?' he said, taking the photograph and frowning down at the large, rose-straggled object that lay half concealed in the shrubbery at the children's backs. 'Strange! I'm sure I recognize that bell shape from somewhere.'

'Ah! Our village VE Day party!'

Smiling broadly, their hostess entered with laden tray. Depositing her load on the low central table, she came and looked over Harrison's shoulder at the photograph. 'That was the first party I was allowed to attend.' There was an uncharacteristic wistful dreaminess in Ruth's voice. 'What was I then? About six or seven I suppose, yet even now I can still remember the exact colour and texture of that gorgeous pink blancmange!' Laughing, she went over and, sitting, began pouring the coffee. 'Mother, I'm afraid, was very disapproving; she was very much a bread and butter pudding person herself.'

'Oh, poor you!' Winnie wheeled to the table.

Harrison glanced again at the photograph of the thin-faced little imp in his hand, feeling a renewed sympathy for her and the amiable-looking bridegroom in the first photograph—imagining them both marooned midst acres of leaks and asparagus, hemmed about by the narrow religiosity of the late Mrs Sarah-Elizabeth Hodge.

'Now do come and have your coffee, Colonel,' said Ruth, holding out a cup. 'I must say I'm intrigued by this unexpected visit. You don't bring bad news, I hope—Dr Cawthorne is not already on the rampage again?'

'Oh, no, nothing like that.' Replacing the photograph, Harrison went over and took the proffered cup. Sitting, he smiled. 'It's merely that my wife and I are intrigued by one of your generous donations to the village fête—a charming little figurine of a monkey, playing what I imagine to be a military fife.'

His hostess burst out laughing. 'Dear me, Colonel, don't tell me you and Mrs Harrison have come all this way just to talk about one of that gruesome little pair!'

'Pair!' repeated Harrison, glancing significantly at his wife. 'So you did own them both, Miss Hodge: *Fifer* and also what I take to be a monkey violinist?'

'Yes, indeed, but what possible interest are they?' Ruth gave a slightly blushing smile. 'Oh, no! I suppose now you're going to tell me those horrible old things were valuable antiques!'

'No, it isn't that,' intruded Winnie hurriedly. 'My husband and I are rather interested in where they originally came from, that's all.' She glanced at Harrison. 'Between us, we've rather cultivated an interest in porcelain of late.'

'Really? How fascinating!' Ruth sipped her coffee. 'But I'm afraid I can't help you very much. After Mother's death, I found the pair secreted at the back of her chest of drawers. To tell the truth, I was flabbergasted—she'd never mentioned them, and really they were the last things I would have expected her to hoard: Mother was not usually one for frills of any sort.'

A look of disappointment crossed Harrison's face. 'I see,' he said slowly as she finished, 'so you presented one—*Fifer*—to the church fête here in the village. And the other—*Fiddler*—what happened to that?'

'I presented it to my other fête, of course.'

'Your other fête?' repeated Harrison blankly, then almost immediately burst out, 'You surely don't mean our fête, Miss Hodge—the cathedral fête —the one organized by the Friends?'

'Yes, of course. I gave one of the figurines to each, together with a donation—I treat both equally.'

'So *Fiddler* was sold at Canterbury!' Rising, Harrison went to the window and stared out a moment before turning back to meet his hostess's puzzled look. 'I take it then, Miss Hodge, that you have no idea how it got back here to Long Ashendon, or how one broken arm came to be in the churchyard while most of the rest of it was lying at the bottom of the village pond?'

'At the bottom of the pond!' Another swaying load of coffin-shaped flower boxes roared past, briefly vibrating the panes. 'Colonel, what it all this about?'

Instead of answering, Harrison turned and gazed again out at the loading lorry. Behind him, there was an awkward silence in the room, thankfully broken by Winnie suddenly saying, 'Yes, I heard how very successful the Friends' fête was this summer—Richard and I were so very sorry to miss it.'

'Of course, Mrs Harrison, in early August you were both away on your Italian holiday. Such a lovely country, Italy! Tuscany especially, I've always considered…'

Ruth's words were abruptly cut short by a sudden exclamation from Harrison; swinging round, excitement contorting his face, he burst out, 'That's it, of course! There's the connection! It must be! Why didn't I see it before? The Friends' fête was held on Saturday, the 11th of August—the very weekend when David Miller was staying in Canterbury!'

'Colonel, I don't understand…'

'It can't be a coincidence, damn it—not the very same weekend, and then his coming over here to the nurseries next day!' Slapping a fist in his palm, Harrison strode across the room, then swung around again to face his bewildered hostess. 'My dear Miss Hodge, pray tell me, when Miller spoke to you that Sunday afternoon, did by any chance the monkey statuette you'd donated to the cathedral fête come up in the course of conversation?'

Taken aback by the urgency in her visitor's voice, Ruth blinked up at him. 'No, I don't think so, Colonel. As I told you after the funeral on Saturday, Mr Miller and I mainly talked about the parish and my work for the church.' She suddenly paused. 'But wait a minute though—you may be right! When we moved on to the subject of my cathedral connections, I do seem to remember mentioning my little donation to the Friends' fête. Yes, in fact,' she continued, 'now I come to think about it, I did tell him the same story I told you about finding the pair of statuettes at the back of one of my mother's drawers. I remember I made a slight joke of the matter: I suggested that the two china monkeys might have originally been won by my father at the coconut shy in the very same Canterbury fête back in the nineteen-twenties when my father was courting Mother—you see, that was the only reason I could think of why she'd kept two such hideous things all these years: that they were a sentimental keepsake from those days she couldn't bear to part with.' Ruth Hodge paused. 'Colonel, won't you please tell me what all this is about?'

'I believe,' answered Harrison, who'd stood listening intently, one hand on his wife's shoulder, 'that David Miller saw and purchased your monkey violinist at the Canterbury fête, then somehow discovered you were the donator. It's purely a guess, but what other reason would he have for coming to see you next day—presumably he was trying to establish how the figurine had come into your hands.'

'But why?'

'To learn its provenance—or, at least, what its recent history had been.'

'You mean he thought he'd found a valuable antique—and when he'd somehow found out it was not, he threw it into the village pond after speaking to me?' Clearly distressed, Ruth shook her head. 'Well, I'm very sorry to hear it is all I can say: Mr Miller seemed such a pleasant man and so sincere. I hate to think his visit was all just some sort of confidence trick—a way of trying to find out if he'd made some wonderful bargain or not!'

'No, no, Miss Hodge. Please don't believe that,' intervened Harrison. 'I can positively assert that David Miller was an honourable man—not some shabby sort of antique dealer out for a fast buck. Whatever the reason,' he continued, walking across the, room, 'he wanted to know how *Fiddler* had come into your hands, I'd stake my life he was not driven by any sordid financial motive.' Halting before the collection of photographs on the side-table, he bent and picked up the silver-framed wedding portrait. For a moment he stared at it, then looked round. 'Miss Hodge, your father, I believe, was once a gardener at Canterbury Cathedral?'

'Yes, for many years. That's why I originally joined the Friends—Daddy was so very happy working there, especially during George Bell's time as dean.'

'Bell? Your parents actually knew George Bell?'

'Oh yes, very well—Dad worked as his private gardener for years. In fact, he married my parents in the cathedral. George Bell was a great bond between my parents and dear old Tom. Indeed, they could actually remember Tom and his brother when they were at the school and used to visit the Reverend and Mrs Bell at the deanery during the holidays.' Pausing, Ruth frowned. 'But, Colonel, I still don't understand—what has any of this to do with that awful old pair of figurines, and why, if Mr Miller was really so interested in them, did he throw the one he'd bought into the village pond?'

Harrison shook his head unhappily. 'I'm afraid I don't know that as yet. At this moment,' he added, replacing the wedding photograph, 'I seem to have reached a blank wall.'

His hostess was about to speak, but before she could do so, Winnie intruded. 'Just to change the subject for a minute,

Miss Hodge, have you seen Joyce since the funeral? She was so brave on Saturday, don't you think?'

Reluctantly, the other turned her gaze from Harrison who stood, hands clasped as in prayer, gazing intently at the collection of photographs. 'Yes, indeed Mrs Harrison, amazingly brave,' she struggled out. 'When I met her after sung Eucharist yesterday, I thought...' She broke off at the slight cry of surprise that came from the other end of the room.

Harrison had once again picked up the small black and white VE Day party photograph, and now he came forward with it to the table, pointing at the thickly garlanded shape he'd noticed earlier. 'Surely that's the old Kington St Laurence font—the one the Roundheads are supposed to have lugged over the vicarage wall. Whatever, was it doing in Long Ashendon in the summer of 1945?'

Ruth shook her head. 'No, Colonel, that picture wasn't taken in this village: it was taken in Kington St Laurence. That's where we lived then—the party was in the old vicarage garden.'

'You lived in Kington St Laurence? But I thought your father opened his nursery business here just before the war?'

'Yes, but as there was nothing suitable to rent in Long Ashendon at the time, my parents were forced to take a cottage in Kington St Laurence. We didn't move here until this bungalow was built in the mid-fifties.' The speaker laughed. 'So you see, I'm a foreigner really, an intruder—a Kingtonite, as they term us here.'

Harrison stared at her a moment, then suddenly slapped his forehead. 'A Kingtonite! Yes, of course you are! Damn it, how stupid of me! Great God in heaven, I should have realized before!'

'Colonel?'

'My dear Miss Hodge, you must forgive me. I've suddenly remembered something my wife and I have to do. Please excuse us if we rush away.' Harrison turned from one bewildered woman to the other. 'Come on, my dear,' he said, seizing hold of the handles of her wheelchair, 'apparently you've also forgotten an uncompleted piece of historical research urgently awaiting our attention!'

'Really, Richard, what's the point of starting this now!' The speaker scowled at the figure groping on his knees amongst the hanging cassocks. 'We're only going to get ourselves cold and hungry! Surely we could have eaten first!'

'Ah, yes, food!' answered the other abstractedly, pushing aside the limp drapery to reveal an antiquated safe of Gothic design. 'I thought,' he murmured, inserting the key, 'we'd have a bite here in the village. Geraldine Gleeson informs me,' he added, opening the brass-decorated door and peering in, 'that the Dun Cow serves a quite excellent lunch.'

'Do you realize the time? It's already nearly quarter to one!' Receiving no reply, Winnie disconsolately looked round the familiar cluttered little vestry as Harrison drew the four church registers from the safe and clambered unsteadily to his feet, brushing dust and mouse droppings from his knees with one hand. 'I know what's going to happen,' she added, 'we're going to be here for hours, hunting again for something without having the slightest notion of what it is!'

'I think not,' answered the other, pushing past to the rickety, worm-eaten table they'd used on their first visit to St Laurence's vestry. 'This time we know where to look.'

'Do we?' Wheeling herself round, Winnie surveyed the pile of heavy tomes doubtfully. 'What makes you so sure?'

'Because,' answered Harrison, bending to inspect the tarnished gilt lettering on each of the spines, 'I believe whatever brought Miller here concerned Ruth Hodge—and as we know her parents were married in Canterbury, it can't have been the marriage register he came for.' Extracting one of the volumes, he laid it aside. 'And as none of the Hodge family died in Kington St Laurence as far as we know,' he continued, removing a second book, 'it can't have been the burial register either. So what have we left? Just the confirmation and baptism registers—and as Ruth was only a little girl when she lived here, it wasn't the former that Miller consulted.' Turning, he held up the remaining book. 'So, *ergo*,' he said, brandishing it, 'this must be what he came to consult.'

'The baptism register?' Winnie looked dubiously at the worn leatherbound volume. 'But what of any significance could be recorded in that?'

'We'll see!' Unfolding a chair, Harrison sat and, putting on his reading glasses, bent over the register. 'Now, where to start? The Hodges moved here just before the war—and from the VE Day photograph, I'd say Ruth was born somewhere around that time. Let's begin working through from the beginning of 1939.'

Buoyed up by his confidence, Winnie wheeled forwards and positioned herself beside him. Apart from the sigh of the east wind about the church, the only sound was that of the turning pages—and what with the few children born to the parish and the stark brevity of each entry, husband and wife were soon flipping on through the early war years—skimming past the invasions of Poland, Denmark and Norway, the Anglo-French collapse, the Battle of Britain, Operation Barbarossa—and by the time the clock struck above their bowed heads, the bells of England were already ringing for El Alamein.

'Nothing!' exclaimed Harrison. Grimacing, he sat back and stared despondently into space—but then suddenly he muttered, 'Dammit! But wait though—Miller was only in here a short time. Clearly he knew exactly where to look!'

Dipping into a pocket, he drew out and unfolded the scrawled-over envelope. Spreading it on the table, he pointed excitedly at the heavily boxed-in date near the top. 'See, Winnie—16th July, 1944! That was what originally misled me, making me automatically link these names to the July Plot and the *Schwarze Kapelle*. Why did Miller note this date? There's got to be a reason. What's the significance of a date four days before the bomb exploded in the Wolf's Lair on the 20th of July?'

Winnie shrugged. 'I don't know—you tell me.'

'Because I bet the 16th July was a Sunday!'

'A Sunday?'

'Exactly—in the unenlightened days of our youth, my dear, remember a christening, like a marriage, was a purely private affair—and a Sunday afternoon was a usual time for the ceremony.' Harrison began flicking forwards on through the register—then stopped. 'There!' he cried triumphantly, indicating an entry, 'the baptism of Ruth Alexandra Hodge! This is what David Miller came to find!'

'But why?' murmured Winnie, leaning over. 'There's nothing here, just her name, her parents' and those of her godparents, none of whom I've ever heard of—and at the bottom, the signature of the officiating minister, the Reverend B. Davis.' She looked up blankly. 'So what's so important about it? It doesn't tell us anything unusual.'

'It's got to, dammit!' Brow puckered, Harrison peered down. 'It must be important: why else would Miller bother to write down and box in the date?'

'Yes, but it's just a normal entry, darling,' said Winnie. 'Listen: *Ruth Alexandra, daughter to Alfred James Hodge and Sarah-Elizabeth Hodge, market gardener, baptized in the presence of...*'

'The date! The date! That's it!' cried Harrison, slamming a fist on the table. 'It's the date itself that's important—the very thing Miller noted down!'

'I don't understand—what's so important about the date?'

'Infant baptism, woman!' Harrison rose from his chair, exultation lighting his features. 'Infant baptism—the normal practice of both the Anglican and the Roman Church!'

'Yes, but...'

'It's obvious—think! A pious, God-fearing woman, notoriously narrow and strict in her religious views, doesn't have a child christened until the age of six! Why not? There can only be one answer: either she was a closet Baptist or Methodist—or that the baby wasn't available earlier.'

'Not available?'

'Exactly!' Ecstasy and agony simultaneously worked in Harrison's face. 'Oh, what a blind idiot I've been! Remember that old gossip of a sexton leering and winking across that grave on Saturday evening? What did the wretch say? *"Rightly was she named Sarah-Elizabeth"*!'

The other's obvious incomprehension served merely to inflame him. 'Sarah-Elizabeth, Winnie! For God's sake, why didn't those confounded parents of yours send you to Sunday School as they ought to have! Sarah was Abraham's wife and the mother of Isaac; and Elizabeth, confound it, was the mother of John the Baptist—the point being, both women conceived long after normal childbearing age! Now don't you see?'

'No, I do not!' answered Winnie, angrily. 'If you'd just calm down and explain, instead of ranting on about gynaecological miracles! Whatever has Ruth's mother's name to do with her daughter, Tom Dove or anyone else!'

'Tom Dove!' At the late rector's name, Harrison's face contorted, and, instead of answering, he crossed to where the display boards of the Gleeson family's celebration of the fall of the Berlin Wall were propped in the corner. 'Yes! It fits!' he muttered, staring as if mesmerized by the photograph of the face-painted youth on top of the graffiti-scrawled wall. 'When did old Mrs Hodge die? Last November, at the time when all this was happening!' Turning, he looked back at Winnie. 'And what would a dying, God-fearing woman ask of her parish priest? Confession and absolution, of course! Christ Almighty, Winnie, no wonder Dove talked of betrayal and forgiveness to Ruth! It's a wonder he could bear to look her in the face at all!'

'Richard, what are you talking about?' said Winnie wearily. 'Just calm down and explain yourself clearly. What are you suggesting—that Tom Dove somehow betrayed Ruth?'

'No, not Dove!' Striding to the table, Harrison pointed again at the baptism entry. 'These two, this gardener and his wife, a bigot and a weakling—they're the traitors, confound them both!'

'My dear, what are you talking about?:

'Centuries of blood, Winnie!' cried Harrison, face contorting. 'The ghettos, the burnings at York, Buchenwald, Auschwitz, Dachau—racial and religious bigotry that has soaked, and is continuing to soak, this world in blood from crust to core!' Trembling, he sat, taking both his wife's hands in his own. 'Oh, you were so perceptive this morning, my dear, and I didn't see it, of course! What did you call Ruth—the ugly duckling? A displaced swan—exactly so!' Turning, he looked back down at the register. 'Ruth Alexandra!' he murmured, as if to a sleeping child, 'poor orphaned mite—you were indeed a bird of a different feather!'

'What? Are you saying that the Hodges were not Ruth's natural parents? That she's an adopted child?' Confused, Winnie shook her head. 'But whatever makes you think so? And even if she is, why all this anger and this talk of betrayal?'

'Because a good man's trust was abused and a child's birth right denied.' Harrison's voice was now calm. 'From where do you think Bishop Bell's middle-aged ex-gardener and his wife managed to obtain a tiny baby at the start of the war, and what did the dying Mrs Hodge confess that caused a barrier between Tom Dove and Ruth? Above all, why did the Hodges have the child baptized so late?' He paused. 'We know, of course, that Bell helped to bring out and settle numbers of refugees from Nazi Germany, and you've heard of the *Kindertransport*—the trainloads of Jewish children sent to safety by their parents who hadn't the visas to escape themselves.'

A look of incredulous amazement rose on Winnie's face. 'Surely you're not saying that...' Breaking off, she shook her head. 'No! I don't believe it! Not Ruth Hodge! The churchwarden of Holy Trinity! The steward of the Cathedral Friends! Are you actually saying that, unknown to her, she was born a Jew?'

'Exactly so—as I say, a bird of a different feather!'

'But...' Winnie's voice died away.

'The Hodges could formally adopt the child entrusted to them,' said Harrison. 'They could have her baptized in the names they'd chosen; old Mrs Hodge could keep her lips sealed for half a century, but what even that narrow-minded bigot couldn't bring herself to do, was to destroy the only link between the child she'd brought up as her own and the world from whence that child had come—namely, a pair of porcelain figurines that the grieving parents must have packed in among the accompanying bundle of baby clothes.'

'Figurines which Ruth Hodge donated to the fêtes, unknowingly giving her own birthright away!' Pained, Winnie shook her head. 'Oh, Richard, that's horrible!'

'Yes, except that, by chance, an elderly sick Jew, who happened to be an expert in European porcelain, saw one of them at the cathedral fête and recognized what it meant. Presumably, already having an idea of the provenance of the *Fiddler* statuette, he guessed the provenance of its donator. That's why he suddenly decided to prolong his stay at Canterbury—he first talked to Ruth herself and then, having found out from her where she was brought up, checked this baptism register to prove his theory correct—and then was finally killed for attempting to restore her stolen birthright.'

'But darling,' protested Winnie, 'if that's all true, then why, when he went to see Ruth and asked all those questions, didn't David Miller tell her of his suspicions at the time?'

'What?' said Harrison with a short laugh. 'With the crucified Christ looking down as they talked? In a room which is almost a shrine to Ruth's imagined parents' memory? Miller was obviously afraid to—anybody would have been! The position was tricky enough, God knows! No wonder the poor fellow was keen to consult an old family friend like Tom Dove who, unfortunately, hadn't by then recovered sufficiently from his stroke to see anyone.'

'And the irony is,' murmured Winnie, 'according to you, Tom already knew the truth—he'd been told it months before by the dying Mrs Hodge.'

'Yes, but was bound by his priestly oath from saying anything of the matter to Ruth.'

'Of course.' Winnie sat silent for a moment. 'And you really think that it was through Bishop Bell that the child originally came into the care of the Hodges?'

Harrison nodded. 'I believe so—it fits. It would have been a temporary wartime expedient at first, and only became a formalized arrangement later. For Bishop Bell, of course, it would have been an act in good faith; being himself such an essentially decent man as well as a lifelong ecumenist, he couldn't have conceived of his good-natured ex-gardener betraying the child. And what happened? Out of bigotry and a blinkered version of Christianity, it was brought up in the narrow orthodoxy of her surrogate mother!' The speaker gave a bitter laugh and grimaced. 'God Almighty, Winnie! Think of the little girl, condemned to a drab bungalow with that woman, caring and sacrificing for her until she was over ninety! Talk about the sad heart of Ruth, sick for home, amidst those alien blasted acres of asparagus and leeks!'

'And her own family,' asked Winnie quietly, 'have you any idea who they might have been?'

'See the name Lipmann here,' said Harrison, pointing down at the envelope, 'next to *Fiddler* and *Fifer*. At a guess, that was the family name, the name Miller asked Ruth if she'd ever heard of—the one he promised she'd hear of again.'

About the church came the sound of the rising wind. At last Winnie spoke. 'But if you're right in all this, Richard, I still don't see why anybody should want to kill either David Miller or Tom Dove. What motive would they have? And another thing, none of this explains how the statuette got broken in the churchyard and finally ended up in the pond.'

Harrison shook his head. 'I don't know the answer to any of that, but I intend to find out. What we need is to discover a little more of the provenance of *Fiddler* and *Fifer*.'

'How will you do that?'

'Easy!' He smiled. 'Get in touch with some of your old arty friends—then perhaps in a few days our two little friends outside in the car can have a small taste of London life!'

'What do you mean?'

'Later, my dear,' said Harrison, glancing at his watch. 'The important thing now is to pack up here quickly.' Closing the register, he got to his feet. 'Talking of tasting the pleasures of the metropolis has suddenly made me anxious to discover what the Dun Cow can do for us by way of a shepherd's pie!'

Chapter Fifteen

Within hours of the visit to St Laurence's vestry, the church weathercock creaked round one hundred and eighty degrees. There it remained, upraised beak and gilded comb facing a few points sou'west of west as a series of depressions drifted in, dragging with them a shroud of drizzling grey. For the rest of the week, the autumn rains fell, rotting the flowers on Tom Dove's grave, wetting and chilling the men working on the western towers of the cathedral and dripping interminably into Geraldine Gleeson's disparate collection of buckets and basins. At last, however, the weathervanes were again on the turn: since dawn, starting from St Mary's in the Scillies, then progressively eastwards, a host of cockerels, arrowheads, galleons and ominous old men with hourglasses and scythes were swinging round—and now, as the figure at the high window gazed out, the sunlight, piercing the thinning murk above, sent a brilliant shaft of light sweeping across London, illuminating the terracotta and yellow of the romanesque palace immediately outside and flashing on the windscreens of the traffic moving along the Cromwell Road.

'Colonel Harrison? Sorry to keep you waiting.'

The door had opened to admit a squat, portly figure, clad in green velvet jacket and yellow bow tie. 'I'm Tom Starless,' he proclaimed, advancing, plump hand extended. 'For my sins, porcelain curator here at the V & A.'

'It's most kind of you to see me,' said Harrison, slightly

surprised by the newcomer's appearance: he'd somehow imagined, presumably from his name, Dr Starless as sombre and tall—certainly not this bright-eyed little toby jug of a man!

'Not at all, only sorry you've had to wait so long.' The curator beamed over half-moon spectacles. 'An unavoidable meeting—nowadays so much museum time is taken up with what our new director enjoys terming "marketing ploys".' He gestured towards various exhibition posters on the walls. 'As you see, since erecting those shiny new turnstiles of ours downstairs, our energies have been increasingly taken up with endeavouring to compel a reluctant clientele to pass through.'

'Really?' Momentarily Harrison wondered about inviting Dr Starless to Canterbury: the council of Cathedral Friends would undoubtedly benefit from the curator's experience of the merits or otherwise of instigating entrance charges—and what he'd have to say would doubtless act as a further brake on Dr Cawthorne's already fast renewing enthusiasm for change.

'But to turn to pleasanter matters,' continued the other, unaware of his visitor's thoughts. 'Your letter was passed on to me by, I believe, an old friend of your wife.' The speaker's eyes dropped to the small battered brown leather case that Harrison held in one hand. 'I must say, Colonel, I can hardly wait to have a peekaboo at these intriguing little discoveries you mention.'

'Yes, of course.' Laying what, in fact, was the dean's vestment case on the desk, Harrison unlatched it and took out the two shoeboxes within. Removing their lids, he displayed the pair of monkey statuettes, each in a deep bed of cotton wool.

'Ah yes! Delightful!' Bending over them, Dr Starless beamed down in such a positively avuncular manner that Harrison half expected to see him actually tickle one or the other under its bearded chin. 'Very nice indeed! I congratulate you, Colonel. Beautiful copies, both of them.'

'Copies?' There was more than a hint of disappointment in the visitor's voice. 'Copies of what?'

Astonishment swept the curator's face as he sat. 'Of the great *Affenkapelle*, of course! My dear fellow, whatever else?'

'*Affenkapelle*?' Harrison's look was momentarily one of stunned incredulity, then suddenly he was laughing. 'Of course—*Affe* is the German for monkey! Monkey Orchestra!' He slammed a fist on his knee. 'Damn it—and all that time I wasted thinking of the *Schwarze Kapelle*!'

Dr Starless regarded the other's merriment with puzzled benignity. 'I must say, Colonel,' he said, smiling, 'your enthusiasm is gratifying, but you'll pardon me for saying that, at first sight, I would never have taken you for such a fervent admirer of the high rococo.'

Harrison shook his head. 'No, it's really my wife who is the enthusiast, but this *Affenkapelle*—it's famous, you say?'

'Indeed so. When the Royal Saxon Porcelain Works at Meissen first produced the set in 1747, it had immediate success. That's why, when the secret of making porcelain eventually reached our shores, pirate copies of the Monkey Band were reproduced by the hundred—and that,' said the curator, rubbing his pudgy hands, 'brings us back to these darling poppets of yours.' Smiling broadly, he again peered down at the figurines. 'Whose copies, my little sweeties, are yours, I wonder—Chelsea or Minton?'

'I believe,' intruded Harrison stiffly, 'that they're authentic Meissen. Both have on their bases what I've recently learnt is the typical blue crossed swords mark and the monograph AR, standing, I believe, for Augustus Rex—King of Poland and Elector of Saxony.'

'Really! True Meissen then, you think? But I warn you, Colonel, there were some excellent forgeries done. Anyway, we shall see!' As if lifting a newborn child, Dr Starless tenderly drew *Fifer* from its box and, switching on his anglepoise lamp, held it close to the light. 'Well, I must say, you just might be right,' he murmured, peering closely. 'The glazing is quite perfect, and as for the...' His voice died, and with an incredulous glance at Harrison, he upturned the figurines and began closely examining the base.

'Anything interesting?'

The curator seemed not to hear the question: still holding

the monkey player upturned in one hand, with the other he riffled through a desk drawer. Pulling out a magnifying glass, he turned the crossed swords mark towards the lamp, squinting through the lens at it with quite extraordinary intensity.

'What are you looking for?' asked. Harrison.

'For something that isn't here,' murmured Starless, still gazing through the glass. 'A dot—a blue dot between the hilts—either that or the add marks used to remove it.' Excited, he looked up. 'But there isn't anything—neither add mark nor dot! And these swords, as you see,' he said, holding the base towards Harrison, 'are heavy-pommelled and wonderfully straight.'

'Is that of significance?'

'Significance! My dear fellow—it's absolutely crucial! You obviously haven't the slightest idea of what you've brought: this isn't just Meissen porcelain, this is the real McCoy! Perhaps you don't know, but after 1756 a dot was included between the hilts; the blades became increasingly bent while the heavy pommelling on the hilt and guard was gradually lost.' Again scanning the base, the curator shook his domed, balding head. 'No, there can't be any doubt: this figurine is from the original mould!'

'And that's good, would you say?'

Dr Starless blinked, then burst out laughing. 'Colonel, if we regard eighteenth-century Meissen as the Rolls Royce of porcelain, discovering one of the original *Affenkapelle* is the equivalent of chancing on a mint-condition Silver Ghost!' Excitedly, his eyes gleaming, he leaned across the desk, once more holding the base towards Harrison. 'Look at those blades, I beg you! As you see, they're as straight as dies, not the tiniest hint of a wobble!' Pausing, the curator again turned the statuette in his hand, scanning it closely, murmuring, 'And this underglaze painting wasn't made by some *dumkopf* apprentice either! No, Colonel,' he said, leaning back in his seat, 'there's no doubt: what you see before you is nothing less than the actual touch of the great J. J. himself!'

'J. J.?'

'Johann Joachim, my dear fellow! J. J. Kändler! Surely you've heard of him, finest and most famous of the Meissen modellers—the Mozart of porcelain! The Michelangelo of the white gold!'

'Kändler,' repeated Harrison flatly—Rachel's potter whose name he'd scribbled down on the evening of the council meeting—then subsequently forgotten all about during the horrors surrounding Dove's death. He looked back across at the curator who had now also removed *Fiddler* from its box and was absorbed in examining Winnie's repair to the one arm with the aid of his magnifying glass. 'These pieces I've brought, Dr Starless,' ventured Harrison, 'would they be valuable, you think?'

'Certainly!' murmured the other, then looked up, his expression one of profound distress. 'But for heaven's sake, Colonel, what happened to this poor little fellow? How on earth did he come to get broken?'

'How?' Turning in his chair, Harrison again stared out at the Natural History Museum across the street 'That's an interesting question,' he mused aloud. 'How indeed? As the broken arm was found in the grass where the scaffolding was laid, however it happened, obviously it was broken before the Holy Trinity tower work was completed.'

The other made no comment; indeed, from his abstracted pained look as he slowly rotated the broken *Fiddler*, the curator had clearly not taken in a word.

'I suppose,' intruded Harrison after a moment, 'it would be possible to discover the provenance of these two pieces?'

'What? Of one of Kändler's original sets? Yes, of course—though it would naturally be of great help if you could supply me with the names of any of the original owners.'

'I think,' said the other, extracting the soiled, creased envelope from his wallet, 'the name you need would be Lipmann. It was, so I believe, through him that they came into the recent vendor's possession.'

'Lipmann, you say?' The curator made a note. 'Well,' he said, sitting back, 'I shall do my best to trace their history, but you understand it will take a few days.'

Harrison sat for a moment, gazing at the list in his hand. 'I wonder,' he said, looking up, 'if at the same time you could look into the provenance of another piece of the same set—it would be titled, *Drummer*.'

'*Drummer*?' Dr Starless's face lit up. 'In that case, Colonel, if you'll bear with me a moment, I think I might be able to help you at once!' Going to a filing cabinet, the curator burrowed among folders and files, finally extracting a broad buff envelope. Returning to his seat, he drew out a large coloured photograph which he held for a moment between the two statuettes, nodded and finally passed over the desk.

'I've an idea this is the chap you're thinking of—the brother, as you might say, of your own two exquisite little friends!'

On the photograph appeared a similar statuette to the pair on the desk, but instead of the fife or the missing violin, the creature held drumsticks poised above a small snare drum slung from the waist. Wonderingly, Harrison looked up to meet the curator's twinkling eyes. 'Yes, Colonel—*Drummer*, the pride of my collection here at the V & A! I only wish I could show it you. Unfortunately, it's presently appearing with top billing at the Metropolitan, New York.'

Harrison glanced at the buff envelope on the desk. 'But you've got a record of its history, I presume; you can perhaps tell me how it came into the hands of the museum.'

'Certainly.' Pulling out a few typed sheets, Dr Starless glanced through them. 'It seems,' he said, 'we purchased it at a Sotheby's auction in 1957.'

'And, the previous owner, the person who put it up for sale? That was Frederick Johann Mendelssohn, am I right?'

'Mendelssohn.' Frowning, the curator bent over the paper and shook his head. 'No, not a Mendelssohn. It was a certain… Ah! But wait a moment though! I see my mistake. Yes, you're quite right, Colonel—F. J. Mendelssohn, as you say. There, you see,' continued Dr Starless, passing over the paper, 'that the reverend gentleman apparently changed his name.'

'Changed his name?' Taking the typescript, Harrison glanced down: immediately, a shadow seemed to run across his face. For a moment he remained staring down at the name in front of him, anguished disbelief in his eyes, then he burst out, 'The scoundrel! The bloody damned scoundrel! But of course, no wonder I couldn't find Mendelssohn's name in *Crockford's*. I should have realized: damn it, I had the example of Müller anglicizing his name, and, of course, I actually heard the archbishop's name!'

'Archbishop?' repeated Starless, blinking at his visitor across the desk. 'Colonel, whatever's the matter? Are you not feeling well—you're as pale as a ghost. Perhaps I should ring for a glass of the museum brandy.'

Partly recovering himself, Harrison shook his head. 'Thank you, no! Forgive me—I was merely remembering something in a sermon I heard: a detail, a mere nothing,' he continued, his face contorting, 'an apparent little coincidence that, if I'd only taken proper notice of at the time, might possibly have saved an old man's life!'

'So, guv, what you think? End in a bloodbath, you reckon?'

'What?' Until then, the passenger had been sitting, case on lap, hardly taking in a word of the cabbie's mournful soliloquy on the state of the world: a wide-ranging analysis encompassing road conditions generally, unlicensed cabs and the present dearth of visitors to the capital. Now, however, jerked from his reverie by the question, he looked up as the taxi squealed to a halt at the bottom of Sydney Street. 'I'm sorry,' he said, 'I'm afraid my mind was drifting—how will what end?'

'That!' exclaimed the other, pointing across the King's Road at the billboards propped outside Chelsea Town Hall. 'Seems to me,' he said, accelerating away as the lights changed, 'that the nutter of Baghdad is set on going the full twelve rounds!'

Glancing left, Harrison read, *'Mother of Battles threatens Saddam'*, and beneath, *'More Tornadoes for Gulf'*.

'Well, what do you reckon then—is Saddam going to back down?'

'I'm afraid I don't know,' answered Harrison, turning back to find the driver observing him in the mirror. 'I've been rather preoccupied with other matters of late. Let's hope,' he murmured, frowning as he glanced at his watch, 'the fellow can be persuaded to see sense.'

'Persuaded!' There was infinite scorn in the other's voice: clearly, just as Harrison's words had disappointed young Simon Barnes on the day of his return to Canterbury, they now had equally failed to satisfy the cabbie. Obviously aggrieved, he slammed down a gear as they swept past the fire station, proclaiming as they swung, across the path of an oncoming double-decker, 'I tell you, mate, the only persuasion that bastard will understand is a short morning walk to a hempen noose!'

A flash of headlights, the blare of a horn, and then they were drawing to a halt in the leafy quietness of Manresa Road.

'Colonel Harrison!'

As he straightened from paying off the taxi, Harrison heard Rachel's call. Looking round, he saw her emerge from the entrance of the block of redbrick nineteenth-century flats at his back. Gone was her gaunt paleness, gone those heavy, sorrowful eyes; instead, it was a cheerful tomboyish figure in sweater and jeans who now hurried down the front steps to meet him.

'I was watching out for you,' she said, all breathlessness and smiles. 'But say, where have you been? Joe Eisenberg is here as you asked—we were both getting worried.'

'Yes, I'm so sorry to be late,' he answered as the taxi throbbed away. 'My interview was unavoidably delayed.'

Something in either his tone or look checked the girl, 'You OK?' she asked, with sudden concern. 'Has something happened?'

'Nothing important,' answered the other. 'It's just that I find London rather a strain.'

'Come on in,' said Rachel, ushering him up the steps. 'You need some coffee. I'm afraid,' she added with a rueful glance as they entered the foyer, 'the apartment's right at the top, and from the look of it, the elevator in this place hasn't worked since India was lost!'

Marvelling at the change in her, Harrison followed her up the stairs. Whatever the horrific implications of the things he'd learnt at the museum, and whatever nightmare consequently lay ahead, at least the removal of the burden of suicide seemed to have allowed Rachel to come to terms with her father's death; free of that crushing load, she seemed a completely different young woman from the frantic, nervy creature with whom he'd shared the garden bench. Now as he—the elderly church official—toiled leadenly upwards weighed down by the secret knowledge of betrayal and murder, she, young and unencumbered, hurried ahead like a precocious child before its wearied parent—the very epitome, or so it seemed, of that irrepressible young republic to which the similarly burdened Cornwallis had reluctantly yielded his sword.

'OK, we're here!' Having reached the top landing, Rachel led him into a spacious open-plan apartment, whose matching corduroy-covered armchairs and settee, metal-framed bookshelves and obviously hand-painted yellow piano, spoke volumes for the taste and personality of its late owner. It was clear that, despite the horrors of his youth, his wife's death, and his partial estrangement from his daughter, ex-Staff-Sergeant Müller had died neither an embittered nor a beaten man. On the contrary, the airy brightness of the large L-shaped room, the pictures, the furniture, that positively Van Goghian piano—all carried a sense of exploration and liberty, of a spirit still recognizably the same as the young man's who had shared the little office with him above Fehrbelliner Platz.

'Hi there!' Joe Eisenberg unfolded from a chair. 'Good to meet you again, Colonel,' he said, crossing to wring the other's hand. 'Look, I'm sorry about this; I don't know if Rachel's told you, but I have a meeting in Frankfurt late this afternoon.'

'This afternoon?' Looking up at this fresh-faced young lawyer, Harrison suddenly felt a painful sense, not merely of the physical limitations of his own world, of the precinct walls and the narrow winding highways and byways of the diocese, but of everything which held him bound: the long past, his schooling and upbringing, the traits of personality and military training—all those determining factors webbing him in obligations, duties and affections, and now leading him helplessly towards the dimly perceived, yet inescapable course of action already forming and swelling like a demon in his mind.

'You just sit down,' said Rachel, indicating the settee. 'I'll make the coffee—you take cream, right?'

'Thank you, yes,' he murmured, placing his small case carefully on the floor and slumping down on the settee. 'Most kind.'

'Now, Colonel,' intruded Eisenberg, drawing forward a chair as Rachel disappeared, 'I don't want to rush you, but that airplane ain't going to wait.' He unclipped a gleaming black document case. 'I've brought along the papers you wanted.'

'I wonder,' said Harrison, 'if first I might establish exactly what Rachel's father was doing in London for your firm. Would I be correct in saying that it concerned claims in regard to properties confiscated from German–Jewish citizens back in the nineteen-thirties?'

'Correct—since the early 'fifties, our firm has specialized in pursuing compensation cases with the West German Federal Republic, but with German reunification coming next week, we've been snowed under with claims in respect of property in what was the old GDR. That's why the firm asked David to come over here to Europe when the Wall came down: they wanted a man on the spot.'

'Quite—and, of course, what with his background and having the language, Miller was the ideal person. He also, I imagine, was committed to the work.'

'Yeah, I guess so.' Opening his document case, Eisenberg drew out a wad of typed papers. 'This is what you asked me to get, Colonel: they're xeroxes of all the claims David Miller lodged on our clients' behalf in the Federal Compensation Office in Bonn. You understand that they're highly confidential?'

'Of course. I shall destroy them when I've read them.'

Having passed the papers over, Eisenberg glanced towards the kitchen recess. 'Colonel,' he said, leaning forwards and lowering his voice, 'you've done Rachel a good service helping her discover that her old man didn't kill himself, but one word of warning. Don't be fooled. She's a hell lot better than she was, but underneath she's still a time-bomb waiting to be triggered off!'

'Thank you—nothing more.'

'Nothing?' Rachel looked round the barely touched dishes with dismay. 'At least try a little of the stuffed eggplant or the macaroni Lyonnaise.'

'Really, no, I'm quite satisfied—it was a splendid lunch.'

'Garbage! You've hardly eaten a thing!' Rachel gave a rueful smile. 'I guess I should have prepared roast beef or whatever it is that you guys eat.'

'The food's fine, I promise,' answered Harrison, surveying the range of salads, rice and vegetable dishes. 'It's just that, for one reason or another, I don't feel particularly hungry at present.'

'Well, at least have some coffee or another glass of wine.'

Harrison shook his head. 'Thank you, but I haven't the time,' he said, pushing back his chair and getting to his feet. 'I have to be getting down to the Aldwych. After that, I've still another call to make before catching my train home.'

Rachel didn't move. Instead, face clouded, she remained seated, staring ahead. Trapped by the etiquette of departure, Harrison hovered beside his chair, certain now that Eisenberg was correct, and that all his companion's former bubbling cheerfulness had indeed been nothing but a brittle surface protruding above the deep shadow of loss and grief.

'I know why you're in such a hurry to go,' said the other, breaking the silence. 'You're afraid I'll ask questions you don't want to answer. I guess you think it's OK,' she continued, her voice hardening, 'coming here for information, then going off without a word when I'm certain you know something about what happened to Dad!' Her voice rose. 'It's the same as the goddamned lunch! You won't say what you mean; you fend people off with politeness—you offer them manners instead of truth! And now you're going to run away with your secrets all safely cocooned inside that frigging cold British reserve!'

Harrison lowered his head. He had been here a thousand times before: it was a different voice, of course, a different accent, different words—harder and coarser—but still from this virtual stranger had come the same bitter recriminations he'd heard in the past so often from Winnie: those cries of protest when, as now again, duty and circumstances obliged him to operate alone in the dark labyrinths beyond public record and view.

'OK—don't say anything! Go and do your own goddamned thing then!' Furiously brushing at her eyes, Rachel turned away her head. 'Get off to your fucking Aldwych, whatever that is!'

'The Aldwych,' began Harrison, reluctantly sitting back down, 'is the area of London into which our Public Records Office has recently seen fit to move. From them, I've arranged to pick up a copy of a certain certificate of adoption. That done, I'm due to inspect some documents, held by a certain specialized private library here in London.' From his expressionless, almost mechanical, delivery, instead of sitting in a sunlit kitchenette, addressing the girl's bowed head, he could have been back fifteen or twenty years before, sitting in the old War Office, delivering a progress report before the perfectly impassive face of Brigadier Greville. 'With the help of the documents lent me by Mr Eisenberg,' he continued, 'and with the proof of the adoption certificate, I then intend completing that act of restitution which your father was killed trying to achieve.'

Rachel looked round, triumphant relief in her eyes. 'So I was right—you do know the reason why Dad was killed!'

It was more accusation than statement, and Harrison stiffened. 'I regret,' he said, 'that for very good reasons, I can't speak about that for the moment. I can only ask you to trust my good faith.'

Rachel stared at him for a moment, then burst out, 'Well, all right then—if nothing else, you can at least tell me how Dad died!'

Harrison momentarily glanced away, visualizing the broken little arm of the monkey balanced on the marble kerbing of the Hodges' grave. 'Your father's death,' he said, again meeting her eyes, 'was sudden and quick—as unexpected to him as I earnestly hope and believe it was to his killer.'

There was a moment of silence, and then he saw realization spring to Rachel's face. 'That means you know who the murderer is! You actually know the goddamned bastard!'

Saying nothing, Harrison met her eyes steadily.

'Are you going to tell the police?' Pausing, Rachel peered at him, then burst out furiously, 'You're not going to, are you? You've no intention of doing so—I can see it in your fucking face!'

Features immobile, Harrison gazed back at his accuser, inwardly cursing his foolishness, not only for having let slip as much as he had, but for ever having risked the inevitable intimacies of a private lunch.

'Well, I don't care what your reason is,' cried Rachel again, 'planned or not, Dad was murdered and the killing was covered up, and I insist you go tell the police what you know! You've just got to!' The speaker's jaw trembled. 'Chief Inspector Dowley, the guy in charge of Dad's case, was down here on Friday, and from what he said, I could tell his investigations are getting nowhere at all—you've got to help them!'

Harrison dropped his gaze to the table. He was weighed down by the dreadful certainty of what duty demanded; there was, nevertheless, a large measure of relief in knowing that he'd been right in his estimation that the police, having so little to go on, were quite lost and likely to remain so. Beyond that, even through the cold numbing horror he'd felt since being handed the details of the sale of the *Drummer*, he experienced a certain pleasure on learning that the hardworking, essentially decent (if somewhat homespun) Dowley had at last achieved his scandalously delayed promotion to chief inspector.

'Colonel, I want whoever killed my father caught and punished,' burst out Rachel again, tears now running freely from her eyes. 'He was a sick old man—and according to you, he died trying to get justice for somebody else.' Pausing, she struggled for breath. 'Well, I demand justice for him too! And dammit, also for me!'

'Of course!' said Harrison, closing his eyes and nodding. 'And he shall have it, on that I give you my word.'

So quietly spoken and so simple was the statement, that momentarily Rachel was silenced. 'I don't understand,' she began again, confusion in her voice, 'if you aren't intending to go to the police, then what…' Breaking off, she paused, regarding the elderly figure sitting bowed at the table before her with an expression that now hovered between concern and awe. 'Colonel, what are you planning to do?'

'Do?' Opening his eyes, Harrison looked directly at her. 'I've told you, my dear—I'm going to collect an adoption certificate. That done, I shall obtain some information from the library I mentioned. After that, I intend returning directly to Canterbury.'

'Yes, I know, but what then?'

'Then? Oh, that's easy,' answered the other with an enigmatic half smile. Turning, he looked towards the window. 'I shall endeavour to go on doing my duty.' He paused, his expression lost in the glare. 'Which, in my case, simply means continuing quietly and discreetly arranging matters in the best interests of the Church and diocese I have the honour to serve.'

Chapter Sixteen

Over the wind came the booms of the bell: five measured hammer strokes as of a gigantic gavel. With each tick of the clock, each imperceptible move of the hands, blackness faded to grey, and gradually, first the cottages opposite, then the archway, the deanery roof and surrounding walls, formed and took shape, contracting the world again to the familiar cobbled court, dreary and desolate now as a prison yard.

Paler grew the greyness—then the sound of a bird—another, and another—and all at once, the blazing rim of the sun, tipping the horizon, threw forth a beam to gleam on Bell Harry's four bronze wind pennants. A fraction later and the light caught the interlace of piping about the balustrades. Momentarily, the cathedral remained a massive dim shadow, crowned in a dazzle of silver and gold, then the sunlight was spilling like liquid honey down the tower to envelop the nave—and flooding outwards across lawn, court and cloister to finally illuminate the face peering between a pair of faded and slightly shabby orange curtains.

'Richard, whatever's the matter?' Blinking the sleep from her eyes, Winnie dragged herself up on the pillow to peer through the gloom at the dressing-gowned figure at the window. 'What are you doing up at this time? Not another bout of your indigestion?'

'No, I'm fine,' replied Harrison, turning to face her. 'Sorry if I disturbed you. I couldn't sleep, that's all.'

Winnie eased herself up a little more. 'What's on your mind?' she asked, studying his face. 'You were very quiet when you got back last night. Are you sure you didn't find out something in London that you haven't told me about?'

'Of course not!' Her husband turned and again looked out into the yard. 'As I said, apart from Ruth Hodge's adoption certificate, the trip was a complete waste of time.'

Winnie frowned. 'And those papers from Joe Eisenberg you insisted on staying up to read: there was nothing significant in those either?'

Harrison shook his head. 'No, nothing at all. Still,' he added, turning back to face her. 'At least we now have proof of Ruth's adoption. I think that's what's keeping me awake—I keep wondering how we're going to break the news to her.'

'Don't worry,' murmured Winnie, snuggling under the blankets. 'As we agreed last night, Ruth's a strong woman—she'll cope wonderfully, just wait and see.'

'Well, I hope so.' Turning again to the window, Harrison peered upwards. 'Incidentally,' he said, 'I notice they've finally got the scaffolding up on the Bell Harry Tower.'

'Sorry, I forgot to tell you,' came a sleepy voice from the bed. 'It went up yesterday. Apparently, George Davidson has already made a preliminary survey of the balustrade supports.'

'Really? And what's his prognosis? Bleak, I suppose?'

There was no answer. Harrison stood a moment, listening to the even rhythm of his wife's breathing, then slipped quietly from the room.

As Winnie slept, the sun climbed a cloudless sky, while the wind, backing northerly and strengthening, continued to rattle the window frames and wrestle the trees in the deanery orchard, sending dry leaves whirling across Ingrams's garden to combine with those scattered from the piles his daughters had spent hours raking together at the weekend. Around her, city and precincts stirred to life, and when she next opened her eyes, the bedroom was brilliant with light and her husband was standing almost exactly where he'd been when she'd dropped off to sleep. Now, however, he was washed, shaved and dressed, and again, just as when he'd left for London the day before, he had the dean's battered old vestment case in his hand.

'You're not going already?'

'Afraid so, my dear—there's a lot to catch up on after yesterday.'

Winnie's eyes fell on the case. 'Why are you taking that?'

'I thought I should lock the figurines in the office safe.'

Pulling herself up a little, his wife sniffed. 'What's that smell? Have you been burning paper?'

'No, no just a slight accident with the toaster, that's all.' Coming over, he hurriedly bent and kissed her. 'Well, I'd better be off then.'

'Richard?' She looked up at him, suddenly wide awake and with a look of alarm in her face. 'Where are you going?'

'Going?' Harrison laughed. 'Where do you think? To the office, of course. Why do you ask?'

Winnie shook her head. 'I don't know—seeing you dressed and leaving early with that case in your hand, I was suddenly reminded of...'

'Shush now!' interrupted her husband, gently smoothing her hair. 'That was another world, all over with long ago—now I'm only going off to see if, amongst other things, I can finally stem those leaks in poor old Gleeson's roof.'

Appeased by both his words and tone, Winnie lay back and closed her eyes. A moment later, however, as she heard the front door open and close, she sat up, listening to his feet on the path, feeling again that same unaccountable chilly dread she'd experienced a few moments before when he'd bent and kissed her.

But then the cathedral clock intervened, and with its reassuring, utterly familiar boom, she was back in Canterbury, back in the precincts, back in the safety of the present—the past was done with, and those footsteps, already dying in the distance, were only those of her husband beginning his daily trudge to his office to take up again all the dull decencies of his diocesan work.

'Ah, good morning, Mary!' Harrison looked up from the letter he was writing as his secretary entered the room. 'Good—you've brought the post. Drop it in the tray, would you—and how was everything here yesterday? No problems, I trust?'

'No, everything was fine, Colonel, though I think Dr Cawthorne was…' The girl broke off with a slight intake of breath as her eyes lighted on the monkey statuette facing her on the desk. 'Oh, isn't it sweet!' she exclaimed, picking it up. 'But you poor little thing!' she added, tracing a fingertip across the creature's face. 'However did you come to get broken?'

Harrison looked coldly at the object in the girl's hand, then glanced round at the window as it rattled in the wind. Through the diamond panes, he caught the gleam of the scaffolding piping capping the Bell Harry Tower. 'You were saying something about the archdeacon,' he said, turning back. 'You told him why I was away, I suppose?'

'Oh, yes, Colonel,' said the other, replacing the figurine, 'I told him just what you asked me to say.'

'Good.'

The girl hesitated, cheeks slightly colouring. 'I'm afraid he seemed a little put out. He said he would call back today.'

'Indeed? Put out, you say?' The speaker gave a wintry smile. 'Well, I look forward to his visit—but now, if you'll bear with me just a moment, I've a small task for you.'

Folding the letter he'd been writing, Harrison inserted it in an envelope; taking matches and a stick of sealing wax, he then dripped a thick blood-red blob over the flap. His secretary watched these proceedings with a look of concern: to her, he seemed more than usually strained and looked as if he'd hardly slept a wink: clearly his day out in London had not been altogether the relaxing break that she'd hoped.

'Right,' said Harrison, applying the diocesan seal to the wax, 'I want you to lock this in the safe. It's addressed to the dean: please hand it to him personally at noon if I'm not in a position to do so myself.'

The girl looked even more perplexed. 'I don't understand, Colonel,' she said, 'are you planning to go away again?'

'I very much hope not.' A bleak smile flickered briefly on Harrison's face. 'But tell me, Mary, who else apart from Dr Cawthorne tried to contact me yesterday?'

'Oh, quite a lot of people: Canon Bedford rang about the dry rot in All Saints; Major Coles dropped by to inquire the date of the first Friends' sub-committee meeting—I told him you hadn't yet decided a time. Oh yes, and Mr Davidson brought round his survey report on the Kington St Laurence vicarage roof.'

'Ah, good! I'd like to see that straightaway.' Harrison paused. 'And you told them all why I was away, as I asked you to?'

'Yes, sir.'

'Right then, if you'll please bring me Mr Davidson's report—oh, and incidentally, Mary,' he added as his secretary turned to the door, 'you'll find a small leather case in the safe. It belongs to the dean. Also return that and its contents along with my letter to him if, as I say, for any reason I'm not here at midday.'

Harrison was deeply engrossed in Davidson's survey report when, twenty minutes later, there was the sound of footsteps on the stairs. His intercom buzzed to announce the archdeacon's arrival.

'Dr Cawthorne! I was expecting you. Come in, please.'

There was already a certain perplexity in the newcomer's face as he entered, but catching sight of the monkey figurine on the desk, his look became one of open indignation. Fists tightening, he faced his subordinate, colour mounting in his face. 'Colonel, I sent you a memorandum a week ago concerning Phase One of our rationalization programme—I have still to receive your response!'

Harrison's expression became icy cold. Since Dove's death, he'd been awaiting Cawthorne's attempt to reassert his authority and try to retrieve his former dominance and control. Obviously the occasion had now arrived, and inopportune as the moment was, he nevertheless felt a certain relief: indeed, with tension already coiled in his stomach like a spring, one part of him actually welcomed a short tussle with this little cock-bantam now bristling and reddening before him. 'Yes,' he answered, calmly resuming his seat, 'I did receive your memorandum, Archdeacon, but as I explained to your secretary, I have been heavily involved with rather more pressing matters of late.'

'More pressing?' Cawthorne's face flushed deeper red. 'I don't understand—I believe I made it amply clear that the implementation of our programme must take precedence over everything else!'

Making no reply, Harrison stared up stony-faced at Cawthorne, who remained standing before him, hands knotted, his whole body now aquiver with rage, 'Colonel,' he managed to breathe at last, 'I am well aware of the esteem in which you are held throughout the diocese. Nevertheless, as your immediate superior, I have a right to know what these so-called pressing matters of yours are—and, in particular, why you saw fit to spend the entire day yesterday away from your desk without any explanation whatever.'

'Forgive me, Archdeacon, but you were informed,' replied Harrison, his voice unnaturally calm. 'As my secretary told you, I was away in London researching early European porcelain china—in particular,' he continued, gesturing towards the statuette, 'the background of this fascinating small curio here on my desk.'

Looking down, Cawthorne gaped a moment at the object indicated. 'No, I'm sorry,' he finally burst out, voice rising, 'I simply cannot believe that a broken china monkey can have anything remotely to do with diocesan administration! I'm afraid, Colonel, I must insist on a full explanation for your London visit and a detailed account of whatever these matters are that have so occupied your time recently.'

Leaning back in his chair, fingertips pressed together, Harrison shook his head. 'I regret that I'm not in a position to enlighten you, Dr Cawthorne. These are strictly executive matters of a highly confidential nature to which I'm answerable only to my board.' Pausing, he allowed his words to sink in. 'Of course,' he resumed, 'if you have any complaint about the performance of my duties, you are free to make representation, either directly to the board itself or to the archbishop.'

For a moment it seemed that Cawthorne would protest—his mouth actually opened to speak, but his position was hopeless: already isolated and unpopular in the diocese, and widely blamed for Dove's death, any official confrontation with the much-respected and long-established secretary of the Dilapidations Board was impossible. There was a moment of anguished struggle in his face, then letting fall his hands, he surrendered. 'That won't be necessary, Colonel.' He took a deep breath and wiped back the strands of red hair that had fallen over his face. 'I'm, of course, entirely confident I can safely leave matters to your undoubted discretion and experience.'

'Think you, Archdeacon.' Again there was the sound of footsteps on the stairs. 'Ah! That sounds like the diocesan architect,' said Harrison, rising, 'I was expecting him also. You'll have to excuse me, I'm afraid—there are a few details he and I need to discuss.'

'Yes, of course.' Backing away, Cawthorne forced a smile. 'Well, I leave you to the good work then.'

'Ah, Davidson, there you are!' called out Harrison as the architect took Cawthorne's place in the doorway. 'Come in and close the door. We need to discuss Mr Gleeson's roof.' Resuming his seat, he bent over the survey report. 'Yes,' he murmured after a moment's reading, 'as usual, a thorough and detailed piece of work.' He turned another page, then closed the document. 'Yes, I entirely agree,' he said, nodding, 'aluminium skylight frames and lead sheeting is clearly what's needed. Who do you suggest for the work? Horne Brothers of Sittingbourne?'

'Whatever you say.'

'Right.' Harrison scribbled a memorandum, noticing that his hand trembled slightly as he did so. 'Now,' he said, looking up at his latest visitor for the first time, 'we come to the question of the Bell Harry. The scaffolding has gone up, I see.'

Davidson was standing exactly where Cawthorne had stood, gazing down, like him, at the grinning bearded face of the monkey. There, however, the likeness ended: whereas the archdeacon had been pink-faced and all aquiver with frustration and anger, the architect, tall, gaunt and dishevelled, face drained of blood, stood before the object on the desk, pale and still as if he too were a thing of glazing and clay.

Harrison coughed. 'My wife tells me that you have had a preliminary look at the condition of the balustrading. I'd therefore like to have your assessment of the likely time the Bell Harry work will add to your original estimate.'

'Perhaps two months.' Davidson didn't raise his head; his voice was a toneless whisper.

'Really—two months! As much as that?' Harrison paused and tapped his desk. 'Well, he resumed, 'in that case we had better go up and have a look at the state of things together.'

As if waking from a trance, Davidson looked up from the figurine. 'You wish to come up the tower with me?'

'Oh yes,' said the other. 'I need to know all the factors involved before I decide on any future course of action.' For a moment he sat, looking directly up at the architect's deathly white face, then rose to his feet. 'Right,' he said briskly, picking up the survey report and his signed memorandum, 'I'll just hand these to Mary and set matters in train. After that, we'll go and see how things look from up on high.'

Halfway to the door, however, he paused and looked round—and going back to his desk, picked up the monkey statuette and carried it out with him.

Through the brilliant autumn sunlight, the autumn gale in their faces, Harrison and Davidson headed along the eastern alley of Great Cloister, the former carrying the statuette grasped like a marshal's baton. Pushing through the Calefactorium door, they entered the shadowy gloom of the lower north-west transept. About them, the cathedral resonated with voices and movement, while from above came the echoing whisper of plainsong.

'Have mercy upon me, O God, after thy great goodness.'

Harrison leading, they began mounting the broad staircase to the upper transept. Above them, the high pitched treble gave way to tenor and bass, the high, ethereal voices of boys balanced and answered by the deeper tones of the men. *'According to the multitude of thy mercies do away mine offences.'*

Morning choir practice had clearly begun, and as the two climbed, the words of the psalm grew increasingly distinct.

'Behold, I was shapen in wickedness.'

'And in sin hath my mother conceived me.'

Having almost reached the top of the steps, Harrison heard a familiar voice call angrily, 'You there, boy! Come here, you blooming little blighter!'

Emerging into the upper transept, he was in time to see the gowned figure of the cathedral venturer shaking an admonishing finger before the upturned face of Simon Barnes. 'Them steps weren't made for running up, nor yet for jumping off!'

'No, sir. I'm sorry, Mr Simcocks.'

'This,' proclaimed the vesturer, 'is the House of the Lord, not an adventure playground!' Drawing out notebook and pencil, he licked at the lead. 'For being late for choir practice and behaving unseemly in the cathedral, I'll now have your name.'

'Excuse me, Simcocks!' interrupted Harrison, striding up from behind. 'I'm very sorry Barnes was late. He shouldn't have been running, but he's been assisting me with some urgent diocesan business.'

It was difficult to say which of the two faces looked the more surprised—the rubicund, moon-round visage of the man, or the dazed, wide-eyed one of the child.

'Assisting you! What—'im, sir!' Simcocks gaped down at the probationer chorister: from his amazed disbelief, it could have been the deanery cat standing on the marble flooring before him.

'Now, Simon,' said Harrison, turning to the equally bewildered boy, 'I have one last little errand for you—go directly to Bread Yard and inform my wife that I've not forgotten her art class—and that I shall be there this evening to take and collect her as usual.'

'Yes, sir.' Barnes's eyes briefly dropped to the porcelain monkey grasped in the speaker's hand. 'Is that all, sir?'

'Not quite.' A brief smile crossed Harrison's face. 'You may also inform her that you are to be given a mug of chocolate and the two sausage-rolls from the fridge. Now off you go—and don't run!' he called as the child darted away.

'No, sir. Thank you, sir.'

Throughout the short interchange, the diocesan architect had remained a chalk-pale apparition at Harrison's elbow—and as the child disappeared, the vesturer peered at him curiously. Before he could speak, however, Harrison intervened.

'Now, Mr Simcocks, if you'd kindly fetch me the Bell Harry keys—Mr Davidson and I are going up to make a further inspection of the tower balustrades.'

Turning and turning up the spiral stair-case, mounting through light and shadow, the two figures climbed the worn, concaved steps in silence, following the unvarying wall, endlessly tramping as if stationary within Master Mason Wastell's massive treadmill-hoist, entombed and decaying below them in the shuttered heart of the tower—until, almost unexpectedly, the final door blocked the way ahead—a rectangle of black haloed by the brilliance beyond.

Drawing the bolt, Harrison pushed out into the open, sending a number of sheltering rooks and gulls whirling upwards. Momentarily bathed by the sunlight, he stood blinking against the glare, then dipping his head, stepped on to the roof—thirty-five square feet of lead, balustraded and cornered by the vane-topped pinnacles, the entire summit ringed at present by the gleaming interlace of steel piping, through which the wind came in great buffeting gusts.

Heart beating hard from the climb, legs unsteady, he crossed the roof to rest a moment, looking down through the pillared supports: beyond the end of the presbytery roof and the ornately crenellated corona, lay the long grassed-over monastery fish pond, from this height looking like a green oval eye. Beyond, behind the oaks, lay the walled garden where he and Rachel had sat, empty now apart from a minuscule figure disappearing through the Queningate. Turning, he looked north, making out the Bread Yard arch in the shadowed corner of Green Court—young Barnes must already have passed under it and be, he hoped, sitting at that moment scoffing sausage-rolls and diverting Winnie with chatter of school, holidays and chums.

He turned to look back at the stairway entry. Davidson had not emerged, but stood watching him, a pale-faced beast in its lair. 'Two months' work, you say?' he shouted over the gale. 'Well, come on out then and show me.'

Bending low, the architect stepped out, the wind immediately ruffling his black hair. Wary and watchful, he faced the other across the fenced-in rectangle of stone and steel. 'To see the condition properly, Colonel, it's necessary to get out on to the scaffolding.'

Harrison glanced up at the sun blazing from a clear sky above his left shoulder. 'Right, let's get on with it then.' He walked past the other to the western balustrades. Placing a foot between the support columns, he paused and, without turning, held out the monkey figurine. 'Hold this while I climb up.'

Heaving himself up on to the stonework, he swung over his legs to sit outwards on the balustrade. Braced against the gusts, he clutched at the lichen-encrusted masonry on either side. Directly beneath was the scaffolding planking with its single guardrail—far further below than he'd imagined, and needing a short ladder to make a safe descent. Below that again, there was nothing but a sheer drop of a hundred and God knows how many feet to the apex of the nave roof.

Feeling the presence of the architect close at his back, Harrison tightened his grip on the stonework, raising his head to look out at the patchwork of lawns and paths on his left, curving and narrowing to meet the Christ Church gatehouse, around which seethed crowds of tiny, ant-like tourists. Gripping tight, he straightened his back, raising his gaze out across the huddled rooftops towards where, on the distant horizon, rose a barely discernible pencil-like shape.

'I take it, Davidson,' he half shouted above the wind, his eyes fixed on that ghostly raised finger, 'that it was in just such a position—with you standing behind David Miller while he looked out from the top of Holy Trinity tower—that you, on a sudden impulse, struck him with the object you now have again in your hand.'

No answer: only the wind in his ears; the cawing and screaming of the disturbed birds wheeling about the tower.

'I further take it,' he shouted again, his voice flat and toneless in the emptiness, 'that you took the opportunity of the Friends' council meeting finishing early to return to Long Ashendon. There, I imagine, you argued again with your godfather as you'd done in the afternoon—and then, when he wouldn't agree to keep silent, you stifled him in an outburst of that extraordinary rage of yours I glimpsed after my unfortunate remark regarding the eviction notice—then afterwards dragged the body out to the garage to make the death look like suicide.'

Again no answer—then from the corner of his eye, Harrison saw the shadow on the balustrade move. Glancing round, he caught the momentary flash of the porcelain as it was raised—and immediately he launched himself forward and dropped.

Harrison landed heavily, causing the planks to dip and flex like a springboard. Toppling sideways, he fell with a jarring crack on his left elbow. Rolling over, he desperately grabbed up at the guardrail and finally lay, sprawled across the boards, head protruding over space, clinging with his right hand to the horizontal bar above him, gasping and retching with pain. Above him, Davidson was leaning out over the balustrade, hair blowing in the wind, the statuette raised like a hammer against the sun.

For moments neither man moved—Davidson gazing down, figurine raised above his head, his expression totally lost in the glare; Harrison helplessly prone ten feet below him, clinging to the rail, spasms of pain pulsing through his arm, staring up at the man who, moments before, had come within a fraction of cracking open his skull.

Heaving down on the guardrail, Harrison half raised himself. 'That's why you were so keen to tidy all those rectory cupboards,' he yelled up, pain bringing tears to his eyes, 'you were after the statuette your godfather had hidden away.'

The apparition didn't move or speak—Harrison could see only the white blur of the face gazing down, black hair whipping about his head.

'Your father's surname was originally Mendelssohn,' shouted Harrison again, hurling his words against the inhuman stare. 'And when he fled Germany in the late 'thirties, he brought with him an heirloom—one piece of Kändler's original *Affenkapelle* that he later had auctioned at Sotheby's to help pay, I imagine, for your confounded education.' Taking breath, he shouted again, his voice growing hoarse. 'And that piece—*Drummer*—was, of course, part of the very same set as the piece now in your hand.'

The raised statuette again flashed in the sunlight as Davidson's arm swung back and then forwards—and seeing the hurled missile come straight at his face, Harrison half rolled over, pain forgotten as it smashed on to the planking beside him, showering him with splinters and chips.

Rolling again on to his back, still clinging to the bar, Harrison felt the blood running from his neck and face. 'Goddamn you!' he bellowed in a frenzy of rage and pain. 'I knew that your father and Tom Dove had been friends, but because of your name, it never occurred to me he could have been Frederick Mendelssohn—the one-time assistant curate in Hove.' Pausing, he wiped at the blood on his face. 'Like David Miller anglicizing Müller, your father took an English name before his Anglican ordination—that's why I couldn't find a Mendelssohn in any edition of *Crockford's*.' A rook swept past, its indignant cry momentarily drowning his voice. 'Archbishop Randall Davidson was Bishop Bell's mentor and friend. Presumably your father took his surname to please the man who'd helped arrange his escape, just as later he had you christened George in his memory—but it never occurred to me to question the link between your names and Bell, any more than it did to ask where the hell you managed to find that convenient little screwdriver in the darkness of the garage!'

The figure above glanced about the tower, obviously looking for a second missile—a block of stone—anything heavy and large enough to silence the shouting man. Next moment, however, he was scrambling on to the balustrade, a black shape against blue—and still almost paralysed with the pain of his cracked elbow, Harrison could only grip hard on the guardrail as the planks flexed and sprang beneath his back.

Davidson was over him in an instant—white face bending low, dark eyes burning. Gripping the guardrail with redoubled strength, Harrison prepared to hang on for his life. Instead of attacking, however, to his astonishment, the other swung round and began tearing at the base of the balustrade, scrabbling and clawing with his nails at the crumbling stone. 'Rotten! Rotten right through!' The architect's voice was a scream in the wind. 'See! See there!' Springing round, he waved fragments of stone beneath Harrison's nose—then, face contorting, he ground the pieces to powder between his palms before finally opening his hand to let the wind whip away the dust like a whiff of smoke. 'Rotten!' he shrieked again, spittle flecking his lips. 'And what was it you said, damn you—"some trowelwork and a touch of patching up"!'

Speechless, aghast, Harrison stared as the architect's face once more contorted in rage. 'Push on! Patch up! Always the same! Cost and time the only consideration—at bottom, you're just the same as the bloody archdeacon!' Wiping at his spittle, Davidson paused, his breath coming in rapid gasps. 'No idea at all—sitting behind that desk without the faintest conception how it feels, risking borrowed money to renovate those Westgate properties, then to have the property market collapse and have the banks threatening to foreclose!'

Apparently exhausted, fury momentarily spent, Davidson slumped back against the tower, hopelessness in his eyes.

'I didn't know about your difficulties with the properties,' said Harrison, forcing himself to speak, 'but why did you risk it, you a family man? Surely, as diocesan architect, you...'

'Diocesan architect!' cried Davidson, scrambling upright, goaded into renewed frenzy. 'What's that—a lifetime patching up other men's work! A jobbing curator! An eternity of peering down into vicarage drains and gutters!' Lurching to the guardrail, he leaned out, a black-headed Valkyrie riding the wind, then swung round to glare into Harrison's blood-smeared face. 'And what was I allowed to create—uncontroversial extensions to parish halls! Crypt conversions! Lavatories for the Mothers' Union!' Harrison stared helplessly up as Davidson continued to rant. 'And suddenly there was a way out, an undreamed-of chance of escape from you and the whole bloody diocese! The Berlin Wall was down, Germany was to be reunited, and I could claim compensation for what had been stolen from my father's family.'

'Ah, yes,' murmured Harrison, fighting against the excruciating pain as he pulled himself up on to his knees and began inching forwards to the balustrade supports, left arm dangling uselessly, 'you are referring to the assets of the old family firm in Dresden—the company of Mendelssohn & Lipmann that appears in your compensation claim against the German Federal Republic.'

'And what did Miller promise me—tens of thousands of deutschmarks!' Face blazing, Davidson sprang forwards, and grabbing Harrison's shoulders, began shaking him, half as if trying to make him listen, half as if trying to pluck him from the planking. Clutching through a gap between the boards with the fingers of his right hand, Harrison hung on desperately as the madman, shaking him with redoubled force, screamed in his ear: 'For no goddamned apparent reason, Miller rushes up here to Canterbury with papers for me to sign one Friday evening, talking of wanting to hurry back to the States—and I, like a damned fool, actually talked him into accompanying my family to the cathedral fête!'

'Where, of course,' grunted Harrison, straining towards the wall, 'he bought the *Fiddler* statuette, knowing as soon as he saw it just what it meant.'

'Damn him to hell!'

With Davidson clinging to his shoulders like a drowning man, Harrison dragged forwards, now nauseous and trembling from the after-effects of whatever damage he'd done to his elbow. 'Then I suppose,' he gasped, reaching up for the pillared balustrade, 'next day he must have rung to announce that he'd actually found you a cousin—a last survivor of the Lipmann family.'

'Yes!' shrieked Davidson. 'And would I care to drive him over to Long Ashendon on the Monday evening! Would I like to help break the wonderful news to Ruth Hodge before he caught his train back to London! Devil take him—the man was a blind, insensitive fool!'

Against the weight of the man clinging incubus-like to him, Harrison heaved himself up to finally get a purchase on the balustrade. Praying it would hold, he hauled himself to his feet.

'Yes,' he gasped, hooking his right arm between the support pillars, 'and on the way over, what did poor Miller do—that insensitive man as you call him? I imagine he admired that beautiful church—and you, of course, knowing where the tower keys were kept, persuaded him to stop off to climb up and see the view. And then what happened after you'd struck and tumbled him over into that isolated graveyard? You hid his body in the back of your car, I suppose, and, after throwing the now broken statuette in the pond as you passed, you drove straight over to the railway cutting. Then, of course, there were his packed suitcases to get rid of—presumably Miller had brought them with him so he could go on to London directly after seeing Ruth Hodge. That made things easy: you had only to buy a single ticket to Charing Cross that night, put his bags on the last train, then slip out of the station and return to plant the unused ticket in his wallet, at the same time powdering a little brick dust in his head wound just as you powdered that stonework under my nose a few moments ago.'

Releasing his hold, Davidson swung away to gaze over the guardrail, black hair streaming in the wind, limp suit pinned and quivering about his body.

'Of course,' shouted Harrison, 'it didn't take your godfather more than a few seconds to guess something of what had happened when I showed him the list of the *Affenkapelle* owners: he knew your father's original name, and perhaps even Ruth Hodge's—also, I presume, the details of your claim on the Mendelssohn & Lipmann assets. Having seen one of the monkey players at the village fête, and perhaps even remembering a similar statuette belonging to your father, he must have understood Miller's scrawlings—and once he'd learnt from me that he had been a lawyer, guessed that his death was connected to your compensation claim. That's why he rang you soon after I left, and no wonder he was so upset: presumably he knew all about these blind rages of yours you'd always managed to keep hidden from me, and might well already have guessed just how and why David Miller had died.'

Davidson remained, back turned, staring out over Canterbury.

'It was damned clever,' cried Harrison again, 'that typed suicide note, obliging your aunt to beg me to cover up your own bloody deeds!'

The knuckles clutching the guardrail grew whiter and the architect seemed suddenly to be quivering like his suit.

'And again you were cunning enough to pretend to be so squeamish and so goddamned law-abiding, forcing Miss Hodge and myself to actually talk you into help covering up your godfather's death!' Harrison's voice increased in volume with his anger. Fear forgotten, he released his hold on the tower and took a few steps, supporting his shattered left arm with his right hand. Standing on the shuddering platform, he saw a second shadow suddenly grow and stretch out beside his own—and, beneath his feet, he felt the tremble of Davidson's approach.

'Why did you bring me up here?'

With the rooks and the gulls wheeling and crying about the tower, Harrison turned to meet the chalk-white face. 'I wanted to give you a choice—a chance for some sort of redemption, a way of avoiding further heartbreak for your aunt and for saving your wife and children from impoverishment.'

There was a flicker of something—was it hope?—in the architect's eyes, but Harrison's voice continued. 'I merely remind you, that as diocesan employees, both our lives are generously insured against any accident occurring during our official duties.'

The import of the words didn't strike Davidson at first,

then, with a convulsion of horror, he involuntarily glanced downwards. Turning away, Harrison looked ahead at the two half blended shadows stretching across the planks.

'Besides you, who else knows?'

Harrison shook his head. 'Nobody—the matter remains entirely between the two of us.' There was a pause, then Davidson's shadow lengthened, blending almost perfectly into his own. Harrison stared ahead. 'However,' he continued, imagining the other's breath on his neck, 'before coming up here, I took the precaution of writing a full account of my investigations. That, together with a copy of Miss Hodge's adoption certificate and the final piece of the monkey orchestra, will be passed directly to the dean if I'm not back in my office at noon.'

For moments there was silence apart from the wind and the cry of the birds—and across the planks, the blended shadows didn't move.

'Goddamn you! Colonel bloody Harrison!'

Ramrod straight, deliberately, Harrison raised his head to look up into the sky. Beneath him, the scaffolding shuddered under the blasts of the wind.

With the throb in his elbow, heart beating hard, he remained looking up, forcing himself to slowly count to a hundred. At last, he lowered his gaze to where, ahead of him, his shadow now stretched alone.

He turned and looked back at the empty platform. Nothing was left but a scatter of crumbled stone and a few white chips of the shattered porcelain, gleaming like bone splinters on the rough, boot-scuffed boards. He remained gazing at them a moment, then, turning to the guardrail, looked down at the tiny figures of the tourists, swirling and spreading out across the lawns from the gatehouse as if a giant hand had recently twisted a stick in an ants' nest. He watched for a moment, then slowly bent and peered directly down.

Far below, a thick streak of bright red ran down the nave roof like the splatter of an insect across a windscreen—and there at the end lay Davidson's body, wedged head downwards in the wide lead guttering, legs akimbo, arms outspread.

Harrison gazed down, dried blood on his neck and his face, his shattered arm cradled in the other, and from his mouth, the whispered words '*Miserere mei, Deus*' were torn away and lost in the wind.

Epilogue

Three mournful blasts of a ship's siren rang through the late winter afternoon, then lights were moving between the sheds and cranes: white stern-lamp, triple row of lit ports, illuminated funnel, starboard navigation lamp on the bridge-wing, appearing in turn as the cross-channel ferry, going astern, slid out between the protruding piers. For moments, the vessel hung as if motionless, a feast of light in the darkening bay, then, with a long single blast of her horn, she was turning and forging ahead for the open sea, water creaming under her bows.

'Is it giving you more pain, my dear?'

The seated figure ceased flexing his left arm and looked round at the woman in the wheelchair positioned beside the bench. 'No, it's fine. I was just giving it some exercise, that's all.' He looked out again between the railings at the ferry. 'I suppose we ought to be getting back: Mrs McNorton will soon be preparing tea.'

'I suppose so.'

Neither spoke with any urgency or enthusiasm, or showed the slightest inclination to move, remaining as they'd been for the last half hour: two elderly figures, muffled and coated, sitting together on the virtually deserted promenade as the short January day drew to a close.

'What are you thinking about?'

Harrison shrugged. 'Oh, I don't know. What's happening out in the Middle East, I suppose.'

His wife made no reply. Given his present insomnia, she hadn't been greatly surprised to wake at three that morning to find him out of bed, crouched over the portable radio. Apparently the BBC World Service had just begun reporting a massive air attack on Baghdad, and with the accounts of the fighting pouring in, he'd continued to sit listening, wrapped in his dressing-gown, until well after dawn. As a result, he'd been even more taciturn and listless than usual all day.

Winnie gazed across the bay. The tide was already on the ebb; from below came the soft, even cadence of the waves; in the far distance, the cliffs of the White Bear gleamed through the gloom, while from away on the right, came the intermittent flash of the Portland light. 'I didn't tell you, Richard,' she said, 'but before we left for Weymouth, I had tea with Ruth Hodge.'

Apparently lost in a reverie, Harrison continued to sit for a moment, gaze fixed on the fading glow of the ferry. Then, with a slight start, he woke from his trance. 'You went over to Long Ashendon? Good Lord! However did you get there?'

'Margaret Ingrams drove me over. I asked her to.'

'I see.' Turning, he stared out again at the already distant ship. 'How was she?' he asked after a moment. 'Still bitter about her foster mother hiding the truth from her all those years?'

'No, she's coping much better now, thank goodness. Very bravely, she decided to go out to Dresden over Christmas to search out the house where her parents lived before they were dragged off to the camps. When she was there, she actually managed to meet someone who had known them: an old woman who remembered her as a tiny baby.' Breaking off, Winnie looked round at her husband who remained staring expressionlessly out to sea. 'Richard, are you listening?'

Harrison nodded, but said nothing.

'Anyway,' continued the other, 'obviously the visit has helped her come to terms with things—according to Joyce Dove, since getting back she's resumed tending the Hodges' grave.'

'Good.'

Winnie sat for a moment in silence, then reaching out, laid a hand on her husband's arm. 'Darling, don't you think it's time that we did the same?'

'What do you mean?' She felt him slightly flinch from her touch as he spoke.

'You know very well: you and I have to face what really happened, that morning up on the Bell Harry.'

'Christ, Winnie! Leave it, can't you!' Springing up, Harrison stood, his back to her, hands visibly trembling on the promenade railings. 'I told you at the time what happened! Do I have to repeat it now?' Face working, he swung round. 'I fell climbing down on to the scaffolding, and Davidson, the poor devil, slipped trying to help me.' He paused, breathing heavily. 'For God's sake, isn't that what I said at the inquest under oath?'

'Yes.'

'Well then?' His raised voice rang through the gloom.

Looking steadily up at him, his wife shook her head. 'It's no good, Richard. Painful or not, you've got to talk about it.'

'Why?'

'Isn't it obvious: the truth is still lodged inside you, poisoning you.' Winnie lowered her eyes. 'And also,' she said more quietly, 'because I can't live with the image of you climbing that tower to kill a man.'

'Kill a man!' Harrison's face again contorted. 'For Christ's sake, woman! What the hell do you mean?'

Winnie sighed. 'Don't bluster, Richard, and do stop shouting. I'm not a fool. Do you think that I've spent these past four months just sitting in this wheelchair, hoping that whatever happened that morning would vanish away? No, I've been making a few little inquiries of my own.'

'What!'

'I've talked to Joyce and to Ruth Hodge, and also to Pauline Davidson and your secretary. Oh, don't look so worried! I've been at least as discreet as you.'

Harrison remained staring down at her for a moment, his expression one of bewildered consternation, then he slumped back down on the bench. 'Well?' he said, determinedly looking away. 'So what have you managed to find out?'

'Mostly what you presumably discovered in those legal documents Joe Eisenberg gave you in London and which you burnt before you left the house that morning,' answered Winnie, 'and also from your researches at the Wiener Library. From Ruth, I learnt that after you and I went over to break the news of her parentage, she had a letter from Eisenberg offering to act on her behalf regarding the assets of a once famous Dresden firm of musical instrument makers. The registered name of this company was *Mendelssohn & Lipmann*, and had been established in the late eighteenth century by two Jewish cousins, then jointly owned and run by both sides of the family until the end of the nineteenth century.' She paused. 'Do I need to go on?'

Harrison said nothing, and, after a moment, Winnie resumed. 'Anyway, from what Ruth has gathered during her stay in Germany, there was then a break or quarrel—presumably because the Mendelssohn branch of the family converted to Christianity. As a result, the Lipmanns bought out the company, but continued to run it under its original name until it was finally confiscated from Ruth's father. Just as you guessed in the vestry, it seems that an original set of Kändler's *Affenkapelle* had belonged to the Lipmanns for generations, and, although the majority of the set was confiscated and auctioned off—along with everything else—by the Nazis, Ruth's father somehow managed to retain two pieces, *Fiddler* and *Fifer*. Those, as you guessed, he managed to send into safety along with his baby daughter.' Winnie paused. 'Then, of course, there remained only the provenance of the final piece of the full orchestra for me to discover—the *Drummer*, which according to Miller's list, belonged to a certain F. J. Mendelssohn.'

Up until this moment, Harrison hadn't moved or said a word. Now, however, his gloved hands gradually clenched and his expression became one of almost physical pain as his wife continued. 'After what happened that day on the tower, I asked Joyce about George Davidson's background. She told me that his father had been one of the twenty Confessional Church pastors Bishop Bell personally guaranteed to support so that they could escape to England in 1938, and that his name then had been Frederick Johann Mendelssohn—the possessor of *Drummer*, presumably a piece of the orchestra once passed as a gift from the Lipmanns to the Mendelssohn branch of the family. Once I knew that, George's motive for attempting to keep the truth of Ruth's ancestry hidden was obvious: any survivor of the Lipmann family meant the total invalidation of his claim on the assets of *Mendelssohn & Lipmann*.' Pausing, Winnie looked round at her husband. 'That's basically what you knew when you left me at home that morning—and what you knew when you and George Davidson climbed the tower.'

Cradling his left arm, Harrison bowed his head. 'It's over, damn it!' he murmured. 'Ruth's claim is lodged with the Federal Compensation Office in Bonn; Joyce is settled in the grace and favour cottage Cawthorne found for her in the Friars; and Davidson's wife and the children have had a generous compensation from the Church as well as his life insurance. Can't we leave it at that? Everything is all right.'

'Yes, except for me and you.' Her own fists now clenched, Winnie took a breath. 'Richard, for both our sakes, you've got to tell me the truth. What happened up there on the tower between you and George. What was it? Some sort of tussle? Is that how you got those cuts on your face and neck?'

Harrison looked away over the darkening sea.

Leaning over, Winnie reached out and touched his shoulder. 'Come on, Richard, I must know—did you kill him or not?'

'As good as.'

The words were so quietly spoken that, for a moment it seemed as if Winnie hadn't heard them—then a look of profound relief crossed her face. 'Then you didn't actually kill him!' she cried. 'Oh, thank God! Thank God!'

'As good as killed him, I said,' burst out Harrison, swinging round, anguish working his face. 'I took the fellow up there, damn it! I cornered him! I was the tempter, the one who offered the poor devil the chance to jump!'

'You allowed him an honourable way out, you mean,' answered Winnie. 'And doing so, given his unstable temperament and those murderous rages of his I've recently found out about from talking with Joyce and Pauline, you knowingly risked your own life for the sake of the Church, the diocese, as well as for Joyce, Pauline and everybody else.'

'Yes, but also for myself—Davidson's death meant that my own part in covering up Tom Dove's murder would never come out: it meant that I could retain my safe little job, my respectable position—keep what Rachel Miller called my perfect retreat!'

Winnie shook her head emphatically. 'I don't believe any of that was in your mind for an instant—and even if it was, it wasn't that that made you risk your life.'

'You don't think so!'

'No, and in your heart, you know it isn't true either.'

Harrison sighed and slumped back, momentarily closing his eyes. 'You know, Winnie,' he said after a few seconds' silence, 'now I'm away from Canterbury, I'm not sure if I can face going back to the place—not to see that damned tower standing above me, day and night.' He paused. 'Surely they'd understand if I threw in my hand now. We could find ourselves a cottage around here—somewhere towards Lutworth perhaps—somewhere with no associations.'

'What, and have a tank gunnery range behind us instead? Hardly my dream of the perfect retirement!' Winnie's smile suddenly faded as quickly as it had appeared. 'No, it's not quite yet time for that,' she added gently. 'People still need you, my dear, and so does the diocese. Remember what the archbishop said in that very kind letter he sent you. What was the term he used? "*Our good and faithful servant*".'

'For God's sake, Winnie!'

'And there's also Matthew, remember,' continued the other. 'He needs your friendship and support more than ever at the moment. Margaret tells me that he blames himself entirely for what happened: in his view, neither you nor George would have been up on the tower if it wasn't for him.'

'That's absolutely absurd!'

Winnie gave a wan smile. 'So is the majority of human guilt—and wasn't it equally absurd, your own about being on holiday when Miller attempted to contact you?'

'You know,' said Harrison after a moment or two, 'thinking about it, I'm sure it wasn't me at all that poor old Miller was trying to get in touch with when he contacted the office—he couldn't have even known I had any connection with Canterbury, and after forty years, I doubt if he even remembered my name. No, all he wanted, I'm sure, was to get in touch with the person who donated the monkey figurine, and someone must have given him my office number because we happened to be dealing with Cathedral Friends' business. Presumably he must have got Ruth's name and address next day from one or other of the Friends acting as cathedral guides.' Pausing, he sighed. 'In other words, that I ever got myself mixed up in the matter was just a piece of wretched bad luck—that and my absurd tendency to read far more into things than are there.'

'Yes, you may be right,' replied Winnie gently, 'but all the same, with your ex-Staff-Sergeant murdered attempting to obtain justice for the little refugee child Bishop Bell sought to help long ago, would you not have wanted to be involved? And would you really have wished Ruth to live and die ignorant of her parents' tragedy, or indeed of her own dark provenance? Could you have borne the idea of Rachel Miller living on with a false burden of guilt and rejection?' Taking his arm, she leant over, pressing against him. 'No, my dear, though I appreciate what it has cost you, if you could go back again to that moment of returning from the deanery to find Rachel in the house, I know you'd act no differently than you did then.'

'You may be right.' Suddenly Harrison smiled. 'Come on, my dear,' he said, gently pulling himself from her and rising to his feet. 'We'd better be getting back to Seaview and Mrs McNorton's toasted teacakes.'

'And to hear the news of what's been happening in the Gulf.'

'Yes,' he murmured, nodding, 'that too, I suppose.'

Turning the chair, Harrison began wheeling his wife across the road past the garishly painted royal statue, now nothing but a dim shape silhouetted against gleaming streetlamps and lit windows. Behind them, the promenade was left deserted, the White Bear a hardly discernible blur above restless waters—but still, unceasingly, unwearyingly, the lighthouse of Portland threw forth a circling beam, its strength and brilliance seeming to increase in the gathering dark.